H.M. RYDER

A Soul In The Shadows

Preface

This work contains content that may be triggering for some audiences. The following pages depict elements of:

Dismemberment

Decapitation

Torture

Sexual Assault

War

Adult Language

Sexual Activity depicted on the page

Prologue

Addie

It's too late. I'm too late.

Addie forced herself up the steep embankment at the cavern's edge. Beads of sweat ran down her face and splashed against the gray stones beneath her unsteady feet. Shadows danced around her as the surrounding trees swayed through the darkness. Patches of ominous, black clouds began to form in the dim moonlight of the autumn sky overhead. Nestled deep in the Alderbrooke Forest, a vast cave system lay sprawled below the land. Few vents into the tunnels were known, and any who found one rarely ventured back. Plumes of stale air emanated from the cave opening. Despite the abundance of life in the surrounding forest, the reek of sulfur and rot filled the air as though death itself claimed this place.

I can't be too late.

Addie's lungs burned and her muscles ached as she pulled her body over the sharp stones at the mouth of the cave. Several strands of long, dark hair fell from her braid and stuck to the back of her neck. Her sweat drenched, emerald tunic clung to her body like a second skin. Catching her breath, she peered ahead and caught sight of Lord Anderson. The tall, lanky man stood just beyond the bend near the darkening

1

waters of the river that carved a path through the cave. Addie pulled herself forward one last time, tearing her leather pants on the stones and settled onto her feet. Striding quickly deeper into the dark, Addie's heart sank. The water before her had already begun to stir and grow murky. The foul stench of death thickened the air.

"Lord Anderson," her voice was a plea, "Think about what you are doing."

Addie moved toward him slowly, ensuring she kept a careful pace so as not to frighten the broken man before her. The sand shifted silently under her feet as she approached. With each step in his direction, the air grew more rancid, churning Addie's stomach and standing every one of her hairs on end. Lord Anderson's words came out void of emotion, unlike the deep, warming timbre she had so often heard from him at court.

"It cannot be undone, I am afraid. The dead will rise, and your father will know my suffering," Lord Anderson turned to face her fully, his vacant stare finally meeting hers.

Splayed below the lord's feet rested a small leather bound manuscript, its pages worn by time. Addie reached the lord's side, her eyes locking onto the self-inflicted, fatal wound on his abdomen. From his lower belly to his rib cage, a large gash beneath his palm seeped blood between his fingers as he held himself together with his left hand. His once warm, tan skin had paled and his body shook.

"Let me help you...please," Addie rasped. "If you die, you will be committing a far worse atrocity than the king ever has. My father may be ruthless, but he is not entirely cruel. Your actions right now would be damning all of Viridia to a fate no one deserves!"

"My wife is dead because of your father's brutality," he forced out through clenched teeth. "He *is* a cruel king that cares not for his people, only for himself! He did *nothing* to protect her, to protect his people. He deserves to suffer!" Lord Anderson shouted with far more life than Addie thought possible, given how close he stood to death's gate.

"I have to heal you. You cannot die. I won't let you become a monster! You and I both know your wife would never want you to do this," Addie stepped closer and reached for the lord's wound with a glowing palm.

Lord Anderson moved with a shocking quickness. Addie didn't have time to pull the dagger at her hip to defend herself. The lord brought up his right hand, revealing a sword she had not seen at his side, and with it pierced through her chest. Addie's scream echoed through the cave, the force of the blade sending her back a step. Her outstretched hand fell to her side as her eyes dropped to the gold hilt of Lord Anderson's sword protruding from her body. Everything seemed to slow. Lord Anderson withdrew his blade and Addie collapsed to her knees. Coughing blood from her punctured lung, the sting morphed into agony. Blood spilled onto the manuscript spread before her.

This was the end. This would be her undoing, her kingdom's ruin.

I have to get up. No one else will come. I have to rise or my kingdom will fall.... I have... failed them all.

Through serrated breath, she fought to remain conscious. Lord Anderson lowered himself to look her in the eyes, his own more gentle now.

"I am sorry, child. I did not want it to end this way for you, but this is how it should be."

Unable to hold herself up any longer, Addie's strength gave way. She fell forward over the leather-bound book that just aided in damning her people, her blood pooling around her body. Her vision faded as Lord Anderson too fell—now lifeless—beside her, their blood mixing into a river that flowed to the pool's edge. As their blood reached the water, Addie's body glowed a dim gold as she unsuccessfully attempted to knit her chest back together. Her breathing hitched.

Was she seeing this right? Figures emerged from the now-black water. Once men and women of wars long since passed, now resurrected as nightmares, stepped onto the sand like wraiths in the dark. Three emaciated, gray skinned beings with unnaturally long, slender limbs approached Lord Anderson's body and stooped in unison to collect his corpse from the ground with clawed hands. Turning slowly, they retreated into the dark. Several rattling breaths left Addie's lungs before the creatures appeared once again from deep within the cave and advanced upon her. The princess's final sight before all went to shadow was that of death peering down at her through milky white eyes.

Chapter 1

Grant

Every time Grant had this nightmare, it began at the Blue Scale Tavern with his best friend, Will. Despite their intoxicated state, both young men were quite skilled at the game of darts. The two poor fools playing them had no clue who they were attempting to swindle.

"Alright gents. You've got us beat again," Will said, collecting darts from the board, as well as some from the wall and floor. "But I feel I've got the hang of this game now. I feel my luck will be changing! What do you think, Grant, old pal? Are you up for one more game?" Will chortled and placed the darts into Grant's hand.

Flipping the darts over in his palm, Grant mumbled, "Sure. What do I have to lose?" He lifted the silver pint in his other hand to his lips and tossed his head back to finish off his drink.

All evening, Grant and Will had spoken at a boisterous volume about their *"wealth"* in hopes of snaring these two travelers. Both newcomers had been seen pick-pocketing the locals over the past few days but they were yet to be confronted by anyone. Grant vaguely recalled the men introducing themselves as Charlie and Randle, or perhaps Chester and Raymond. Now, several ales and games in, Grant wasn't quite sure, nor did he care. In a few short moments, those men—whatever their names were—would be leaving the Blue Scale, and hopefully the town of Shepherd's Glen, with empty pockets and a newfound respect for the people there.

"Double or nothin'," Charlie or Chester grunted with a slimy grin. "We ain't playin' for free now."

"Yeah, losers. What Chester said!" his weaselly friend chimed, practically licking his chops and rubbing his grimy hands together, "We ain't gonna play you two for free."

"Sounds great. I'll go first so I can order another drink," Grant said, glancing at Chester before taking his position. "I'm going to want to celebrate our win."

Grant threw the first dart. From the corner of his eye, he saw Chester and his weasel friend stiffen.

"Hey…" Grant grinned . "Would you look at that? Bullseye!"

"Psh, pure luck!" Chester scoffed, stepping up to take his shot. "We still got you drunk fuckers beat." He took his aim and fell just short.

"We'll see, *friend*," Will grinned, more sober than he had seemed all night. He came up for his turn, aimed slow and focused, then matched Grant's shot.

Throw for throw, Will and Grant outplayed their new acquaintances. Grant put the final nail in their proverbial coffins with another shot, dead center.

Grant turned to face both infuriated men. "Well gents, it's been interesting. Now pay up."

"You two cheatin' sons of bitches ain't getting shit from us!" Chester spat. "Go fuck yourselves! You played us!"

"Now, boys," Grant tisked, "we made a fair bet and you lost. Rules are rules. But…we *are* feeling generous tonight. Aren't we, Will?" Grant glanced at Will, then lowered his chin to stare down both men and stepped closer to block their exit.

"Super charitable!" Will lifted his chin and grinned wide before stepping beside Grant.

"You two can either return the items you have stolen from the lovely town folk and pay us what you wagered, or Jeremy, our bar keep here, will loose an arrow through both of you," Grant dipped his head in a subtle bow and gestured a hand behind the men. The stout man standing behind the bar raised a heavy crossbow over the counter and all the color drained from Chester's face.

"F-fuck you. Th-this ain't worth my time," Chester stuttered, fishing several handfuls of coin from his person and throwing his satchel to the floor. As they ran from the tavern, Will moved forward, chuckling to himself, and collected the dirty canvas bag and several glittering items from the ground.

Grant watched as Will stood once again and walked the several paces to the bar to hand the portly, gray haired man a simple brass pocket watch, "I believe this is yours, Jeremy."

"Thank you again, Will. It was a gift from the misses. I'd be at the other end of this crossbow if she knew I'd lost it," Jeremy rested the bow on the counter top and nudged Will's arm with a playful shove before tucking the watch into his vest pocket.

An hour later, Grant and Will were enjoying their sixth –possibly seventh– pint of the night when the doors to the rundown establishment swung open. A sharp gust of cold autumn air flooded the tavern. Red and gold leaves flurried across the wooden floor boards.

7

"Grant, where is Grant Anderson?!" shouted a balding, middle aged man, as all heads turned in his direction. "Sir! You must hurry!" His breathing was labored as he made eye contact with Grant and Will at the far end of the room.

The man bent at his waist and placed his hands on his knees as Grant's mind quickly sobered at the sight of his father's personal guard covered in blood. With both hands, Grant shoved himself away from his table. The chair beneath him groaned before it crashed to the floor. Stumbling forward, Grant tossed aside several other scattered wooden chairs and made his way to the gore coated man's side.

"Where are you hurt? What has happened, Ren?" Grant demanded as he placed a hand on Ren's shaking shoulders. Ren's thick, bushy brows knit together and Grant's racing heart filled with fear as he took in his father's closest friend's appearance more fully. Something truly terrible must have happened if one of the strongest people Grant knew now stood before him a quivering mess.

"They've taken the grounds, sir," Ren exhaled a shuddering breath. "I'm- I'm fine. Most of this blood is not mine. I got Maggie to safety but I could not get back into the house. Your parents need aid quickly. I fear I may be too late."

"Will," Grant turned, and before he could finish his sentence, Will was standing by his side. His friend's jovial demeanor from moments before was replaced by a stark seriousness.

"I'm right behind you, brother. We can get what we need from my house and I have already asked Jeremy to ready the horses," Will stated without hesitation, brows furrowed and face grim.

Within a matter of seconds both young men were running

the several blocks from the tavern to Will's family home. The flickering lights from several windows cast uneven shadows across the cobblestone beneath their feet.

Following his mother's death several years prior, Will lived alone in a small, white stone bungalow with his father, a man he barely knew and rarely saw. Will's dark, empty house greeted Grant and his friend as they burst through the front doors.

"I'll grab the bow from the den and I have my long swords in my room," Will directed.

Grant stepped down the narrow hall to the left of the main sitting room and instantly sprinted toward the small room in the back. Dread pooled in his stomach as he pushed open the thin door to his best friend's broom closet sized bedroom and stepped into the inky black.

"I really wish you would move into the manor with me, Will," Grant yelled toward the open door. "This place is eerie in the dark."

Will entered the space strapping several daggers to his tan, leather vest, "We can discuss your fear of the dark later. Jeremy brought the horses around. Let's go!"

The ride from Will's home to Grant's was a blur. The cobblestone streets quickly turned to dirt and the beautiful white stone buildings in the city turned to the darkened emerald of the surrounding forest. The moon was full and high as both riders finally passed through Grant's front gate. The dark rod-iron fencing was nearly torn from the gray stone pillars on either side of the road leading to the brick manor beyond. Dozens of lifeless bodies littered the ground just outside the ajar grand entry doors. Blood coated the marble steps.

"Be cautious, Grant," Will advised in a whisper as both still inebriated men dismounted their horses and made their way to the large oak doors.

From somewhere down the hall, a gargled groan cut through the otherwise silent home. From the foyer to Grant's parent's personal rooms were several more fallen men and women. The faces of the Anderson's family guards, as well as faces Grant had never seen, engraved themselves into his memory.

Grant stepped through the broken door of his parents' sitting room and beheld the greatest horror he had ever witnessed in his twenty-six years of life. Will inhaled a shocked breath and stepped beside Grant, sword drawn. Three men grinned wickedly and stood over Grant's mother's and father's broken bodies. Entrails covered the floor, blood splattered the white lounge chair against the far wall, and it appeared Grant's father, Lord Gregory Anderson, had put up the fight of his life in an attempt to save his wife but had ultimately failed. There was no chance she still drew breath. Her skin was far too ashen, all color gone. Her eyes stared ahead unseeing and the absolute terror frozen in her expression chilled Grant's blood. Lord Anderson's breaths were too shallow and infrequent. He needed a healer quickly but all Grant knew was unfettered rage.

Grant stood in a puddle of his mother's blood and his body went rigid. His cold voice was the only warning, "You are all dead men." Then his powers were unleashed.

For the first time since he was seventeen, Grant did not hold back his gift. Despite nearly a decade of being suppressed, his magic lurched forward like a sentient being and cut through the three remaining intruders' minds like a blade in search of

10

their greatest nightmares. Within seconds their own greatest fears tore apart their minds. The only physical tells were the trails of blood leaking from the men's eyes and nose before their bodies crumbled to the ground.

"Fuck man…" Will breathed.

Grant fell to his knees and let out a heartbreaking, guttural roar.

Unlike every other time he relived this nightmare, Grant felt a shift he had never experienced before. Like a hand pulling him from the dark, Grant could feel something yanking his soul out of his despair. He could feel he was being watched as he rose to his feet. He saw no one but knew, in the depths of his soul, he was not alone.

In a nearly inaudible female voice, a faint "help," echoed through his mind before Grant startled awake, drenched in sweat in his bedchamber.

"Who the fuck was that?" Grant groaned under his breath and rubbed his face.

Movement in the shadows near the drapes covering the large window of his room caught his attention. Still slightly unsteady from sleep and mind brimming with rage, Grant stood and hurried to the curtains, brandishing the dagger he pulled from his bedside table. He quickly pulled back the fabric ready to destroy whoever hid in the darkness to reveal nothing but empty space.

Grant's voice was low and gruff as he spoke to the silence surrounding him, "I'm loosing my fucking mind."

Chapter 2

Addie

Addie couldn't see anything in the darkness that seemed to consume her and felt only the cold chill of death down her spine. Lost somewhere between the world of the living and the land of the dead, Addie's soul lingered in an unending abyss. This wasn't right. She should have found peace in death, not this void.

Where am I? What is this place? How long has it been since I've seen light?

Her memories were hazy and broken but she knew she must be dead. Despite no physical form, she still felt a sharp pain through her chest and warm, thick blood coating her skin. But why was she still here? Wherever *here* was.

It is too dark. Empty.

Without warning, Addie's soul lurched forward toward the sound of utter grief. Someone was in pain, total and all consuming, soul deep agony. Regardless of her current turmoil, she knew she needed to help whoever it was that was calling to her. If there was anything she could do, she knew she had to try.

The flickering light of a room became visible just ahead in the seemingly never-ending darkness. With blurred vision, Addie stood in the middle of a tragic scene. There was so much blood, so much gore she didn't know what she could possibly do to help these poor people. At the center of the room was a couple in a final embrace on the floor. A middle-aged man shielded a once beautiful woman from where their attackers once stood, now nothing more than additional bodies in the chaos of the room. The woman's silver-brown hair was stained a deep crimson. The man had ultimately fallen in his pursuit to save her but still drew haggard breaths. Addie somehow knew he was not the soul that called her here.

Pulling her gaze from the bodies on the floor, she focused on the man on his knees in a puddle of blood that was clearly not his own. Terror and pain etched itself into the most beautiful face she had ever seen. She knew his face; he looked so much like the woman butchered before him. Somewhere in the recesses of her shattered memories, Addie knew him but could not quite recall who she was seeing.

She needed to help him, needed to end this awful pain that had begun to tear into her very being like it could rip her soul apart. When she tried to speak, no words formed. She tried to offer her aid however she could, but still nothing happened. She yelled as loud as possible in an attempt to let the broken man before her know she was there to help and he was not alone.

Only a faint "help" echoed through the world as the young man's head snapped up and then she was falling into darkness. Her offer of aid resounded as though it had been shouted down a long tunnel but now her screams were just the echo from another time and place entirely.

The room shifted around her as she tumbled through existence once more. For a short few seconds, Addie saw the same beautiful man sitting upright in a bed she'd never seen before. His dark hair was disheveled by a restless sleep and sweat coated his face and the tan skin of his chest. Anger and agony drew two harsh lines between his brows.

He said *something*. She was sure he had said something but she felt too far away to hear him clearly, like her head was sinking below water deep in a cave somewhere far away. Addie desperately tried to hold on to the world around her but she continued to fall into a void between worlds. The young man quickly approached her from across the room. Just as he pulled back the fabric that concealed her in shadow, she was ripped into emptiness once again.

Chapter 3

Andrew

"Father, we can't just let her stay out there alone," Prince Andrew's voice was stern.

Standing before King Poneros Colvin's throne, Addie's eldest brother pleaded with their father. Despite his efforts over the past week, the king continued to refuse to send a search party into the Alderbrooke Forest to find the princess.

Andrew ran a hand through his sandy brown hair, "I know you say we don't have the manpower to send a large party to find her, but I am not asking for more than *two* men to accompany me."

King Colvin rose from his seat and stepped down from the dais with regal grace, "As I have already stated, I will not be sending anyone after your sister. She made her choice to disobey my wishes in the middle of the night. I will not risk my heir to find her."

"She could be hurt or dying, father; possibly even dead already!" Andrew shouted.

Spinning hard on his heels, the king wrapped his large fist around his son's throat, "I am not in the business of repeating myself, *son*. You will not ask to send aid for Addie again. Do you understand?"

"You don't care at all," Andrew's powers drifted through his father's thoughts. "Have you lost your humanity entirely?" Andrew spoke through raspy breath, his father's fist tightening unnaturally.

"You ungrateful swine! I am not your equal. You have no right to use your gifts against me. Addie made her choice and it appears you have made yours. You will learn your place, as your brother has. I will teach you not to speak to me like that! Vern…" King Colvin bellowed and Andrew's vision began to darken at the edges as he slowly lost consciousness.

When he woke, Andrew's head pounded. His hands and feet were pulled tight on either side of his body; secured in place by rusted metal shackles. The room was dark and cold around him as he faced a mossy, damp stone wall. Goosebumps rose over his entire body and the metal shackles bit hard into the bare skin of his wrists and ankles. Instantly, the prince knew where he was. The thick smell of mildew filled his nose as he inhaled a shaky breath.

"Hello, Prince. I am happy to see you again," a cruel voice sounded from the doorway behind him.

"Vern, always a pleasure," Andrew replied dryly.

"It's been a while, hasn't it? I think this has been the longest time we've gone between these… *visits*," Andrew could hear the smile that etched itself into Vern Accor's ugly face.

"Almost six months, I believe," Andrew took a deep breath through his nose and tried to brace himself for what he knew was coming.

"Then I won't waste any more time. The king has asked me to ensure you remember your place. He has left the lashing total to my discretion. I think we will start with fifteen and see if you are still conscious."

Andrew clenched his jaw as the barbed whip in the king's interrogator's hand snapped through the air and tore through the bare skin on his back. After years of punishment from the man at the door, Andrew had learned to avoid counting each lash if he could and to avoid screaming. Vern was never one to stick to his word; fifteen lashes usually meant a minimum of twenty. If Andrew made any sound, Vern would start his count over after the prince was silent once again.

Crack after crack of the whip, Andrew's fist tightened around the metal chains of his cuffs. Several trails of blood ran down his back, soaking the top of his tan trousers. Layers of skin split and soon Andrew struggled to remain conscious through the pain.

"That's probably fifteen," Vern laughed with a shrug. Despite his best efforts to avoid counting each strike, Andrew knew it was more than fifteen; seven more to be exact. "Now, prince, will you be speaking out against your king again?"

Spitting onto the floor, Andrew winced as he tried to stand tall, "I will always do what is right for those I love; even if that means I do not agree with my father."

"Such a shame. For *you,* I mean. I, myself, *thoroughly* enjoy this," Vern pulled his arm back once again and several more snaps of his whip pulled Andrew into the oblivion of blinding pain.

Just as it always was after every visit to Vern, Andrew woke alone in the confines of his own room. The injuries that should mar his skin were nowhere to be seen. The smooth plains of his muscular body showed no sign of the torture he became accustom to at a young age. The sound of sloshing water from the bathing chamber in his rooms drew his attention.

"Who's there?" His voice was rough. At some point during his punishment he must have begun to scream before he passed out.

"I'm sorry, your highness. I didn't realize you would wake so quickly," a young woman stepped out into the sitting room.

"Who are you?" Andrew reiterated.

"My name is Elinore, sire. The king..." Elinore's voice wavered, "The king recently employed me as his *personal* healer."

"Where is Shawn, his last *personal* healer?" Andrew asked.

Lowering her eyes to the floor, Elinore shook her head and whispered low, "Shawn liked to talk, sire. I believe he was taken to Vern."

"Why did you take the position?" Andrew demanded.

"I don't think I had the choice to refuse *his majesty*," Elinore spit her final words with complete discuss before she lifted her head and looked into the prince's sea blue gaze. Panic momentarily flashed in the young healer's eyes, "Please forgive me, your highness. I should not speak in such a manner."

Andrew froze momentarily as he looked over the young woman's face. Despite being far too thin for her health, she was quite beautiful. Her honey brown eyes were kind and a soft smile graced her blushing cheeks at his intense gaze.

"No," Andrew spoke, clearing his throat, "You have done nothing wrong, miss. I do hope you always feel comfortable speaking freely with me. Anything you say will not leave the confines of this room. I promise you."

Andrew watched as the pink in her face deepened and she ran her palms down the front of her apron. A loud crash from his chamber doors caused both the prince and Elinore to jump slightly.

"Out. Now! I must speak with the prince," Vern barked before stomping through the room and wrapping his hand around Elinore's forearm.

Andrew was nearly certain he heard bone snap as Vern pulled the small woman forcefully toward the door. A sharp wine slipped from Elinore's lips and anger boiled in Andrew's chest.

"There is no need for that, Vern!" Andrew stepped forward grabbing Vern's wrist, "Let her go! You will not lay another hand on her!" Slowly, a malicious smile spread across the interrogator's face as he looked from the prince to the king's chosen healer.

"Please," Elinore whispered through silent sobs, "You will make this worse."

"Quiet, bitch!" Vern tossed Elinore through the open door, sending her stumbling to the marble floor of the hall beyond, "Fix that arm and head to my chambers now."

Silent tears streamed down Elinore's face and dripped from her chin, "Sir?"

"Are you deaf or just stupid? Get to my room!" Vern barked, causing Elinore to wince.

Vern pulled his hand free of Andrew's grasp and slammed the door, closing him in the room alone with the prince. "I do not care who you are, *boy*. You do not order anything from me. I had no intention of harming that young woman any further but now you have peaked my interest. I am going to leave this room and I will touch that healer *any way* I please. She actually is quite lovely, you know. The way her skin flushes. It is enticing, is it not? I am going to enjoy the next few hours so much more knowing it tortures you too. The best part is, you won't even be able to do anything to stop me."

Andrew leapt forward and smashed his fist into Vern's nose, splattering blood down his bare chest. Quickly, he moved to strike the mammoth of a man as many times as he could. Despite the prince standing at nearly six and a half feet tall, Vern still towered over him by several inches and out-weighed him significantly.

Andrew knew he wouldn't win this fight but he refused to let Vern leave unscathed. Vern spun hard and drove his elbow into the prince's chest, knocking the air from his lungs. In one swift movement, he lifted Andrew from the ground and threw him back to the floor. In an instant, he was on him, slamming his fist into the prince's chest and face. Andrew freed his right arm from beneath Vern's knee and landed several sharp blows to the larger man's ribs. Bones snapped along the large man's side with each hit. Blood from Vern's nose dripped down onto the prince's bruised face.

"Fuck. You broke my nose, mother fucker," Vern spat, "I was going to have the healer fix it but I quite like the way my blood looks on you. I think it will look delicious on that delicate little thing's back," Vern grinned wide, red staining his gnarled teeth. The sound of his grimy voice made Andrew's skin crawl.

"Fuck you," Andrew spat around a mouth full of blood before Vern's large fist threw his head back into the ornate tile floor, pitching him back into unconsciousness.

Chapter 4

Grant

Despite trying his best to forget the agony of last night's nightmare and his strange, abrupt wake up this morning, Grant couldn't help but continue to mull over the strange plea he'd heard. The woman's voice seemed achingly familiar but he couldn't seem to place when or where he had heard her in his past. Lacing up his pants, Grant looked at himself in the floor length mirror in his bathing chamber.

   Since his father left, Grant no longer needed to fill his time keeping Lord Anderson from drinking himself into a stupor every morning. His days were no longer spent ensuring his father saw the light of day at least once while it was still high in the sky. Instead, most mornings this past month, Grant found himself training in the courtyard. His already toned body became more defined and his skin looked like as if it had been kissed by the sun's golden rays. Only in his eyes could you see the exhaustion that weighed him down. They seemed gaunt and more hollow than they had just weeks before, likely due to his terror-filled sleep nearly every night and the recent stress of his father's journey to see the king alone.

In need of a distraction, Grant found himself returning to his father's study earlier than usual. Like he had the past several days after his training, he searched for any clue regarding his father's plan and location. With the anniversary of his mother's death now less than a week away, Grant knew his father wanted to confront the king again about protecting those that lived in the outskirts of the kingdom. He had a terrible feeling his father's plans were far more nefarious than a sit down meeting with their ruler, however.

One evening before his father had left for the capital, Grant overheard him discussing some sort of ancient text with a spindly woman with long moon white hair. Most of their talk had been difficult to hear until the woman raised her voice in concern.

"This is all ill advised, Anderson," the woman seemed to be objecting to something his father had said but as soon as Grant entered his father's study, they both fell silent. As the woman turned to leave, she brushed against Grant's arm and froze mid-stride. Her bright green eyes appeared to take a milky hue.

"You and the shadow can save us all," she whispered low enough that Grant was certain his father most likely had not been able to hear.

Now, standing in the same place, Grant's memory of that day came flooding back and he couldn't help but think the woman's statement may be more relevant than just the ramblings of a crazy old witch. Did this have anything to do with the movement in the shadows this morning or his altered nightmare last night? How was his father involved with the voice he had heard?

While Grant sifted through the papers on the desk, a phrase was frantically scribbled across multiple parchments like it was something his father had been obsessing over:

Find the cave
Find the cave
Find the cave

"I need to find the witch you were meeting with, father," Grant whispered to himself. "She has to know something."

Grant returned to his room with several papers and began to pack a satchel with everything he thought he might need for a journey of unknown dangers and an unclear final destination. The knock at his bedchamber door drew his attention away from his packing.

"Sir, it's Ren. Maggie would like to know if you were going to be in need of breakfast this morning," Ren stated from behind the closed door.

"Come in, Ren. I may need a few things beyond breakfast from you and Maggie both," Grant responded.

"Are you leaving, sir? How long might we expect you to be gone? I can let Maggie know right away," Ren bowed his head as he entered.

"I don't know yet. At least two weeks I believe. I need to find my father. He's been gone far too long and I'm beginning to think something has happened. I do have a question for you though, Ren," Grant turned from his nightstand to face his father's oldest friend.

"Anything, sir," Ren nodded.

Grant stepped closer to the last member of his family's personal guard, "Before my father left, he met with an older

23

woman. I believe she may know something about what he had been getting himself involved in. Do you know who she is or what he needed her aid with?" Something in Ren's expression sent alarm bells ringing in Grant's head.

"Sir, I do not believe that woman is someone you, or your father for that matter, should be associated with; not given the current climate with the king," Ren stated sternly despite the color draining from his face.

"That was not my question. I need to know who she is and where I can find her. Now, Ren. Please."

"She is a necromancer, sir. Her magic is unpredictable and wicked. I," Before he could finish his thought, Grant interjected.

"And mine is not?!" his words were clipped, a hint of pain in every word. Instantly regretting his tone, Grant rubbed the stubble on his face. "Sorry," he breathed slowly and looked away, "I'm on edge and this week is… h-hard," Grant stated through clenched teeth.

"No need to apologize. I do understand more than most," Ren replied gently and placed a hand on Grant's shoulder. The same sorrow Grant felt each day filled the older man's eyes.

As one of the few people to survive the attack last fall and know of Grant's powers, Ren truly was one of the very few who understood Grant's turmoil. He had always been a great source of advice and a familiar comfort after his mother's death.

"Thank you, Ren, for everything," Grant sighed, "I'm going into town to see if Will would like to join me on my fool's adventure to find my father. Could you ask Maggie to pack a bit extra for him, please?"

24

Ren gave Grant a small grin in gratitude and answered, "Of course. Would you like me to prepare our horses as well then? I can accompany you both."

"I will need you here, my friend. It will not be an easy trip to the capital and I fear this place may fall apart without you," Grant tried to keep his concern for the aging man from his face and failed.

"Do you truly think me that old? I am not yet ready to be put out to pasture," Ren said with a joking tone.

"I know you can hold your own with the best of them," Grant grinned, "but, as I said, I need you here. If word arrives about my father, or he returns, I will need you home; not traipsing through the wilderness or heaven knows where."

Nodding again, Ren turned for the door, "Then let me get you a map to the necromancer's cottage and hopefully enough food to keep you and your bottomless pit of a friend fed for some of your journey."

"Thank you again," Grant stated with the utmost sincerity.

"It has been, and will always be, my honor, sir," and with a nod of farewell, Grant was again alone in his room.

Grant returned to his packing once more and decided to travel light and bring only the essentials. After closing his bags, Grant made his way into the kitchen down the hall where he found Ren and their cook, Maggie. It was clear the two had a personal relationship despite Ren's attempts to keep their feelings private.

"Well, it's nice to see you young man. It's been a while since I've been able to see your handsome face," Maggie lovingly scolded.

Growing up, Grant and Will spent quite a lot of time in the kitchen with Maggie, sneaking treats and supplies for their adventures as boys. Maggie stepped forward and wrapped her arms around Grant in a warm embrace. He inhaled her familiar honey sweet scent and smiled. She had always felt like a part of his family.

"Maggie and I were just discussing what gift you should bring to the necromancer. We cannot have you showing up, asking for favors from her, empty handed," Ren stated.

"Oh, yes. When she was here last for your father, I recall he requested a large supply of black mustard seed and juniper berries in our deliveries before she arrived. I may have some left of the mustard seed but I am afraid I am out of the other," Maggie remarked and patted Grant's arm.

The plump woman quickly made her way into the pantry closet near the large wood fire stove, her skirts swishing across the recently swept tan tile floors. She returned moments later with her apron filled with several cloth bags and jars with various colored spices.

"There isn't much of the mustard seed left, as I thought," she began, "however, I do have quite a collection of exotic goods we can put together instead. I believe these should be quite the gift, if arranged well."

"Where is this all from?" Grant asked, looking over the array of delicacies Maggie placed atop the butcher block at the center of the room. "This must have taken forever to collect Maggie. I couldn't possibly take these from you."

"Relax child. They are just spices. I have been holding onto them for something special, and what could be more special than helping my family," the older woman smiled kindly.

"Don't go inflating his ego, Mags! His head is already too big as it is," Ren joked and bumped Grant lightly.

"It is not. My head and my ego are perfectly proportionate

26

for my greatness," Grant rebuked, a small grin pulling at the corners of his mouth.

"While you two boys continue your banter, I am going to find my smaller jars and a case for them," Maggie bowed her head slightly and again entered the pantry. After several minutes of her absence, an elated squeak sounded from the pantry door and out flowed a grinning Maggie with two metal tins and a beautiful mahogany box.

"I found a couple of teas! And look at this lovely case. It will do splendidly! The jars are a bit of a mismatched bunch. I broke two of the original ones from the set a while back but there are a few good replacements in here," Maggie said glowing. "Now, let's pick some spices and I can make some labels for them."

After quite a bit of debate, Grant, Maggie, and Ren decided on the six best luxuries to include in the offering for the necromancer and Grant thanked them both several times before making his way out into the stables for his horse, Whiskey. Grant had always enjoyed riding and the effort that went into caring for his horse. As he stepped into the dim stable, Whiskey greeted him with a quiet nicker and chuff. After a quick brush down Grant saddled, loaded and mounted his beloved horse and made his way to the front gates to meet Ren.

"I have outlined the best route to the necromancers for you here. The turn is easy to miss. If you keep a steady pace, you'll need to keep an eye out for two mangled trees about five hours into your ride after you leave Will's," Ren handed Grant a rolled map of Viridia. "The path is overgrown to keep any travelers from stumbling upon it by mistake but if you know what to look for you cannot miss it."

"Thank you again for everything." Grant said, taking the parchment from his friend. "I will return as soon as I can. Please keep things in order for me while my father and I are away."

Ren bowed with a nod and patted Grant's leg, "Of course, sir. Now go, before the morning has left and you must arrive to greet a witch in the dark."

Grant ushered his horse forward at a light trot that quickly picked up pace. The cold morning air whipped his dark hair as he rode into town. The entire ride, Grant pondered how he planned to pitch his quest to his best friend Will without everything sounding foolhardy. Ultimately, he decided there was no way for him to minimize the absurdity of his half-baked plan. The best course of action was to be forthcoming with his friend. Grant would simply ask Will if he would be interested in joining him on a journey to meet with a known necromancer to discuss what his drunken and deranged father enlisted her help with and what that had to do with the king.

There was no true destination Grant knew of beyond the witch. They would be embarking somewhat blindly to find his father. They would need to figure things out as they went along. Within a half of an hour Grant stood at Will's front door, ready for whatever decision his friend would make. Luckily for him, Will was one of the most optimistic, and sometimes foolish, people he knew. Grant was quite sure his friend would be willing to go anywhere, and do just about anything, if it meant he would have a good story to tell.

Chapter 5

Will

William Banks had never been one to shy away from an adventure, regardless of the dangers that may be involved. As a boy, he spent much of his time with his mother in the castle where she served as the queen's lady's maid and where he trained with his uncle, General Thomas Banks. In that time, he befriended a young lord's son who would soon be his closest and most trusted friend. It was no surprise that when that same young man knocked on Will's door this morning, Will had not hesitated to accept his request to join him on a journey of unknown peril.

Grant quickly divulged what he planned to do and that his first stop after Will's would be with the necromancer his father had been meeting with. Both young men were now in the confines of Will's small bedroom while he began to eagerly pack his bags.

"Thank you for this, Will," Grant said, adjusting the wool cloak on his shoulders. "I don't know how long we will be gone or what my father has done but I need to find him."

"You are my brother, Grant, in every sense but blood and your family has always been here for me, no matter what. I am happy to join you. I'm actually quite excited! Work at the shop has been slow lately with more folks leaving the city for the security closer to the castle," Will replied with a half smile.

Will was quite skilled with leather and created beautiful artwork with every piece he was commissioned to create, from bridals for livestock to the most intricate leather clothing pieces. The summer after his fifteenth birthday, he had apprenticed with one of the king's personal leather smiths and had taken to the craft like a fish to water.

"I do have a question though," Will stated and Grant raised a brow. "What did you have Maggie pack for us?"

Grant rolled his eyes with a grin, "Of course you are more concerned about what *food* I've brought than the fact that in just a few hours we will be face to face with a woman who communes with the dead and practices black magic."

As they made their way to collect Will's final few belongings from the sitting room at the front of the small town home, Will saw the lines of concern on Grant's forehead. Looking around, he couldn't help but notice how bare things had truly gotten. He had hoped his best friend would have been distracted enough not to notice as well. Collecting his final belongings, Will turned for the door and Grant shook his head.

"Where is all of your furniture, Will?" Grant asked, skeptically.

"Things have been a little tight at the shop, like I said. I just sold a few things. That's all," Will shrugged, nonchalantly, despite the true fear he knew he wouldn't be able to hide from Grant.

"Your home is *empty* and this was in your room. Why didn't you tell me it was so bad?" Grant held up a notice of eviction and raised a brow.

It was overcast as Will and Grant stepped out into the chilled fall air. The golden strands of Will's short, wavy locks glistened a pale auburn against the yellows, oranges, and reds of the leaves covering the cobblestone streets from the large maple that grew near the town's center. His deep blue eyes glassed from the chilly air, or perhaps his suppressed emotions, as he admitted the truth of his current home life.

"My father stopped sending money home for the town-house and sent a letter letting me know he would not be returning to Shepherd's Glen. He has remarried and does not wish to return to the memories here again. I had planned to tell you I just never found the time to, I guess," Will breathed.

The two young men walked in silence for several minutes as they neared the boarding stables. Turning the final corner, Will approached a young woman no more than fifteen years old.

"Morning, Grace. Could you bring Brandy out for me?" Will smiled.

"And Whiskey as well please, Grace. He is still saddled in the stall near Brandy," Grant added, cheeks flushing lightly.

As teenagers, Grant's father had gifted Will and Grant two beautiful horses after completing their schooling. Both boys thought it would be fitting for the prized horses to be named after the amber colored liquid they had been known to sneak from Lord Anderson's liquor cabinet. Both Will and Grant thought it quite amusing at first; now it felt almost childish when the two horses were referenced together.

Grace giggled brightly and turned to collect the horses while Grant and Will retrieved Will's saddle from its mount in the tack storage room. The stable had once been a hub for the town but now was at a point of dilapidation very few in Shepherd's Glen chose to keep horses boarded.

"She's the oldest of five children," Will nodded in Grace's direction. "She works here almost every day and she takes random jobs like running supplies for me when I can afford her help. Her parents can't afford to leave yet but they are doing their best to make their way north as soon as they are able if things don't change here soon."

"Something has to change. The king needs to either help his people relocate or secure all borders, not just the northern front. Our kingdom is shrinking and rebel attacks are growing far too prevalent," Grant groaned.

Grace approached the young men leading the two horses behind her. Will tossed a sand colored riding blanket over Brandy's back before placing his beautiful leather saddle down.

"Thank you, Grace," Will said, handing the young girl four copper coins; far more than was necessary and more than Will could truly spare.

"Of course, Will. If you need anything else, you know where to find me," Grace waved her thanks and walked back into the supply shed, grinning happily.

After tying his bags down, Will stepped into his stirrup and threw his right leg over his saddle gracefully then turned to face Grant. It hadn't been more than a couple of days since he had seen his friend, but Will thought Grant looked like he had aged and knew he obviously hadn't been sleeping well.

"How are you holding up with all of this, Grant?" Will

32

asked, knitting his brows together in concern.

"It's going to be a long ride. We best head out," Grant diverted.

Taking the hint, Will nudged his horse forward and Grant swiftly mounted Whiskey and followed his friend onto the empty cobblestone street. The mid-morning sun was covered by darkening clouds, turning the sky a deep gray and promising a coming storm.

"We need to make good time if we want to reach the cottage before the storm hits too hard," Grant motioned to the sky with a jerk of his chin.

The ride through town was silent apart from the sound of the horses' shoes against stone. The center of town was empty except for two shops; one selling baked goods and the other a general store that routinely sold out of most things except for a horrible bitter root flavored candy. The smell of freshly baked bread filled the air as Will and Grant passed the bakeshop.

"Did you happen to bring any cake? Or scones? I would love a lemon scone if you have any," Will closed his eyes and imagined one of the crumbly lemon glazed scones Maggie had perfected, his mouth watering at the memory. Moments later, Grant rode up beside Will and smacked his shoulder lightly.

"I only have two scones, so only one now. Maybe another at lunch if we have time to stop," Grant said, placing a loaf wrapped in a white, waxed, linen cloth into Will's hand. The beautiful, golden glazed scone made Will's heart sputter as he took his first bite. This delicacy was the first thing Will had eaten since he had last seen his friend that wasn't either covered in mold or didn't involve a game of roulette with his intestines; a game he had unfortunately lost more times than he would care to admit.

Both Will and Grant fell silent as the sound of horse hooves against paved roads was replaced with a softer crunch of gravel and dirt. Soon the buildings on the outer edge of town began to disappear behind them in the distance. The path north towards the necromancer's cottage was nearly a full day's ride through the pine forest that surrounded most of Shepherd's Glen. If they made good time, they could reach the hidden path Ren had drawn on the map just before lunch. From there, it was most likely another three or four hours through the forest, given the terrain in the thickest area of the woods.

Will's mind began to wander the longer they remained silent. Soon his head was filled with what he expected to find once they reached the witch's cottage. As someone who practiced black magic and had regular interactions with the dead, Will assumed her cottage had to be filled with spiders and critters of all shapes and sizes. He imagined it probably smelled like mold and dust and was poorly lit by large, black, drippy candles.

He was sure he hadn't ever met a necromancer in person and could only imagine how dreadful she would look. He pictured a small hunched woman with stringy, dark, gray-black hair and putrid green hued skin like the witches he'd seen depicted in the story books he read as a child. He could almost see her face covered in warts and a large goiter on her neck.

"Are goiters contagious?" Will's voice broke the silence.

"What?" Grant furrowed his brow as he looked over to his best friend beside him.

"Like a wart? Can you catch one like a wart? Because I don't think I want to have either but I think I could manage a wart or two. I don't know about a goiter," Will admitted.

Grant shook his head before he burst into a deep belly laugh, "I don't think they are, so I think you are going to be alright!"

"I bet the necromancer has them," Will said quietly.

Still chuckling to himself Grant asked, "Is that what you have been thinking about for the last twenty minutes? I can assure you she does not have a goiter or warts. She is an older woman but she looks quite lovely, actually."

"Oh, right, you have met her. I forgot. She does probably live in a dirty old hut though" Will thought aloud.

"That may be true. I don't know. I guess we will see soon enough," Grant replied.

"Did Ren tell you what we should expect from her?" Will asked.

"Not really. He just told me necromancers are people you don't want to cross and it's best to avoid them if you can. And if you can't, it's best to bring a gift or offering to get you into their good graces," Grant reached into his bag and pulled out a wooden package.

Will leaned forward slightly in his saddle to see what Grant held in his hands. "What's that?" he asked, tentatively.

"Ren and Maggie said my father gifted her spices when she was at the manor so I asked Maggie to bottle some of her best spices and a few teas in these glass bottles. Hopefully this will be enough to get a few questions answered," Grant admitted, opening the parcel's lid.

Inside the wooden box rested six glass jars nestled in velvet-lined cubbies. Two of the vials had simple cork stoppers while the remaining four were capped with beautiful intricate glass knobs shaped like budding flowers. Each was labeled with a paper tag and a dark green ribbon.

"What's in each one?" Will squinted to read.

"There is saffron, mustard seed, vanilla bean, cinnamon, cumin, and white pepper. They are the best we have so I hope they are things she can use. I also have a metal tin of black tea and another filled with a red tea as well," Grant patted his satchel again as he placed the box gently back inside.

The next several hours passed quickly. It was difficult to tell where the sun sat in the sky through the clouds as they rode but Will could see Grant regularly checking his gold pocket watch.

"It's past midday," Grant said, "we should be coming to the path soon and we can stop to eat."

Will's eyes lit up and he grinned widely. "Thank the heavens! I am starving!"

"How you are able to eat the way you do and still remain as you are, is perplexing, Will," Grant chuckled.

"I don't really know how to respond to that," Will admitted with a shrug. "What all do we have to eat?"

"To be honest, I don't know yet. We can check once we get to a good place to stop. I think that may be the path just ahead." Grant picked up his pace to a trot and steered Whiskey to a break in the shrubbery.

The two trees on either side of a poorly defined dirt path matched the ones Ren had described for Grant. Both trees were twisted unnaturally as though they had been wrung out like wet rags. The overgrowth made the path almost invisible to any passerby that was not looking for it. Will and Grant both had taken this road to the castle likely hundreds of times and had never paid any special attention to this section of the forest as though it had been shielded from sight.

"This is it I think," Grant almost whispered.

"We can't stop in the middle of the road though, Grant. If anyone sees us here and knows this place, word could get back to the king. I don't know if that looks good for us, *for you*, given your father's history with the king, if we are rumored to be consorting with a known necromancer," Will's caution was evident in his gentle tone.

"I know. Lets ride in a little ways and see if there is a safer place to stop off the main road and we can discuss the plan," Grant admitted.

"We have a plan?" Will's eyebrows rose, mocking surprise. "I figured we could give her your spices and I would use my magnificent charm to woo her." Will's goofy smile spread across his face.

"Your charm might be enough to get us into trouble," Grant jabbed, playfully, "I think it's best I do the introductions and most of the talking."

"Ya, that's probably best. I wouldn't want to be kept as her pet if she falls in love with me," Will joked. "I'll let you take the lead this time."

Roughly ten minutes from the main road, Will and Grant stopped in a small meadow next to the path that would lead them to the witch's cottage. Along the edge of the field of wildflowers was a small slow moving creek and an apple tree. The two riders dismounted gracefully and tied both horses to the small fruit tree at the water's edge to graze. Will stood next to Grant and watched his friend pull out a large bundle wrapped in cloth and tied with twine, as well as a smaller sack, from his saddlebags.

"Well, moment of truth my friend. These are the items Mags said were for today," Grant said, handing both items over to Will.

He accepted the packages and both young men took a seat near the creek's edge, "I hope there's a scotch egg in here," Will exhaled.

Opening the smaller sack, Will placed two beautiful, fluffy rolls down followed by a small brick of cheese. In the larger cloth, Will found dried meats, four strips of crisp bacon, two apples, a handful of carrots, two baked potatoes and another smaller package wrapped in bee's wax cloth with a note that had his name scribed on the outside, tied on by a velvet ribbon:

Will

I hope you have chosen to accompany our dearest Grant on his journey. I know you will keep him out of too much trouble or, at the very least, be by his side and have his back when you two inevitably find yourselves in a tight spot.

-Love, Maggie

Will handed the note over to Grant to read as he opened the last package. Resting in Will's hands were the two most beautiful sausage wrapped eggs he had ever seen. He looked up to find his best friend grinning at him with a small container in his hands that looked like Maggie's homemade stone ground mustard.

"She asked that I keep those a secret until we stopped for lunch today," Grant placed the mustard into Will's hand and began to eat a strip of bacon. "Both of those are yours. They won't last long on this trip and I don't have much of an appetite today."

Will smiled knowing that was not entirely true. Grant had always made a point to look after his friend as one would a little brother, even before their accident when they were kids. Even as adults, Will knew Grant looked out for his welfare constantly. Grant was most likely starved from their long ride but insisted on Will eating more than his share.

"Thank you, Grant. I am going to kiss that wonderful woman when I see her when we return!" Will picked up one of the eggs and took a bite and closed his eyes with a pleased groan. "These are the absolute best!"

"Good! I ate one on my way out this morning when they were hot and it did not disappoint," Grant remarked. "Now, let's discuss how this all might play out with the necromancer. I believe we should get a look at the house before we head in and, as politely as we can, offer her the goods Maggie and Ren suggested. Then, hopefully, we will have the opportunity to ask what she may know about my father. If she accepts, that is the best case scenario and if she does not, we will hope we haven't offended her in any way and head for the castle to see if, by some miracle, my father actually made it there as he said he intended."

"Sounds like a good plan to me," Will sputtered through a mouth full of food, small crumples of meat tumbling into his lap from the corners of his mouth.

Following their quick meal, Grant and Will remounted their horses and were surprised to find the remainder of the path leading to the cottage was not at all as rough as the map had suggested.

"Is that it already?" Will asked, an hour later, pointing to the cottage through the thicket of trees just ahead. "It's much more ordinary than I expected."

"I don't know. The map says it should be a good distance away still and should not have been so easy to get to. But who else would be this far from the main road?" Grant questioned and dismounted his horse. "Let's tie the horses here and walk in to get a better look first."

"Good idea," Will slid from Brandy's saddle and tied her next to Whiskey just off the path.

Both men moved off the trail and slowly made their way closer to the small cream colored home. As they approached, they saw the beautiful colored flowers that ornamented several window boxes. The front stone walk appeared clean and well manicured. At the edge of the white fence, a dark haired young woman knelt with her hands in the dirt. She was clad in dark leather pants and a white flowing blouse that was rolled to her elbows. Will froze instantly when the young woman stood and wiped her hands on the apron tied around her waist then turned to face where Will and Grant stood in the shadows. Dark strands of soft curls tumbled from over her shoulders and shone in the dim sun light.

Will stumbled out from his vantage point before Grant could stop him. "I think I might be in love," Will spoke without thought as though he was enchanted.

The young woman's emerald eyes darted to Will then back to where Grant stood still concealed in shadow. Without warning, she sprinted for the door of the cottage where the necromancer now stood with a small basket in hand. Will's eyes followed her movement until the young woman reached the necromancer's side. Quickly, she picked up a small, uncorked vial full of dark blue liquid from the basket and threw it in his direction, splashing the contents over his head. His vision instantly began to change. He was shrinking lower and lower to the ground. Grant quickly stepped forward with his hands raised.

"Please ma'am, don't harm him any farther. I just have a few questions," Grant pleaded.

"Well hello again, Grant Anderson. Your friend will be just fine. A few hours as a… what has he become? Ah, *a newt*, never hurt anyone. Please, come in," The older woman raised a brow and spoke gently, then ushered Grant forward to collect his friend from the pile of Will's discarded clothing on the ground and follow her inside.

Chapter 6

Grant

Grant stood above the small, orange speckled amphibian, that moments ago was his closest friend, and slowly bent to pick him up gently from the ground. The moment his hands touched the creature's moist skin, Grant's mind was flooded by vivid memories.

* * *

A young Grant and his father walked through the long halls of the castle toward the guest suites in the east wing. Lord Anderson had been called to the castle for a meeting with the king's council and Grant had been elated to have the opportunity to get to stay here this week. As they rounded the final corner that led to their rooms, a small boy with blonde hair and freckles splashed across his nose, crashed into Grant, spilling the contents of his arms and knocking both children to the floor.

"I'm sorry," the boy's small voice sounded.

Grant giggled, "Is this sugar?" Looking down, Grant saw the front of his light green tunic and dark brown trousers covered in a layer of a powdery white substance.

"Yes," the boy admitted sheepishly, picking up several sugar dusted balls of dough. "They had extra pastries Mama said I could have after the queen's tea. I didn't mean to ruin your fineries, my lords."

Lord Anderson swept away some of the sugar that had managed to make its way to his pants as well. "There is no need for an apology," Gregory Anderson smiled and helped the two boys to their feet. "What is your name, son?"

"Will- William Banks, my lord," Will bowed his head.

"Hello Will. This is my son, Grant," Lord Anderson gestured to his son with a graceful hand.

"Hi!" Grant grinned wide.

"Will, do you think you could help us out? You seemed to be in a bit of a hurry but I am in need of some assistance," Lord Anderson raised a brow curiously.

"Of course, sir. How may I help?" Will replied eagerly.

"I shall be in meetings quite a lot this week. If you are around, and free for it, do you believe you could show my son around the grounds a bit and help keep him busy?" Lord Anderson smiled.

"Really father!?" Grant bounced excitedly.

"Of course, my Lord!" Will beamed. "Do you want to see a really cool tree? We can eat these too," Will lifted a pile of goodies in his small hands.

"May I, father?" Grant asked Lord Anderson enthusiastically.

Lord Anderson nodded and instantly both children were running down the hall headed toward the gardens. The memory of Grant and Will's first meeting began to fade from Grant's view and was replaced by another memory. Both boys, now in their early teen years, had climbed to the top of one of the larger trees near the castle, hoping to see into the council room.

Laughing loudly, Will hooted, "Could you imagine flying, Grant? That would be amazing! Perhaps someday when we are older, we can capture a giant crow from the isles when it is a baby and raise it as a pet. Then we could fly anywhere."

Playfully, Grant nudged his friend as he climbed higher, "And what will you feed it?"

"It can eat my leftover scraps of course," Will decided happily.

"Then it will surely starve," Grant joked and both boys lost themselves to hysterics.

Grant's memory faded once again and a new scene unfolded before him. This time Grant's mind began to race in a panic. He had done his best to forget the specifics of this day but now every detail manifested in stark resolution. It had been nearly a decade since their first meeting and hundreds of adventures. He found himself now standing in front of his friend atop the castle's tallest parapet that led from the main building to the tallest watch tower. From the lookout, Grant and Will would be able to see over the forest surrounding the castle all the way to the cliffs by the sea.

"We're almost there," Grant shouted. "I didn't realize it would be so windy this high up."

"This is amazing!" Will shouted back to Grant.

Grant looked down just before taking his final few steps to

the lookout and his breath caught in his throat. "How high do you think we are? It has to be close to 200 feet, right?"

"Definitely! Maybe higher! It's almost like flying!" Will grinned.

For years Grant and Will had dreamed of getting to climb to the top of this tower and see the sea beyond but had never been given permission to take the tower stairs. Last night, after sneaking into Lord Anderson's liquor case, Grant and Will decided this morning would be the day they made the journey across the parapet while the rest of the castle was still asleep. Finally, both young men looked out over the trees to the rising sun. The sky was painted with strokes of oranges, pinks, and yellows. This view was everything Grant and Will had hoped for and more.

"You know, the ocean is beautiful and all but I think this is the closest I hope to ever get to the deep," Will breathed nervously.

"Are you scared of the ocean, Will?" Grant teased.

"Not the ocean itself but what hides below its surface is... terrifying," Will admitted. "It is beautiful from here though."

"We should head back soon, before the castle guards find us and we are forced to clean the stables again like when we *tested out* the royal carriage last year," Grant laughed.

"Oh, but what a story that is to tell!" Will beamed. "Do you remember your father's face when we rode back into the courtyard and the entire guard was there? That was worth every minute of stable duty!"

"Ya it was," Grant smirked. "Watch your step here, this stone is a bit loose." Grant pointed to the stone at the edge of the parapet as he stepped past Will back toward the castle.

Several steps later, Grant heard the shift of stone behind

45

him as Will's feet stumbled. He whirled around in time to watch his best friend stumble backward and roll his foot over the loose stone. One moment Will was mere feet from Grant and the next he was falling. Grant reached forward to grab his friend's hand and stop his fall but unintentionally something dark broke free from Grant's mind and wrapped itself around Will's subconscious. Wicked tendrils clawed through Will's thoughts and nightmare clouded both young men's vision. In a matter of seconds, Grant too was tumbling from the tower's edge, still lost to the strange images of crashing waves and wicked mer-folk before all went dark.

* * *

Grant's eyes refocused on the newt curled into his palm. He wasn't sure how this had gone so terribly wrong so quickly or why he had just seen what he had. Was there some sort of ward surrounding the cabin that made Will expose himself like that? Will was usually a little reckless but not stupid. He would have never endangered himself or Grant like that on purpose.

The older woman at the door again startled him when she spoke. "Lord Anderson, you do have questions, do you not? I have quite a bit to tell you if you would please follow me."

Grant blinked in surprise, heart breaking slightly. "I am not Lord Anderson ma'am. Not unless you know about something that has happened to my father that I do not."

As he stepped across the threshold to the necromancer's home behind the two women, Grant was stunned silent. The interior of the small cottage was far grander than would be expected given its exterior facade. From outside the cottage, it appeared as though there should be only one main living space and perhaps a separate bedchamber and possibly a small attic. The inside, however, consisted of a grand entryway and a long hall with several doors to adjacent rooms on either side. The staircase just off the front door swept to a landing on a second story as large as the lower level.

"How?" Grant whispered to himself.

"The house is enchanted. It was my mother's and someday it will be my daughter, Cora's," the older woman waved her hand towards the dark haired young lady beside her. "Many women in my family have worked very hard to keep our home's appearance as it is. Now would you please, follow me to the drawing room. We have a lot to discuss and not enough time, I am afraid."

Nodding, Grant and his amphibian friend followed. No part of the house had been as Will or Grant had expected. The walls were a light taupe color with beautiful artwork hung throughout. The floors were a pale, polished marble with delicate veins of gold. Huge windows allowed an abundance of natural light to fill the space, while the furnishings in each room they passed were vivid and cheerful.

When they turned to enter the drawing room, the air seemed to chill slightly and Grant and Will's original expectation of the home's decor was more accurate here. The walls were lined in deep purple velvet with multiple shelves housing neatly organized jars and vials of various objects. The largest jar at the back of the room held a clear liquid encasing a massive grayish pink hand tipped in four long black talons.

"Please have a seat, all of you, so we may begin," The necromancer requested pulling out two black leather armchairs in front of a large table.

"Thank you, ma'am. I am here to discuss your dealings with my father and I have brought you this," Grant placed Will on the table and retrieved the box of spices and teas from his satchel.

"Oh, dear child, we have far more to discuss than just your father, but that should be as good of a place to begin as any other. And thank you for the offering. I do love a good vanilla and cinnamon tea," the necromancer smiled without opening the box and sat in the large wing back chair on the other side of the table.

Puzzled, Grant spoke "How? Never mind, I'm glad you are pleased. What can you tell me about my father."

"After Lady Anderson's murder, your father came to see me with the hope of speaking with his wife. I did my best but her soul searched for peace and did not wish to linger in this world. I was able to contact her briefly to give your father closure but, in his grief, Lord Anderson requested he hold on to my spell book a little longer to try on his own. I did not believe it wise and should have listened to my feelings then. I returned to your home a couple of weeks ago to retrieve my book. He asked if he could return my manuscript when he left for the capital to see the king and I reluctantly agreed, despite my mistrust. That is when I met you," the woman furrowed her brows curiously.

"I don't think my father ever made it to the castle to see the king," Grant admitted.

"Nor do I. My book is filled with ancient spells and wisdom

from my ancestors and I fear your father may use it when he does not truly understand what it can do. When I touched you as I passed you in your father's study, I saw what you are, Grant." The older woman leaned over the desk and narrowed her eyes on him. "How you have kept your powers suppressed without losing yourself to them is fascinating. You are lucky the king has not discovered what you are capable of yet but I fear that may soon come to pass."

Grant's brows knit together forming two parallel lines, "My power is not a gift. It is terrifying."

"You are correct. Power can be terrifying to those who care how it is used. This kingdom teeters quite precariously on the edge of a very sharp blade, Grant Anderson. Magic flourished throughout our continent once, centuries ago, but greed is a dangerous thing. Kings of our past have staunched the flow of magic to ensure only nobility can access it. But magic is a living thing that needs balance and for decades the southernmost regions of Viridia have felt a resurgence. Gifts like yours are... *uncommon* and Viridia's king has been working very diligently to ensure that power like yours does not exist at all. Even those of royal blood have met tragic ends because of King Colvin's hunger. That being said, our princess needs you or she will not survive the shadows her father and yours have damned her to and this kingdom will fall," the necromancer warned.

Grant's heart dropped into his stomach. For year's, Addie had been a true friend in the castle and was the main reason he had refused to return to court after his accident with Will. Without control of his cursed nightmares, Grant feared he could harm another person he deeply cared for and that was something he could not live with; especially if that someone was the young woman he had loved as an adolescent.

"How is the princess involved?! Are you saying the shadow from my dream was Addie? How is that possible and how do you know about any of this?" Grant questioned. He had not even told his best friend about his strange encounter this morning with the woman in his nightmare.

"Unless you are like my Cora and were *born* with the gift, foresight is a difficult magic to master. Things are always changing. I cannot say, with absolute certainty, what has or will happen to the young woman in your nightmare. But yes, the voice in your dream was very much real and the princess is lost between life and death at your father's hand no less. You will need to embrace your own powers if you wish to save her and this kingdom," the necromancer explained. "Like your own, many gifts are not understood and thus not trusted but you will need to trust yourself and the princess. Some gifts that are given are *multifaceted*. Some who possess talents, like yours and Princess Addie's, are a dichotomy. You may be able to destroy with one's own fear and tear a soul from existence but in turn, you also possess the ability to mend a lost soul if you are able to find balance."

"No, that can't be true. I would know if I could help people. My powers are not a gift, they are a danger to everyone," Grant protested.

"Tell me, Grant, when was the last time you intentionally used any aspect of your power. I believe it is safe to say it was the night your mother died. Was it not? Or perhaps, more recently, with another young lord?" the necromancer asked, not needing an answer. "You seem to utilize moments when your emotions are high, like when your mother was butchered or when you and William fell. You seem to grab onto that power, that terror, but it can also bring immense joy as well if used correctly and not feared."

Cora shifted slightly in her seat at her mother's words and cleared her throat to speak. "Mother, I think it would be wise to discuss our concerns about Lord Anderson's current location."

"Ah, yes. Of course," Cora's mother sighed hesitantly.

"You don't believe my father ever intended to return your book and speak with the king," Grant stated.

"No, I do not believe he intends to ever return what is mine. However, I do believe the castle will be his ultimate destination. I fear he may have entered the Alderbrooke Forest in search of retribution for your mother's death. In my book, there is a prophecy that tells of a great army that can be risen if one is willing to forfeit their own life to control it. It is written that whomever raises such an army may doom us all. But, as I said before, foresight is difficult," the necromancer explained in a foreboding tone.

"Give me your hand so I may be able to see your roll more clearly," the older woman held her palms up for Grant.

Reluctantly, Grant placed his hand into her outstretched arms. Quickly, the necromancer's ice-cold fingers gripped Grant's right wrist like a vice, bruising the skin. Grant struggled and attempted to pry free with his other hand but found his shoulders pinned in place by Cora now standing just behind him. The necromancer effortlessly held his arm still and pushed the small newt in front of them aside before she drew a small dagger from her hip. As she ran the knife across Grant's palm, a thin bead of blood bloomed in its path.

"What the fuck?!" Grant protested as the woman behind the table leaned across the distance and ran her tongue over

51

Grant's wound. "Why did you do that?"

"Shh!" Cora chided. "Be quiet and let her see, you fool."

Cora's mother had gone still in her chair, eyes fogging a milky white. In a voice that sounded like it belonged to the old and young, both male and female, the necromancer spoke:

> *"Find the cave and set them free*
> *Do not forget there is a fee*
> *A sacrifice by more than one*
> *He tries to raise the dead*
> *To right a wrong that should not be*
> *Will fill the world with dread*
> *Shadowed fear and healing hand*
> *May revive this cursed land"*

Just as abruptly as her tone had changed the necromancer relaxed into her chair and spoke again in her previously melodic tone, "You will stay here tonight. In the morning, you and your companion will leave for Alderbrooke Forest. Cora will be your guide."

"What did all of that just mean?" Grant demanded. "The army my father is searching for is an army of the dead? He wouldn't do that. And he would never intentionally harm Addie. He is a good man."

"Grief and anger can rot one's heart and make even the strongest of us do the unbelievable, my dear child. Losing one's mated bond is like having your soul cleaved in two. Once a bond is accepted, your souls are tethered to each other completely, for eternity. It was believed, long ago, that the strongest of bonded could even feel the other's pain as their own. I believe Lord and Lady Anderson may have been one

52

of those few. Your father losing his wife and possibly even feeling her pain in death was far too much for his shattered soul to handle, it would seem. His desires are abhorrent, yes, but what remains is not the father you knew, Grant. Please remember that and try to find the light in him that once was."

"I do not believe your father has succeeded in his plan entirely or we would not be here now. Something has gone wrong. What exactly went wrong… I do not know. This will be your task to discover. Now, you need to rest. It is a dangerous journey ahead," The older woman rose gracefully to exit the room.

Grant sat frozen in his seat for several seconds before he spoke, "What about Will? He can't stay like this."

"Ah, yes. Cora dear, could you make a draft to turn him back for us, please. We cannot have your mate stuck in this form forever." The necromancer called to her daughter over her shoulder.

"Of course, mother," Cora sighed. "I do wish you would have kept the last part to yourself though," Cora exhaled.

Grant's eyes widened. "Mate? How is that possible? How could you know that?"

"Most of those with gifts have one in order to ensure their power passes to the next generation. It is like your soul calls for them when you are near; like a pull or a push together," Cora stated dismissively as she collected vials from the wall and began to mix them into a small black pot near the hearth. "I knew who he was before he let his foolish heart guide him and he stepped out from behind the bushes an hour ago. I discovered who he was to me the day I saved his life at the castle as a teenager. I saved your life too that day for that matter." Soon the smell of burned vegetation filled the room.

53

"What? Does that mean he has a gift too? Do I have a mate as well?" Grant questioned.

Cora stepped back to Grant and the newt version of Will on the table. "Yes to both, you fool. He is a shifter. Do not tell him what my mother has said about his and my relationship or I will gut you, lordling," Cora threatened.

Grant nodded and asked gingerly, "How long will it take before he is human? Will he remember anything?"

"He won't remember anything after stepping into the garden. He didn't shift naturally, so it will take longer than if he were to be able to do it himself. Becoming human again is much slower than becoming a newt. I would guess it will be at least three hours or so before he is back to himself. Luckily, he is nicely toned; he won't need to reform excess body mass. Newts are quite lean. It would take much more time for him to reshape if he were a larger man. You will need to keep an eye on him though so he doesn't have any ill effects," Cora ladled a sticky spoonful of the concoction she created over Will's body and his color instantly began to change. "I'll take you to your room and have food for you both soon. He will be quite hungry when he returns."

Grant scoffed, catching Cora by surprise, "He is always hungry, even before any of this. I would recommend something hardy."

"Of course he is," she exhaled, frustration lacing her words.

Cora guided Grant through the house to the staircase at the front entrance and left them both in the second room from the landing, Will still in his ever-changing state. Grant impatiently watched over his friend's unconscious body resting on the large bed in the middle of the room. Within an hour Nathan, a small green-skinned forest sprite, quietly introduced himself with a bow and delivered several steaming trays. Under the covered domes on each tray was a large meal of roast boar meat and carrots with red potatoes and onions for both young men, along with a large pitcher of cool water. Grant ate quickly, never letting Will out of his sight.

In just an hour, Will had gone from a fleshy looking reptilian creature to a near human-sized, fidgety beast with a disturbingly inhuman face. Grant had worried the entire evening that his friend would never be himself again and he would have to find a way to communicate with him in this new terrifying form. He had paced the length of the room nonstop and was surprised he had not worn a line from his path into the delicate looking rug beneath his feet. Within three hours, Will sat wrapped in a blanket before Grant's horrified expression.

"What the fuck happened?" Will croaked. "I'm starving!"

Grant shook his head and wrapped Will in a tight embrace. "Oh, thank all that is holy! You were a newt for most of this evening. Then you were something in between for some time as well. We will be staying here tonight. I can tell you more in the morning. Now I need sleep or I am going to lose my mind. There is a plate of food for you on the nightstand that is surprisingly still warm," Grant waved to the steaming plate. Grant made his way to the other side of the large bed to rest and quickly drifted off; finally relieved to have his best friend back to his human self.

Chapter 7

Addie

It was hard for Addie to tell how much time had passed. She seemed to be suspended in darkness, with no sense of direction, for what could have been minutes or hours or even days. Her mind spiraled and she once again felt like she was being lurched forward toward an overwhelming feeling of terror. When her vision cleared, Addie stood in the grass near a large stone castle wall. Instantly, all of her memories flooded in from her childhood here and who she had been in life.

Her attention shot upward toward the two young men atop the lookout tower. Both figures appeared to be on the verge of a terrible fate. Without warning, Addie's vision tunneled as though she looked through another person's eyes. Tendrils of dark shadow framed her thoughts. The young blonde man's face before her was filled with fear as he fell from the parapet. Without warning, the scene surrounding him changed abruptly.

The near two hundred foot fall was replaced by crashing

waves and broken seas. He was being pulled under the water's surface by pale blue-green webbed fingers. A beautiful voice echoed over the water, drawing Addie's attention to the face of a gorgeous woman. Along her neck, the slits of gills peaked out from behind her long silver hair. She grinned widely, revealing two rows of razor sharp teeth. Each point stained a sickening red. The siren's wicked smile widened further and her teeth sank into the young man's throat spraying blood into the water, cutting off a broken scream. His body when limp and his head sank below the surface. Addie's own screams replaced his.

Just as abruptly as before, Addie was yanked out of the haunting vision. As the two young men's bodies crashed to the ground in front of her. The impact seemed far softer than a fall from the tower high above should have created. Castle staff instantly flooded around the men on the ground. A young woman with long dark hair and brilliant green eyes stood near the familiar face of the necromancer.

"I tried to stop them, mother," the young woman wiped blood from her nose.

The nightmare began to shake apart in Addie's mind. The vivid scene blurred. The colors melted into nothing more than thick, inky smoke. A familiar deep voice shattered the illusion surrounding her completely.

"Princess, can you hear me?" The voice echoed in her mind. "Addie, are you here?" The deep vibration in his tone traced down her spine like a caress before she found herself suspended in darkness in front of the same man she had seen the last time she had awoken.

"Grant?" Addie breathed.

"Addie, where are you? What is going on?" Grant pleaded,

57

concern pouring from him.

"I... I don't know. I can't remember. It's dark and I think something awful has happened. I think I might be dead. I don't feel anything but cold." Addie's voice wavered, "I'm afraid, Grant. I feel like I'm slipping away. How am I here, like this?" Addie's shadow shifted, gesturing to her corporeal form.

Her body was nearly invisible, as though she stood like a specter composed of the same dark smoke she had just felt tear a man apart in this nightmare. The only visible color emitting from her was a near iridescent sheen from her eyes, like that of a beast's gaze reflecting firelight. The details of her face were hazy. Her hair swirled around her head like she was floating in an invisible pool of water.

"I'm coming for you. I will find you and my father, I promise," Grant vowed.

"Lord Anderson... your father... he's" a fractured flash of a memory crashed through Addie. For a moment she stood in wet sand, warm sticky liquid clinging to her chest.

"He's done something terrible. I tried to stop him, I think," Addie's eyes closed and her shadow dulled.

"I'm going to find you. Please, Addie, hold on a little longer," Grant pleaded and Addie could hear the fear and desperation in his voice.

"You have to stop him. I feel like I'm sinking and I can't stop it," Addie panicked.

"Wait, please. Where are you?" Grand asked frantically as she began slipping away. As she fell deeper into the cold empty darkness, Addie thought she heard despair and longing in Grant's voice before everything went still, "Please, Addie, I can't lose you."

Chapter 8

Cora

In the early hours of the morning, Cora found herself wandering through her home toward the room she had left the two young men last night. Grant had rightfully seemed overwhelmed by everything that had transpired yesterday; from his best friend becoming a newt, to the wealth of information her mother had dumped at his feet. She had not helped much by adding her own relationship with Will onto Grant's growing worries.

Having Will so close felt like it was nearly impossible to keep away and it was driving Cora insane to have so little control over her own thoughts and actions. Her entire life, she had been taught to master her feelings so they would not cloud her judgment. As she stopped in front of the door she knew Will rested behind, anger filled her every cell. She wasn't sure why she was even here or what she would do if he actually opened the door at this early hour, but she reached forward to knock anyway. As her hand neared the wood, she froze and her vision began to blur, eyes going a clouded white.

In her vision, Cora saw the young princess on her knees in blood soaked sands. The air was rancid and Lord Anderson's dying form towered over Addie before they both fell flat to the ground. Cora's hand slapped against the door in front of her to steady herself. It had taken years of training to control her visions and only a matter of moments in Will's proximity for her resolve to falter and her powers to unintentionally manifest. She knew her ire towards the young man was not his fault but she could not help her distaste for her lack of restraint because of him.

The door swung open abruptly and Grant stood before her shirtless and panting like he had just seen a ghost. Cora had not yet gained control of herself as she met his gaze and spoke through her vision, eyes still murky.

"She is not quite dead but drifts through worlds. Lost. Time runs short. We must make haste if we hope to stay the dead. Her words are true; what she speaks of Lord Anderson. I fear he may be too far gone to save and you must soon choose for all our fate," Cora's attention turned to Will who had propped himself up onto his elbows on the couch near the fireplace, his eyes wide.

"You will be my undoing, shifter," Cora's words were a hiss through clenched teeth as her eyes slowly returned to their natural emerald green.

Grant's worried tone caught Cora's attention once more, "Where is Addie? What has my father done to her? We can be ready to leave within the hour."

"I cannot tell for sure. But I believe she is in the cavern system in the Alderbrooke Forest. There is only one accessible entry point that looks like my vision. I will wake my mother and collect a few things for our journey," Cora said looking back at Will and taking a steadying breath before turning from the room.

Cora quickly made her way to her mother's quarters and found her awake and drinking a cup of steaming tea in her large armchair by the window. The sun had not yet crested the hilltop but the sky had begun to shift. Hints of orange and red broke through the clouds that blanketed the sky promising a wet journey.

"You do not have to guide them if you do not wish, my child," Cora's mother spoke as she brought the tea to her lips. The scent of warm cinnamon and vanilla filled the air.

"You know as well as I do that I cannot let them walk into that forest blindly. If the scum that hides within doesn't kill them, the beasts will," Cora sighed.

"And Will's connection to you has not impacted your choices at all then?" her mother asked tilting her head slightly and raising a brow.

"Of course it has and I hate it. But the fact that I know it has, should mean something, right? I won't let either of them fail and I won't let the shifter distract me more than he already has," Cora decided aloud.

"Very well then. I do not think he knows what he is capable of yet. He may need you to force his abilities out more prominently. I believe he unintentionally adopts other individual's traits with his powers without realizing," the necromancer stood, placed her cup on the small table near her chair, and made her way to stand beside her daughter.

"I may be in over my head with all of this, mother," Cora admitted, embarrassed.

The older woman reached forward and collected her

daughter's hand in her own, "There is no one alive who would be prepared for what you may face in the caves if Lord Anderson was successful. I just hope you are able to deliver the young lord there in time. The rest is in his and the princess's hands, I am afraid."

"And if he fails, what then?" Cora shook her head.

"Then this kingdom will see more bloodshed than it ever has before and we may not all survive through the winter," the necromancer's brows knit together and her mouth formed a thin line.

"I should ready the horses. The two with Will and Grant were brought to the house last night while we spoke with them, correct? " Cora asked as she followed her mother toward the door.

"Yes. I sent Nathan to fetch them as soon as I saw the two young men sneaking toward the cabin yesterday and asked him to board them both with Shea," the older woman smiled warmly at her daughter. "Be careful, child. You know better than anyone the dangers you will find once you leave here." With that, the necromancer stepped into the hall and vanished in the direction of her drawing room.

Cora stepped into a large closet just outside of her mother's room and collected several healing potions and vials of various herbs before she made her way into the main entry to meet with Nathan.

"Could you ready the horses for us Nathan? My companions and I will need to leave as soon as they are ready," Cora asked.

"They have been fed and are already saddled at your mother's request, madam," Nathan bowed his head.

From the top of the stairs, Will's voice echoed down to Cora,

"We're prepared to leave immediately if you wish." Cora's heart skipped suddenly.

She spoke sternly in an attempt to compose herself, "We'll ride through the morning and travel to a small town about an hour from the edge of Alderbrooke Forest. We need to pick up something important before we continue."

"Very well," Will made his way down the stairs, Grant on his heels.

"Let's move then," Grant ordered and stepped through the front doors, out into a light rain that was just beginning to fall.

Chapter 9

Elinore

Elinore rolled off her small bed in the servants quarters and stretched her neck and shoulders. The tight space seemed to creep in on her more this morning as she prepared herself for her day. After leaving the prince's chambers yesterday, she suffered through Vern's filthy hands on her skin for what felt like an eternity. Every fiber of her being crawled and an undeserved shame filled her chest. When she left her home in Onyx Hollow for this mission, she knew there would be sacrifices to make but had no inkling she would give up so much of herself. If she was successful, she told herself it would all be worth the cost. She just hoped yesterday's assault would never be a price she would have to pay again.

"Miss Elinore," a woman's voice sounded beyond her door, "the king has requested you aid the prince this morning."

Dread polled in her belly. Apart from herself and Vern, Prince Andrew was the only person in the castle to know what she had been through yesterday. If the king had ordered her aid for his son, it also meant the prince must have put up a fight after she left his chambers and was in need of discreet healing. Standing to her feet, Elinore refused to let herself crumble under the weight she felt building in her heart.

With a deep breath, she forced a smile on her face, "Thank you. I'll head to his chambers now."

As she made her way through the halls, Elinore repeated a new mantra in her head with each step, *"I am not weak. I will not let this break me. I am not weak. I will not let this break me,"* until she stood in front of the prince's large, double doors. Elinore raised a hand and knocked lightly.

The prince's muffled voice responded, "Please leave."

"Your highness, I'm afraid I cannot do that. The king has sent me to tend to you." Elinore's voice shook slightly.

A small crash boomed several seconds before Prince Andrew was fumbling with the lock to his door, "Elinore?" His voice sounded sorrowful as the door swung open.

"Yes, your highness," Elinore's eyes stayed glued to the floor, her chin tucked close to her chest. She slowly began to nervously curl and uncurl her hands into fists at her sides.

"Come in, please," Elinore winced instinctively as the prince reached forward toward her before he recoiled, causing a weight to sink in her chest.

She hadn't realized how long she stood frozen at the threshold to his chambers until Prince Andrew's hand eased slowly into her line of sight once more. Elinore inhaled again and inspected his outstretched palm.

"My apologies, highness," Elinore bowed lower and placed a trembling hand into his. The moment Andrew's fingers closed gently around her own, the small weight she felt moments ago lifted slightly from her heart until she saw the broken skin across his knuckles.

"Sire, your hands," Elinore gasped, snapping her head up only to see the prince's swollen and bruised face. Her eyes went wide at the sight of the beautiful man's broken appearance.

The prince stepped aside, still holding her hand softly and ushered her into his sitting room before closing the door behind them both. "Are you alright, Elinore?"

"Of course, your highness," Elinore forced on a smile that did not touch her eyes. Her voice wavered, betraying her falsely portrayed optimism, "Not a mark to be seen."

"Just because your flesh has been healed, doesn't mean there are no wounds," Andrew narrowed his eyes on her and led her to the lounge at the center of the room. "I'm going to ask again, my lady. Are you alright?"

"I do not have any other choice but to be," Elinore's reply was just above a whisper.

"It is alright to *not* be alright," the prince took a knee at Elinore's side, "If there is anything you need from me, I am here for you."

Tears clouded her vision as she tried to keep herself composed. Shaking her head frantically, Elinore tried to clear her troubled mind, "I feel like I'm drowning and I can't get enough air or like I'm being crushed."

"Would you like to talk about what happened?" Andrew's voice was free of judgment.

"I don't think I'm ready for that today. Would it be alright if I work on your injuries and discuss *anything* else?" Several tears ran down Elinore's face and she swallowed hard.

Andrew slowly pulled an embroidered fold of fabric from his pocket and held it out for her, "Of course. What would you like to discuss while you work? I'm normally unconscious for any healing."

"I'm sorry," Elinore began and accepted the ivory cloth to blot away her tears. "Are your injuries like yesterday's common?"

Elinore watched the flash of pain on the prince's face before he composed himself. Still on his knees, she couldn't help but wonder if this sort of interaction was commonplace for the man before her. Several seconds passed silently; both lost to their own thoughts.

Realizing she may have overstepped or struck a similar frayed nerve like her own, she began to ramble, "I'm so sorry, your highness. I have overstepped. I shouldn't have asked something that is none of my concern at the present moment. I can continue in silence if you would prefer."

"You haven't overstepped and please, call me Andrew. I do hope we are able to speak freely with each other. Despite my title, or maybe perhaps because of it, I do not have many people to confide in besides my sister and she still has not returned from the forest," Andrew grimaced. "And to answer your question, yes, the punishment you healed me from yesterday is a common occurrence."

Elinore placed the handkerchief in her lap and took a steadying breath. A soft golden light began to radiate from her hands, "I am sorry for that, as well. May I touch your nose? It looks like it may be broken." The prince nodded slightly before Elinore ran her finger tips down the bridge of his nose, eliciting a wince of pain. "Sorry. It is, in fact, broken but not terribly so. The bone beneath your eye is also fractured but I can have you back to your beautiful self in just a few minutes."

By the time she realized what she had said aloud the words

had already reached the prince's ears. "Beautiful, huh?"

Crimson stained Elinores cheeks and warmed her skin with embarrassment. "I'm sure you know you are a charming man, your high…" Andrew raised a swollen brow in reprimand, "*Andrew.* I can guarantee you have heard more flattering statements from many young ladies at court."

"Not from any so stunning," the swelling in Andrew's face had begun to diminish and the prince smiled a coy half smile.

"Thank you for that but I fear you may have some serious brain damage if what you see before you is nothing more than damaged goods after… after yesterday," Elinore said with a self-depreciating tone, tears once again lining her eyes.

"You, Elinore, are not damaged goods. Do you understand me? Your value as a person has not and will not change because of anything that man has done," Elinore could hear the anger in Andrew's voice.

"He took everything from me," tears began to fall freely from her eyes, "my virtue was all I had left to give and he stole it. I… I can't get that back. I felt so helpless."

"I am so sorry that happened to you Elinore. You are far braver than you realize. Talking about it takes tremendous courage and you are a thousand times the person that *monster* could ever dream to be. I know you don't know me well yet, but I am here to listen if you need me," Andrew moved to sit beside her.

Overwhelmed by her grief Elinore buried her face in her hands and nestled herself against Andrew's chest. The prince ran a gentle hand down her arm and held her head in a loose embrace against his body. The rhythmic thrumming of his heart in Elinore's ear eased her through her tears.

"Thank you," Elinore finally spoke and inhaled an achingly

familiar scent.

"I will be here if you need me," the prince offered a kind smile, "any time of day or night."

For several long moments, Elinore allowed herself to find comfort in the prince's arms. The silence between them eased the strain on her soul.

"I best be going," Elinore rose to her feet several minutes later. "I do hope we do not need to meet for my services again any time soon, Andrew. But, I will keep your offer in mind, always."

The prince stood at her side once again, "Any visit from you will be welcomed, my lady."

With a small bow, Elinore retreated to her other duties for the day. Shortly after leaving the prince, she walked through the castle gardens. Dark clouds hung low in the sky and a misty rain began to dust the field leading from the castle into the forest beyond. The caw of a raven overhead drew the young woman's attention to the windows of the servant quarters. Quickly, she collected the basket of vegetation she had been gathering and slipped quietly back to the castle and into her small room.

Atop Elinore's bed sat the onyx plumed bird; a small slip of paper secured to its leg. After slipping the note free, Elinore read and reread the parchment before tossing the scrap into her apron pocket to burn in the kitchen hearth later.

C and her companions will reach Onyx Hollow before night.
Did your father complete my order?
Are you safe?
-R

Elinore knelt down and pulled a small stack of papers and a quill with an ink bottle from beneath her bed. Hastily, she scribed her reply.

As safe as would be expected.
We may have a valuable ally here.
Their weapons are ready to find the princess.
-E

With deft hands, Elinore rolled and secured her reply to the raven's leg. "Take that home to your master, friend," Elinore whispered and lifted the bird through the open window.

Chapter 10

Will

The ride back to the main road was slow and wet. Shortly after departing the cottage, the light rain began to turn to a steady deluge soaking all three riders to the bone. Will rode between Grant and Cora and his mind was racing with questions and the overwhelming urge to shield Cora from the whipping wind and rain. Right after Cora had left them this morning, he had asked Grant what she had meant when she called him a shifter but Grant was reluctant to explain much. He couldn't understand how he could have lived his entire life not knowing what he was.

Will turned to speak to Cora, "How did you know what I was?"

Cora's shoulder's stiffened, "I, I didn't for certain until I forced you to shift at the cabin with my mother's potion."

"That isn't very helpful. How could I not know?" Will questioned aloud.

Cora shook her head, rainwater falling from her hair. "I don't really know but my mother has her suspicions that I feel inclined to agree with."

"Care to share that with the group?" Grant spoke from beside Will.

"Not particularly, no," Cora exhaled an irritated breath, "I would rather get to Onyx Hollow without conversation."

"Anything you wish, my love, but it is going to be difficult for me," Will teased. "I have always been one to enjoy the comforts of pleasant small talk."

Cora rolled her eyes and picked up her pace to a faster trot, leaving Will and Grant to follow suit. The next hour passed with little discussion and Will once again felt the confusing need to get ahead of Cora to shield her from any dangers they may encounter on the road. His mind continued to mull over his recent enlightenment about his apparent gift. No matter what Cora's assumptions were as to why he was unaware of his gift his entire life, Will couldn't wrap his mind around the fact that he was gifted at all. Since setting out on their journey this morning, he had tried his best to shift into every manner of beast imaginable but all he managed to do was give himself a massive headache and make himself hungry.

"I need to make two stops once we enter the village and I need both of you fools to promise you won't speak to anyone," Cora said, breaking Will's current fixation. In the last several minutes, the rain had slowed to a light mist and Will couldn't help but notice how Cora's black tunic clung to her body.

"What is it that you need?" Grant asked.

"I need to pick up a few weapons my mother ordered among other things that do not concern you," Cora replied frankly.

"Take my cloak," Will unclasped the pin at his throat and offered the beautiful woman beside him the wet gray fabric.

Cora raised one brow and shook her head, "Why? I have

my own."

"You are soaked and your top is… revealing. You wouldn't want strangers to ogle," Will admitted. The laugh that escaped Cora's throat sounded like music to Will's ears. It was a genuine, wholehearted laugh and caught him completely by surprise.

"'Ogled huh?! I can guarantee I will not be *ogled* by anyone in the village. I believe it may be only you who is brave enough to gawk at me, shifter," Cora continued to chuckle as she pulled out her own cloak that appeared much drier than his and threw it over her shoulders. "Onyx Hollow is just beyond the next bend. This stop should not take long. Then we will be about an hour from our stop for today, if conditions hold."

Will kept his eyes fixed ahead as much as possible and tried to avoid watching the way Cora's body moved rhythmically atop her horse as they rode toward the village. Grant, too, seemed on edge at his side. Will caught his best friend turning several times to watch the road behind them as they moved closer to Onyx Hollow.

As they finally reached the outer edge of the village, Will couldn't help but notice the streets here were not paved like the ones in Shepherd's Glen and the houses were far from pristine. Many of the structures were in desperate need of repair and looked as though they may have been better suited for livestock than the small children he watched run in and out of them. Despite the gloom that seemed to saturate everything, the sound of laughter from the children echoed down the street behind them as they passed.

"Do those children not attend a school?" Grant asked and Will could tell his friend was riddled with the same grief he felt seeing the children splashing in the filthy puddles along the muddy road.

"Even if a school still existed for them here, who would make them attend?" Cora's voice sounded as though she were on the verge of rage filled tears.

"Their parents are not here with them?" Will knew the answer before Cora could respond but her words felt like ice in his chest.

"No, shifter. They are not here. Some were exiled or executed for their powers by the king and many others were killed by the 'rebel' camps in the Alderbrooke Forest for information," Cora said, slowing her horse in front of a small shack before dismounting. "You two stay here. I need to collect my order."

"Like hell!" Will began to protest.

"Will, I think it's best we remain out here. Cora knows these people, we don't. She will be fine," Grant assured his friend.

"You two can take the horses to the trough on the side of that building and let them rest there for a moment. I will be there shortly." Cora pointed a delicate hand toward a large wooden basin near the most solid looking building down the street.

Will nodded and obliged Cora's request reluctantly but never let the shack she entered leave his sight.

"You need to control yourself, man," Grant's voice was low.

"What are you talking about?" Will snipped.

"You know what I'm talking about. Don't play stupid; it's not a good look," Grant chided. "You need to get a hold of yourself with Cora. She is fully capable of taking care of herself and you can't let this thing between you two distract you."

"What thing? Cora despises me. I don't really understand why," Will countered.

"You are my best friend and I need you to know something but Cora can't know it was me that told you what I am about to tell you. That woman scares the shit out of me," Grant whispered cryptically.

"For heaven's sake, spit it out, Grant," Will groaned.

"Did you know that those that are born with powers often also have a *mate* as well?" Grant asked Will, prodding.

"No. Why?" Will's brows furrowed.

Grant ran his gloved hand down his face. "You and Cora were both born with magical abilities. Did you know *that*?"

"Not until recently but what the hell does that have to do with any of this?" Will said, waving his arm around him.

"Are you really that thick?" Grant shook his head in disbelief.

The two were silent for a moment as they dismounted and tied the three animals to the watering post. Will's mind was racing. He wasn't sure if what Grant was suggesting could possibly be true.

"Cora and I are mates," Will exhaled softly, "I don't understand how that's possible. Until this morning, I was just a normal man but now I'm a shifter? I don't even know how to do that."

"I don't know but Cora told me last night and said if I told you she would gut me. But I didn't technically tell you. Not exactly," Grant grimaced. "I do think you should try to figure your shit out soon though. I can't ever watch you shift like you did yesterday," Grant shivered in disgust.

Will stared at the mud caked on his boots. In a matter of hours, everything he knew about himself had changed and he felt like he was in a spiral. When he lifted his head, he saw Cora step out of the shack down the road and shook his head.

"What am I supposed to do?" Will asked Grant.

"Fuck if I know. Just take it a day at a time. I still have no idea how to keep my emotions from impacting my power," Grant admitted. "Just try to keep this knowledge to yourself for now if you can. I'd like to keep my guts inside my body."

It took only a couple of minutes for Cora to reach both Will and Grant's side. Despite where they stood, the air around them smelled sweeter than expected. Cora stopped at the front of the building and smiled. Strapped to her back, Will saw a strange double headed ax and a long swords in each hand.

"These, gentlemen, are yours," Cora held out the swords.

Will looked at Cora confused. "What do you mean?"

"I mean, these swords now belong to you two idiots," Cora shoved the two sheathed weapons into Grant and Will's hands.

"How?" Grant unsheathed his sword and grinned. "This is a stunning blade."

"My mother and I knew you would be coming and that back there is the home of one of the most skilled blacksmiths in the entire kingdom. Somehow he has kept himself in the king's good graces despite his fire wielding magic," Cora beamed. "My mother imbued the metal with an enchantment so it will never dull. The same goes for my ax."

"This is magnificent! It must have cost a fortune!" Will stated absolutely baffled. "I can't accept this."

"You can and you must," Cora shrugged. "Now, I have one last stop before we continue on. We will need to make it to the edge of the forest before nightfall."

Will and Grant both nodded and Cora disappeared into the brick building. As they stood near the horses and waited for Cora's return, Will had the feeling they were being watched.

"Do you see those two men over there," Grant gestured subtly with a nod of his chin.

"The two near the blacksmith shop Cora just left?" Will questioned.

"Yes. I think I saw them in the forest while we were on the road this morning. I wasn't sure with the amount of rain but now I'm nearly certain it was them. I think they've followed us here," Grant murmured.

Will turn to face Grant fully, "Should we confront them or see if Cora recognizes them?"

"Let's see if Cora knows if they are locals or not. I'm hoping they are residents of Onyx Hollow, but I don't have a great feeling about them," Grant admitted.

"Nor do I," Will agreed.

Moments later, Cora rounded the corner with the most beautiful smile Will had ever seen plastered across her face and a brown package in her hands. A small dimple graced her cheek. Cora's smile quickly dropped and her dimple vanished the moment she caught sight of Grant's expression.

"What's happened?" Cora frantically searched Will from head to toe curiously.

"We are fine but I think we're being watched," Will directed Cora's line of sight with a nod.

"Of course you're being watched," Cora sighed with fleeting relief before she saw who Will had motioned to.

"Do you know those two men," Grant asked.

Will couldn't help but notice the unease that coated Cora's voice as she spoke, "I do not think they are from Onyx Hollow.

We best not linger here. We should try to lose them through the back half of the village and make for Alderbrooke quickly."

Grant made quick work of the knots that bound the three mounts to their place while Will eyed the package Cora cradled in her hands, no larger than his fist. He assumed the contents must be of great importance if Cora insisted they stop here after the blacksmith's shop, regardless of the village's notorious reputation.

"May I ask what the final provision was that you needed to collect before we left Onyx Hollow?" Will attempted to get a better look at the package.

Cora's face flushed a beautiful scarlet and she held tight to the contents in her hands. "They are personal and none of your concern."

"Now I must know," Will teased and quickly plucked the paper wrapped goods from her hands before she had the chance to hide them away.

"Give those back you thief," Cora barked. Will held the package over his head as Cora jumped in an attempt to retrieve her belongings. Finally, she admitted defeat. "Fine, have a look then," she conceded, rolling her eyes and taking Shea's reins from Grant.

Will gingerly opened the brown paper wrap and was instantly puzzled. Inside, there were four golden brown cookies stacked atop each other, each containing several chunks of chocolate morsels.

"These are cookies," Will stated, raising a brow. "Are they special in some way?"

Cora took the stack of baked treats back and stored them in her pack before mounting. Will and Grant both climbed atop their horses and the three directed themselves behind the bakery.

"They are quite special, yes," Cora grinned.

"Do they have some sort of magical power or something?" Will questioned hesitantly.

"No they don't. They're ordinary chocolate chunk cookies but they are special to me. I never pass through this village without stopping at *Ms. Alma's Bakery* for a few of them," Cora admitted.

"So they're just cookies?" Grant spit the words out with disgust. "We wasted time here and are possibly being followed so you could stop for a sweet treat?! Addie is in trouble and my father has done the gods know what and you wanted to buy a bunch of fucking *cookies*?"

Cora squared her shoulders and faced Grant, fury boiled in her blood, "First, Grant Anderson, do not, for one second, think that you have the right to speak to me with that tone. No matter what power you possess, I am far more skilled with a blade than you ever will be. Second, we added only a matter of minutes to a stop we already needed to make for the weapon you now carry at your side; weapons that may just be the difference between life and death for us all in the coming days. And finally, until you have fully experienced Alderbrooke Forest first hand, as I have, you have no right to question what my possible final indulgence in this life may be. We may not all survive this and I will be damned if I do not get to enjoy one of the few pleasures in life one last time."

A large smile spread across Will's face as he attempted to contain his pride. Since their accident, there had been very few instances where Will could remember someone other than Maggie, Ren, or himself chastising Grant. And now, Grant sat atop Whiskey slack jawed and speechless. The most stunning woman Will had ever met just thoroughly reprimanded a man nearly twice her size over a stack of cookies.

"I don't think I have ever been more attracted to someone than I am right now," Will exhaled a shaky breath.

Once again, Cora's cheeks flushed a beautiful red and Will was sure he saw a small smile crack her normally stoic expression before she cleared her throat, "There may be something seriously wrong with you then, shifter."

Will glanced over his shoulder as they rode to find Grant once again scowling. The trio rode for several more minutes in silence before Cora made an abrupt turn down a dark alley between two, three story buildings at the village center.

"If we are truly being followed, we will soon know for certain. This alley only leads in a circle behind this inn and back to the main square. Once we exit around the other side, we will wait across the street to see if the two men have followed us in," Cora explained.

Quickly, the three exited the trap they had laid out and sat in silence watching the shadows of the alley. Two cloaked men on horseback emerged from the shadows and made eye contact with Will and Grant. If there had been any doubt before, there was none left now.

"How do we lose them through the village," Grant whispered urgently to Cora.

Cora shook her head, "We will need to be quick and head away from the forest for some time and double back to enter farther north. It is a shorter distance to the caverns that way but far more beasts roam that region. I had hoped to avoid the northern wood but it may be necessary. Those two now know they have been seen but that doesn't answer who they are or why they are following us. My hope would be grifters. We are quite obviously more wealthy than the people of this town. If we are lucky, they just hope to rob us."

"And if luck is not on our side?" Will asked hesitantly.

"They may be the king's scouts and we are in much more danger than I hoped to encounter just yet," Cora's voice was low, "Once we move, do not slow until I do. Do you understand? Are both of your horses in good health?"

Grant and Will both nodded simultaneously and dread began to pool in Will's stomach. Without warning, Cora whipped her horse around and kicked her mount into a full gallop down the street behind them. Grant and Will were behind her in seconds. The sound of shouts echoed through the square.

"Hurry! Cut them off!" a male voice boomed. "Don't let them reach the fork."

Soon, the village disappeared and overhanging trees shadowed the muddy road ahead. Will pushed his horse as hard as he could for what felt like a lifetime before Cora veered hard right off the road into the thicket just before a three way split in the road appeared. She slowed her pace and held her index finger to her lips to silence any questions from Grant or Will. The path they now took was far too narrow and resembled a wild game trail more than a road meant for travel. After several hundred yards from the main road, Cora took another slight right again over a creek.

"I think it is safe to assume we've lost them for now but we must remain as quiet as we can," Cora's voice was just above a whisper. "We will need to ride a little longer today before we reach a small clearing at the edge of Alderbrooke Forest where we will rest tonight."

Several hours passed and Will's mind began to mull over the unprocessed knowledge Grant had shared. Cora was his mate, he was a shifter, and they were about to enter the deadliest place in the kingdom with a few magical weapons and the unlikely hope that Lord Anderson hadn't already doomed them all. Will breathed slowly through his nose to calm his racing heart and Cora's eyes filled with concern as she looked him over.

"Are you alright, shifter?" She asked tentatively.

"I am in a tailspin. There is so much going on that I can't control and it is infuriating," Will admitted.

"Then focus on the things you can control. There is no need to let your emotions force you into a panic over things that are not in your hands," Cora said like it was really that simple.

"But what can I control? I am apparently a *shifter* that doesn't even know how to shift," Will groaned.

"We are born with the inherent ability to wield our power to some extent. Mastery takes practice and patience. You need to believe you are capable and trust yourself," Cora's words resonated through Will's mind. "That goes for both of you," Cora looked over to Grant who had been dreadfully quiet.

"My nightmare's are dangerous. It may be safer for them to remain suppressed as much as possible," Grant's voice was hoarse.

"I wouldn't even know where to start though," Will added. "How do I make myself turn into something else if I don't understand the process?"

Cora scowled at Grant, then eyed Will, "Start small. Don't assume you will be able to shift into your alternate form without trying something more realistic first. The records I've read about your kind of gift state you should be able to adopt other's human traits. Just try changing a small physical feature. Work your way to a full shift. Visualize your hands smaller and close your eyes. Will yourself to become what you are seeing in your mind's eye."

Will closed his eyes as they rode and took a deep breath through his nose. He imagined his fingers thinning and becoming more delicate. In his mind he saw the blunt tips of his fingers turn to fine pointed nails. His skin began to warm and hum softly.

"Holy shit, Will!" Grant sputtered and Will's eyes flew open. Holding his reins were the two most beautiful female hands Will had ever seen. "Those look like your hands, Cora," Grant noted, confused.

Cora's head snapped to Will's lap where a near perfect rendition of her own hands rested, one atop the other. "If I ever find out you have touched any part of your body with my hands, I will cut them off! Do you understand me, William?"

Will's heart sped up and his head swam. He had done it. It wasn't a large shift but he had intentionally changed part of his own body. Slowly, Cora's words broke through his elation and disbelief. A belly deep laugh escaped Will's throat.

"I promise you Cora, that was not even close to my first thought. But, I'm pleased to know that your hands on my body is on *your* mind," Will teased and gave Cora a flirtatious wink.

"That's not... I wasn't... Fuck you," Cora fumbled over her words and Will's smile grew wider.

"You two are incorrigible," Grant groaned.

Will sat up taller in his saddle and beamed, "I think you

meant incredible."

"Will, could you please shift your hands back right now. And could you two keep your voices down? We are almost to the clearing and I would prefer we are not heard by anyone. If the two men that were following us earlier headed this way, by some crazy chance, I want to see them before they see us," Cora explained changing the subject.

Will couldn't help but notice the pink that stained Cora's cheeks as they rode on. Closing his eyes, Will tried to focus on his hands again. He pictured them as he remembered them before but struggled to keep thoughts of Cora's actual hands touching his body, out of his mind. When he opened his eyes, her perfect hands remained. Shaking his arms loose, Will tried again and thought about his leather work; what his hands looked like as they manipulated hides and created beautiful pieces of art. When he opened his eyes again, Will was amazed to see he had, once again, succeeded in shifting his form, however slight it may have been.

Holding his hands up, Will whispered in disbelief, "I did it. Holy shit, I did it!"

Both Grant and Cora looked at a beaming Will. Grant patted his friend on the back in congratulations and Cora raised a brow with an upside down smile and nodded her head forward in a bow of approval. Once again, the trio fell into silence as Will continued to admire his success.

Soon, the woods around them began to thin and the dark gray light of evening began to peak through the canopy. Cora brought her horse to a stop and dismounted gracefully. Will joined her as they both edged closer to the opening of the brush. The clearing before them was quiet apart from the sound of sunset wildlife beginning to chirp.

"I think we're alone, for now. We can set up camp over there across the field in that narrow valley and we can continue on tomorrow," Cora stood pointing to the ravine just beyond the small hill covered in hundreds of white wildflowers.

Still on his knees, Will's eyes traveled the length of Cora's body, taking in her entire form. His heart began to thrum faster as he came to the realization that he would very likely be sleeping mere feet from this goddess of a woman tonight. His chest began to ache and he had to take several steadying breaths before he could stand.

"Lead the way and I will follow you anywhere," Will stated and bowed low.

Chapter 11

Cora

The sun had nearly set completely as Cora made her way through the brush at the edge of the forest collecting firewood and kindling. Although a fire was ill advised, she knew it was a necessary risk. She had advised Grant and Will to build something small to keep from drawing too much attention. If they were not able to get their spare clothing dry enough by morning, there would be no chance that any of it would be dry once they entered Alderbrooke Forest. Building a fire in the forest was an almost certain death sentence and the sun did not breach the heavy foliage enough to provide any aid. Quickly, Cora made her way back to the makeshift camp both Will and Grant had begun to set up tucked in the small valley at the forest's edge.

"The deeper we get into the forest, the worse the creatures become, so do not wander. And do not, under any circumstances, get into the river. If you have any hopes of making it to the end of this, do not look into the trees if you hear a cry," Cora said sternly.

Grant narrowed his eyes on her, "Why, pray tell, is that?"

"Why what? The river or the trees?" Cora replied, dropping her firewood and moving to lay out her bedroll.

"Both?!" Grant and Will echoed each other's thoughts simultaneously.

"The river is filled with wicked river sprites. They are horrid little creatures! They have beady yellow eyes and dark gray flesh and they will pull you under faster than you can imagine possible. They aren't very large, probably the size of a house cat but they are numerous. They will rip your skin from bone before you are able to drown. As for the trees, the sound is a ploy. They are shape-shifting beasts and they are not small by any standard. If they know they have been seen, it's already too late for you. They stand over 8 feet tall and look almost human in build. Some believe they once *were* human. I think they are a nightmare of their own making," a chill ran down the length of Cora's spine at the thought.

Will gave a mock smile and sat atop his own bedroll near Cora's. "Well that's not haunting," he breathed.

"I've tried my very best to never have the misfortune of seeing one alive up close. From what my mother says, their skin is nearly translucent when they still breath and has a pinkish hue, but after death, they become a grayish color. Each hand is massive and tipped in four black talons. Their faces are smooth with narrow slits for eyes and several rows of razor sharp, venomous teeth. They can change form to resemble other creatures, but the eyes and teeth always remain the same." Cora warned.

"The necromancer has seen one. That was what was in the jar in her spell room," Grant stated as a matter of fact.

"Yes. It was from a smaller dead one I came across several

weeks ago while I was collecting other supplies. There wasn't much of the creature left when I found it. It looked like a larger beast had feasted on it and left the less desirable parts behind. My mother has encountered them more than once. Parts of them are crucial for her spell work and their venom is vital for certain elixirs like this one," Cora dug through her bag and held up a glowing green vial.

"I'm quite glad all she did was turn me into a newt," Will joked with little humor.

"First, you must remember, she did not do that; *I* dowsed you in a revealing potion to force you to use whatever gifts you possessed and *you* changed on your own. Second, don't be too relieved, shifter. Newt's eyes are quite prized as well," Cora joked and offered Will a playful smile over her shoulder.

"If you two are finished with your flirting, could we discuss what we plan to do about the men we saw in the village today?" Grant said seriously.

"We were doing no such thing!" Cora flushed embarrassed.

"Speak for yourself," Will winked at her, earning an elbow to the ribs.

Shaking her head, Cora addressed Grant, "We will sleep in shifts. I will take the first watch, then I will wake you after a few hours. You can wake Will when you see fit. Unless whoever was following us in the village was a scout, I doubt they will follow us farther into the forest," she stated hopefully. The moon crested the treetops as she rustled through her pack and removed her water skin and some dried meat.

"How can you be so sure? Quite a few of the folks we saw in town seemed far from savory," Will remarked.

Cora's eyebrows knit together, "Because only reckless fools and the desperate venture here. I fear we may be both. Now, sleep while you can. We will move at first light tomorrow. We will need as much rest as we can get. There will be very little once we reach the heart of the woods."

Grant and Will both tucked themselves into their bedrolls near the fire. Across from them, Cora had finished laying out the rest of their wet belongings. She moved to take her seat at Will's other side, creating a final barrier between him and the forest to her right.

"Do you genuinely believe I have been using my gifts unknowingly my entire life?" Will asked as he propped himself onto his elbows and rolled to face her.

"Not your entire life, but a large portion of it. Shifting was a gift that was known to present itself early in many children. I've read it was quite often missed when more people like you existed. Have you never wondered why you seem to get along so well with other people?" Cora asked, puzzled.

"I thought I was just charming," Will baited.

Cora responded without filtering her thoughts, "I'm sure that helps but I don't think that is it entirely." Her face blanched the moment she realized what she had admitted aloud and hoped Will wouldn't be able to see her reaction in the low light cast by the small flames flickering at her feet.

Laying back, Will grinned, "If I didn't know any better, I would think you just agreed that you find me charming."

"Then I am glad you know better then," Cora sniped without any true malice. "Back to my point, I think you routinely shift into the person you are speaking to subtly. At least in their mannerisms, in order to protect yourself."

"Protect myself from what?" Will wondered aloud.

"That is for you to truly reflect on, but I would assume it would be because of a fear of being seen for who you truly are and rejected for it," Cora wisely exhaled and pulled a cookie from the small parcel she had collected in the village. She caught Will's gaze and rolled her eyes. "Would you like to try one?" she asked reluctantly.

"If you are offering, I would gladly have a small taste; but I would not want to rob you of such an important delicacy, my love," Will smiled flirtatiously.

Cora shook her head and broke off a small piece of the golden treat and ensured she gave him a piece with a chunk of delicious salted chocolate. The attractive look of surprise on Will's face made her heart sputter. She watched him place the morsel past his full lips into his mouth. Cora swallowed hard as Will closed his eyes and moaned softly.

"Shit, that's good," he exhaled and slowly blinked his eyes open.

Cora choked lightly. She hadn't expected to be so distracted by his enjoyment of her favorite treat. The sounds he made caused a delicious heat to pool in the stomach.

"Are you alright?" Will sat up abruptly, concern painting his expression.

Cora could only imagine what he must have seen. Her jaw still hung slightly open, lips parted. "Ya, ach, yes," She sputtered, "I'm fine. I'm glad it wasn't a waste for me to share. But don't think I'll be sharing any more with you. Now sleep." She chided and turned away from him to compose herself.

Cora swore under her breath and heard Grant chuckle to himself from Will's other side, his back to both of them. Will may not know it yet, but he was slowly but surely destroying every last shred of control she had left and she knew there was nothing she could do about it, no matter how hard she tried. She sat in silence for some time, trying to decide how she was going to tell Will about their bond when a snap in the distance drew her out of her spiraling thoughts. Heart pounding, Cora instinctively shifted her body in front of Will's sleeping form to shield him from whoever approached.

Placing a hand on Will's shoulder, Cora shook him awake gently and whispered, "Wake up. Someone is coming. Quietly wake Grant and arm yourselves quickly."

Chapter 12

Addie

Once again Addie found herself pulled into Grant's sub-conscious. She now stood in the great hall in the castle surrounded by nobles and performers enthusiastically cele-brating the winter solstice. Trays of food and sparkling wine circled the room on silver platters. The walls were adorned with beautiful emerald and gold banisters and vases that held bundles of vibrant purple flowers and crimson berries. The air smelled of warm spices and roasted meats. The sound of a lively orchestra filled Addie's ears. As she spun on her heels to look for Grant in the crowd of revelers, she recalled the day clearly. This night was the last celebration Grant attended the day before his and Will's accident. The chimes echoed midnight and Addie knew that in a matter of hours the two young boy's lives would change.

Addie's eyes stopped scanning the crowd when she caught sight of two young people laughing and spinning together in the middle of the dance floor, entirely carefree. She moved closer and felt her own heart begin to race. Grant stood almost a foot taller than the young woman before him and he looked like an absolute god in his deep blue fineries. His dark hair swept freely across his forehead and two small dimples graced both of his cheeks. From behind, Addie admired the skirts and shape of the dark viridian, velvet dress she wore. The two teens moved like magnets as they spun and Addie felt her chest tighten as the young Grant leaned close to her ear in the memory.

"I have never seen a creature more stunning than you, princess," Grant's deep voice sent chills down her spine once again.

In a soft voice, Addie's younger self responded, flushing with embarrassment, "I can't recall the last time a person has ever called me a *'creature'* and made it sound so lovely. You are quite dashing yourself tonight, if I might add."

The music ended and began again much slower than before and Grant bowed at the waist playfully. "Why thank you, Highness. That is quite the compliment. Would you like a drink?" Grant gestured to the table against the wall covered with several sugar covered treats and a collection of crystal glasses filled with a golden colored sparkling wine.

"That sounds great," Addie breathed. "And I would like some air in the gardens for a few moments. If that's alright with you?"

Grant nodded with a smile and took the young Addie's hand. Her soul followed the memory of the two younger versions of herself and Grant as they collected their drinks and moved into the garden. Joy filled her instantly. For years, Grant had become a person she had grown to trust and someone that she felt truly saw what she was capable of. She had even believed she had started to fall in love with the wild

93

and reckless boy. Grant stopped and placed his drink atop the stone railing at the foot of the garden steps and stepped close to Addie's side. Gently, he took her face into his hands, her heart stopped like it had that night.

"May I kiss you, Princess? If I do not know the feel of your lips on mine I know I will regret not asking for the rest of my existence," Grant asked in a sultry voice.

A near silent "Yes," left Addie's lips and instantly his mouth was on hers. Their kiss started gentle and soft but was filled with both of their restrained desires. The moment was cut short when Addie's brother, Gavin, stepped out onto the garden steps and cleared his throat forcefully.

"I think it is time you said goodnight sister and set off for bed," he said, looking down his nose at Grant.

Grant stood in the garden for several moments after the young Addie walked back into the castle with her head down behind her brother. Grant returned to the festivities disheartened and quickly found his friend at a table filled with various meats and cheeses. Grant approached Will and soon both young men vanished from the room in hopes that they might drown their night with Lord Anderson's personal liquor cabinet.

Addie stood in the center of the garden's open doors as the memory around her shifted. Now the room was empty and the light of late evening shone through the stained glass windows. All hints of revelry had been replaced by dust and gloom. Several maps littered the large table that ran the length of the room. Grief replaced Addie's joy from moments ago. Grant stepped through the large double doors and Addie instantly knew this was a much more recent memory. The softer edges of Grant's boyish face from before were replaced

94

by sharp angles and a more defined jaw. He had aged almost a decade but his eyes looked as though they had seen a lifetime of darkness. Shadows haunted his expression.

Lord Anderson stood beside his son, a shell of the man he once had been. The king sat at the head of the table tracing lines over several pages. As he looked up at his guests, the king's expression hardened.

"Your Majesty, we must speak," Lord Anderson's voice was raspy.

"Then speak quickly, Anderson. I do not have time for your worries today," the king barked.

"The rebels have made it past the town of Shepherd's Glen and are hiding in the Alderbrooke Forest. We must do something!" Lord Anderson demanded.

The king's voice boomed, "You do not get to order me to do anything. Do you think I do not know my kingdom is being invaded? Do you think me naive?"

Addie couldn't recall a time she had seen her father stressed to this degree. She knew this must be a memory from this last spring. Since the winter solstice before Grant and Will's accident, Grant had not returned to court until now.

Grant stepped in front of his father and bowed before the king. "Your majesty, my father means no disrespect, but we do have genuine concerns about rebel movement near our home. We do not wish for any other family to suffer the same fate we have. We ask you to please look into extending your forces past Alderbrooke Forest and aid in relocating some of your kingdom closer to the castle," Grant spoke sternly.

The king shook his head, "I do sympathize with your loss, but as it was last fall. We do not have the manpower nor the resources to extend farther than we already have to the south.

Those that are able to make it to the castle will find sanctuary here in the city, but I cannot afford to risk more men when the larger fight is coming from elsewhere."

"There must be more you can do. If you do nothing, hundreds of people will be at risk," Grant protested.

"I will not continue to have this argument with you both. I cannot and will not send any further aid," the king said forcefully.

"What aid have you sent?! We are alone in the south. If you do not send assistance, many of your citizens, *your people*, may decide the rebel cause is worth supporting. And worse than that, those who do not secede will face death," Lord Anderson growled, the smell of liquor coating his breath.

The king rose to his feet and slapped his hands against the table, "There is nothing worse than treason and that is what you threaten, Lord Anderson. I will not take that threat lightly. This conversation is over. You're welcome to stay the evening. However, I do advise you leave the castle by morning."

"Your majesty, please," Grant began

"Dinner will be served shortly. The young Lord Stevens is joining us. You are welcome to as well if you'd like," the king said dismissively.

Grant sighed and Lord Anderson slumped, defeated. "Of course, your Majesty. Thank you," both men said bowing and made their leave.

Addie's mind followed both father and son through the castle as they entered a smaller dining room where a smug looking Lord Stevens sat reclined near the head of the table.

"I heard you decided to *grace* us with your presence," his arrogant voice felt like broken glass in Addie's mind. The overwhelming sensation of disgust flooded her senses.

"Hello, Rodger," Grant gritted through clenched teeth

"You will address me correctly as Lord, Grant Anderson," Lord Stevens tisked.

"Of course, Lord Stevens," Grant mocked a bow.

"It will be your highness soon if things go my way," Lord Stevens grinned, "The king needs access to my land in the north and I want a promise of the princess as a trade. Seems like a fair exchange. A debased princess for access to land," Lord Stevens gloated.

"I think it wise you speak carefully if you hope to keep your tongue, *Rodger*," Grant growled.

"My tongue matters little. It is *her* tongue I intend to use for my needs. And there is nothing you can do about it, Grant! Your family is one step from a true fall from grace; you have no sway with the king," Rodger taunted.

Rage boiled in Addie's heart. Grant's eyes closed. Dark tendrils of shadow leached from Grant like talons. Lord Anderson placed his hand on his son's shoulder.

"Grant, you need to control yourself," his father warned but Grant struggled to restrain his gift.

The shadows wrapped themselves around Lord Stevens' mind and his nose began to bleed.

"Grant! Stop!" his father ordered and Grant mustered the energy to release Lord Stevens.

The young lord slid from his chair before collapsing to the marble floor on his hands and knees, eyes wide and panting for breath. There would be no undoing what the lord must have realized. Dark magic like Grant's was dangerous and Addie's father strongly believed those that possessed such powers were going to be the kingdom's demise.

"You are a monster," Lord Stevens finally croaked out, shaking. "The king will not be pleased to know what you are."

Lord Anderson stood taller and spoke firmly, "You will tell no one. If you value your own life, you will remain quiet."

Lord Stevens shook his head in disbelief, "Even if I do not speak of this, the king will find out. I promise you. He already suspects something is amiss in your home." The young lord collected himself from the floor and hastily made his way to the door wiping blood from his nose.

Grant's deep voice caressed Addie's mind, "That was not something you were meant to see. I'm sorry, princess."

The world around Addie slowly dissolved into dark whispers of smoke and she found herself standing in the comfort of Grant's troubled mind. She knew he must still sleep as she held her hands before her and, for the first time in she wasn't sure how long, Addie could truly see herself. Grant formed before her like a phantom.

"Where are we?" Addie asked.

"In my mind somewhere between dreams, I would assume. I felt you here and tried to stop my memories from reaching you but I couldn't. I'm sorry for Lord Stevens," Grant sounded ashamed.

"I already knew of his intentions. He is a vile, self-serving man. What he said does not shock me. He has done far more disturbing things than vocalize his *urges,* I am ashamed to admit. You have no need to apologize. Your actions were valiant," Addie admitted uncomfortably.

"Addie," Grant's form stepped closer stiffly and he placed his hands on either side of her face. Tenderly, he brought her eyes up to meet his. Fire burned behind his gaze, brows knitted together creasing his forehead, "What did he do to you?"

"It's not important and it wasn't that terrible really. My lady's maid, Jade, interrupted everything before things were taken too far," Addie tried to shake her head but he held her still with gentle hands.

"Please, Addie, tell me or I will assume the worst and I am not strong enough to contain that kind of anger," Grant sounded like he might be hanging on by a thread.

Addie took a moment to steady herself. "A few years ago, I think he may have slipped something into my drink at a winter celebration. I didn't realize why I had felt so unsteady until it was nearly too late. He had offered to walk me to my rooms when I stumbled from my chair in the great hall. Once we reached my doors, he tried to kiss me. I pushed him away but it was like trying to push against a wall. I don't really remember what exactly happened next. All I remember after that was falling back onto my bed, my dress was gone, and the ties on my corset were ripped open. Lord Stevens had his hands under my skirts and I felt like I couldn't move my limbs to protest. Luckily, Jade had seen us tripping over ourselves down the hall and she came to make sure I didn't need her help readying myself for bed. Lord Stevens left quickly and Jade and I told no one because nothing really happened."

Addie could tell her words had not eased his thoughts. She could feel the rage pouring over him like it was her own.

"Princess, that is *not* nothing. He assaulted you. He would have had his way with you had it not been for your lady's maid. If I ever see that man again, I will shred him apart slowly from the inside," Grant said deathly calm.

"Who would that help?" Addie questioned, "You would be

hung."

"He will suffer, Addie, I promise you," Grant vowed.

After several moments in silence Addie cupped Grant's hand on her cheek, "I am alright, Grant. Well, in that regard anyway. I still don't know what is happening here," she gestured around them with her other hand. "Can we please discuss how I am here and what is happening?"

Grant let his hand's fall to his sides and Addie instantly missed his warmth. "We aren't sure but I'm with Will and the necromancer's daughter, Cora, and we are coming to find you. We will stop whatever my father has done."

Just as the words echoed in her mind, Will's voice was a whisper through her thoughts.

"Grant, wake up. We have company." Will's voice warned and Addie's soul was thrown through worlds once again.

Chapter 13

Grant

Grant stood with his back to Will and Cora, sword in hand. It had taken less than a minute for the trio to ready themselves as best they could for potential intruders. The moon was still high in the sky, shrouded by rolling clouds as the shuffle of approaching feet sounded from all around them. Addie's shadow was heavy in the air as anxiety radiated through Grant's entire being. He wasn't sure he was fully ready to use his gifts and fight off their attackers.

You can do this, Grant. Just breathe. Addie spoke directly to Grant. Her voice sounded like it had echoed from all around him and helped steady his racing heart slightly.

"You are outnumbered six times over," an arrogant male voice called from the darkness, "It would be in your best interest if you handed over your enchanted goods and leave this place. We will not harm you if you comply."

Cora's voice was wickedly dark as she spoke, "We will be doing no such thing. If you have any sense of self-preservation you will all turn around and return to the holes you crawled out of *now*, while you still draw breath."

A chill ran down Grant's spine as a chorus of laughter sounded around them. The man's voice spoke again much closer as he stepped out into the dim light of the dying fire.

"We will gladly take your things from your dead bodies then. It makes little difference to us. Your king will pay us either way, perhaps more so when we bring him your heads," a maniacal smile showed the intruder's broken yellow teeth. His filthy hair was slicked back against his head and his clothing hung from his body in tattered rags. The two men from the village this afternoon stood on either side of the man, all armed with long swords.

"If you touch a single hair on anyone here, it will be the greatest mistake of your very short lives," Will's voice was filled with a new predatory malice.

Before anyone else spoke again, chaos erupted from all around Will, Cora, and Grant. Nearly two-dozen men and women swarmed the camp with the sole intention of ending their lives and taking everything they carried. The sound of steel clashing against steel echoed.

"Grant, you need to do something or we won't survive very long," Will's voice called from the edge of the forest where he had pushed several of their assailants into the brush.

Addie's shadow expanded and tendrils of darkness reached into their attackers and brought them to their knees where Grant could cut them down.

You can do this, Grant. I'm here with you.

Grant took a deep breath and let his powers take over and reached for the closest mind. A nightmare flooded his senses and instantly Grant knew he had made a mistake. Cora's greatest fear manifested before his eyes.

* * *

Cora knelt in a puddle of melted snow on a field decimated by flames and littered with charred flesh and bone. Ash rained from the sky above and the clouds reflected red from the fires that burned around her. In her lap, she cradled a man's broken body. Blood soaked his normally golden blonde hair. Tears ran down her face in an unending cascade as she rocked Will's limp form in her arms. His eyes had closed but he still struggled for breath.

"Please, Will hold on! You're going to be alright," Cora pleaded to unhearing ears knowing it was a lie.

He was not going to be alright. He was going to die in her arms and she could not help him. Five deep gash marks ran across his throat from ear to ear where a creature had caught him by surprise and shredded his flesh. Will's chest rattled and rose once more with a gurgle before stilling entirely. The soul-shattering scream that left Cora's chest was excruciating.

Addie's voice broke through Grant's trance, "Let her go, Grant. You're going to kill her."

* * *

Grant's vision refocused on the fight surrounding him and his companions. It had only taken a matter of moments for him to experience Cora's deepest fear and unlock one of his own. He felt as though he had experienced the death of his closest friend, his brother, first hand. A single drop of blood dripped from Cora's nose. In her brief distraction, an archer at the edge of the fire was given a large enough window to draw back his bow and release a single arrow in her direction. Time seemed to slow before the arrow pierced the center of Cora's torso just below her sternum.

Will roared in anger and swung his sword through the man in front of him, dropping him to his knees. Turning quickly, Grant watched as his best friend moved like silk through the throng of men and women, cutting them down one by one, until he reached the archer. Will raised his sword into the air and brought it down on the man's neck swiftly, separating his head from his shoulders before sprinting to Cora's side as she hit the ground.

Grant's pain and fury churned in his stomach at the scene around him. The remaining eight men made to flee. Reaching his hand forward, Grant directed Addie's shadow to intercept the men.

Like talons, Addie's shadow form sank into the men's bodies and dark lines spread like ink under their skin. Large yellow-green blisters began to form and rupture over every inch of the attackers as the men screamed in agony. The putrid smell of decay filled the air with each bursting pustule. All eight attackers went still and crumpled to the ground in heaps of festering flesh. The remnants of their bodies became nothing more than sludge and rotted bones. Grant too fell to the ground with a ragged breath, succumbing to his exhaustion. Unconsciousness pulled him under, leaving Will alone holding Cora's injured body in the darkness.

Chapter 14

Will

Will was in shock; utter and complete dismay. Cora lay in his arms, barely conscious, an arrow still protruding from her core. Dark shadows seeped into Grant several feet away and Will feared the worst for his friends. He watched Grant's chest rise and fall steadily for several seconds before his fear subsided slightly and reality of what he had just done sank in. Looking around, he saw the aftermath of their battle. Their makeshift camp was a graveyard of bodies. In his life, Will had seen death up close but never delivered by his own hand. Despite the pain in his heart, Will knew he would be willing to do anything for the woman he cradled close to his chest.

"Cora, I need you to tell me where your healing elixir is in your packs. We can't stay here much longer. There may be others close by," Will spoke urgently.

"It's, it's the bright green vial I showed you earlier. It's in my satchel by the fire," Cora managed between pained breaths.

Will got to his feet and rested Cora's head down gently on the soil. Quickly, he rummaged through Cora's trampled bag

105

and swore profusely.

"Fuck!! They're all smashed! Every single bottle is broken!" Will threw the bag down hard and knelt next to Cora once again. "What do I do? We aren't safe here and you need help."

Cora attempted to sit herself up and winced, "I need you— fuck— I need you to get some things from the forest to make more healing potion. I can't collect it on my own. Hand me my journal and quill out of my bag."

Will retrieved the writing supplies and handed them to Cora. She frantically scribbled a list of ingredients for him to collect and tore the page free.

"Most of this will be relatively easy to identify and collect. There are two items here that are going to be dangerous to procure but I don't think I can survive this if we don't get them," Cora admitted.

"I will collect anything you wish but first I'm going to need to move you and Grant into the cover of the woods," Will said nearing where the three horses had been tied for the night just outside of their camp.

Quickly, Will hoisted Grant's unconscious body over Whiskey and rested him on his stomach, then made to help Cora to her feet.

"Can you stand or ride on your own?" Will asked, gently lifting Cora. She took a shaky step forward before collapsing into Will's waiting arms.

"You will ride with me and your horse will follow. I cannot have you fall in your current state. You've already lost a lot of blood," Will's voice did little to hide his terror.

Lifting her slowly, Will set Cora atop Brandy's back. As he swung up behind her, Cora's body jostled forward slightly and a groan of pain escaped her lips.

Will's heart ached, "I'm sorry, Cora. I will try to keep you as still as I can but it's going to be a tough ride."

Will led Brandy to Whiskey's side to collect the reins and Cora's horse followed behind obediently. The three moved silently into the forest and were quickly swallowed by the dark; very little light broke through the dense canopy above.

Cora leaned her head back against Will's chest and spoke in a whisper, voice breaking, "If we head east for about fifteen or twenty minutes we should reach a large fallen tree. It's hollowed. If we are lucky, it will be empty of any beasts for the night. We can stop there and you can continue on for what we need."

Will kept the horses' pace steady and attempted to brace Cora's body at every sharp movement without touching the arrow shaft. Despite his efforts, Cora still groaned in pain frequently as they rode. It had taken only about five minutes before massive trees that seemed to grow unendingly upward replaced the smaller red alders from the forest's edge. The bases of some trees were so large it would take nearly ten grown adults with their arms spread wide to circle a single one.

"I've never seen trees like these," Will admitted, stunned. "I didn't understand how a hollow log was going to help us here but now I see. I thought you were delusional."

"To be fair, this place is the only place I've ever seen them and I *am* delusional. The chances of the tree being uninhabited are slim. I just hope whatever creature has claimed it for the night is more afraid of us than the other beasts of the forest," Cora managed.

Ahead in the darkness, Will could make out a wall of solid black completely impermeable to light. Fireflies danced through the air and provided some reference for him to follow toward the massive structure.

"That's it," Cora attempted to raise herself upright, "you'll need to clear it before we can set up inside."

Will swung down as smoothly as possible and gingerly approached the rotting tree. Drawing his sword he slammed the pommel against the mouth of the entrance. The sound of the steel against wood echoed through the forest. A low snarl responded from deep in the cavern eliciting a sigh of relief from Cora still seated atop Brandy.

"That's a good sound?" Will turned slightly toward Cora.

"Yes. Probably the best we could have expected. It sounds like a fox or possibly a badger, not anything magical. If we feed it something it might leave willingly. Do you have my bag with my food in it?" Cora asked.

"It's tied to your saddle," Will pointed to her horse beside her. Cora tried to dismount on her own and nearly fell. Will was by her side, instantly cradling her shaking body. Slowly, he led her to the tree and helped settle her against the mossy surface.

"Stay there, I'll grab the bag," Will directed, leaving Cora to brace her body against the wet surface of the log.

"The cookies will be the most enticing. Just toss half at the entrance and the other half of one at the edge of the shrubs over there," Cora pointed to the large bush several feet from the mouth of the tree.

"Damn it," Will swore. "The cookies aren't here. A biscuit will have to do."

The flaky, golden biscuit broke apart easily into three crumbly pieces. Will tossed one into the hollow tree, another at the opening, and the final chunk into the dirt just outside the tree. Will and Cora fell silent while they waited for the small creature to take their bait and exit the tree so they might find sanctuary within. Movement inside made Will's heart race. He raised his sword before Cora's hand came to rest on his forearm, gently lowering it.

"As little blood as possible. If there is too much it will draw in something larger that hunts in the dark," Cora breathed into his ear.

Will furrowed his brow and bent low so his lips were at her ear and spoke with unease, "How have you forgotten you are covered in your own blood. As soon as that arrow is removed, you will unfortunately bleed even more."

"That *is* unfortunate but inevitable at this point. Whatever exits this den can be spared tonight," Cora exhaled.

From the mouth of the giant fallen log, a red fox stepped tentatively into the chilled air and sniffed. With a loud clap, Will startled the animal, causing it to run for the cover of brush just feet away, clearing the tree for the trio and their horses to enter. Will slowly stepped into the once grand wonder of nature that now slowly decayed on the forest floor.

"It's clear," Will announced quietly as he stepped out to the cold and wove his arm beneath Cora's shoulders. "It looks deep enough that we might be able to light a small fire if we are far from the entrance and not draw any unwanted visitors."

Cora nodded slowly as they made their way to the far end of the long tunnel. Will softly lowered Cora to sit on the damp ground and hurried out to usher Grant and the three horses inside as well. Grant's limp body slid swiftly from his horse and Will had to use his entire body to brace his friend's weight as he laid him to rest near Cora.

"He will be safe to recover his strength here Will, I promise," Cora said in an attempt to ease the worry Will knew would be apparent across his face if either conscious party member could see in the pitch black. "In my bag there should still be a few matches left."

Will blindly rummaged through the bag he had collected the biscuit from moments before and pulled out a long, smooth, metal tin he had seen Cora pull matches from at their last camp. Kneeling slowly, Will searched the ground for Cora and Grant's waiting forms. The soft velvet fabric of the inside of Cora's cloak brushed his fingertips and Will inched closer to Cora's body. His hand came to a rest atop her leather-clad thigh and Will instinctively pulled his hand back.

"I'm sorry. I can't see and I have your matches here," he rambled and placed the tin where his hand had just been.

The melodic chuckle that escaped Cora's throat would have brought Will to his knees had he not already been on all fours. "You're alright, shifter. But you could have just lit one of the matches to see if you needed. They are enchanted and can burn for hours," Cora said, striking a match and letting the yellow glow of the flame illuminate both of their faces.

"Oh, that's good to know," Will's cheeks burned crimson. "I will collect something more substantial to burn anyway, then set out to find the supplies."

Will stood and patted the pocket of his tunic before he turned for the exit to ensure he still held Cora's list. The weight of what he must do to save Cora's life and protect his friends was heavy as he stepped out into the cold once more. He made quick work of finding several small pieces of mostly dry wood and returned to find Cora with her head lulled back, eye's closed, and skin ashen. Dread swelled in his heart.

"Cora!" Will pleaded, "Wake up! You must stay awake."

"I'm not dead yet, shifter. But I will need you to hurry. I can't leave the arrow in much longer," Cora's voice seemed to hint at humor but fell short.

"Will you be safe here while I'm gone? I should be able to collect everything in less than an hour," Will said looking over the list from his pocket in the flickering match light.

"As safe as anyone can be bleeding out in a forest where everything here can smell my death a mile away," Cora deadpanned.

"That isn't funny. I will move as quickly as I can. Just stay here and stay quiet. I'll be back soon," Without thought, Will leaned in and placed a light kiss atop Cora's head. If she was disturbed by it at all, she did not let him know as he stood and quickly ran from the tree into the dark, frigid forest.

As Cora had said when she wrote him the list, Will had no trouble collecting the first eleven items. Most of the list consisted of common herbs and plants Will was quite familiar with and were easy to identify in the dark by their smell or shape. The final two items, however, were going to prove to be more dangerous. The second to last item was a slimy green, aquatic weed that Cora specified grew at the bottom of the river near the forest's edge; the same river she had previously bayed them to avoid. In his mind, Will tried to imagine the creatures she had described and decided his best option would be to attempt to reach the plant in a form he assumed they too would fear. Will stopped at the edge of the ice-cold river and stripped off his clothing and sword before he willed himself to shift into a beast from his own nightmares.

His hands grew pale, thin membranous webbing between his fingers. A massive dark scaled fin replaced his two strong legs; each scale an iridescent onyx reflecting the scattered light from the moon peeking through the dark clouds and canopy overhead. The moment his head sank below the water's surface his lungs began to burn as water filled his airway. Panic-filled memories of his greatest fears filled his mind. His hands grabbed his throat as he struggled to concentrate for several seconds before finding his composure and willing four slatted gills to open on either side of his neck just below his ears. He ran his tongue over his teeth and found a row of razor sharp daggers replaced his normally beautiful smile. Disbelief and astonishment momentarily clouded his thoughts before he was moving through the water and dove deeper into the dark river to find his prize.

As he swam, he found the water oddly comforting despite his original fear. Smaller beasts and fish quickly evaded his approach to the river floor, evoking a confidence and thrill he had not expected to find in this place. The bright green weed seemed to glow and call to him as he neared. Several river sprites darted towards him before they quickly thought otherwise and took cover in the lustrous vegetation below. In a matter of seconds, Will ripped the plant from the murky floor and swiveled his body to head for the surface. Icy hands wrapped around Will's wrist and slatted bright blue-green eyes met his own.

"You are not from here, child," a beautiful, ancient voice gurgled through the water. The creature before him had the face of a beautiful young woman in the shadows. Only the light from the moon overhead illuminated her true decrepit form in fractured waves. Her sharp teeth resembled his own

112

but were stained by centuries of feasting on the poor souls that ventured too close to the water.

"I mean you no harm," Will managed to croak out.

"Pity, I do love a good fight. And you seem … tasty," the woman's sharp nail drew blood before she released Will's arm and brought her webbed fingers to her lips. Instantly, the creature's eyes went wide with ravenous hunger. Her thin pupils dilating wide, nearly blocking out the blue entirely. "You are not our kind… You are a *delicacy*! What a treat indeed!"

As the creature moved to strike, Will forced himself past her with a swift thrust of his fin. His sword lay just at the edge of the water. He had no other means to protect himself in this form. Pushing himself hard, he forced his body through the current and out onto shore as the woman sank her claws into the flesh of his fin, tearing deep into his lower half. Blood poured from the wound as Will grasped for his sword. The woman snarled and bared her sharp teeth. In one swift movement, Will drove his blade through the creature's eye socket all the way to the hilt. Quickly, Will shifted into his mortal, human form and used his uninjured leg to force the blade free from the creature's skull. The woman's body went slack and slipped motionless back into the running river. Before disappearing entirely from view, dozens of small shadowed forms swarmed the siren's body and began to shred her apart.

Will tore a strip of fabric from the bottom of his tunic and tightly wrapped it around his bleeding leg. In his human form, the cut did not appear nearly as deep as it had moments ago but would most likely need to be cleaned as soon as possible to prevent infection. Quickly, Will added the glowing plant to his collection of goods in his bag and stood. The final item was going to be the most treacherous and time consuming. As he stood to his feet, Will realized he wasn't sure if he would be this close to their original camp again.

With one goal in mind, Will sprinted for the remnants of their old camp to collect whatever remained of Cora's cookies. As he neared the brush edge, there was absolute silence like the creatures that lurked in the woods could sense the death that had been spilled here and quieted to pay their respects. Will stepped out into the empty clearing and noticed the bodies that once adorned the ground were gone, only blood and decay were left behind. Several warm embers still shone in their fire pit. Less than three feet from the fire was a small brown parcel Will knew contained the deliciousness he was here seeking out. He collected the package quickly and entered the woods once more to collect the final item on Cora's list.

Will knew time was limited. He would need to cover an extensive amount of forest ground to reach the cave Cora specified on the list in order to collect the venom she would need to complete the healing elixir. In a hurry, Will shifted into a large spotted cat-like animal he had read about as a child that was capable of covering large territory in a very short time. Will secured his sword over his body and collected his belongings between his teeth.

Although the creature from the story books was better suited for flat, dry lands, Will flew through the forest swiftly jumping over large limbs and rocks. He slowed his pace when the terrain began to elevate steeply and shifted back into his human form. Crouching low, Will eased to the edge of a rock face that seemed to match Cora's description. Just around the bend in the rock was an opening into complete darkness.

Entering the cave in his human form was going to be impossible and he wasn't sure what he would be able to shift into at this moment. Exhaustion had already begun to take its toll. He had a terrible idea he hoped would not be the death of him. Once again, Will removed his sword and dropped his clothing before he began to shift. Shrinking low, he morphed into a near invisible winged insect. He was absolutely vulnerable to every creature now but he would most likely be of no interest to the massive shape-shifting monster he needed to acquire venom from. Will flew silently into the cave where he could see a single massive form resting against the cave wall.

This would be his only opportunity to apprehend the beast. Without hesitation, he flew straight for the creature and directly into the beast's eye slit. The monster roared its irritation and swung its massive clawed hand toward its face just as Will shifted again. Adrenaline fueled his every movement. He focused all his efforts and concentration on shifting into the largest beast he could imagine. One moment Will was nestled in the cavity of the pink skinned creature's eye, and the next, his massive, scaled body erupted through the top of the unsuspecting beast's skull. Blood and brain matter exploded and covered the cave walls. Will picked the beast up in his black, talon tipped claws and easily drug the carcass from the cave. Pausing to pick up his sword and belongings between his razor sharp teeth, Will spread his wings and took flight.

In just a few short minutes and two attempts to lift from the forest floor, Will was soaring back to the fallen tree where he had left Cora. His entire life he had dreamed of flying.

Although he wished it was under less dire circumstances, he reveled in the feel of the crisp, cold air against his scaly skin. Every part of his new body felt like it was operating on an entirely different level. His senses were heightened and worked overtime as he flew over the trees below. He could only imagine what Cora or Grant's faces would look like once they learned he had successfully shifted into a massive dragon. As Will approached the hollow log, his heightened sense of smell caught the overwhelming scent of blood and his heart sank. Something had gone horribly wrong in his absence. He landed hard on the packed soil and shifted back into his human form in a single stride before he was sprinting toward Cora, sword drawn. Will abruptly skid to a stop as the flickering light of their small fire illuminated Cora's silhouette. At the far end of the log, Cora stood on shaky legs, ax dripping black blood at her side.

Her back was still to him when he spoke, "Cora, are you alright?"

Cora turned to face the fully exposed shifter. Her gaze met his and the look of utter rage that painted her face softened at the sight of him. He stepped closer and Cora's last ounce of strength failed her and she fell to her knees. Immediately, Will was kneeling before her, holding her face in his blood stained hands.

"It wanted to take Grant," Cora lifted a shaking finger to the black winged monster left to bleed out on the hollow log floor.

"What the fuck is that thing?" Will asked, then shook his head dismissively. "It doesn't matter. I have what we need to heal you."

Cora's look of surprise was quickly replaced with something more animalistic as her eyes lowered down Will's naked, gore coated body. A faint pink flush brightened her pail skin.

"There will be time to admire my physique after you are healed," Will's normally jovial flirting was staunched by the urgency in his tone. "How do we make your elixir?"

Chapter 15

Cora

"First, I need you to be a little bit less of a distraction. At the bare minimum, put on your pants before you freeze to death," Cora closed her eyes and rested her head against the inside of the log. "Then, I need you to grab all of the ingredients and the small iron pot that's in one of Shea's saddle bags."

Will rose to his feet and quickly ran for the tunnel opening to collect the supplies he had left outside in his hurry to get to Cora.

Cora's entire body screamed in pain. She supposed it was probably a good sign that she still had feeling in her extremities and she hadn't gone cold yet. She hadn't lost too much blood despite her encounter with the vampiric creature at her feet. The now broken arrow shaft still lodged in her torso continued to staunch the blood. Will slid to his knees in front of her in bloody brown trousers and his shirt left unbuttoned, his arms filled with all but one of the ingredients she would need.

"Were you unable to find a skin-walker?" Cora asked

inspecting the pile of herbs and plants before her. "That will be alright... I think... I can manage without it. The elixir will still work some just not as well and it will be very painful."

"My love, you wound me. I will be right back with the last of your supplies and something for you to bite on when we remove that arrow," Will's white smile radiated with satisfaction in stark contrast to the blood that splattered his skin.

Cora sat stunned as she watched Will enter the tree once more. Thrown over his shoulder with ease was the carcass of a massive beast; the top portion of its skull missing just above its nasal cavity.

"Where did you find that? It's still fresh," Cora ran her hands over the creature and felt its pliable skin.

"What do you mean? I killed it," Will stated puzzled. "Your list said their nests were in the rocky mountain face. I went and got what you needed."

Panic filled every cell in her body. Instantly, Cora shot to her feet, her injury be damned. Startled, Will dropped the creature to the ground with a thud. Cora circled Will frantically. There was no way in her mind that Will, a shifter who just discovered his ability, would have been able to bring down one of these fully grown beasts unscathed.

Confusion soaked Will's expression. "What are you doing?" he asked and tried to settle Cora back to the dirt floor. Cora swatted his hands away weakly and proceeded to search his bare chest for injuries, running the tips of her blood stained fingers over his body.

"How are you unharmed?" Cora breathlessly dropped to her knees with a groan and began to pull Will's pant leg up over his knee. "This was not from the skin-walker. What did this to you?" Irrational rage began to broil in Cora's core.

Will took Cora's hands gently, "I'm alright. The cut to my leg is from a siren in the river. As for the, what did you call it, a skin-walker?" Cora nodded her head in confirmation and took a shallow breath. Her heart rate began to steadily decline once more as the concern knitting her brows together subsided. "As for the *skin-walker*, I was able to shift several times tonight. That's a pretty amazing story I will be more than happy to tell you *after* you are taken care of."

Cora reluctantly nodded and directed Will to prop the pot over the fire and fill it with the remaining water from her water-skin. Methodically, she began to measure out the components she needed and handed them over to Will to mix into the cast iron. A sweet smell filled the air in the tree once all but the venom from the skin-walker had been added. Unsteadily, Cora rocked herself forward to kneel over what remained of the creature's head.

"This part is a little bit more difficult," Cora exhaled. "I need no more than seven drops of venom from the creature. If there is not enough, our healing will take longer and any serious damage may have more permanent side effects. Too much venom and we could accidentally paralyze ourselves for the gods know how long."

"Our healing?" Will's brows came together.

"Yes. *Our* healing. If that gash on your leg is not taken care of, you could end up with an infection. I will be damned if that is how you die William!" Cora snapped.

Gently, Cora placed the rim of her water-skin against the longest protruding fang in the creature's mouth and pushed the tooth up and forward just like her mother had instructed as a child. A translucent, viscous yellow liquid seeped into the container.

"That is more than enough," Cora said, turning to the iron pot simmering over the small fire. Slowly, she counted each drop as it sizzled in the concoction below.

"Six, Seven. Perfect," Cora dipped the tip of her two smallest fingers into the water-skin before she capped it and set it aside. The smell in the air became richer, like burning caramel or toffee.

"Come over here," Cora gestured for Will to sit at her side. "Roll up your pant leg please." Will obliged without refuting and Cora ran her fingers over the flesh surrounding the open cut up his thigh. "That will numb most of your lower leg and minimize the burn once you drink the elixir. "

Gently, Cora began to unbutton her sticky black tunic. A large amount of her blood had already begun to congeal. She watched Will try to turn away slightly.

"Ever the gentlemen. Unfortunately, I will need your help with this next part. Did you get something for me to bite down on? I can't let my screams draw in other predators. Although, with those things in here, skin-walkers are probably our only real threat tonight," Cora said, gesturing to the bodies on the floor.

"I have a leather strop you can use," Will pulled a long piece of leather from his pocket and handed it over to Cora.

"That will do just fine. I'm going to need you to pull the arrow out. Alright?" Closing her eyes, Cora leaned back and placed the leather between her teeth and gently rubbed the remainder of the venom from her fingers around her puncture wound.

"On three," Will confirmed in a soothing tone, "One, two," Before he reached three, Cora felt the arrow rip free of her body and a muffled curse left her clenched teeth, "Fuck. I'm so sorry, love. It will be alright soon. I promise. How much of that do you need to drink?"

Will pressed one hand firmly onto her abdomen. She wasn't sure when he had done it, but Will now sat shirtless again and held his bunched tunic to her body to stop her bleeding. With his free hand, Will ran his fingertips down her cheek and wiped away tears that had begun to stream down toward her chin.

"We need to drink as much as we can without vomiting," Cora managed between silent sobs.

Cautiously, Will reached over and grabbed the wrapped handle of the iron pot and brought it to his lips but did not drink. Cora couldn't help but notice the charming look of surprise on his face.

"It's cool," Will said, baffled.

"That, too, is enchanted. The liquid inside should be a palpable temperature as well," Cora confirmed.

Will lowered the pot to Cora's lips and she swallowed deep as the viscous, pungent liquid coated her throat. No matter how many times she needed to use this elixir, it never seemed to be any easier to take. Cora could feel her bleeding slowing and her skin knitting back together. After several filling gulps, she choked and pushed the container toward Will and lifted his hand from her torso to reveal her healing injury.

"It will begin to work quickly. See? But it will not taste as it smells, so prepare yourself, shifter," Cora coughed out.

As Cora watched Will swallow down the first mouthful, she was surprised to see very little response from the man before her. Only the slightest of winces and subtle scrunch of his nose told her he even tasted the bile like bitterness as we drank it down.

"That is absolutely horrid," Will finally spoke. "It's a good thing I have a remedy for that too."

Will stood gracefully and walked to where he had discarded his cloak. He bent low and Cora's heart exploded in her chest at what he held. In his hands, Will approached with a small brown paper package.

"Is-is that what it looks like?" Cora stuttered in disbelief.

"It is," Will said, sitting next to her on the floor. Slowly, Will opened the package and removed several large crushed pieces of chocolate chunk cookie. "I know you said you wouldn't share these again, but I do hope I've earned one and this could be an exception."

"My gods, Will. I think I love you," The words left Cora's lips before she could truly process what she was saying. They sounded like an echo of Will's own words just a day ago. Her heart fluttered hard at the realization that she might have meant what she just told this man she hardly knew. Heat flushed her face with embarrassment.

"Cora, I..." Will began.

"Please don't," Cora interrupted.

Will smiled sweetly and leaned in to kissed the top of Cora's head, "Thank you for sharing, beautiful," Will's voice was like velvet against her hair as he spoke. " I don't just mean the cookies either."

Both companions sat in silence as they enjoyed their just rewards. Cora's mind continued to race while the elixir pieced her body back together. Huddled close, she could see the hint of a faint pink scar on Will's calf. The chill of the late fall air was blocked out by Will's warm body cradling her own.

"I doubt I will find sleep anytime soon. I think now is a good time to hear how you were able to manage whatever the hell you did to that thing," Cora pointed to the skin-walker.

Will leaned back into the tree and pulled Cora's body closer to his. The heat from his bare chest radiated from him like a flame. "I suppose you are right and it's quite exciting, if I do say so myself. I would then like to know what happened after I left. If you are up for it."

Cora's body relaxed into him fully, "That seems like a fair trade." The grin that spread across Will's face melted Cora's heart and made it difficult for her to concentrate on the story he began.

"Well, I collected everything except the weird glowing weed and the skin-walker until last. I figured the best way not to be ripped to ribbons by the river sprites would be to shift into something they are afraid of too. So, I climbed into the river and grew a fucking siren's fin and dove to the bottom. I didn't have any issue until I moved to return to the surface and a creepy female siren attacked me. I was able to get to the bank of the river and I ran her through with my sword." Will thrust his right arm forward dramatically in demonstration and Cora chuckled softly.

"You fully shifted into a siren?" Cora asked and lifted a brow in astonishment.

"Oh ya I did! Then I was a mountain cat for a bit to run through the forest," Will continued with a grin.

"That's uncommon..." Cora spoke to herself under her breath.

Will tilted his head slightly and knit his brows together, "What is?"

Cora shook her head to clear her thoughts, "Most information I've ever read about shifters states they can only choose from two forms to shift between. Adopting other's *human* traits or physical features seemed to be common but not multiple species. I assumed the newt was going to be your alternate but then you said you were a siren. For a moment, I thought maybe my mother's potion forced you into a newt and perhaps you were truly a siren shifter. But a cat too? Your gift isn't common in Viridia any longer so my books are probably just outdated."

"I have no idea but when I got to the cliffs, I shifted again into a tiny insect," pride coated every one of Will's words as he spoke.

"Why would you do that?!" Cora tried to keep her outrage from becoming too apparent.

Will shrugged his shoulders, "It seemed like the smartest way to be unseen."

"Perhaps, but it was also completely reckless! You were beyond vulnerable, you fool!" Cora barked and smacked Will's arm.

Laughter erupted from him, "It was a good idea. Just listen to the rest. It gets better."

"Gods, help me. I don't know if I can handle what you think *'better'* is," Cora rubbed a hand down her face.

"I flew into the cave, right into that creature's eye. Guess what I did next," Will beamed.

Cora shook her head in disbelief, "I think it's safe to assume you blew up that thing's head when you shifted."

"*Ya I did*! I shifted into a huge, black dragon," Cora could feel Will's pride deep in her soul. "Then I flew all the way back here to you. I have always wanted to fly."

"You are either the bravest or stupidest person I think I

have ever met," Cora admitted. "But, I am glad for it and I don't mean just for the ingredients I needed."

"Anything you need I am more than happy to oblige," Will stated with full sincerity.

Cora couldn't help but think about the nightmare Grant had revealed just hours ago in the clearing. She knew it wasn't just her fear she had seen, but a glimpse into a possible future she hoped she could keep from unfolding. Will would be willing to die for her and she wasn't going to let that happen if she could stop it. Will watched as concern deepened the lines between her brows.

"Are you alright, Cora?" Will placed a gentle hand against her cheek and ran his thumb over her skin.

"I will be. Do you still want to hear about the blood sucking beast over there?" Cora tried to say lightly but fell short.

Will's concern did not ease from his expression but he nodded nonetheless and Cora began, "A little while after you left, I could hear something moving outside. I tried to drag Grant a little closer to the fire. Then that thing flew in here."

The creature splayed out on the floor had large membranous, bat-like wings and a sickly wolf-like body. Patches of wiry black fur covered its dark gray skin. In her lifetime, Cora had encountered several of the rabid creatures in the woods and hated the reek of their breath more each time.

"They feed on warm blooded creatures. Apparently, I was not worth the trouble because it went straight for Grant. I had to cut it down before it could pull him away. I don't normally have such a hard time handling them, but I was already bleeding out so it was a bit more of a struggle than I care to admit," Cora rolled her eyes in annoyance.

"How much time have you spent in these woods?" Will

exhaled.

"As a child, my mother wanted to make sure I was prepared for the world. She would bring me here to make sure I never let my fears or emotions cloud my judgment and abilities. I don't really know for sure how much time I was here as a child. Now I frequent here before every full moon to collect supplies with her," Cora stated. She knew how insane and cruel that made her mother sound. She was grateful for having the control she did; that was until Will had arrived and completely derailed her.

"That sounds terrible," Will's voice was soft but somehow she didn't feel like he was judging her or her mother but simply reflecting on her upbringing and acknowledging what she had been through.

"It was. But, I don't regret any of it or hold any ill will toward my mother for it. I would not be as strong as I am now without her guiding me through all of this. I don't think she would have ever truly let me be in real danger even to this day. That's why she had the blacksmith make us the weapons," Cora kicked the handle of the ax with the toe of her boot.

"Why an ax?" Will asked.

Cora laughed lightly, "Despite my mother's best efforts, I never took to a sword the way she did. I've never liked the feel of one in my hands. The ax has always seemed like a much more well-rounded tool to me."

She watched Will close his eyes and exhale a relaxed breath, "That makes sense. It's quite difficult to throw a long sword, but I bet you could get a good launch from your ax." Cora yawned wide and covered her mouth with her left hand. Will rolled his neck to the side and looked down at her fully, "I think you should rest a while and let your body heal. I can take watch for now."

A sudden wave of exhaustion seemed to seep into Cora's bones, "That is probably wise. Wake me in a few hours if you can so I can let you rest as well."

"I will be doing no such thing. Grant will relieve me when he is able. I have slept enough tonight. Now please sleep while you can. I am going to clean some of this blood off of me before it really starts to stink," Will adjusted and helped Cora settle to the ground.

As she drifted into unconsciousness, Cora could hear Will's deep voice quietly singing one of the most beautiful and haunting melodies she had ever heard. His deep baritone lulled her to a restful, dreamless sleep. She stirred only once when Will came to sit with her once again. His clean, spare clothes smelled like warm, rich leather and smoke. She drifted back to sleep feeling like she was wrapped in a peace she had not yet known.

Chapter 16

Grant

The memory of Grant's final moments, before fatigue pulled him into darkness, circled his mind as he slept. In seconds, Grant had watched and somehow aided in melting nearly ten men to nothing more than rotting fleshy puddles. He wasn't sure if the thought made him fearful of the young princess or impressed at their shared power. The grotesque display should have been enough to turn anyone's stomach, but for some reason, Grant felt a resounding sense of pride and relief. A selfish thought flashed through his mind.

If I am a monster, at least I'm not alone.

"You are not a monster," Addie's voice was a welcome sound in Grant's endless turmoil and confusion. "That was almost entirely my own doing."

"How can you be so certain? I haven't ever really seen the extent of what I'm capable of," Grant admitted. "And I am a monster, princess. After my powers surfaced... I was, fuck..." Grant hung his head in shame, "I *am* responsible for the deaths of innocent people. I couldn't control what I was capable of and one night in a panic, after an argument with my father about me not wanting to return to court, I lost control and five members of my family's staff died because of me. People I knew and cared about, that cared about me, died because of the monster I am. I saw all of their greatest fears. I felt their terror and anguish as I ripped them apart from the inside. In a matter of seconds, I took the lives of innocent people because I was afraid. I destroyed so many families, Addie. Their memories haunt me."

"That doesn't make you a monster, Grant. What you experienced was terrible, yes; but it was an accident. Your remorse and regret are just proof that you aren't a monster. I know what happened in the forest was me because that is not the first time I have intentionally done something destructive like that. I wanted them all dead," Addie's voice filled with disgust. "When I was about fifteen and still trying to master my healing powers, I nearly killed a woman; one of my teachers in fact. She had been injured in a riding accident and I had been asked to heal her but I didn't want to, despite knowing it was my duty as a healer. She was not a kind woman, at least not to me. When I put my hands on her body, all I could think about was how unfair it was that I was meant to heal a woman that had struck my hands with her cane for misbehaving and been cruel for no real apparent reason. Before I realized what I had done, it was too late. I had let my anger and hatred for a person nearly destroy her. The smaller cuts and injuries on her hands had gone gangrenous and the larger internal injuries were rotted far beyond my own ability to heal at the time. My father has kept my failure a secret and pretends, to this day, as though that facet of my power doesn't exist. But, I nearly killed a woman because

I did not like her. It took my father's personal, specialized healer to repair what I had done and even he could not fully save the function of her right hand. The scariest part of all of it though, is that I don't regret hurting her, not even a little bit."

"I'm sorry, Addie. I don't think you are a monster. I didn't mean it that way. I was just… honestly, I don't really know what I meant. It just felt like I wasn't so alone. Like there might just be another person that may be able to understand what it's like to contain so much," Grant spoke softly.

In the darkness of Grant's mind, Addie's form manifested. Grant thought hard for several seconds before the lush palace gardens came into focus all around them. Addie's beautiful golden brown hair hung in a loose braid down her back and her silk blue gown shifted as she stepped closer and took a seat next to him on the edge of a large fountain.

"But I am a monster. I've never done what I just did,"Addie squeezed her eyes closed and shook her head, "not to that magnitude, but that was undoubtedly my magic, not yours."

"I'm the reason you were put into that position though and it was my shadow, my nightmare, that held them still. I felt their fear. You are not alone in any of what just happened."

Addie sighed, "Thank you for that, I guess."

Grant studied Addie's face a moment before he spoke. "I don't think my memories of you do you any justice in my mind."

"What?" Addie turned to face him.

"I mean, as children I remember you being brave and honest and kind but not…" Grant shook his head and struggled to find the right words to explain how he was feeling.

"Not a walking plague?" Addie questioned.

131

"That was not what I was going to say. You're not as delicate as I thought you were. You're far more resilient." Grant's heart tightened as he watched the small smile crack Addie's expression.

Without warning, Grant's mind recalled another memory from tonight. "Did you see Cora's nightmare?" Grant asked with a heavy heart.

"That was not your fault, Grant. It was an accident. I'm sure she will be alright." Addie tried to reassure him.

"Gods, I hope so. But I was talking about her actual nightmare, the thing she fears most. That's what I see when I use my power."

"Yes, I saw it but that isn't going to happen either," Addie tried to argue.

"Cora has the gift of foresight. I don't think that was just her fear. I think it was a vision of what's to come if I fail to stop my father. I think Will's life is in danger," Grant inhaled a shaky breath. "I don't think I can handle losing him. I fear I've already lost my father. My mother is gone. Will is all I have left. And knowing your life hangs somewhere in the balance too, feels like far too much to bear."

"If my life ends, it was my own stubbornness and pride that led me to where I am. Please do not mourn me yet," Addie shrugged. "I do think your father may be lost to us though. It's all hazy, but I'm nearly positive he may have tried to kill me. Judging by where my soul is stuck here in this purgatory, I fear he may have succeeded."

"He wasn't always like this, you know? My father. He was a great man and now he is just... well *broken* is probably the best way to describe him. When my mother was killed, everything that was good and hopeful and honest about him seemed to die with her. He was just completely lost after that."

"I know. And I know it doesn't really change anything but, I'm sorry your family had to go through all of that, that you had to go through all of this now. I know he was a good man though," Addie spoke as though she could feel Grant's guilt and despair.

After a moment, Addie continued, "Would you like to know something a little more lighthearted? Do you know your father is the reason I was ever educated on... um... how do I say this in the least mortifying way... he is the reason my mother had to explain 'oral relations.'"

"Excuse me?!" Grant choked, "I do hope you aren't about to tell me that you and my father..."

"Oh gods, no!!!!" Addie interjected, "I should have worded that better..." She pulled her lip between her lips as she mulled over her word choice.

"For all that is holy, I beg you Addie, please continue quickly before my mind goes wild with assumptions" Grant's face blushed.

"It's far more innocent than it sounds and it actually led to me learning a lot about my parents and love in general, actually. It's quite a funny story thinking about it now. I was sixteen, I think, and my father had called a council meeting so all of his advisors were all roaming around the castle. And, as always, I was told to leave once the discussions of war began but I never went very far. There was a closet just outside my father's map room where the council would meet and I could hide inside and hear everything."

"You were a shadow even then!" Grant teased.

"Oh, I was quite good at eavesdropping," Addie smiled playfully, "Anyway, as I was saying, I was listening in to a

133

particularly heated argument about some groups' movement in the northern part of the kingdom near the boarder or something, I can't really recall now, but your father said something that I will never forget and when I asked my mother about it she nearly choked to death. Your father asked, I think he was speaking to my father's interrogator, if he wanted to *'just get down on his knees and blow the king already'* and I had no idea what he meant. So, being the dutiful daughter I was, I ran straight to my mother's chambers and told her that someone wanted to blow up the king. Of course she seemed alarmed by that and asked how I knew. I told her everything I remembered and she turned about as red as you are now. She then proceeded to tell me what your father meant. I still don't fully understand why anyone would want to do that or have that done but that's neither here nor there."

"You'd be surprised what a talented tongue can do, high-ness," a momentary wicked grin graced Grant's face before he realized what he had just spoken aloud, "Not that I have a talented tongue. Or, or that I was planning to show you... shit I'm sorry. I'll stop talking," Grant rambled nervously.

If she were able to feel her heart, Addie was sure it would have been doing summer salts in her chest. After a few awkward moments, she continued.

"Ummm, as for the whole learning about love, I watched your parents more closely then, and they taught me about that too. I always knew my parents didn't love each other. Don't get me wrong, they care for each other some, I think, but their marriage is one of duty and loyalty. They were married for political reasons, not for love. Every time I saw your mother and father together I knew they had so much more! They would sneak little kisses when they thought no one was looking and they seemed to be drawn to each other like magnets that needed to be touching in some way all the time. I liked to see them in court when they came because they gave me hope that love still existed or ever really did at all for that matter. It was written on their faces, in their eyes and anyone who cared to look could see it as clear as day. I think that's why my father can't understand the lengths yours would go to for someone he loved. My father wouldn't do that for my mother. Not that he doesn't care if she were to die, but he wouldn't burn the world for her."

Grant wiped a hand down his face, "Thank you."

"What for?" Addie asked softly.

"For caring enough to look," Grant replied nearly inaudibly, "and for wanting to share that with me. I do have a question for you that I haven't quite figured out yet." Grant stated raising a brow curiously.

"I'm an open book, my friend," Addie said with a smile in her tone.

"How did you end up where you are now, involved in this whole mess in the first place? This isn't your battle to fight and I know things are still a little bit difficult for you to recall but what made you go in search of my father in the first place?" Grand asked tentatively.

"Oh. Um, well when Rose came to warn my father about your father's plans," Addie began.

Grant raised an eyebrow in inquiry, "Rose?"

"Yes, Rose, Cora's mother. Didn't you speak with her? She came to see my father and warn him but he wouldn't listen. I heard it all from my broom closet. And when I stepped into the hall to confront her, it was like she knew I was going to be there and she told me everything she knew and some

135

crazy prophetic sounding stuff about becoming the weapon of fear," Addie concluded.

"She failed to mention having met you when we spoke. She also did not give me her name for that matter," Grant mumbled to himself.

"She was my father's magic adviser until I was nearly fifteen. When Andrew, Gavin, and I turned six we were all taken to see her so she could tell father of our gifts, if we had any. My father was elated when Andrew showed signs of telepathy and Gavin showed immense strength around their sixteenth birthdays, just as Rose predicted. But when I turned six, Rose warned my father that I would be damned to shadow and embody fear. My father panicked a little at first. Around my fifteenth birthday my healer's magic started to surface and the king never trusted her the same after that."

Grant cocked his head to the side inquisitively, "Because she was wrong?"

"No, I think he thought she intended to instill fear and unrest. But now I think she was seeing beyond my healing gift to our more current circumstances," Addie surmised, shaking her head.

"Do you think what we did tonight is what she meant by '*embody fear?*' The shadow part I understand but the rest I don't get how a healer can embody fear. That sounds more like my power than yours," Grant laid back against the edge of the fountain and laced his fingers behind his head, weariness sinking into his soul.

"Perhaps. But you can't actually manifest a person's fear into existence. Can you? It's all in a person's mind, right? I do, however, believe it all has to do with us being connected to each other." Addie breathed. "And, I do think we should

136

learn to master your nightmare gift together."

"There isn't much time for that and the only mind I do not know is yours," Grant shrugged.

Smiling to herself, Addie continued, "I am more than happy to help you in any way I can but you should regain some of your strength first. I can feel your exhaustion."

Grant nodded his agreement and the illusion in his mind faded to black. Addie's soul drifted into the darkness and Grant's control of his dream began to slip away. Before his mind went blank, he heard Addie call from the shadows, "Find me when you wake."

Chapter 17

Will

Will watched Cora's chest steadily rise and fall as the hours passed and dawn approached. The worry lines that had been carved into her face since they left her cottage were relaxed, making her look younger and far more at ease. Grant's face too seemed more at peace than Will had seen it in years. The faint gray light of the dismal morning sun broke through the dense canopy overhead illuminating several large holes in the hollow log Will had not noticed in the dark. To his right, Grant groaned and began to stir.

"It's nice of you to finally join us again," Will spoke softly in an attempt to not wake Cora; who's head still rested in his lap.

"Gods, my head hurts," Grant slowly sat up and rubbed his hands over his eyes.

"You look better than you have in a while," Will raised his brows at his admission.

Slowly, Grant propped himself up on his elbows and hummed to himself; a sound that mirrored Will's growing relief before he nodded to the woman sleeping in Will's lap, "How is she?"

"She's going to be alright, I think. A lot of shit went down after you fainted on us," Will joked.

"I wouldn't say I fainted," Grant frowned in protest.

Will laughed quietly, "Then what would you say you did? Because from my perspective, it looked like you fainted."

Grant angled his head to the side and shrugged, "I would say I collapsed into unconsciousness as a result of over exertion."

"That sounds a lot like the definition of fainting to me," Cora's voice echoed through Will like the melodic chime of a golden bell ringing through a silent room.

"Well, good morning, beautiful," Will ran his hand over her shining dark hair.

Instantly, Cora shot up to a seated position and her beautiful alabaster skin flushed a deep pink. Will wasn't sure if her embarrassment was caused by the fact that she just had her head in his lap or if it was because she was only covered by her cropped under layer and his cloak. He couldn't help but admire the flush of her skin nonetheless. In truth, it was probably a combination of both factors accompanied by Grant's now skeptical gaze on them both.

"It seems I may have missed quite a bit," Grant raised a brow.

"You missed Will saving *both* of our lives and getting us here," Cora scolded and gestured to the hollow around them.

Will filled with pride once more at all he had accomplished last night. Leaning forward, he picked up two pieces of somewhat dry wood and added them to the low burning embers of their small fire.

"Let's get some food in our stomachs before we kill each

139

other," Will got to his feet and picked up the remnants of their food. All that remained was a small supply of dried meat and four severely bruised apples. "Well, maybe not."

Cora stood and pulled her clean dry shirt over her head, "You washed my shirt?" she said, confused.

"I couldn't find a spare in your bag so I used my water and cleaned it the best I could. I hope it was able to get dry enough," Will smiled.

"Thank you," Cora smirked before Grant cleared his throat drawing her attention. "Um, right. I can head out quickly and collect a few things to eat. Most of the creatures here hunt at night so they should be tucking themselves into their holes about now."

Will watched as she quickly collected her ax from the floor and made for the exit. "Be careful. I know you can handle yourself with that thing but you literally had an arrow inches from your heart just a few hours ago. Please don't go too far."

Cora nodded and was running for the exit in a flash. Will looked over to Grant's wide eyed expression. He was certain his friend was going to want a lot of explanation. Breathing in a sigh, Will shook his head with a goofy smile on his face.

"So tell me, what all happened while I was unconscious and where the hell are we right now?" Grant asked, looking around.

"We're in the Alderbrooke Forest in a massive hollow log," Will deadpanned. With a roll of his eyes Grant cocked a brow at Will and smirked knowingly. "After everything at the camp, I loaded us on the horses and Cora directed us here to find cover for the night. All of her healing elixir was destroyed so I went into the forest alone and collected what she needed. It was crazy. I blew that thing's head off when I shifted into an insect in its eye then into a giant dragon," Will motioned toward the exit. "I also killed a river siren after I collected the weeds Cora needed at the bottom of the river."

Will looked at his best friend. Stunned disbelief was the only emotion he could see in Grant's face.

"You are insane," were the first words out of Grant's stunned mouth. "What about that thing over there?" Grant pointed to the body of the winged creature near the entrance of the tree. Will had pulled it farther away from their small camp after Cora had fallen asleep.

"That was Cora. She killed it while I was gone. It tried to eat you but she fought it off with that fucking arrow still in her chest," anger laced Will's words.

Grant's lips formed a tight line before he spoke, shame and regret in every word, "Will, I'm so sorry for what happened to Cora. That was entirely my fault."

After a moment, Will spoke with less fire in his words, "I think everything happened the way it was supposed to. Plus, you weren't the one to shoot her. That sorry excuse for a man is dead."

"I didn't ever want any of this to happen the way it has. None of this should have ever been on your shoulders, Will. There's been far too much blood spilled and it's all because of my father and the king," Grant pushed himself to his feet and started to pace.

"I have a feeling there is going to be a lot more death if we aren't able to stop your father," Will admitted quietly.

Cora entered the tree on silent feet and dumped her armload of goods on the ground before the small, steadily burning fire. Will watched as she pulled a small dagger from her boot he hadn't seen before. Just as methodically as she

141

had handled the ingredients for the potion last night, Will watched Cora swiftly chop wild mushrooms, onions and a strange purple root-like plant into diced pieces and dump them into the now empty iron pot from last night. The sizzle of vegetables filled the silence before Cora spoke.

"I agree with you, Will," Cora's face was filled with what looked like dread. "When Grant saw my nightmare yesterday, I saw a vision of what's to come if we fail. There will be war and it will not end well for many in this kingdom." Cora looked over to Grant with a knowing expression.

Grant stood next to Will when he spoke, "How long do we have if we aren't able to stop my father?"

"There was an abundance of snow on the palace grounds, so I would assume the brunt of whatever war we are going to face is going to happen once winter has hit full force," Cora admitted. "We will most likely see three more moon cycles before the true bloodshed begins."

"Then let's eat and get a move on so we can keep innocent people from dying," Will said optimistically.

He couldn't quite decipher the exchange that passed between his best friend and Cora but assumed it was because of the severity of what Grant and Cora had seen. Given the destruction and horrors both had experienced in their lives, Will hoped deep in his soul whatever future Cora had witnessed could still be avoided.

The trio ate quickly in an awkward silence. The purple vegetable that Cora had collected was sweet and reminded Will of a potato dish he had a few times at the castle with his mother. After snuffing out the fire and packing the remainder of their belongings, they headed east toward the cave system once again.

Grant rode just behind Will and Cora on the narrow game trail that led deeper into the forest. "How long before we reach Addie?" Grant asked.

Cora's voice was grave, "We will be able to ride for a few hours before the terrain gets a little bit tougher to travel through. We can either attempt to go around the rock mountains; which I don't think we have the time for. It could take days and there is the chance that the river is flooded from the storm and we would have to double back. The other option is to climb over the ridge and down the steep embankment on the other side. It's more dangerous to cross with the horses but it would mean we can reach the cavern I believe Addie and your father were in, by tomorrow midday, or tomorrow morning, if we are lucky."

Will shifted slightly in his saddle and looked at Cora as he rode, "These are the same mountains I was in last night, correct?"

"Yes. I may need you to guide us away from the cave you found so we can avoid any skin-walkers that might have smelled the beast's death in the cave and come to scavenge whatever may have remained," Cora admitted.

Nodding his agreement, Will's shoulders tensed, "All that was left in the cave was blood and brain matter I'm sure, but I will do my best to keep us clear of the area." Will said and hoped he would be able to identify the area in daylight from the ground.

They traveled for hours with very little conversation. The weight of what they were facing hung heavy in the air around them like a wet blanket. The sun had most likely reached its highest point but the dense trees coverage above blocked out the majority of the light. It looked as though it could have been just before dawn or dusk. Surprised he hadn't done it before, Will thought about his eyesight and tried to think of what animals he knew had excellent nocturnal vision.

Opening his eyes, Will could see the world in sharp clarity. Although most color was nearly gone and their surroundings were mostly grays and blacks, he could see the finest of details on everything. The dew on the ferns below were like drops of crystal refracting even the faintest light and every slight movement of the small rodents on the ground and in the trees easily caught his gaze. Looking over to Cora, Will's heart skipped several beats. The contours of her face shone like the brightest star in the blackest night; the ethereal glow that radiated from her beautiful dark hair encased her entirely as though she were one of the gods themselves.

"Holy shit," Will involuntarily exhaled aloud, completely and utterly awestruck.

"What's wrong?" Cora snapped her head to Will in a panic. "*Holy shit* is right! Your eyes are incredible!"

Will jerked his head back stunned slightly, "What do they look like? I couldn't see very well so I tried to shift my sight. The best animal I know with excellent vision is a white owl."

Grant brought his horse to Will's other side and leaned over curiously, "They're completely yellow and your pupils are huge."

"They're stunning," Cora said in awe. "They look like the moon has blocked out the sun."

Cora's words felt like a caress to Will's soul. He wasn't sure he would ever get used to hearing words of praise or admiration from such a magnificent woman. Growing up, Will had felt like he had spent so much of his time trying to please those around him and tried so hard to never do or say the wrong things. Now, without trying to seek approval from everyone, he felt like he had somehow found the only favor he would ever need.

"I can see everything," Will finally spoke. "It's strange but so clear. It's like I can see a completely different world. It's a little overwhelming if I'm honest."

"Well don't shift back just yet," Cora nodded her chin ahead without breaking Will's stare, "we are nearly to the base of the mountain."

"I came in pretty fast but none of this looks familiar. I think I was farther north of here," Will surmised. "I don't smell any blood either so we should be alright to start here to pass."

Grant rested back into his saddle and pulled his horse behind once more, "I haven't spoken to Addie since I woke."

Will and Cora's head's both snapped back to where Grant now rode with his head down.

"You can see her when you are awake, like an apparition?" Cora asked, confused. "Or is she just in your mind?"

"In my sleep, she is herself but in our world here, she is my shadow. She is like my nightmare given a human shape instead of just smoke. She has been with me when I wake for a short time over the past two days, but not today," Grant confessed with his brows together. "I fear I may have lost her until I find her in sleep again."

Cora pulled her horse to a stop, causing Grant and Will to do the same. She reached her hand out for Grant, "May I try something?" Cora asked tentatively.

"You aren't going to cut me are you?" Grant pulled his arms close to his chest and Will noticed the thin cut that already ran down Grant's palm.

Cora shook her head in reply, "No, Grant, I have the gift of

145

foresight by *birth*. I do not need to rely on blood magic like my mother. It's just easier for me to focus if I can touch who I am trying to see." Grant slowly placed his hand in Cora's.

Closing her eyes Cora inhaled sharply then spoke with the same tone she had when she stood in the doorway in her home, "You and Addie are bound together. If you call to her, she will come."

Chapter 18

Grant

Grant wasn't even sure where to begin. How was he meant to call to Addie when it was his unconscious mind in control? "What am I supposed to do?" he asked with little hope for a clear answer.

Cora shrugged gently and shook her head as her eyes opened and faded back from an eerie white to their normal deep green. "I'm not entirely sure but your souls already call to each other in your sleep. If you are able to concentrate on how she *feels* when she is in your mind, you may be able to reach her."

"I think we should take a quick break and let the horses rest and eat before we continue on," Will suggested with a smile. "That way you can try to find Addie."

"That's a good idea. The horses are going to need their resolve to get over the pass and down into the forest beyond the mountain," Cora agreed.

Grant dismounted and stretched his arms over his head

before shaking out his limbs from their ride. After setting Whiskey up with access to the creek nearby that Cora had advised was runoff from a fresh spring, he filled his waterskin and found a quiet spot near his friends. Will stepped close and offered him a small portion of their limited rations before he too took a seat and began to eat in silence.

Closing his eyes, Grant concentrated on what it had felt like each time he had seen and spoken to Addie in his dreams. His original recollection was that Addie always appeared in moments of fear and pain but then remembered their last dance. His heart had been filled with joy and an overwhelming sense of wholeness. With a deep breath, Grant spoke into the darkness of his mind.

Addie, are you there? Can you hear me?

He waited several moments before trying again. This time Grant reached further into the recesses of his soul to find her.

Are you still here, Addie? I need to hear your voice and know I have not lost you. Grant had not stopped thinking about her since they had left Cora's home and the longing in his plea resonated into the dark.

Addie's gentile voice echoed in his ears but she still did not appear, *Grant, I'm here. Open your eyes.*

Slowly, Addie's shadow form came into focus before him. Her eyes shone in the dim light of the Alderbrooke Forest around them. Despite her being shrouded in darkness, Grant could see the relief on her face.

"Have there been any changes?" Grant asked, concerned.

Her shadow moved like smoke on the wind as she neared Grant. *I am still here but I don't know where 'here' is or what condition my body is in. I feel weak.*

148

Will turned from his seat. "You found her?" He asked hopefully.

"Yes. She is here as she was in the camp outside the forest. Can you not see her?" Grant confirmed.

"I cannot. But, if we are ready to continue on, we should get moving soon. We can find a safe place to camp on the other side of the mountain. That way we aren't stuck in skin-walker nesting grounds after dark," Cora stood and ran her hand down Shea's ivory main.

Both Will and Grant got to their feet and mounted their horses. Grant hadn't traveled with Addie still present in his conscious mind and wasn't sure how she would continue on with them through the mountain. As they began on the trail once more, Grant could feel Addie's soul being pulled alongside him. Looking to his right, he could see her drifting like a specter in the dark through the trees. Even if he hadn't known who she was, she would have been a magnificent sight to behold. Her hair seemed to float behind her on a phantom wind and her beautiful dark cloak flowed from her shoulders, making her look like death incarnate searching for souls to claim in this world.

Cora looked over to Grant, "She is still with us. I can feel her like a chill down my spine. She makes the air heavy as though death surrounds us."

"Then we must hurry," Will spoke from her left and kicked up their pace.

After clearing the ridge of trees halfway up the mountain, the terrain gave way to sharper rock faces and steeper grades. Their trek was slow but within a couple of hours they reached the top of the peak with no issues from any wildlife.

"This will be where things get more difficult and we must

lead your horses on foot," Cora advised as she gracefully slid from Shea' saddle. "The path here will be narrow and if Brandy or Whiskey begin to slip, let them fall. Their lives are not worth yours."

Looking over the back of the mountain, Grant could see a path not much wider than his shoulders that would lead them down the steep cliff side. Loose rocks shifted underfoot as they all stepped out onto the only path down into the forest on the other side. If any one of them were to fall, it would be certain death.

Will cleared his throat and asked Cora, "Wouldn't it be faster if I shifted into a dragon and carried us all down one at a time?"

"I don't think that would be wise. With the sun now on its decline, the creatures that hunt at night will begin to stir soon and a massive dragon flying overhead with prey in its talons would be like a beacon to scavengers and we wouldn't want that," Cora responded.

"Then we will proceed with caution but try to do so with haste. We need to be off this mountain before darkness falls," Grant asserted and again the three found themselves moving toward an unsteady fate.

Grant knew Addie lingered in his mind despite her silence. He couldn't help but wonder what this all must feel like to her. How was she managing to keep any sliver of hope when all Grant could focus on was the horror he hoped he would not find?

I don't really have much of a choice except to have some optimism. If I don't, then why am I here? What was the point? Addie answered Grant's unspoken thoughts.

"Can you hear every thought I have?" Grant asked curiously.

I haven't tried to hear more than what you are thinking at the moment. It felt like an invasion of your privacy. Addie admitted.

Will looked over his shoulder as they walked on. "What did she say?"

"She said she has tried to give me my privacy and not search my thoughts. But I feel like I, of all people, don't deserve that," Grant muttered under his breath.

Annoyance that was not his own flooded his senses. *You can't truly believe that. The gifts we are born with are not something we choose. How we decide to use them is what matters, Grant. You could very easily have become a true monster but you have chosen to isolate yourself from court, from me, because you wanted to protect people. You should never take your sacrifices lightly, no matter how ridiculous they were.*

"Ridiculous?! How was me leaving court and staying away from you foolish if it ensured your safety, princess?" Grant's frustration clouded his mind.

I would have been more than happy to be by your side for everything you have gone through but you chose to ostracize yourself. You were one of the few people I felt I truly trusted and you abandoned me. I know it was with the best of intentions now, but at the time I was absolutely devastated! Addie fumed.

Grant felt like Addie had physically struck him in the gut. He hadn't ever thought about how everything must have seemed from her perspective. Leaving court after their accident was understandable but giving her zero explanation for never returning felt cruel in hindsight.

"Addie, I'm so sorry. I didn't," Grant began.

I know. Addie interjected. *I'm in your head, remember. It's not just that either. It feels like I can feel your every emotion right now too. I can taste the bitterness of your regret and I hate that you feel that way. It is done and I now understand why you acted as you did. If my father knew what you are capable of, you would have met the guillotine I fear. I believe he has become more paranoid with age as well.*

Grant was silent for some time as he processed Addie's effortless forgiveness. Ahead, Cora and Will spoke silently about where they planned to make camp in a few short hours. As he moved forward, still distracted by his own shortcomings, the rocks beneath Grant's feet shifted forcing himself and Whiskey to lurched forward. The small ledge they had been walking along began to give way and tumble down the sheer rock face.

Cora's voice was filled with terror, "Move!" She shouted over the crash of stone tearing down the mountainside. Swiftly, she pulled Will by his tunic closer to her body.

They had only made it about halfway down the hundreds of switchbacks on the trail that cut across the mountain and Grant knew there would be no chance they would all make it to the bottom of the ravine as he watched the collection of rocks build in size and speed and demolish section after section of the path below.

"We're fucked," Grant exhaled. "Is everyone alright?"

Will's voice was far too cheerful, "We're good."

Grant looked over to find his friend pressed close to Cora's chest, shielding her from the world. Looking around it was apparent there were only two options left and neither were going to be ideal.

"I think we might need a dragon, Will," Grant raised his brows. "I refuse to add more time to this journey and further endanger Addie's life and the lives of the rest of the kingdom."

"Unfortunately, I reluctantly agree with that foolish plan. We will need to fly close to the mountain all the way to its base to limit our chances of being seen," Cora gently moved out from under Will's arms.

Grant could almost feel the joy radiating off of his best friend. "I can do that I think," Will beamed.

In the blink of an eye, Will stepped several paces forward and his body twisted and grew. In the place he once stood, now perched a massive dragon the same tan color of the rocks that surrounded them. Bowing his head to Cora, Will pushed free from where his black tipped talons had found purchase and he plummeted down the mountainside before he spread his wings and circled back around over their heads, his body near inches from the rock. As he descended toward the group once more, Will and Grant's horses went wild with fear. It took all of Grant's strength to restrain Whiskey. He wasn't sure how Cora had managed to keep Brandy from a lethal fall.

As Grant braced himself and his horse, Will's front leg wrapped swiftly around Cora and his rear feet tucked under Brandy. Then they were plummeting to the earth below. Grant briefly lost them in the trees at the mountain's base before Will was once again soaring up the side of the mountain and turning to approach. Grant tucked his arms in tight, just as Cora had, and tightened every muscle in his body just before he too was falling; Whiskey bellowing her protest behind him in Will's back claws.

The feeling was exhilarating and terrifying. Grant could feel Addie's trepidation but still she didn't speak as they came to land in a small meadow with Cora and Brandy. Once again, Will was soaring high overhead for his final flight to retrieve

Cora's horse.

"Shea has seen and been through a lot with me," Cora's voice was far calmer than Grant knew his would be. "It takes a lot to spook her."

A sudden gust of wind signaled Will's landing before he stepped out from the shrubbery behind Grant, leading a content Shea.

"Why the fuck are you naked?!" Grant barked in shock.

"I forgot to take my clothes off before I shifted and they are long gone now," Will laughed. "I guess I was just excited."

"You could say that," Cora joked and nodded to Will's nudity.

"My love, was that a *dick* joke?" Will bellowed with joy.

"I can be funny you know," Cora scolded lightly and attempted to avert her gaze from Will's body. "You do have spare clothing still, right?"

"I have a cloak," Will shrugged.

Grant shook his head at his friend and laughed, "You can wear my spare pants and you can have my vest." Grant stepped to Whiskey's side and pulled a pair of black slacks from his saddle bag and unlaced his leather vest.

Addie's voice startled Grant when she spoke. *Do you think he has any sense of self preservation? I vividly remember him always being a little reckless.*

Speaking loud enough for all to hear, Grant answered Addie aloud, "No, Addie, I don't think he had any sense of self preservation. He is an idiot." At that, Will smacked Grant playfully with the back of his hand.

Once Will was somewhat decent, the three mounted their horses again. The sun had just begun to sink below the horizon as they made their way back into the thicket of trees that were far more reminiscent of those at the outer edge of the Alderbrooke Forest. Gone were the giants they had been buried beneath.

"We are just a few hours from the caves now but it would be wise to camp near the stream up ahead tonight so we are rested for whatever we face in those caves," Cora suggested.

Despite his desire to find Addie, Grant knew Cora was right. He unhappily agreed, "We will leave at first light tomorrow; tonight we can rest and prepare."

Grant soon found himself seated near a small fire next to Will and Cora. Addie's shadow lingered quietly as they ate and readied for sleep.

I do hope Cora's assumptions are correct and I am not too far gone already. Addie's thoughts were heavy with dread.

I don't think she is wrong. Grant thought for only Addie to hear. *After we landed on this side of the mountain, it felt like I could almost reach out and touch you.*

We will see tomorrow, I guess. Addie's shadow swayed and settled near Grant's side.

I shouldn't keep you awake any longer. Addie's voice was soft.

Breathing in slow deep breaths, Grant relaxed into his bed roll. *And what if I lose you tonight while I sleep?* Grant's eyes began to heavy.

Then I will find you again in your dreams. Addie whispered.

With a voice like velvet, Grant continued to speak directly to Addie in his thoughts. *And what if my dreams are of the wicked sort?*

Then I will be beside you in your nightmares as long as you need me. Addie replied.

Grant gave a half smirk with his eyes now fully closed. *Not that sort of wicked, princess.*

What felt like hours passed and Grant struggled to find sleep in Addie's absence. After they had spoken, her soul silently drifted into the darkness. Grant couldn't help but think of her. He and his father spent days in court and when he wasn't getting into trouble with Will, he remembered seeking out the young princess on multiple occasions to help her train in secret. She had confronted him once after he and Will had finished sparring with General Banks, and asked for his assistance with training her for combat. At first he had thought it a joke but Addie insisted and, for some reason, Grant couldn't resist her. She seemed fearless and headstrong, even a bit reckless for a young princess. He knew now she was not at all the delicate thing he had believed her to be.

Once, Grant could recall seeing her beautiful golden brown hair tucked beneath a woolen cap. She had been attempting to disguise herself in order to listen in on discussions that her father deemed too violent for a princess. He had been intrigued by her curiosity even then.

For several months, he met with her in secret as young teenagers, until his accident with Will, causing their budding relationship to end. He stopped attending court with his father and became far more reclusive. Now, as he finally drifted off to sleep, she filled his mind with wonderfully wicked thoughts.

* * *

Grant found himself in his bedchambers at his family home. The sky outside his window was clear and a blanket of stars glimmered overhead. The cold late autumn air swirled through the room raising the hairs on his skin. This dream felt as vivid as the nightmares he so often lived through but different somehow. It was far more pleasant. There was no underlying sense of doom or fear lacing his emotions, only a peace he so rarely knew.

As Grant turned to face the hearth adjacent the open window, he realized he was not alone. The silhouette of a beautiful woman was outlined in the glow of the fire. Her golden brown hair cascaded down her back and ended just below her shoulder blades. Her light blue satin slip left little to the imagination, becoming nearly transparent in the flickering light. Slowly, she turned to face him and his heart skipped. Less than five feet in front of him, Grant stared at Addie's radiant smile.

"Hello, Princess," he purred and stepped closer to her side and took her hand in his.

"Hello," Addie responded in a delicate sultry voice.

Without warning, Addie stood on her toes and kissed Grant lightly. Grant's breath hitched and he was sure his heart had stopped. She had kissed him and he was ruined. All coherent thoughts left his mind as he reached for her waist and pulled her body against his. Each inch of her was like the most beautiful map he had ever known. Every curve and valley perfectly placed like she was drawn by the most skilled hands. His fingers lightly traced up her ribs to her chest, then her throat, before finally resting on either side of her face as he pulled her closer for another kiss. Unlike the first, this kiss was more fervent and filled with Grant's growing passion and need.

Addie laced her fingers through his hair and sighed softly

into him. His name escaped her lips on a breathy moan and Grant was undone. He spun her toward his bed and guided her until the back of her knees hit the plush green duvet atop his bed. Gently, Grant lowered Addie back and pressed his body over hers. Slowly, she ran her hands down the front of his chest and began unbuttoning his white tunic exposing his beautifully sculpted body.

Grant pulled his shirt off and knelt before the edge of the bed, spreading Addie's knees to either side of his broad shoulders. He grabbed Addie's hips and pulled her toward him, causing her slip to ride up and pool around her waist, exposing every inch of her beautiful legs. Grant's heart quickened and his entire body hummed.

"Fuck, you are perfect," Grant breathed leaving kisses up Addie's leg from the inside of her knee to the apex of her thighs. Her body jolted and arched as Grant ran his hand up her stomach to cup her peaked breast. "Absolutely perfect."

He moaned into her and ran his tongue up the inside of her thigh before stopping to press a line of soft kisses along her hip and begin a path across her lower belly below her navel. He paused for a moment before continuing his ministrations with his tongue, stopping to circle her sensitive bud. A gentle moan left them both. With his other hand, Grant slowly teased his fingers through her slick center.

"Grant please," Addie's voice echoed through his mind.

"Asking for permission? Good girl, princess," Grant praised, "that's it," he continued stroking his tongue over her warm skin.

"Please, Grant... Wake up," This time Addie's voice was more breathy and urgent.

Snapping his head up, the Addie before him lay with her

head leaned back against the bed, eyes closed, bottom lip pressed between her teeth. She had not been the one to speak.

"Grant," Addie's voice resounded in his mind again and his head turned to the curtain by the window where Addie's shadow stood.

"Fuck, Addie..." Grant stood as the fantasy around him dissolved and Addie's shadow ripped away.

* * *

Sitting up abruptly next to the fire, Grant's heart raced as the gray morning sun began to crest through the trees. Cora turned to him with a knowing grin.

"Pleasant dreams I take it?" Cora chuckled, raising her eyebrows and nodding toward Grant's lap.

Looking down, Grant flushed and sighed. "I may have just scarred the princess. And now I cannot see her," Grant said standing to his feet.

"Addie, are you still here?" he called out with no response. "Addie!?"

Several moments passed before Addie abruptly materialized before him from the shadows, breathless and shaking.

"I'm so sorry, Addie. I didn't mean," Grant started.

"It's alright. I, I just woke up in the cave, Grant. For a moment I was really there not like this ... in this form but in my body. I think I'm going to die," Addie said, panicked.

Chapter 19

Addie

Addie woke in Grant's room at the Anderson manor. The air was cold and her heart was racing. She found herself once again tucked into the shadows near the curtains framing Grant's window. The wind blew lightly chilling the air in the room.

This was a new dream Grant had not yet shared with her and Addie scanned the room quickly to assess where the threat from this memory might stand but found no terrors in sight. Instead, she found Grant without a shirt, on his knees facing away from her.

He's not alone. Addie realized as she caught sight of what lay spread before him.

She quickly averted her eyes knowing this was an intimate moment she was not likely meant to see between Grant and a past lover. Addie assumed whatever nightmare was about to unfold would most likely interrupt his current distraction and put an end to her embarrassment. She was quickly surprised however when the moan she heard leave the young woman's mouth sounded like her own.

Addie hesitantly glanced back to the bed and was instantly confused. This was not a memory. Addie knew this was not an event from the past or a nightmare because that was her body indecently exposed on Grant's bed with his hands trailing her skin. Her heart rate spiked and her body hummed as she watched Grant grip her breast and run his other hand up her thigh to her core.

For a moment she almost thought she could actually feel him touching her; his callused hands gliding over her sensitive skin; his mouth leaving kisses on her inner thigh. It was like peace and joy and the greatest pleasure she could imagine. But this wasn't real. Abruptly, she was snapped from her trance. Once he discovered she loomed as an uninvited audience to his private thoughts, she knew he would be mortified if she let him continue his fantasy, regardless of how much she too wanted to see where this train of thought might lead. She had to stop him; had to stop this before it went any further.

"Please Grant," Addie breathed, her voice unintentionally smooth like silk.

"Asking for permission? Good girl, princess," Grant's voice was deep and smoky and sent a delicious shiver up Addie's spine, "that's it."

She was on the verge of coming apart and letting him continue his thoughts, repercussions and humiliation be damned. Instead, Addie's logical mind won and she again began, "Please, Grant... Wake up."

Addie watched Grant's eyes widened and he stared at the Addie laid relaxed before him.

161

"Grant," Addie tried to sound calm but her voice was shaking and her heart was pounding like a drum in her chest. She needed to assure him this was alright and she was sorry she had interrupted. Grant looked like he was going to be sick. His cheeks flushed and Addie knew her face would probably match his if she could see it.

"Fuck, Addie…" his tone seemed to be filled with repentance. Then he stood and Addie was falling hard out of his dream. The peace that had just overwhelmed her was replaced by physical agony. Addie realized as her soul continued to tear through reality that this pain was real. This was her *body's* pain. She was in the cave with Lord Anderson. She tried to open her eyes. She tried to move but she was frozen. All of her mind focused on her pain and the strain she felt in her chest as her heart struggled to keep beating.

A voice somewhere close startled her but she wasn't able to fully comprehend what they were saying. Were they talking to her? The voice was low and gravely but also sounded like a chorus of voices speaking in tandem.

"She is close, my lord," the voice echoed, "her body stirs."

"Good," a familiar male voice replied.

Was that Lord Anderson? How? I watched him die. Addie thought.

Just then Addie's pain began to fade. The bone deep chill she felt moments ago subsided and she was being pulled away once again.

* * *

"Addie!"

162

Addie stood in the shadows trembling, unable to catch her breath. She felt as though she had just been kicked by a horse and her lungs were going to fail her.

"I'm so sorry, Addie. I didn't mean," Grant was panic-stricken before her. Addie's mind was reeling. She needed to tell him everything.

"It's alright," Addie cut Grant off. "I, I just woke up in the cave, Grant. For a moment I was really there not like this," she gestured frantically to the specter before him, "in this form but in my body. I think I'm going to die."

From over Grant's shoulder, standing near the embers of their fire, Cora's voice was sharp, "I can see her, Grant…"

Addie moved past Grant to stand near Cora.

"Can you hear me?" Addie hesitantly asked, all embarrassment from Grant's dream lost to her current terror.

"Yes. Just as I hear Grant or Will," Cora stated with true fear in her tone.

"What does that mean, Cora? Is she dead? Have I lost her?" Grant pleaded.

"No, I don't believe she's dead yet but I don't know if it's a good sign that I can see and hear her. I feel her soul more like that of the dead than those of the living," Cora said, turning to kick dirt on the embers of their fire and bent to collect her weapons from the ground. "We are about four hours from the cave. If we hurry we can be there in less than three. We must be quick."

"We will not let you lose her, Grant," Will said, placing his hand on Grant's shoulder.

"Collect your things," Grant directed, "We need to make a plan. Addie, what can you tell us about the cave entrance."

In hopes of lightening everyone's somber faces, Will gave

a mocking grin, "Great! Now I'm going to be left out of this conversation."

Addie relaxed her shoulders slightly and spoke to Grant and Cora, "One of you let him know he isn't missing much. I can't really remember the outside of the cave. I just remember that it's dark and smells of rot. The air was thick and humid."

"She can't recall much just the smell," Grant repeated for Will.

"You need to look into her memories, Grant. See her nightmare. I have a feeling the death she faces, or rather the one she already has, will be her greatest fear. It might give us a better idea of what we are walking into," Cora stated with a tremendous amount of sympathy.

"I don't know if I can do that to her," Grant paused and looked toward Addie, "I don't want to hurt you."

Addie could see the battle that raged within him. She couldn't remember everything that had happened but knew it would be devastating to relive. In her heart, she knew this was their only chance to save her and her kingdom. She breathed deep and settled next to Grant. Tendrils of her dark shadow wrapping around him in a smoky embrace.

"I know you will not hurt me, Grant. I need you to do this for me; for my people. There is no one I trust more, with this, than you. It will be alright," Addie spoke with more conviction than she truly had, as though she was also aiming to convince herself that what she was about to face would not be devastating.

"Are you certain?" Grant's voice was unsteady.

"Yes," Addie said, "Whatever happens, I trust you have my best interest at heart."

"What if I can't stop? What if I destroy you, Addie?!" Grant

164

demanded.

"I will be by your side. You can do this, Grant," Addie said gently.

"Alright," Cora tolled, "let's do this then."

* * *

Addie tried to brace herself for whatever Grant would see in her mind but no amount of preparation would have readied her for what unfolded. As Grant's nightmare wove its way through her memories, flashes from her past flooded her mind until everything around her was consumed by her recollection of the evening she went in search of Lord Anderson.

Both Addie and Grant stood as spectators in her bedchambers in the castle, watching Addie strap several daggers and a bow to her dark leather clad body. Addie's hair was pulled back into a tight braid down her back. Turning toward the window, she pulled her black cloak over her head and slipped out into the setting sun of the early evening.

Why didn't you tell anyone? Grant spoke directly to Addie's mind. *You should have never left the castle alone.*

Addie's rage began to simmer before she spoke through clenched teeth, *I was so tired of never being seen. My father didn't care and my mother wouldn't have been able to help me even if I had told her my plan. Andrew was already being watched by my father's men and I wasn't willing to risk his life if I failed. I tried to tell my father that he should listen to Rose but he disregarded everything I said. If no one was going to try to protect the people of this kingdom, I decided I was willing to do whatever it took to stop your father. Even if that meant I was alone.*

Addie's memories leapt as she rode through the forest east of the Alderbrooke mountains. The cave system Rose had warned her of was just a matter of hours from the castle through the densely packed trees. The woods were dark as Addie's memory surged and she approached the sunken entrance to the cave. The full moon shone bright through the trees overhead as she dismounted. Her dark tunic stuck to her skin with sweat.

Sliding down the steep embankment to the mouth of the cave, Addie and Grant's minds followed wearily. The entrance was large but filled with sharp stones that projected from the floor and ceiling just beyond the threshold. The tear of fabric broke the silence as Addie's leathers ripped before she hit the sand.

"Lord Anderson, think about what you are doing," Addie's voice echoed through the dark, damp cave.

"It cannot be undone, I am afraid. The dead will rise and your father will know my suffering," Lord Anderson's voice was strange.

Blood poured from Lord Anderson's middle and Addie glanced over to Grant's apparition. Dread and agony that was not her own ripped through her soul.

"Let me help you... please," Addie's memory drew her attention back. "If you die, you will be committing far worse atrocities than the king ever has. My father may be ruthless, but he is not entirely cruel. Your actions right now would be damning all of Viridia to a fate no one deserves!"

"My wife is dead because of your father's brutality. He *is* a cruel man that cares not for his people, just for himself! He

166

did *nothing* to protect her. To protect his people. He deserves to suffer!" Grant's father roared, his voice so unlike Grant had ever heard.

"I have to heal you. You cannot die. I won't let you become a monster! You and I both know your wife would never want you to do this." Addie lifted her golden, glowing palm.

Addie's soul braced for the pain she could see coming. She couldn't understand how she had been so foolish to trust Lord Anderson. Grant's animalistic roar reverberated in her head as his father lifted his sword and pierced through her chest; his murderous intent filled her every cell and the memory began to fade.

Wait, Grant. Hold on a little longer. The creatures are coming, Addie spoke to Grant.

I can't. I'm going to hurt you, Grant struggled to speak.

Look! Addie's voice was filled with fear as she tried to focus on the beast that pulled themselves from the black water.

Large, distorted, human-like creatures with sickly gray flesh slunk across the sand to Addie and Lord Anderson's bodies. The once human beings had been reanimated into something from a true nightmare. Each face no longer resembled the person they had once been in life but instead now were grotesque with decay from decades, some even centuries, trapped in the freezing waters of the caves. Large clawed hands lifted Lord Anderson and Addie from the ground before everything disappeared into shadow.

* * *

Reality crashed in around Addie and Grant. Grant fell to his knees at Addie's feet, blood dripped from his nose.

"Are you both alright?" Cora spoke softly and placed a hand on Grant's shoulder.

"He killed her. I watched them both die," Grant's voice was heavy with despair. "There's no way she could have survived that, Cora."

"She is still here, Grant. There is still hope that you can bring her back. Her body is still in that cave right?" Cora asked.

Grant shook his head, "I don't know. The creatures my father created took her somewhere."

"I'm still in the cave. I think I'm just deeper in the dark," Addie replied.

Will stepped to Grant's side, "Let's go find her and end all of this now if we can."

Chapter 20

Cora

Grant's shoulders stilled and his body petrified into a statue of flesh and bone while Cora watched in stunned silence. Minutes had passed slowly before several drops of blood dripped from Grant's nose and he dropped to his knees. Addie's form weakened and nearly faded from Cora's sight, causing panic to race through her. The moment Grant inhaled a sharp breath through his teeth, Addie was once again as clear as Will was at Cora's side.

Quickly, Grant explained everything he had seen and Will paced the grass near the small creek that ran alongside their camp. Cora had already seen the cave but had no idea what the living dead would be able to do or if they would even be stoppable.

"We will need to keep however many creatures your father has created distracted so you can get Addie's body out of the cave and find where your father is," Will declared. "Cora, do you know how to make an explosive with anything in this forest?"

A small grin spread across Cora's face, "I do indeed. I'll start a list and we can split up to collect everything more quickly."

Cora hastily pulled a slip of paper and quill from the bag tired to Shea's saddle and tore it in half before hurriedly scribbling down several items for Will and Grant. Both scraps of paper consisted of three individual ingredients and a general location where each item could be found. She, herself, would collect the two most difficult ingredients. One of which was a fine black pollen from a carnivorous plant that grew near the banks of some creeks and rivers in the Alderbrooke Forest. If inhaled, the dust would cause paralysis or convulsions and, if in large enough quantities, possibly even death. The second and final ingredient Cora needed to collect made her stomach turn just at its memory.

Not far from where they had set up camp last night was a small meadow Cora had avoided her entire adult life. The meadow was the only place in the entire kingdom where a small white and purple bush grew. The milky sap from the plant acted like an acid and could easily melt through even the thickest of hides. When combined with the powdery pollen, the two would cause a series of sparks. With the remaining components, Cora could create several small explosives. They wouldn't burn for long without adequate fuel but could create a loud enough bang and enough smoke to hopefully distract whatever guarded the caves for a suitable amount of time for Grant to stop his father and get to Addie.

"We will meet back here in fifteen minutes," Cora ordered and the party separated in agreement.

Assuming the pollen would be the least painful to obtain, Cora sprinted for the sound of rapid moving water down stream from their camp. When she reached the creek's edge, several small budding flowers sprinkled the ground. The soft pink petals curved inward on themselves near their base before reaching outward into a beautiful five pointed star. Thin black lines traced the veins along each petal toward the center where several sharp barbs awaited its prey. At the center of the flower, inside the bud, was the dark pollen Cora needed. If she moved swiftly as she severed the vibrant green stem from its roots, the plant hopefully wouldn't open and release the toxic dust into the air. Taking a deep breath and using her shirt to cover her nose and mouth, Cora knelt down and pulled her ax free. She swiftly brought the blade down hard on a flower that faced away from her.

Despite her best effort, the small plant expelled a small plume of soot colored pollen into the air. Quickly, Cora covered more of her face with her velvet cloak and prayed she wouldn't breath in too much of the toxin through her tunic and the thick velvet. She shuffled away from the bank, clumsily kicking a smaller flower near her boot that she had not seen. The black spray coated her hands and cloak over her mouth seconds before her limbs started to lock and her spine went rigid. For several minutes, Cora lay staring into the early morning sky unable to stop the uncontrollable tremors that ripped through her muscles. Slowly, the shaking came to a stop and Cora inhaled an unsteady breath.

When she had regained control of her limbs, she stood and once again approached the edge of the quickly moving, white capped water. Stepping close to the largest flower along the bank, Cora removed her cloak and threw the hood over the bud to trap the pollen from escaping into the air and severed the stem from the root with the dagger from her boot. She knew more time had passed than she had intended to spend here. Collecting her prize with steady, cautious hands, Cora was again on her feet and running to the clearing where the acid shrub grew.

There wouldn't be enough time here to extract the sap safely before Will and Grant would return to their meeting point. With great reluctance, Cora entered the clearing and collected the lower half of her cloak into her hands. Every inch of the field before her was a beautiful display of white and deep purple leaves. Had she not known the horrors this plant could cause, the scene would have been one of absolute wonder. A shimmering, ethereal glow blanked the meadow with an iridescent sheen. Hesitantly, Cora grasped the smallest bush she saw at the meadow's edge with her cloak-covered hands and pulled the entire plant free of the soft soil by the root.

A hot exhale of breath passed through her lips as she stood and sprinted towards their camp. Cradled in her arms was her hood tied closed and filled with black pollen and the remainder of her cloak wrapped around the small shrub. She could see Will and Grant just yards away when movement from her right caught her attention. A light brown creature bounded through the trees on graceful hooves toward her friends, toward her mate. At a glance, the beast appeared to be a large deer but Cora knew instantly that it was not. The thin slatted eyes and overbite of sharp tipped teeth was a clear sign of what the creature truly was.

She knew she would never be able to reach Will before the skin-walker but could see it was far closer to her than its distance to Will. Skidding to a stop, she dropped her cloak to the ground, withdrew her ax and ran her palm down the length of the blade. The skin-walker's prance ceased as the smell of her blood filled the air. She had never taken down anything this large on her own but she had to try to give Will and Grant a fighting chance.

"RUN!" Cora's voice broke through the sudden silence of the wood surrounding her.

Will snapped his head in Cora's direction in time to witness the skin-walker shift into its horrific true form and make for Cora's waiting attack. Core bent her knees slightly and held firm to her ax as the monster tore through the brush. The beast lunged for her with a snarl; razor sharp teeth ready to tear her to shreds. Lifting her ax over her head with both hands, she reared back and threw her blade end over end through the air. The razor sharp edge buried itself in the monster's chest with a sickening crunch of flesh and bone. The skin walker stumbled several steps before it continued forward clumsily once again.

As the creature closed the distance between them, Cora's final thought flashed through her mind and silenced her fear, *If this is to be my end, I am going to take this beast with me.*

Swiftly, Cora spun and picked up the small shrub from the pile behind her. With both hands, she grabbed a small limb and stripped its bark to the base of the plant. White sap instantly began to ooze from the exposed branch. Cora snapped the limb free; the smell of melting flesh filled the air as the sticky syrup ran over her knuckles. The creature froze inches from her face in stunned realization but it was too late for it to escape unscathed. Cora rammed the broken end of the branch through the beasts open, snarling mouth, upward into its skull, shredding her skin on her arm on its bared teeth. A blood curdling roar echoed from the creature as it pulled away from her and clawed at its face in an attempt to remove the spear that had already begun to burn away flesh.

The pain that radiated through Cora's hands moments ago ceased as the acid ate through her nerves and began to dissolve into the muscles and tendons. The whaling skin-walker was suddenly ripped from her line of sight by a beautiful, massive, black dragon. The wet sound of flesh tearing and bones snapping was drowned out by her own screams of terror as she beheld her hands melting before her eyes. Cora's hands and arms were destroyed beyond anything she had ever experienced. Several trails of corrosive sap and blood ran from her palms to her elbow and began to eat into the gashes left behind by the skin-walker's teeth.

Will's hands quickly rested on either side of her face, "Look at me, Cora. Breathe. Look at me." His voice was soft but demanding. "We can fix this, love. Just breathe."

Cora lifted her gaze and found Will on his knees before her, completely naked. Grant ran to their side, leather satchel in hand.

"It's in the inside pocket in my water-skin," Will spoke to Grant but never let his eyes leave Cora's. Grant quickly removed Will's water-skin and handed it over. "Drink, Cora. Please."

Tears streamed down Cora's face as Will brought the mouth of the container to her lips. Swallowing deep, Cora welcomed the horrid tasting remnants of the elixir she and Will had brewed. At some point while she had slept in the hollow tree, Will had thought to preserve what little was left of the potion. Although only a few mouthfuls remained, the skin on Cora's arms and hands began to slowly knit together.

"That's it, beautiful. All of it," Will's voice coaxed. "Your hands are looking better already."

She wasn't sure when she had closed her eyes but as she opened them and looked at the blood coated man on his knees before her, she made a vow to herself that she would never let her vision for him come to fruition. There was nothing she wouldn't do to keep him safe. A small smile spread across Will's face.

"Thank you," Cora managed shakily.

"There is nothing to thank me for. We should be thanking you. That was the most reckless thing I have ever seen anyone do in my entire life and that's saying a lot coming from me," Will chuckled softly. "I owe you my life."

"You owe me *nothing*," Cora's voice was laced with a deep agony she knew Will would not understand.

Grant threw his cloak over Will's shoulders, "I don't have any spare clothes left for you."

Will shrugged, "Clothing was the least of my concerns."

"I have spare pants and my wool shawl but the pants are much too small for you," Cora's voice was ragged.

Warm air radiated from Will like a furnace. In seconds, he shifted into a petite golden haired woman huddled beneath Grant's cloak. The soft lines on the familiar looking face were stunning. Will's blue eyes and long lashes remained on a feminine version of his own fair skinned expression.

Cora's mouth fell open in shock, "I guess that solves that problem."

"I've always wondered what it would be like to be a lady for a day," Will smiled playfully.

"You are the farthest thing from a lady, Will. No matter what form you wear," Grant chuckled.

Chapter 21

Will

Will wrapped Cora's shawl around his torso, the dark fabric a stark contrast to his soft pale skin. Cora tossed a pair of tan pants in his direction as she spoke, Will hanging on every word.

"We will need to be as careful as we can when we put all of the ingredients together. The sap, as you both saw, will have devastating consequences if it touches your skin," Cora's shoulders shivered in disgust.

Grant stood facing the shredded remains of the skin-walker with his back to both of his companions, "What do you plan to do with the bombs once we have them all put together?"

Will grinned a wide mischievous grin before he spoke, "Cora and I will do what we can to cause a large enough distraction to buy you the time you need to get to Addie and stop your father."

"If we are lucky, the acid sap and the black powder can take down a substantial number of the creatures your father created," Cora stooped down and picked up one of the round yellow fruit she had directed Will to collect.

"Why do we need rose apples?" Will asked, picking one up and tossing it in the air.

Cora ran her dagger through the fruit splitting it in half. The crisp yellow flesh separated evenly revealing a large brown pit in the center. "Each half will hold either the black pollen or the sap. For some reason the interior flesh is resistant to the sap's corrosion. Grant, were you able to find the leaves I needed?"

Grant reached into his bag and withdrew more than two dozen silver hued leaves, each roughly the size of his palm. An iridescent sheen coated the top surface of the unusual plant. Will stepped closer to Grant and turned a leaf over in his petite feminine hands. Light from the morning sun reflected off the surface casting a kaleidoscope of color onto Will's face.

"And what are these intended for?" Will asked as he handed the foliage over to Cora's waiting hands.

"With a little bit of pressure, the veins in this leaf secrete a glue like liquid we are going to use to keep the two reactive ingredients separate," Cora explained. "When we throw the fruit it will cause the seams to split and the black pollen and the sap will mix, causing the explosion we need. Once the sap dries, it's not going to burn flesh. After the bombs go off, however, do your best not to touch any wet sap that remains if you can help it at all."

Will stood in quiet contemplation for a moment before he spoke, "I am extremely intrigued as to how you know how to do any of this. Don't get me wrong, it's amazing, but it's also slightly unsettling that these plants exist in the first place."

"One of the perks of having a necromancer as a mother,

I guess," Cora shrugged, "I came across the acid sap shrubs by mistake once when I was here as a child. I thought the leaves were a beautiful purple so I snapped off a branch to show mother but when I realized what I had done, I panicked. Luckily, my mother and Shea weren't too far and heard my screams. They were at my side in an instant and my mother healed my hand before any real damage was done."

An unexplained rage started to rise in Will's chest at the thought of Cora left in these woods as a child. He knew she had faced more than he could possibly imagine, but after seeing what damage the white sap could inflict, he could not understand how any person could possibly let their loved one near something so deadly.

"The more stories I hear about your mother, the less I like her," Will gritted out.

Cora scoffed nonchalantly, "Like I said before, I don't regret any of my childhood; nor do I hold any ill will toward my mother. In all truth, she is my closest friend and I love her more than, well, *almost* everything."

Silence fell over the trio as they stood over the bags of supplies. Will couldn't help but think about his own relationship with his parents. He knew his father never loved him like a father should... the way Grant's father had loved his own son. Will couldn't even recall a time when his father even acted like he liked him. There was always disgust behind his eyes no matter how hard he tried to be the son he thought his father wanted. Most of his childhood was spent in the castle with his mother and uncle who both cared for him far more than his father ever had. His uncle, General Banks, had even insisted on training him and Grant as boys and had spent countless hours showing both young men how to survive in his hunting cabin before the king had sent him away just before Will's mother's death.

He wondered if Cora had a relationship with her own father. She had not mentioned him but he figured that was understandable if there was any trauma there. As he mulled over his thoughts of his parents, Will knew Grant must be turning over troubled thoughts about his own mother and father as well.

Clearing her throat, Cora cut off Will's downward spiral, "I think it would be best if we got started on these bombs; that way we can get to the cave and end all of this."

Cora proceeded to methodically lay out the components into stations. The first step would be to remove the pit from each fruit and scoop out a small amount of the fruit's flesh to make the cavity larger. While one person focused on that task, the other two would strip blackberry vines and use the bark to create a flexible cordage to bind the fruit halves together once they were loaded. Will had been instructed to collect both the berry vines and the rose apples as well as several large fig leaves. Grant had collected the iridescent leaf, a small yellow shrub, and the cap of a massive mushroom that would be large enough to hold roughly three pints of clean warm water.

"The fig leaves need to be used as a mask when we collect the pollen. I'm hoping most of the pollen was expelled into my cloak when I covered the bud but just in case the flower decides to fuck us all over, put the leaf over your mouth then cover it with a cloth like a filter," Cora placed a large green leaf over her mouth and nose, pulled a scarf from her satchel, and proceeded to wrap the material around her head. "I should have just waited for this to collect the plant in the first place.

179

I was just hoping I could have saved us time."

"What do you mean," Grant asked with furrowed brows.

Cora removed the makeshift mask before she spoke. "That plant wasn't the first one I attempted to harvest," she responded, gesturing to her cloak. "I had a bit of a fumble with the first one and temporarily paralyzed myself in the process."

"What the fuck, Cora!?" anger and frustration leached from Will's soft voice, "You had us picking berries and leaves and you were collecting plants that could kill you?! Are you fucking kidding me."

"Why are you angry? I was doing *you* a favor. I was keeping *you* safe!" Cora snapped back.

"By risking *your* life! You say I'm the fool and yet you pull that shit? What were you thinking?" Will protested.

"I was thinking that we had to get everything we needed quickly and I'll be damned if I put you at risk for any reason! I cannot risk failure here," Cora spoke the last words under her breath.

Stepping closer, Grant placed a hand on Cora's shoulder, "We will not fail, Cora. I know what we stand to lose if we do."

Will watched as Cora and Grant exchanged a look of agreement before they both faced him with a look of determination in their eyes. Quietly, Grant and Cora took a seat in front of a pile of supplies and got to work processing blackberry vines, leaving Will to cut and hollow out the rose apples. In thirty short minutes, all twenty eight apples were pitted and ready to be filled and the pile of vines had become a collection of cream colored twine.

"Now the fun part," Cora murmured and began to re-secure

her face covering.

"How can we help," Will followed Cora's lead and placed the fig leaf over his mouth and nose and pulled the dark shawl Cora had lent him over the bottom half of his face.

"I need Grant to heat three or four pints of water and fill the mushroom cap while you crush up the leaves of the yellow shrub into a paste," Cora directed. Grant knelt down and started a small fire to heat water.

"What are we using the paste for?" Will asked as he made quick work of plucking each leaf from its stem.

"I want a barrier on my skin when I collect the acid sap. The paste can create extra layers for the sap to dissolve instead of my skin," Cora bared her teeth with a grimace.

"And the water in the mushroom?" Will questioned.

"Once I start to feel the heat of the acid, I need warm water to wash away the paste and then reapply more," Cora replied.

"I don't think you should do that all by yourself. Let me," Will started before Cora raised a hand and vehemently shook her head.

"You have never done any of this before and I have. I'm doing this portion myself. You can help seal them shut and bind them," Cora smiled.

Will realized there would be no changing Cora's mind and decided it would be best to follow her lead and not cause any unneeded stress. Cora slid a small flat stone from the nearby creak over to Will and instructed him to use the surface as his grinding stone. The thought of Cora and most likely her mother doing this same process ran through Will's mind.

"Why would you have ever needed to build a bomb? What poor idiot crossed you?" Will finally asked.

Cora laughed softly to herself. "It was to get rid of the

vermin that kept eating my vegetables back home, actually," she admitted shyly.

For the first time in several minutes, Grant spoke with a light tone, "Good to know that the big and powerful Cora is afraid of squirrels."

Will struggled to restrain a laugh before Cora responded, "First I am not afraid of them, second they are disgusting. Do you know how many illnesses they carry?"

Grant and Will silently made eye contact before they both erupted into hysterics. Will watched as Cora too relaxed her shoulders slightly and joined their laughter. The lighthearted, jovial moment was severed by the wailing sound of a beast in the distance.

"What was that?" Grant asked skeptically.

"I don't know," Cora admitted. "but I can guarantee Addie does."

Will watched Cora and Grant face the small oak tree near their set up. It was clear Addie was speaking to them but Will was still unable to see or hear anything from Addie's apparition.

Leaning near Cora quietly, Will asked, "What did she say?"

It wasn't Cora that responded but Grant, in a voice full of rage, "It's the creatures my father created. They're waking up. Addie has slipped away from me a few times now and has woken in the caves with the beasts. My father called them his death wraiths."

"We need to hurry," Cora palmed a small handful of the paste Will had just started to grind and smeared the yellow substance over her hands up her forearms.

She made quick work of peeling back the bark from the acid sap shrub. Will watched in amazement as each drop of the viscous white liquid landed in the rose apple cavities he had scooped out. Will too coated his hands in paste and with light pressure between his thumb and forefinger, he began to easily secure the iridescent silver leaves to the now filled fruit halves. Despite having to wash her hands clean twice, Cora and Will worked smoothly filling half of the fruits before moving on to the grainy black pollen. Opening the hood of her cloak slowly, Cora breathed in an obvious sigh of relief at the minimal amount of loose dust that escaped.

"It won't take much pollen to cause the reaction we want," Cora admitted, scooping a small amount of the dark powder with the tip of her dagger. "This will be more than enough to cause a spark."

Together, the trio filled, sealed, and bound all of the rose apples together. Standing to his feet, Will picked up his large saddle bag and dumped the few remaining contents into the dirt before offering it to Cora to gently load the bombs.

"We will need to be careful not to cause any major trauma to any of those or whoever carries them will likely lose a limb or worse," Cora spoke softly as she lowered the final deadly fruit into the leather bag.

Will grinned widely, "I will be sure to ride carefully then."

Grant helped Will load and mount Brandy smoothly. "Please be careful. If you feel anything wrong, do not hesitate to speak up and we will stop for you," Grant held firmly to Brandy's lead rope.

"Are you worried about me, Grant? How sweet," Will joked, playing with the leather strop nervously.

Without another word, the trio set out in the direction they had heard the beast's call, in search of Addie and Lord Anderson. In less than two hours, Cora pulled her horse to a stop and lifted her right hand to silence her companions.

"We'll go on foot from here," she whispered and dismounted on silent feet. "The entrance to the cave is just beyond that rise. If the beasts are able to roam freely, I want to see them before they hear us approach."

Grant stood at Will's side the moment his feet hit the soil and helped ease Will's smaller frame from his saddle without disturbing the large bag draped over Brandy's body. Together, Will and Grant lifted the bombs from the horse and followed Cora's slow ascent up the hill. Despite being quite light, the significance of the bag's contents felt heavier with each step up the steep incline. As they approached the top of the hill, Cora dropped to her knees and inched to the edge of the overhang that lead to the cavern below.

"Do you think we can use this spot as our vantage and barrage the creatures without meeting them face to face?" Will asked skeptically.

Cora scrunched her brows together and let her eyes survey the small clearing just outside the cave entrance below. The line of trees just past the dark sand was only a few yards away. A slow moving stream of strange, dark water cut the area below nearly perfectly in half. The world around them seemed to be muted by some unseen force weighing down the air.

"I think this will be our best bet, yes. We can start a few explosions at the treeline and hopefully draw as many of the beasts out and give you the chance to slip inside to find your father," Cora said, facing Grant.

Will's heart was thrumming so loudly he hardly heard the remainder of Cora's plan. He and Cora would hopefully be able to incapacitate whatever left the cave and if all went well

Grant would be able to save Addie and stop his father. As they spoke, movement down below caught Will's attention. Inhaling a sharp breath, Will drew Grant and Cora's attention from the map they had scrawled in the dirt at their feet, to where Will stooped at the edge of the cliff.

"What is it?" Grant asked.

"You both need to see this," utter disbelief and dread consumed Will's tone, nearly stanching his voice entirely.

The color drained from Cora's face. She opened her mouth to speak but no words left her lips. Grant shifted uncomfortably at Will's side shaking his head.

Rubbing a hand over the base of his neck, Grant's voice was low and shaky, "They are far more disturbing in the light than they were in Addie's memories."

Now standing in the clearing, were seven beings only a nightmare could conjure. It was impossible to distinguish if the things below were male or female. If Cora's mother had not told them Lord Anderson intended to raise the men and women lost to ancient wars, no one alive would have guessed these things were once human. Their leathery, gray skin and sunken solid white eyes looked like that of a corpse left soaking in the frigid waters of the deep for centuries, unable to decay completely. Sparse patches of hair sat strewn across the tops of many of their heads. Unnaturally long slender limbs, ending in feline-like clawed fingers, stretched from the creatures' concave shoulders. Their sunken ribs lead to midsections that seemed far too thin to be able to house a single organ.

"Are you both ready," Cora said, voice filled with a stoic resolve.

"As much as one can be when that's what we face," Will

185

gestured to the landing below.

Grant shifted away from the edge of the cliff and stood to his full height. Drawing his sword, he shook out his arms and legs and nodded to Will and Cora, "Be careful, both of you." With one final deep breath, Grant turned for the small game trail that led down to the cave's entrance.

Will could have sworn he heard Grant whisper to himself something that sounded like, 'Let's finish this,' before disappearing into the brush. At his left, Cora opened the leather bag that held their collection of weaponized fruit. Will watched as she slowly armed herself and let the first bomb fly. The yellow fruit soared over the clearing and struck the base of a large tree at the river's edge. On contact, an ear splitting boom ran out and the tree surprisingly burst into bright white flames. Over a dozen of the horrifying wraiths below flocked from the cave to the unnatural glow of the flames, moving with horrifying speed on all fours like demonic primates.

"What are you waiting for? Let's go," Cora spoke sternly over the ringing in Will's ears.

One after another, Will released bomb after bomb striking down the monsters in the sand. The smell of rotted, sizzling flesh assaulted Will's nose. High pitched wailing echoed through the forest like a death knell signaling when each creature hit the sand. Looking down, Will saw only four bombs remained as the final creature hit the ground.

"We did it," Cora breathed in a steadying breath. "That was far easier that I expected. Let's hope Grant is as successful."

Will rose to his feet, "Let's go give him a hand and make sure he is."

Quickly, both Will and Cora navigated their way down the embankment. The moment their feet hit the clearing an overwhelming sensation of dread coiled in Will's gut. Up close the sight and smell of the creatures charred, rotting skin turned his stomach. Their scent was far worse than it had been on the hilltop. Looking over his shoulder, Will saw the concern and utter disgust that contorted Cora's beautiful face. She snapped her head to her right at the same moment as Will. The first wraith they fell slowly began to push its mangled, smoldering body from the ground and rise to its feet. In a matter of seconds, nearly all of the creatures were beginning the stand on blistered legs in a near circle around Will and Cora.

"For the love of all that is holy… We're fucked," pure terror sank deep into Will's core at Cora's words.

"What do we do?" Will spun frantically realizing they had just trapped themselves with their backs to the cave and were surrounded, heavily outnumbered.

"We can't kill them," Cora breathed to herself in realization.

"Is there a way out through the caves?" Will asked.

"Not one we could survive," Cora admitted. "I can try to stall time but I don't think I can do it for very long; maybe two minutes at most."

"What?!" Will choked out stunned. He wasn't sure he had heard her correctly. "You can *manipulate* time?"

Cora shook her head, "Not well, but yes. I can slow time for those around me if I focus hard enough, but it's dangerous. You will need to get Grant and Addie and run."

Will nodded, "I won't leave you."

"I'll meet you at the top of the hill by the horses," Cora nodded, "now go quickly."

Instantly, Will was sprinting for the cave entrance as the beasts began to move closer to Cora's waiting form. As

187

he made his way over the sharp stones, Will began to feel a sluggish pull deep in his chest. Looking back over his shoulder, he saw Cora's hands outstretched on either side of her body and eyes closed tightly. From her side profile, Will could see a crimson trail of blood leaking from her nose. With a deeper sense of urgency, Will turned and made his way to the wet sand beyond the mouth of the cave. It struck him then what Cora had meant when she said it would be dangerous to stall time. She hadn't meant that it would be dangerous for him or those around her but that it could be deadly for *her*. Panic coursed through his blood at the thought. Just then, Will saw Grant on his knees before a wicked version of Lord Anderson. Once again, Will was sprinting into the darkness.

Chapter 22

Grant

The moment Grant left Will and Cora on the ridge he knew time was running short. Addie's consciousness drifted between his own mind and her body, tucked somewhere in the darkness of the cave before him; leaving Grant with the uneasy feeling that he wasn't going to make it to her side in time.

Feet skidding around the final bend, Grant glanced at the horrendous wraiths swarming the flames at the clearing's edge. Quickly he entered the shadows that would lead to his father and Addie's body and pulled himself over the pile of stones. Sliding down the back side of the embankment, he made sure to avoid the sharpest of protrusions from Addie's memory. The air was much heavier than he had expected. Death weighed down Grant's every breath with the stench of decay.

He's here, Addie's voice quivered, causing Grant's already pounding heart rate to spike. The only other sounds were the crunch of Grant's boots through the wet sand and the constant echo of water dripping from the sharp jagged rocks on the cave's ceiling.

A cold empty voice shattered any hope left in Grant's fragile heart, "Hello, son."

"Is that title still fitting? Does my father still remain or has he truly been lost to whatever this darkness is?" Grant's pain for his father saturated every clipped word as he spoke to the crazed version of the man he once knew.

Lord Anderson stepped over a dark mount at his feet and walked several steps into the dim light that broke through the mouth of the cave. His face was far more gaunt than Grant had ever seen, as though death had already claimed him but somehow he still drew breath. His father's once warm, welcoming eyes were shrouded by a hollowness Grant was not prepared for. The last time he had seen his father was when they had said their farewells only a few short weeks ago at their home. Although Lord Anderson's eyes were filled with grief, they still had some light left and the remnants of hope for his kingdom. Now there was no hint of joy or promise there, only his sorrow clouded by hatred and rage.

"Parts of the father you once knew still remain but only those riddled with anger and fear and driven by the need for retribution," Lord Anderson's voice was not his own.

"Then he *is* lost to us all. The man I knew was kind and cared for his family and his kingdom. He would never have considered the atrocity you aim to commit," Grant breathed.

"I will destroy the man responsible for this agony and anyone that stands to get in my way. The king will know what it is like to lose what he cares about most! He will feel it all, as I have," Lord Anderson bellowed.

"Where is *Addie*?" Grant barked.

Looking over his shoulder to the small crumpled form he had stepped over, Lord Anderson scoffed, "Do you think *she* was what I meant? She means *nothing* to him, or anyone of importance. The princess has become an unfortunate collateral that has inadvertently trapped me here," Lord Anderson's rage was palpable.

"What does that mean? She can't be dead," Grant shook his head in disbelief and stepped forward towards the body at the water's edge.

Lord Anderson raised his sword in Grant's direction, his head still turned to where Addie's body lay, "Do not move any closer or you too will join her."

"Look, Grant. I am not dead yet. My chest still rises and falls," Addie spoke and Lord Anderson's head snapped to where Grant stood. The lord's eyes were wide and his nostrils flared with vicious delight.

"She is with *you*?! I knew she was not here entirely. Her physical body, yes, but her soul seemed to escape me. I did not realize she was bound to *you*," Lord Anderson's expression shifted, an insidious grin spreading across his face.

"How is that possible?" Grant exhaled.

Lord Anderson shrugged, "My blood was willingly given. Addie's was not. I do not know what exactly happened but Rose's book is filled with *ridiculous* spells with even more absurd consequences when dealing in death. When my blood mixed with the princess's, I must have linked her to me, trapping me here. You are my child and are of my blood. When her soul left her body after I ran her through with my sword, it found you instead of peace."

"How do I save her?" Grant spoke through clenched teeth.

"That I do not know either. I do believe once she is no

longer tethered to me, or you, I will not be stuck in this horrid place any longer. I will be able to lead my death wraiths as intended," Lord Anderson straightened his spine proudly and smirked, "That will be a decision you will make for this kingdom. If Addie dies, I fear I will cease to exist and you will lose all that remains of your father completely. Forever. The creatures guarding this cave will fall when I do. If you restore her soul to her body, I will be freed and I promise to finish what I started. But you will have your beloved Addie. Do you care for her enough to chance that?" Lord Anderson's grin widened.

Grant scowled at his father's shell, "Addie doesn't deserve any of this and neither does this kingdom... Neither did you!"

"Your father is gone. Protect my people, Grant. Please." Addie's voice was filled with unshed tears.

Grant looked at Addie's slow breaths, "I refuse to let either of you go," he spoke in a whisper.

Closing his eyes, Grant focused on his father and every happy memory he could imagine of him and his mother together. Slowly, Grant's nightmares spilled free and wrapped themselves around his father's inky mind. Lord Anderson's thoughts were unlike any he had ever encountered. There was so much pain and rage. Grant could hardly stay on his own feet. Pushing through the darkness of his father's turmoil, a dim light shown that felt like his mother's warmth. It took every ounce of his will power to reach the single brightest memory.

* * *

Lord Anderson stood in his large living quarters near a low burning hearth. The sound of a baby's cry echoed through his mind. Grant floated through the room like the dense morning fog of early spring. The sun had just begun to set and a young woman stepped out from the main bedchamber, wiping her face with a clean white towel as several other women left the room behind her.

"Mother and babe are both doing splendidly," the woman smiled and placed a hand on Grant's father's shoulder. "You are welcome to see them both now if you wish, my lord."

In seconds, Lord Anderson rushed through the large double doors to his wife and newborn child. Seated atop the large four poster bed, surrounded by dozens of large fluffy pillows, sat Grant's mother holding a swaddled bundle. Grant watched the memory through his father's eyes. Every flicker of candle light seemed to glow a soft gold and cast radiant light throughout the room. Lady Anderson's flushed cheeks were rounded by the smile that graced her beautiful face. Grant's heart swelled with the overwhelming pride and love that radiated from his father's recollection of his birth. Of all the memories he thought he might find, this was not one he would have ever imagined to see.

Grant held back his own emotions as he spoke to his father's soul, "This is the man I knew. This is the love and life he believed in."

"Grant, my boy. I fear that man has been gone for far too long. I cannot recall the last time I felt such joy," the warm vibrato of his father's familiar voice seeped into Grant.

"I need you to fight. Hold on a little longer. Let me save you," Grant pleaded.

Lord Anderson's memory began to fade into the darkness

that surrounded them both, "Save Addie. I may be able to hold on long enough for you to collect her body and flee this horrible place. My mistakes will be my own to face at judgment but she should not suffer my fate. I need you to promise me you will not let her fade away into darkness. I cannot allow you to bear the same weight I have since losing your mother."

"I won't leave you here," Grant protested.

The image of Grant's father sank into shadow as his voice echoed through his mind one final time, "I love you son. I need you to run."

* * *

Grant rocked back onto his heels steadying himself. The rancid air of the cave flooded his senses, bringing him back to reality. Instantly, he was sprinting for Addie's body. Lord Anderson stood petrified in place, sword still raised to where Grant had been standing moments before. A thick trail of congealed blood oozed from his father's nose.

Dropping to his knees, Grant wrapped one arm under Addie's legs, careful not to move her more than necessary, before he reached forward to move the strands of hair from her face. The instant his fingers grazed the chilled skin on her forehead, Grant felt like he was being ripped open. A blood curdling scream pierced the silence of the cave just before Addie's eyes flew open wide and Grant wasn't sure if he or the princess had uttered the sound. Pain emanated through every cell in his body and a fire tore through the center of his chest. A bright golden light filled the cave and illuminated even the darkest cove. Every beam of light emanated from the would-be fatal wound to Addie's chest. Grant watched as the skin rapidly knit itself back together completely and once again Addie's eyes snapped closed and her body went limp in his arms. The all consuming pain Grant felt dissipated slowly as the light from Addie's chest flickered out. A cold laugh drew his attention away from the princess's now steady breaths. Lord Anderson stood between Grant and his only path to salvation.

"Love makes men foolish," what once was Lord Anderson grinned. He flipped the blade in his hand with a flick of his wrist and stretched out his neck. "But I must thank you for that stupidity. My freedom is all thanks to you and of course the lovely Ms. Rose and her book."

"What do you want?" Grant rested Addie's body in the sand, stood to his full height, and lifted his sword.

"I strive for revenge. I want suffering. I want the king to feel trapped in chaos and fear. I will be his pain and suffering incarnate. I have spent far too long trapped in this place alone." The skin on Lord Anderson's face sank deeper into the hollows of his cheeks and eyes, leaving only pail taught skin stretched too tightly over bone. "I will not allow you to leave this cave. You pose too great of a risk to me now. I am afraid I must kill you both, my son."

"I am no son of yours," Grant's rage filled his every word, "but if pain is what you seek, I will readily oblige."

Charging forward, Grant lifted his sword to block Lord Anderson's first strike before he swung his blade up the length of his father's spine. An animalistic roar echoed through the cave and dark blood dripped to the sand from the older man's back. Spinning on his heels, Grant faced his father once again. Rage lit Lord Anderson's eyes with a fury Grant had never seen. Both men stood feet apart and matched each blow with skilled movements. Grant deflected a strike that should have severed his head from his body but instead sliced through the fabric of his sleeve and tore through the skin and muscle down the length of his left arm from his shoulder to his elbow.

Strike for strike and blow for blow, Grant and Lord Anderson spun through the cavern like dancers trapped in a never ending, fatal ballet. Grant's father showed no sign of slowing while Grant's strength was beginning to fail him. He knew if he let his fatigue win, he and Addie would never see the sky again. They would never laugh with Will or enjoy Mag's delicious food. If he failed, Grant knew there would be no stopping Cora's vision for the future and the kingdom would burn. Lifting his sword with shaky arms, blood slicked his grip on his blade. In the darkness of the cave it was hard to tell how much of the blood that now covered his body was from his own injuries or his father's. Lord Anderson charged like a rabid animal and brought his chipped sword down hard on Grant's razor sharp blade, knocking it into the sand just out of Grant's reach and forcing him to his knees.

"You have defended yourself valiantly but it ends now, child," Anderson's cold voice was strained by an exhaustion he did not show in his movements.

Grant looked over to where Addie's body still lay. Once he was dead, whatever now guided his father would surely dispose of her as well. He slumped forward and looked down at his hands, sticky with blood; small pebbles sticking between his fingers. Grabbing a fist full of damp sand in each hand, Grant looked up to his father and swiftly tossed the grains into Lord Anderson's face. Time slowed and each speck seemed to hover in the air as the older man's arm lifted to block his eyes.

"Get up, Grant!" Will's melodic voice was a welcome sound from the entrance of the cave. "Cora can't hold time for very long. Grab Addie! Move!"

Grant's shock subsided as Will reached his side and both worked together to lift Addie's body from the ground.

Chapter 23

Cora

The world around Cora had begun to shake and her vision began to fail her. The taste and smell of iron filled her mouth and nose. She wasn't sure how much longer she could hold the wraiths at a stand still. Lifting her gaze from the creature only a few feet away, Cora's heart filled with relief at the sight of Will and Grant hoisting Addie's unconscious body over the rocks at the mouth of the cave.

"Get to the horses," Cora's voice was gargled as blood splattered to the ground at her feet.

In a few quick strides, Will was by her side, terror in his eyes, "We need to move you out of here."

Cora shook her head, "I can't," the rest of her admission sticking in her throat. She knew that she would lose the last strand of control she held the second her hands fell.

Confusion swept through her groggy mind as Will hastily pulled his borrowed clothing from his body, "What are you..."

Before she could finish her thought, Will shifted into the dragon she had seen take down the skin-walker in the forest.

With a turn, Will's massive tail collided with the three closest wraiths, sending their frozen bodies soaring through the air and slamming into the earth with a bone shattering thud.

A wave of heat flowed over Cora's back just before Will's bare chest crashed into her. His strong arms wrapped around her body, spinning her and lifting her over his muscled shoulder.

"Problem solved," Will breathed out as Cora's hold slipped and she watched the creatures begin to move toward them once again.

She could feel her tunic clinging to Will's skin as he ran over the embankment back to where the horses had been left before their fight. How much blood had she lost? What internal damage had she done if her clothing was soaked through?

"Fuck!" Grant's frantic voice drew her attention from her sprawling thoughts. "They're gone."

In her haze, Cora struggled to focus on her surroundings as Will lowered her to the ground next to Addie's semi-conscious body. Wiping some of the blood from her nose, Cora took a deep steadying breath before she spat blood into the grass and spoke.

"The explosions must have startled your horses away," Cora's voice was breathy with fatigue, "Shea is not like most *horses*. She is probably close." With a high pitched whistle between her fingers, Cora called to Shea. From the brush near the river, Shea responded with a chuff and trotted back into view from behind the foliage.

Grant shook his head, "One horse won't be much help if Addie and you are both unable to ride."

"You take Addie on Shea and I'll make sure Cora and I make

199

it back to the castle with you for aid. Is that alright, Cora?" Will asked, kneeling at Cora's side.

"Grant and Addie can take Shea but if your plan is to fly us back to the castle, we will both be dead before we reach the inner gates. The grounds are heavily protected," Cora exhaled.

"Cora is right," Addie's raspy voice momentarily stopped Cora's heart. She was sure hers wasn't the only one to skip a beat.

"Addie," dropping to his knees, Grant gently held Addie's face in his hands. "How do you feel? Can you stand? I don't mean to rush you after everything you've been through, but we aren't safe and can't linger here."

Addie gingerly shook her head from side to side, "I don't think I can stand or ride on my own, not yet, but I think I will live thanks to you all."

"I will get you back to the castle princess, I promise," Grant vowed. "May I lift you onto Cora's horse?"

Addie gave a weak nod as Grant slipped his arm under her knees and hoisted her into the dark leather saddle as Will moved to help Cora.

"Cora can ride with me at your side. I doubt the king and his guard will shoot down his daughter and her companions," Will stated.

Cora shifted up onto her knees to face Will fully, "Have you forgotten we are without a horse once they leave? I know I'm disoriented right now, but is there something I've forgotten? You cannot ride into the castle as a *dragon*."

Will's brilliant, mischievous smile widened across his face, "I can shift into *any* beast I choose, remember. You can ride me into the castle grounds as a horse." Cora mulled over

Will's statement for several moments before she agreed to Will's plan.

Leaning in close, Will whispered softly into Cora's ear, "Don't worry, beautiful. I won't let you fall. I'll make sure your ride is smoother than our last one together"

Heat filled Cora's body and she wasn't sure if it was from Will's tone in his whispered confession or him shifting at her side. Gracefully, in his new form, Will lowered his golden brown body to the ground to allow Cora an easier mount. Tentatively, she rose to her feet and held firmly to his dark brown mane before swinging her leg over his back. Will stood slowly and followed behind Grant and Addie seated atop Shea. From the clearing outside the caves, an angry, wicked bellow echoed through the forest.

"We need to move now. They're coming," Grant warned and held tighter to Addie.

A soft neigh escaped Will's muzzle, encouraging Cora to hold tight before the group was racing through the dark forest toward the castle. Despite the few short hours that had passed since they had woken up this morning, so much had transpired. Addie was alive but, adversely, Lord Anderson had raised the dead. By some miracle, they all were now headed toward their safe haven in one piece. The dark, ominous sky above once again seemed to promise a violent storm ahead as they rode. The screams from the death wraiths behind them began to slip away and were replaced by an eerie silence in the trees. After several hours at a brutal pace, the forest began to change; the trees becoming more sparse.

The feeling of relief Cora had expected to find as she and her companions exited the thickest parts of the woods never

201

came. Instead, unease settled into her bones as they hurried over the small green hills that separated the Alderbrooke Forest from the castle walls. Perched atop every lookout tower were the royal guards in the deep greens and golds of the kingdom. Cora looked to her other companions in the hope of alleviating some of her discomfort and was momentarily satisfied to see the light in Addie's face shine as the princess looked upon the gray stone walls of her home. All traces of comfort were dashed away in seconds.

One instant Grant held tightly to Addie seated on Shea and the next both were tumbling to the ground, a black fletched arrow protruding from Grant's already injured, right shoulder. Cora watched in horror and disbelief as dozens of the king's royal guards swarmed. Will swiftly skidded to a halt alongside Shea and reared up in an attempt to shield Cora from attack. Raising her hands, Cora could see no possible escape that didn't result in unnecessary bloodshed.

She leaned forward and spoke low for only Will to hear, "I think they knew we were coming. Do not shift. Find us when you can get away."

A large heavily armed soldier swiftly pulled Cora to the ground by her wrists, throwing up a puff of dust. Will turned and reared up over the man, knocking him into the dirt beside her as voices rang out from all around.

"Someone secure that animal and take it to the stables!" one voice shouted.

"Get those two into custody by order of the king. Seize them as enemies to the crown and get the princess inside now!" a gruff voice ordered.

Cora, now pinned, face pressed down hard into the dirt, watched as Grant struggled to keep his hold on Addie, who too strained to cling to him desperately, as several soldiers ripped them apart.

"Please, stop!" Addie screamed through sobs.

"Let her go!" Grant bellowed before taking another blow to the abdomen and dropping to his knees once more.

Addie's guttural scream echoed the pain Cora was certain Grant must be feeling as if his pain was her own. It took several men to pull Addie into the confines of the castle walls out of sight. Her screams of pain and anger reverberated through the halls.

Cora could feel Grant's rage before she witnessed his power unleashed once more. Like it was nothing, Grant's gift reached six of the closest guards and dropped them all in an instant, blood dripping from their eyes, ears, and noses, just before a deep voice silenced everyone.

"Bring them down now," the voice boomed and a wet, fragrant, cloth bag was thrown over both Cora and Grant, pitching them into a dark unconsciousness.

Chapter 24

Addie

Addie struggled against the several sets of hands that pulled her down the hall into her bed chambers. The overwhelming pain in her ribs subsided as exhaustion clouded her vision. The room around her began to spin and her arms and legs felt limp. Before she had time to brace herself, she was falling to the cold floor.

"Someone get the king's healer," the man at her side ordered and the sound of shuffling feet exited her bedroom door.

Through fogged consciousness, Addie could vaguely hear a young woman's voice speaking to someone else in the room. She struggled to remain conscious and held on to every word she could hear.

"There's no reason she should still sleep," the woman's voice was tentative.

"What is wrong with her?" King Colvin's voice boomed.

"I'm not sure, sire. Has the young man woken yet?" a soft hand ran down Addie's arm in soothing strokes.

King Colvin stalked for the door. "That criminal is none of

your concern, healer. Just do your job and figure out what he has done to the princess," he barked before slamming the door behind him.

Sighing, the healer placed a glowing palm on Addie's head, "I know you can hear me, your highness. I'm doing my best to fix whatever this is."

After several hours, Addie finally felt the fog lifting, "Where is Grant?"

The exhausted woman shot to her feet from the chair at Addie's side, "Your highness!"

"Where are they?" Addie continued.

"I'll send word to the king that you have woken," the woman's voice was frantic.

"No, please," Addie besieged. "I need to know where they are. Did my father order an execution?"

Shaking her head, the woman's voice was soft, "I don't believe so, miss. But I do think they were taken to the east tower."

Dread pooled in Addie's gut, "Where is the king now." She stood to her feet and looked down at her dark green sleep gown. "I need to change and speak to my father."

"I believe he is in his map room with several other lords, ma'am. Would you like me to send for your lady's maid?" the healer asked, sidestepping toward the door.

"That won't be necessary. What is your name?" Addie pulled a clean pair of dark gray pants from her wardrobe and a thick white tunic.

"I'm Elinore, your highness," the small woman spoke. "The king employs me for discreet scenarios like your own."

Squinting, Addie looked the woman over from head to toe, "Can I trust you?"

"With your life, Highness," Elinore bowed.

Something in Addie's gut told her the frail looking young woman before her was telling the truth. "No one can know what I ask of you. The king cannot know. Do you understand? It is both of our lives at stake if anyone discovers what I need," Addie warned.

Elinore bent at the waist and dropped her head, "I mean no disrespect to the king but I do not trust his intentions with our kingdom, ma'am."

"Neither do I... I need you to find out what you can about Grant and Cora and come find me when you can, please. But be safe," Addie pleaded.

"Of course, your highness. I will be back here as soon as possible," with a nod Elinore departed.

Swiftly, Addie made her way through the castle to her father's map room. The late evening sun sat tucked behind dark ominous clouds as it sank below the horizon, casting dark shadows through the hall's of the castle. Addie slipped into the small closet outside the map room and settled her racing heart in order to listen to the commotion within the adjoined room.

"They have become more brazen, your majesty," General Banks's voice radiated concern. "I fear if we don't send aid south of Alderbrooke now we may lose vital townships and possibly Shepherd's Glen."

"We need to keep our focus to the north," Lord Steven's slimy voice gritted out.

"Lord Steven's is correct," King Colvin chastised General Banks, "Your foolish request for aid is *again* denied."

Frustration rose in Addie's chest. This kingdom was crumbling quickly and she wasn't sure if it was stubbornness and pride or ill-intent that drove her father's actions. Addie could no longer sit in the darkness and watch her people suffer. Bursting through the door of the closet and straight into the map room, Addie announced her arrival with a flourish.

"Father, you and Lord Stevens are either blinded by fear or have lost your sense of duty as rulers if you aim to continue to ignore the plea for help from the south," Addie barked.

"You are out of line, daughter. This is no discussion a princess should be a part of. Now leave," the king snipped.

"I will do no such thing," Addie stood her ground.

"What has that villainous creature brainwashed you into believing, child," King Colvin stepped to his daughter's side and grabbed her shoulders roughly.

"I am not a child," Addie pulled away hard.

"No, you are a woman; that's much stupider than a child," Lord Stevens snarled.

"Fuck you! You have no right to speak to me," Addie bit out.

Lord Stevens laughed, "As a woman, you are insignificant and cannot order anything from me. In fact, you are to be my bride. The deal has already been made, my dear, and you will obey what *I* say."

Addie stepped forward and raised her right hand and brought it down hard across Lord Stevens' smug face. Gasps of shock cascaded through the room. A red hand print bloomed where she had struck the lord. Small white blisters began to form over his cheek.

"You bitch!" Lord Stevens shouted, grabbed Addie by the shoulders, and threw her to the floor. "How dare you?!"

"How dare *I*? How dare *you* touch me? I will not let your

vile advances persist any longer!" Addie stood once again.

"What are you talking about, your highness?" General Banks asked with concern and offered a hand to her.

"This isn't the first time the *lord* here has put his hands on me without consent," Addie addressed General Banks, "I believe he drugged me once and forced me into my room alone with him."

"Don't listen to this harlot, General," Lord Stevens groaned.

"Shut up, Stevens," General Banks snapped, "Addie, did he hurt you?"

"No, luckily my lady's maid interrupted his pursuits," Addie admitted.

"You wanted me, you whore," Lord Stevens stepped toward Addie but was intercepted by the general's large frame.

"If you hope to keep your life, I advise you stop where you are before I must defend my princess," General Banks scowled down at the cowering lord.

"These are grave accusations, Addie," King Colvin stated with a disbelieving tone. "If you are saying Lord Steven's attempted to assault you, I will be obligated to act as your father and your king."

"It's true," Addie faced her father. A low groan slipped from Lord Stevens' mouth.

"Guards, take Lord Steven's into custody," King Colvin ordered. Several guards filled the room and pulled the young lord away in protest.

A strange grin spread across the king's face before Lord Stevens yelled from the closing doors, "You're going to regret crossing me, your highness!"

Turning to her father, Addie spoke again, "Thank you father, for all of that, but none of this was the reason I came here. I need to know where you took Grant and Rose's daughter, Cora."

"They are not your concern. Both criminals will be disposed of soon," the king replied coldly.

"Those *criminals* saved my life! They aren't the bad guys here! Set them free!" Addie demanded.

"Do not speak to me with that tone, *child*. They already face their judgment as we speak. Now leave this room before I choose to keep you sequestered to your quarters indefinitely," Addie's father nodded to the two guards at the door to escort Addie back to her rooms.

A flash of remorse and gratitude shown across General Banks's expression before Addie turned and stomped back down the hall toward her rooms to await word from Elinore. As Addie turned the corner outside the map room, Prince Andrew rushed to her side.

"Are you alright, sister?" Andrew's genuine concern poured from his words.

"I'll be alright but father, I fear, is not," Addie whispered to her brother.

"I know. We need to…" Prince Andrew looked over Addie's shoulder at the trailing guards. "Not here. When you are feeling up for it and can get away, we need to meet for a game in the garden." Andrew tilted his head with a wink at his younger sister.

As children, Addie and Andrew met every chance they could, under the old willow in the forest beyond the castle grounds as a way to escape the pressures of royal life with their father. Any time one of them needed to talk away from listening ears, they would ask the other if they wanted to join them for a game in the garden and sneak into the woods for peace.

"Of course, Andrew. I always enjoy a game in the garden," Addie smiled softly. Catching sight of Elinore moving swiftly through the hall, Addie bowed to her brother, "I will see you soon," and made her leave.

Quickly, Addie shuffled through the hall back to her rooms and slipped inside. The look of fear and terror on Elinor's face sent alarm bells sounding through Addie's mind.

"They are going to kill them both, your highness," Elinore sucked in a breath.

Outside Addie's window, sheets of rain pelted the stain glass and lightning cracked through the dark sky. "I need to get them out," Addie rushed to the large window.

Cracking the window open quietly Addie bent down beside a large desk and pulled a rope from behind the heavy piece of furniture. She efficiently tied the rope around her legs and waist and proceeded to climb onto the window ledge.

"Princess! What are you doing?!" Elinore protested.

"Shh," Addie hissed. "I will be fine. No one saw you come in here, right?"

"I don't think so, why?" Elinore asked, puzzled.

"If anyone comes to the door, pretend you are me in the bathing chamber and do not let them in. I will be back soon. I need to get Grant and Cora out and find Will," Addie threw herself over the window's edge and eased herself down the stone in the dark heavy rain.

Chapter 25

Grant

The pungent scent of mildew, decaying wood, and stagnant water flooded Grant's senses. His head throbbed at his temples like he had been kicked by a horse and eyes felt far too heavy. Slowly, he shifted his extremities. Iron cuffs secured his wrists and ankles in place with nearly no room for movement. Below his bare shoulder blades, Grant could feel the bite of the uneven wood table he had been strapped down to. Foggy memories rushed through his mind of him and Addie tumbling from Cora's horse and the sound of Addie's screams echoed through his thoughts.

"I'm glad you could finally join us, Grant Anderson," a deep voice sounded from the dark.

With immense effort, Grant pried his eyes open. The space around him was poorly lit by flickering candle light and the distant tap of water against stone made Grant realize he must be in the dungeons below the castle's east tower. As young men, he and Will had discovered the holding cells at the entrance of the dungeons by mistake while looking for the king's private wine reserves. When they were found by a castle guard, they were warned the east tower was the only secure place for dangerous prisoners and not anywhere they would ever want to find themselves again.

"Where is Addie?" Grant responded finally.

The sound of heavy boots against cobblestone edged closer until a tall, tawny skinned man with jet black, shoulder length hair stepped into Grant's line of sight. The man had broad shoulders and large muscular arms. Grant knew he, himself, was by no means a small man. But in comparison to the behemoth at his side, he wouldn't stand a chance against him with brute strength. Reaching deep, Grant felt for his powers and found nothing. Confusion must have shown in his expression, eliciting a wicked laugh from the man at his side.

"You can't use your gifts, traitor," the man spoke. "The potion that knocked you out also subdues natural abilities. Since we are probably going to be here for a good while, let me introduce myself. My name is Vern Accor. I am King Colvin's favorite interrogator." A devious grin split through the man's short beard.

"I don't give a fuck who you are. Take me to Addie now," Grant demanded, gritting his teeth and pulling hard on his restraints. The wound from his father's blade and he arrow in his shoulder began to leak blood down the length of his arm pinned at his side.

Stepping closer, Vern placed his large hand on Grant's chest lightly before patting softly, "I don't think I will just yet. I need to know a few things first; like what involvement you had in aiding your father in the forest and why you both went to see the necromancer."

"I went to stop my father from doing something stupid and to save the princess. Now let me out," Grant barked.

A low clicking sound startled Grant slightly as Vern began to turn a tarnished metal knob near Grant's right hand. The table beneath Grant's body began to tilt, pitching his bare feet slightly higher than his head.

"You see, I don't believe you and neither will the king. We are going to need more if you have any hopes of ever seeing the princess or the sky again," Vern's voice took on a crueler tone. "For each answer I do not believe — or *like* for that matter — I will take something or break something of yours. For answers I *do* like I will answer a question you may have. Does that sound good?"

"Fuck you," Grant spat. No matter what Grant told the man at his side, he knew he probably wouldn't be leaving this cell in one piece.

"Now, now Grant. That is an excellent example of an answer I. DO. NOT. LIKE." Vern snapped each word. "And now I will take something of yours."

With a razor sharp knife, Vern stepped to the end of the table and ran the tip of his blade up the length of the underside of Grant's left foot.

Despite his best effort, Grant let out an animalistic roar of pain. "What the fuck do you want from me?!"

"I have already told you. I want answers I will like. If you continue to provide ugly quips and unhelpful responses, the things I take will become more severe. Understand?"

Through clenched teeth, Grant replied, "Yes."

"Good. Let us begin again. Maybe a *smaller* question," Vern smiled sickly, "When did you decide to see the necromancer?"

"The morning I left Shepherd's Glen," Grant stated bluntly.

"Great. I believe that. But why did you go to see her?" Vern continued.

"You said you would answer one of my questions first," Grant snapped.

Vern thinned his lips, "That I did. What is your question?"

"Where is Addie?" Grant blurted.

"She is in the castle," Vern grinned.

Anger boiled in Grant's chest. "Is she safe in the castle, you prick?"

Rage flashed through Vern's eyes before his blade slammed deep into Grant's upper thigh without warning. The tear of the blade through flesh elicited another scream from Grant. Blinding pain radiated through him as Vern slowly pulled the steel free, the edge grinding against bone.

"I answered your question, fucker," Vern's voice was cold. "I am losing my patience with you. Now, tell me why you were going to the necromancer's!"

Through silent tears, Grant sucked in a shaky breath, "She met with my father after my mother died to try to contact my mother's soul. I needed to know what happened during their meeting."

"The princess is guarded in her rooms and is safe, for now. Tell me what she told you."

Grant knew he wouldn't be able to tell Vern the whole truth if he wished to be free. "She said my mother's soul was at peace and my father was devastated."

Exhaling a deep breath, Vern shook his head in discontent and pulled a chair next to Grant. Blood from Grant's injuries on his foot and thigh had run up the length of his body and was beginning to drip off the table past Grant's head. The constant tapping of blood in the growing pool below him seemed to mirror the water dripping from the walls around him.

"Do you know what my gift is, Grant? No? I'll tell you. I have a special type of telepathy that allows me the ability to know when I'm being lied to. I know you are telling the truth but I also know you aren't telling me everything. When you said you went to stop your father, that wasn't entirely true," Vern leaned back in the chair slowly, spinning the bloody blade over his fingers before resting it on the table near Grant's head.

"I'm telling you the truth," Grant growled.

"Not *all* of it," Vern placed his hand atop Grant's and collected his middle finger into his palm, "And in all honesty, even if you were telling the total truth, you've already proven you are far too great of a threat to this kingdom regardless of your intentions with your father. So, I am going to continue to do my job here — a job I love by the way"

Pulling hard Vern snapped Grant's finger back cracking through the bone. A stifled grunt escaped from deep in Grant's chest. With gentle hands, Vern lay Grant's hand back down against the bloody wood table, his finger bent at an unnatural angle, and picked up his knife once again.

"And then I am going to throw you back into the darkest cell in this place and wait for you to rot away without any remorse," Vern stood and ran the tip of his blade across Grant's face from his cheek to his temple, a thin line of blood beading in its wake.

Lifting his head swiftly, Grant opened his mouth and sank his teeth into the thick flesh of Vern's right thumb. Dropping his knife, Vern's roar echoed through the empty hall. Blood ran out from the corners of Grant's mouth before he spit in the interrogator's direction, splattering Vern's tunic in his own blood.

"Mother fucker!" Vern howled, "You nearly took off my thumb! Maybe when I finish with you I *will* have a visit with the princess and have her pay for your treason too!"

"Fuck you," Grant's voice was low and vengeful, "You better hope I never get out of here or you will regret that threat!"

From the shadows beyond the cell door, a smaller man stepped into Grant's view on silent feet. "She's awake, Vern," the newcomer whispered.

"Good. I'm done with this trader for now. Send me the healer for my hand and I'll go visit with Rose's daughter," a predatory grin overtook Vern's scowl. Cradling his injured hand to his chest, he lifted his left arm over his head and smashed his fist into Grant's skull, thrusting him into darkness once again.

Chapter 26

Will

Will's heart pounded hard in his chest as he fought against the two men pulling him along into the castle stables beside Cora's much calmer horse. Her words played over and over in his head. Shea nipped his side lightly, drawing his attention. Something in the horse's expression cautioned him to calm himself. Heeding Cora's words and Shea's reprimand, Will eased his struggle slightly. He was going to need to find a way to get to Cora as soon as he could free himself but exposing himself as a shifter now would help no one.

"Put them both in the back and bring the farrier around," the woman holding Shea's lead ordered once they entered the cover of the stable. Nodding, the two men pulled both horses into a dark stall in the far corner of the large space.

Quickly, the two men tied Will and Shea to a post and made their way out of the stables in search of the farrier. In a few short moments, a tall lean man made his way inside with an arm full of tools. At the far corner of the room was a small chimney and stone pit where the man placed several of his items down. A small fire roared to life as he collected a long rod with the kingdom's insignia inverted in iron at the end. Placing the end of the rod into the flames, Will's heart sank. If he hoped to avoid the brand he knew was coming, he would have to shift but he would need to incapacitate the innocent man to avoid being discovered. Mulling over his options, Will reluctantly decided it would be best to wait for the farrier to leave after he was branded and stage his escape. He and Shea could then head into the forest after nightfall to avoid discovery.

"Hello you two beauties," the man's voice was soft and kind. Slowly, he ran his hand down Shea's mane, "I fear this will probably hurt and I hate to mar either of you with that *awful* man's emblem, but I must do my duties. I have a salve here to ease some of the burn once I've finished."

Turning away, the man pulled the glowing iron from the flames and approached Shea tentatively, "I hear you are more mild mannered, sweetheart. I'll do my best to move quickly."

The smell of burning flesh and hair reeked but Shea hardly winced at the assault. Quickly, the man slathered her freshly branded skin with a thick cream colored paste.

"At a girl," stepping back around Cora's horse, the man returned the brand to the fire and fished a large purple carrot from his sack of supplies and fed it to Shea. "You're up next, young man. Please don't kick me if you can help it."

After several minutes in the flames, the branding rod once again glowed a brilliant orange. More hesitantly than before, the man approached Will's side and placed his hand on Will's neck. Stroking slowly, the man radiated kindness with every touch.

218

"Here goes nothing, friend," fear laced the man's voice as he put the brand to Will's rear haunches and pressed the burning metal against his flesh.

Will had no intentions of hurting the man at his side. Every muscle in his body tensed at the overwhelming pain that seemed to last forever. How Shea had barely moved, Will wasn't sure.

"All done. Let's get you some relief," An overwhelming chill spread from the brand up Will's spine. Turning his head, he watched the tall man's scrunched expression relax, "I'm not sure what the guards were talking about. You both did splendidly."

Shea let out a chuff of insult at the man's words. In a mock whisper, the man addressed Shea, "I think they were referring to *him* more than you, my dear." Earning him a flick from Will's tail.

Chuckling to himself, the man collected his bag and doused the fire with sand, "I'll let you both rest tonight and fit you for shoes tomorrow morning."

Once again, Will and Shea were alone. The late afternoon sun sank slowly behind the trees outside the stables casting dark shadows through the coming storm. Several young children came and left shortly after the farrier departed, leaving two large stacks of hay at Will and Shea's feet. The hours seemed to pass slower, each moment consumed by Will's fears of what Cora might be facing. Finally, the tower tolled nine bells and Will was sure now was his best chance for escape.

Heat billowed through the chilled air and instantly Will stood in his human form. "Alright Shea, let's get us both out of here." Will winced with each step moving around to untie

Cora's horse. The distorted brand on his hip protested his movements as he continued to check over Shea's body for any injuries. As Will approached her rear, he couldn't help but see the lack of a brand on her pristine white hide.

"How?" Will questioned aloud and ran his hand over the perfect skin.

Shaking his head dismissively, Will turned from Shea and continued to move quickly through the stall, quietly breaking down several posts to stage their escape. A loud crash snapped Will's head to where Cora's horse had been. Now there was only empty space and a large hole through the stable's wall leading to the northern edge of the forest nearly a hundred yard away. From the tree cover, a loud neigh broke through the silence. Shouts began to sound from the entrance for the stables and Will found himself sprinting nude into the heavy rain.

Will skidded to a halt once he was fully tucked out of sight below the dense tree coverage. The tightly woven branches overhead blocked out most of the downpour from the sky above but the whipping wind threw rain in all directions and the ground below Will's bare feet had become a slick mess of mud and decaying leaves. After several minutes on his knees in the brush, the guards' shouts slowed then silenced completely. Cora's horse stepped to his side and nudged his shoulder with her soft velvety nose then nodded slightly back to the castle.

"I need to figure out how to get into the east tower as soon as possible," Will's voice was a whisper as he attempted to wipe some of the rain from his eyes. "I think it's safe to assume that's where I'm going to find Cora and Grant."

Slinking through the trees, Will and Shea circled around

to the east side of the castle grounds, stopping several times to avoid detection. Three quarters of the expansive property surrounding the castle lay nestled against the forest tree line as though a large portion of the old forest had been cut away to make room for the large stone structure.

Speaking to himself, Will pondered his current turmoil, "I think I know how I can get in ... but how am I going to get *them* out?"

The longer Grant and Cora spent in the king's stronghold, the higher the likelihood that Will would be attempting a retrieval mission instead of a rescue. There was no way he could sit idle any longer while his friends were most likely being harmed. After nearly an hour of scouting the safest exit, Will arrived at a plan he hoped would allow both Grant and Cora to escape in one piece at his side.

"I can't believe I'm about to do this, but I'm going to need your help here, Shea," Will ran a hand over his face, clearing some of the frigid water from his skin. "I need you to be ready, right here, when I whistle for you to run. Can you do that?"

Shea lowered her head as if to nod in agreement. "I really hope I haven't lost my mind and you really do understand me," Will sighed to himself then shifted into a discreet dark plumed raven and took flight.

Flying over the castle wall, Will landed softly in the grass just outside the entrance to the east lookout tower. The sound of gravel shifting under petite boots made Will's heart race as a small woman exited the tower and passed his side.

"I hate that horrible man," the woman murmured with tears in her eyes and wiped her hands down the front of her wet apron, leaving a smear of blood behind. Will couldn't help but notice the faint golden glow of a healer that emanated from the woman's wrist in the shape of a large hand. Someone had grabbed her arm hard enough to bruise. Furious, Will moved closer to the building, shifted into a small gray mouse and squeezed under the door.

Farther down the hall, past the staircase to the lookout, a man roughly Will's usual size approached, key's clanging at his hip. Through the flickering light from the sconces along the walls, Will could see and hear no other person nearby. A bright flash of lightning illuminated the space more fully, confirming Will's assumption. Now was Will's chance to ambush the man before him and find Cora and Grant.

As the sound of thunder crashed, Will lunged forward and shifted midair and forced the guard to the ground. Stunned, the man didn't have time to shout before Will had his mouth covered, had stolen the guard's sword from its sheath, and was dragging him into the first door on his right. Will knew the stairwell to the holding cells below was at the far end of the long hall and hoped this room wasn't occupied. Luckily, there was nothing more than a large table and several empty chairs strewn around the space.

"I need you to listen to me and answer my questions with a nod 'yes' or 'no' or I will snap your neck right now," Will's voice was cold and detached. Frantically, the man nodded his agreement.

"Are there two new prisoners below: one a dark haired woman with alabaster skin and the other a tawny skinned, dark haired man?" Will asked aggressively.

Nodding once in confirmation, Will's heart tightened in his chest. "Are they alone?"

An ugly grin spread across the man's face. Nodding a "no"

in response, he squirmed under Will's weight. With a sharp twist, he brought his knee up into Will's rib, causing Will to lose his hold over the man's mouth.

"You don't stand a chance down there alone with him no matter what *gift* you have," the man retorted.

"Then it's good I won't be alone once I get down there," Will replied, holding the sword against the man's throat, drawing a bead of blood.

A slimy laugh escaped from behind the man's yellowing teeth, "Your friends won't be much help in their current state."

"What have you done to her ... to them?" unbridled rage poured from Will.

"Your little man friend is unconscious and probably won't be walking out of here anytime soon if he hasn't bled out already and as for the little *minx*," the man smirked and ran his filthy tongue over his bottom lip, "She is currently being *tended* to. Wish I could have stayed to watch."

Without hesitation, Will ran the sword across the man's neck cutting his laugh to nothing more than a choked gargle. Blood sprayed from the guard's throat, covering Will's face and body. Crimson coated the length of the blade and splattered across the floor in an ever growing puddle at Will's feet. The guard grasped at his throat for several seconds before his body went limp below Will's grasp and hit the ground with a thud. With shaking hands, Will removed the man's leather jacket and pants. Dressing himself as he walked through the door into the hall, Will could see nothing but the burning fire in his soul. If anyone had violated Cora, he was certain their head would be the last thing he removed from their body.

As he approached the large wooden door at the end of the

223

hall, a muffled high pitch scream broke the deafening silence. Swinging the door open silently, Will ran down the spiraling stairs into the darkness, shifting his vision as he went.

A deep voice sounded down the corridor at the base of the stairs, "I'll only ask one more time, you bitch. What sort of necromancy have you and your mother been practicing?!"

Will sprinted down the hall on silent feet and stopped in the shadows just outside the door the voice had come from.

"I study *alchemy*, you uneducated moron. I see enough death with my own gifts. I do not need to practice necromancy to know a person's fate," Will peered through the doorway and watched Cora lean forward and spit her mouth full of blood onto the dirty cellar floor. "I also don't need my power to know your fate is looking more grim with every second I spend here."

"Are you threatening me?" The man laughed. "You're strung up like prized game. What could you possibly do to me?"

"That is true at the moment," Cora breathed hard, "but it's not *me* you should fear." She grinned a bloody smile and glanced toward the flickering light pouring through the open cellar door.

Confusion washed over her interrogator's face, "Do tell. Who should I fear?" The large man raised the whip in his hand into the air before it was stopped abruptly.

A voice full of wicked promise cut through the frigid cell. "*Me.*"

Will stepped into the blinking candle light and yanked the whip free from the grimy hands responsible for the many cuts and bruises that now scared Cora's bare flesh.

In one quick movement, Will snapped the whip around the

large man's throat and pulled his body to the floor before he had the chance to draw his sword.

"Well now I don't get to make *him* suffer," Cora attempted to joke through restrained sobs.

"I don't think he's dead yet," Will shrugged unaffectedly and stepped over the man's still body.

"The cracking sound of his skull against stone might beg to differ," Cora smiled, blood coating her teeth .

"I can hear his heart still, he is seriously concussed, I'm sure, but he will live— for now," Will reassured Cora as he pulled a ring of keys from the pocket of his pants. Slowly wrapping his arm under her body, he unlocked the cuff that held her suspended just over the ground. The sudden release dropped Cora's injured body into Will's arms.

"I must say, I'm not a huge fan of this side of bondage," Cora exhaled as Will helped her settle into a lone wooden chair.

With a sly wink, Will cocked a mischievous grin, "Lucky for you, I don't mind being tied down."

A soft laugh escaped Cora's lips, eliciting a wince from her most likely cracked rib.

"Are you alright? How badly are you hurt?" Will's eyes scanned over Cora's body slowly looking for every injury.

"I'll be fine. Our new friend Vern over there just got in here with me not too long ago," Cora responded, settling her feet to the cold floor.

Knitting his brows together and looking Cora in the eyes, Will's voice lowered to a near whisper, "Cora, did he touch you?"

"Obviously," Cora waved her hands gesturing to the lashes over her stomach and chest. Scraps of her under shirt held on by threads.

225

"*Intimately*, Cora." Will's breathing was heavy with anger. "I will relieve him of his manhood if he has."

Realization shown on Cora's face as she looked down at herself clad in just her under layers, "Gods no! Will, I'm alright."

Exhaling hard, Will's shoulders relaxed, "I'm still going to kill him though."

"I think that will need to wait," Cora stepped toward the door on bare feet. "His partner just left and will be back soon."

"Who's pants do you think I'm wearing?"

"I assume that's his blood then too?" Cora asked, raising a brow.

Will replied with a shrug and nodded, "You would be correct in that assumption. He inferred he wanted to watch Vern have his way with you. So I slit his throat."

"I promise I'm alright, Will," Cora placed her hand on his shoulder. "But, I still don't think we have time to waste on Vern. We need to find Grant and get out of here. I hope you have a plan for that."

"Ya, we need to find Grant," Will stated, standing to his full height.

Cora held tight to Will's hand for a moment longer, "Grant's probably in worse shape than I am. He took down six guards when they drug Addie away screaming. They had a sleep draft on hand. I think they knew we were coming, Will. We need to be careful."

"When am I not careful?" Will asked rhetorically.

"I'm serious. If they know what Grant can do then they may know what you are capable of now. The king doesn't take powerful gifts like yours lightly."

"I know. I have a feeling the king is hiding more than we

know," Will admitted.

"Me too. I would love to get close enough to get a reading from him but that doesn't seem like a possibility any time soon," a shiver ran through Cora's body as they eased through the dark, deeper into the dungeon.

Will held up his hand, stopping Cora abruptly. Turning his head, the sound of raspy breathing filled his ears.

"He's down here," Will pointed to the door near the end of the hall. "I think we're just below the entrance to the tower now."

Pulling the door open Will's heart began to race. Propped with his feet slightly higher than his head, was Grant, slowly bleeding out onto the floor.

"Fuck," Will ran to the table and spun the metal nob leveling him back out.

Cora made quick work of the restraints at Grant's feet with Will's stolen keys then tossed the key ring back to Will to unlatch Grant's wrists and belted middle. Will ripped the bottom portion of his pant leg free and wrapped it around Grant's upper thigh to slow the bleeding.

"I have Shea waiting for your signal at the tree line. Once we make it to the forest edge, if we get separated, I need you to run due east into the forest until you hit a large willow tree. Then head north until you reach an old hunting cabin," Will spoke quickly as he lifted Grant into his arms.

"We aren't getting separated," Cora protested.

"I hope not, but if we do, I will meet you back there," Will said firmly.

Reluctantly, Cora lowered her chin, "Okay. We are going to need a healer for Grant soon though."

"I don't think I can get Addie out of the castle right now

but I have an idea of someone that might be willing to help you both," Will swept down the hall and up the stairs, Cora just behind him. The hallway above was still empty as they made their way to the exit. Cracking the door slightly, Cora leaned into the storm and whistled into the dark.

Chapter 27

Grant

Cold, wet air assaulted Grant's bare skin, startling his senses. Everything around him seemed distorted like he was looking at the world through a crystal ball. The crack of lightning overhead was far too bright and struck too close for comfort. The sound of thunder never met his ears. He could feel his body being cradled against a warm chest who's heart thrummed rhythmically against his cheek. Shifting slightly, Grant saw the ground below him zipping by before he saw hooves strike the wet grass pushing him and his rescuer forward. It struck him then that he was in someone's arms atop a horse racing from the east wing of the castle but something about his position felt wrong. Where was the horse's head? Was he being rescued by a *centaur*? He knew he must be delusional; there hadn't been a centaur alive in centuries. Despite his trepidation and desire to remain alert, Grant struggled to stay conscious. All concepts of time eluded him as he drifted into a dreamless dark.

"Grant, can you hear me?" Will's voice was far away. "Come on, Grant. I need you to wake up so we know nothing was too seriously damaged in your head."

Groaning, Grant's eyes fluttered open. The room was small and familiar. Lamp light illuminated Will and Cora at his bedside, as well as a young golden haired woman. The air was dusty and smelled like an old leather boot.

"Are we in the General's cabin?" Grant pushed himself into a seated position against the headboard, "Who are you?"

"I'm Elinore, a friend of the princess. I was able to heal most of your injuries enough but you lost a lot of blood and are going to need to rest. Please lay back down," Elinore's eye's were tired but her smile was kind.

"Is she safe?" Grant asked hurriedly, ignoring the young woman's request.

"She's fine for now, Grant," Will answered, "how is your head?"

Grant ran a hand over his temple, "It's okay. Sore, but I'll be alright. Cora, how are you? The last thing I remember was the king's *interrogator*, leaving me to come for you."

"Will got to us before any irreversible damage was done. Elinore helped with the rest," Cora admitted.

Will leaned forward resting his elbows on his knees, the wooden chair beneath him groaning. "When I went to find Elinore I heard some of the castle guards talking about Lord Stevens. I think Addie may have done something."

Grant's brows rose, "Like what?"

"I couldn't hear everything but it sounded like there was some sort of argument with Addie and the lord and she struck him," Will stated hesitantly.

"And?" Grant gestured for Will to continue.

"Before he was forced out of the castle, his face was festering. The guards are talking and they think her power is from what happened in Alderbrooke Forest with your father," Will admitted.

"I need to speak to Addie," Grant moved to stand.

Elinore placed both hands on Grant's shoulders and forced him back against the bed, "You, my lord, *need* to rest for the next few days. I am happy to carry a message to the princess if you wish when I return in the morning."

Grant groaned in frustration, "Fine, but I want to see her soon or I am going to tear the castle down, stone by stone, to get to her. Do you understand?"

"I will be sure the princess gets to you as soon as she can slip past her guards," Elinore said walking toward a cot near the hearth. "Now, if you don't mind, I am in need of rest as well. Healing two seriously injured people and a large stupid buffoon's thumb is tiresome."

"You were the one to heal Vern?" Grant tilted his head.

Leaning back into the pillow on her cot, Elinore closed her eyes, "Unfortunately. I would have rather he lost his whole arm to some awful infection."

Will silently rose to his feet and headed toward the door leading to a small kitchen space. Before leaving, Grant watched as his friend leaned down and placed a light kiss atop Cora's head. Grant couldn't help but notice the slight limp in Will's step as he walked away.

"I'll take up watch until sunrise," Will rolled his neck and pushed the heavy door open.

"Why are you limping, Will?" Grant asked skeptically.

"I'm alright," Will deflected.

Cora rose to her feet quickly, as if just noticing his uneven steps, "Will, Why are you limping?"

"I was branded," Will's voice was even.

Elinore's sleepy voice drew Grant and Cora's attention as she slowly stood from her cot, "I can try to heal you."

"Only if you have the strength for it," Will turned to face Elinore now just an arm's length away.

"A brand should be no trouble. Burns are something I'm quite skilled with, actually. My father is a great smith in my village and I learned at a young age how to heal burns," Elinore smiled and held out her hands for Will.

He gently placed his large hand atop the young woman's palms. Confusion swept across her face almost instantly, "I cannot feel a brand? Was the burn treated by someone?"

Shaking his head, Will replied, "Not by a healer and I can assure you the brand is real." Will gingerly pulled the waistband of his trousers low enough to reveal the angry red blisters on the outer side of his hip. The king's warped insignia vivid on his skin. "The farrier that branded Shea and I used a salve to ease the pain though."

"Whatever the healing cream was, I think it's preventing me from healing you," Elinore admitted confused.

"Why didn't you say anything?" Cora stepped to Will's side.

Will faced the door again, "Because it didn't matter. I needed you both safe. My skin will heal in its own time"

"Will," Cora placed a gentle hand on Will's shoulder, eyes watering.

"I'm *fine*, Cora, truly. I will gladly bear this brand and every other mark on my soul for the rest of my life knowing that what I have done and endured gave me the time I needed to figure out a plan and get to you. My only regret is that either of you had to suffer at all because of my hesitation."

"We are alive because of you, brother. Don't for a moment think we do not know that. So ... thank you for that," Grant said with all sincerity, placed a fisted hand to his heart, and bowed his head in respect.

A heavy silence filled the room as Elinore returned to her cot and Cora ran a gentle hand down Will's arm. Despite the torture he had faced only a few hours ago, Grant felt an overwhelming thrum of pride in his chest. Regardless of the danger they all faced, Grant's closest friend had run head first into the lion's den to rescue him and Cora and brought them here safely. Exhaustion seemed to creep in over Grant the moment Will bowed to him and again kissed Cora's head before stepping into the adjoined room.

Deep sleep pulled Grant's conscious mind into a peaceful darkness. Dream's of Addie filled his mind and when Grant woke the gray light of the midday sun lit the floor at his bedside. Rustling and whispered voices from the kitchen drew his attention.

"She can sneak away tonight if he is recovered enough to get to the willow but if he is still too weak, we cannot risk bringing her here in case she is followed," Elinore's voice was wary.

Slowly, Grant pulled himself to his feet and his vision tunneled slightly. In three long strides, he stood at the door and pushed through, feigning a strength he wasn't sure he possessed yet.

"I *will* meet her tonight," Grant stood tall.

A grin spread across Will's face. "Did you get enough beauty sleep, your highness?" he joked, earning an elbow to the ribs from Cora.

"Plenty, thanks," Grant smirked, "Elinore, how is Addie?

Has anything changed?"

Elinore shook her head, "She is still accompanied at all times by the king's men but I do have some information about Lord Stevens. This is all hearsay from castle staff, so it must be taken with a grain of salt."

"What is it, Elinore?" Grant pushed.

"Some of the staff believe that Lord Stevens had some sort of leverage over the king and that is how he was able to secure his now severed betrothal to the princess," Elinore began. "The king had him taken into custody after the princess arrived but he is nowhere to be found."

"The king was really going to force Addie to marry that scum," anger rose in Grant's chest.

"Whatever he knew about the king must have been damning," Will inferred. "We need to find out what he knows. Cora, can you use your gift to see what Lord Stevens planned to do with what he knows?"

Cora took a bite of a crisp green apple and spoke around a mouth full, "If I can get close enough to Lord Stevens or King Colvin I can see what their future holds but that doesn't tell me what he has on the king. It could be helpful to know the king's intentions though."

"You're not setting foot in that castle with the man that had you whipped," Will said ominously.

Scoffing, Cora faced Will, "Thank you for your concern but I will do as I please. If you are worried about my safety then you are free to join me."

"We can see if Addie can get you both in when we meet tonight," Grant nodded.

Elinore collected her basket from the table at the center of the room. "I will head back now and let her know we are on

234

for tonight then. I must collect a few supplies for the kitchen so no one questions my being in the forest for so long. I will relay everything to the princess."

"Thank you again, Elinore. We know this is not a safe task for you to take on," Cora gave a small nod of gratitude.

"Many in this kingdom feel the king no longer has their best interest at heart. I am glad to aid you in any way I can," Elinore smiled sweetly before departing to set their meeting into motion.

Chapter 28

Addie

"The princess has requested my assistance," Elinore's shoulders held firm as she stared down the two large guards standing on either side of Addie's doors.

"The king has specifically stated no one is to enter the princess's chambers without his approval," the fair hair guard refused to look at Elinore.

From behind the closed door, Addie spoke with undeniable authority, "Then it will be your heads when my father discovers you denied his daughter aid from *his* personal healer."

Fear flooded the young guard's face. Turning to his counterpart, both men nodded to each other and pulled the doors wide for Elinore to enter.

"Wise choice gentlemen," Addie smiled wickedly before slamming the door shut behind her new friend. "How is he? When I saw him escaping last night I was sure he was near death. I should have followed them into the woods but the guards were everywhere. I couldn't risk them being caught because of me," Addie's voice was low.

"His strength is returning. I think he may still be more worn than he lets on but he wants to see you tonight under the willow if you are able to get away," Elinore whispered skeptically.

"Will you be able to take my place here while I am gone? I know I ask a lot."

Elinore laughed lightly, "Oh yes princess. Being trapped in a well heated room with a plush bed and a library at my disposal tonight will be very difficult."

Addie scoffed, "You know that is not the danger. If you are discovered ... I am asking you to put your life at risk for me."

"If you aim to help this kingdom, I am more than happy to play my role here, even if the cost is ultimately my life, your highness," Elinore's voice was serious. "I have spent a lot of my life trying to get to where I am now to help my family. After what you did, going after Lord Anderson, I have faith you want the same things many of *us* do."

"Thank you Elinore, and please, it's Addie," Addie placed a soft hand on Elinore's shoulder. "I will need you here tonight unseen so I can get to Grant."

"I will be here when you return from dinner," Elinore bowed before departing.

The hours before dinner felt like they crawled by. Alone in her rooms, Addie prepared as much as she could for any dangers she might face once she left her rooms after nightfall. She had spent most of the early evening ensuring her favorite dagger was honed to a razor sharp edge and everything was ready for her escape. Beneath her full billowy gown she donned her leather pants and vest.

"Your highness, dinner has been prepared and your attendance is requested by the king," one of the guards spoke from the hall.

Addie sheathed her dagger at her thigh and made for the door. "Fine," She huffed and the door swung open slowly.

The hall's were empty except for Addie and her two assigned guardians. As they entered the great hall, the king rose from the head of the table with an obviously forced smile. On his right, the queen sat looking more emaciated than Addie had remembered. Her eldest brother entered just behind her.

Bending low, Prince Andrew spoke quietly into Addie's ear, "We should meet in the garden for a game tonight."

Shifting to see her brother, Addie's eyes were wide, "I have a previous engagement with a friend. Can it wait?"

"I believe we should all play together if your friend is who I believe them to be," Andrew raised a brow.

Addie nodded slightly and took her seat next to her mother. "Hello Mother. How are you feeling today?"

For the past several years, Addie's mother, Queen Arma, had been suffering from an unknown ailment not even Addie had been able to cure. Seated next to her now, one would assume the queen had been the one recovering from a sword through her chest.

"I'm tired, my dear, but I am so glad to see you home. I have missed you these past days. Your father said you were on an adventure. Did you enjoy yourself?" the queen's voice was weak.

Tear's filled Addie's eyes. Her father had lied to the queen about her whereabouts and Addie struggled to find the words she needed to speak.

"Oh, my sweet girl?" Queen Arma placed her too frail hands on Addie's cheeks, "Have I misspoken? Please don't cry."

"No, mama. I have just missed you too," Addie wiped unshed tears from her eyes. "My journey was quite difficult but I discovered a lot while I was gone."

"Good. Sometimes the most difficult journeys teach us the most," her mother smiled softly and kissed her daughter's braided hair.

Addie's father cleared his throat loudly, silencing the room. "I would like to make a toast to you both, children." Addie looked to Andrew for clarification but her brother shrugged and shook his head in confusion. "To you, princess, I toast to your safe return and your health, may you thrive in your recovery and to you, my *son*, I toast to your gifts, may they always lead you clear of danger."

Addie watched her brother swallow hard before he raised his glass at his father's side, "Thank you, father."

The echoing chime of crystal glasses rang through Addie's ears as she tried to decipher her father's cryptic toast. The strangely bitter wine lingering on her tongue. Despite the seemingly pleasant wishes, a deeper malice lay within the king's words that Addie did not fully understand. The remainder of dinner passed without conversation, only the occasional scrape of someone's utensils against porcelain broke the deafening silence.

"May I be excused and retire for the evening? I am surprisingly tired," Addie hadn't expected to feel the exhaustion she claimed but an odd sluggish feeling settled in her belly.

A sharp grin stretched across the king's face, "Of course, daughter. You need your rest after your journey."

Standing swiftly, Addie swept through the halls and back

to her rooms on clumsy feet. Once the double doors to her chambers closed behind her, Elinore exited the bathroom.

"Princess! Are you alright?" Elinore rushed to Addie's side and took in her clammy, pale skin and weary expression.

"I'm tired," Addie's words mirrored the queen's words before dinner. Realization bloomed across her face.

"What is it, Addie," Elinore reached out with a glowing palm and took Addie's hand. "Holy shit... I think you've been poisoned!"

"I think you may be right. What should I do?" Addie made her way into the bathing chamber.

"You need to purge your stomach. Who do you think did this?" Elinor swept several loose strands of hair from Addie's face as she leaned over the large tub at the center of the room.

"I think," Addie forced out the contents of her stomach, "I think it was the king... I think he has been poisoning my mother. I need you to help me get to her room."

Elinore pulled a small linen towel to Addie's side, "Of course, princess. Was anyone else at dinner with you three tonight?"

"My brother was there too. After I leave my rooms I need you to get to him and make sure he is alright," Addie stood and wiped her face.

"I can get a few things from the kitchens on my way to Andrew's chambers to combat whatever you ingested," Elinore replied.

Elinore's comfort using the prince's first name did not go unnoticed by Addie but in her current situation she knew it would be a topic for a future discussion with her new friend. After forcing every drop of food and wine from her body, Addie hurried unsteadily through her room and collected two more daggers from a hidden compartment in her bedside table.

"Are you sure you will be alright on your own?" Elinore worried aloud.

"Yes. I can already feel the fog lifting. I think my healing gift will help eliminate the rest of the toxins. You need to get to the prince quickly."

Together, Addie and Elinore stepped to the window and began their descent to the floor below Addie's room. Slowly, Addie pried open the large stained glass window in the hall and slipped into the dim light on shaky legs. Just behind her, Elinore landed with immense grace and followed her for several minutes before silently splitting down a separate hall leading to the kitchens and the prince's chambers beyond.

As Addie neared the king and queen's suites, dread pooled in her gut. Utter silence filled the air. Peaking low around the final turn, Addie had expected to see the two men that had been assigned to her mother's protection detail for the night, but instead, the room was left entirely unguarded. Quickly, Addie sprinted for the door and threw herself inside. Frantically, she scanned the sitting area and headed to her mother's bedchamber. Atop the large bed on the far end of the room, Addie's mother's body lay motionless.

"Mother?" Addie's plea fell from her lips.

Moving to stand by her side, she lay a glowing palm on the damp skin of her mother's arm. A nearly inaudible groan escaped the queen's throat.

"I need you to vomit, Mother. Please, I think father poisoned us all," Addie pulled the chamber pot from beneath the bed and forced her mother onto her side.

After several attempts to rouse her, Addie was finally able

to open the queen's eyes and forced her index and middle fingers into her mother's mouth and down her throat.

"That's it Mother. Get as much of that out as you can," a small sigh of relief left Addie's chest.

"Addie," Queen Arma choked out, "If he has started to poison you too, I need you to leave this place. Find your brother and take him with you."

"I am not leaving you here. Andrew is being helped as we speak," Addie ran a caressing hand over her mothers sweat slicked hair, "I need you to rest."

Without another word, Addie's mother drifted to sleep; her breaths once again even and steady.

"I'm going to fix all of this. I promise," Addie leaned forward and placed a soft kiss on the queen's brow before going in search of Andrew.

Chapter 29

Elinore

The kitchens were surprisingly empty as Elinore skidded around the open door from the main hallway. She threw all caution out the window the moment Addie's confession of Andrew's involvement left the princess's lips. There was no obstacle Elinore wasn't willing to overcome to make sure the prince survived whatever toxins most likely coursed through his system.

Throwing open the pantry doors, Elinore collected the hem of her skirt in her hands and filled the makeshift pocket with every herb and possible ingredient she could think of that might help counteract the poison. In less than a minute, she was racing through the final short hallway that led to Andrew's rooms. She did not stop to knock at the door, instead barreled through the entry and found the prince on his hands and knees halfway between his bed and his bathing chambers.

"Andrew," Elinore shrieked as she dropped to her knees,

spilling the contents of her skirt and a small slip of paper across the floor before the prince. "You need to get everything you consumed tonight out of your body now."

Andrew's voice was breathy as he spoke, "Elinore, what is happening to me? I can't breathe."

"We believe your father poisoned you all at dinner. Now, throw up in this," Elinore dumped the bouquet of floral greenery from the large ceramic vase that sat on the table at the edge of the lounge over her shoulder.

Forcefully, the prince began to purge his stomach into the ornate container. Elinore wasn't sure she had ever heard a more beautiful sound until the prince spoke again, his voice was rough, "Who is 'we' and who all did my father poison?"

"Addie and I. And we both think he poisoned you, Addie, and the queen," Elinore raised a hand to calm the startled panic in the prince's eyes before she continued, "Addie is fine now and is tending to your mother as we speak. Let me help you and I will tell you everything as soon as you are healed."

Andrew rocked back and leaned his shoulders against the large velvet chaise. It was then that Elinore realized the state in which she had found the prince. Wearing only his under shorts, the prince's muscular legs stretched out before her and his beautifully sculpted chest and core glistened with sweat from having just vomited the entire contents of his stomach.

Clearing her throat, Elinore clenched and unclenched her hands in her lap, "I'm not sure if my gifts are much help in this type of scenario but I brought other supplies just in case I cannot help."

Andrew closed his eyes and tried to pull in a deep breath but failed, "Anything you can do will be greatly appreciated."

"I'm going to have to touch your chest. Is that alright?" Elinore raised a glowing palm.

Andrew opened his eyes slightly and cocked a devilish smile, "You've healed my body before, Elinore. Except for the fact that I am awake and nearly naked this isn't any different."

"I guess you're right," Elinore swallowed hard then stretched forward to place her right hand on the prince's chest. "Your lungs feels like it's filled with glass but I think I can fix it for the most part. I have no idea what the king used to cause so much damage."

The skin under Elinore's hand began to glow a faint white and thin curving tendrils of light swirled across the plains of the prince's chest. Slowly, Andrew's breathing became less labored and the faint blue hue of his lips faded back to their normal rosy color.

Panting slightly, Elinore lifted her hand from Andrew's body and braced herself on her hands and knees, "That. Should. Help," she managed between breaths.

"Elinore," concern soaked Andrew's voice, "are you alright? What did you do?"

"I'm alright. I'm not the most powerful healer. The closer you are to death, the more exhausted I become," she replied, rolling to her side and resting her head on the arm of the lounge beside Andrew.

"Would any of the things you brought with you have been a better option then?" Andrew sifted through the pile of goods scattered around them both.

"Probably, but none of them would have worked as quickly and I couldn't risk that," Elinore exhaled.

"Cinnamon sticks would have helped?" the prince raised a curious brow and held up a jar with several rolled cinnamon

245

sticks inside.

"I've used it for a lot of things, like fungal infections, for my father when I was young. It seemed like a smart grab," Elinore shrugged.

"What about th.." Andrew began to speak but paused before he continued, "What is this, Elinore?" In his hand, the prince held up a small scrap of rolled parchment.

Elinore felt like the floor was falling out from beneath her. Still unable to catch her breath completely, she watched the prince open and read her most recent correspondence she had yet to burn. There would be no way for her to deny or misconstrued what he read. In her heart, Elinore had no real desire to lie to the prince anyway.

"Who is 'R' and why do you carry a note about my sister? And do not lie to me Elinore. I can see your thoughts," Andrew moved to stand over her, sharp probes of his power scraping her mind, anger and wariness in his eyes.

For a moment, Elinore saw a flash of Vern standing over her in his chambers; both of his vile hands reaching forward and forcing her to kneel before his exposed body. Instantly, Elinore recoiled into herself. Voice low and filled with fear, she tucked her head against her propped knees, tears filling her eyes, "I know what power you possess. I have no intention of lying to you."

"Oh gods, Elinore. I'm so sorry," genuine remorse stained Andrew's words as he dropped to his knees before her, "I saw… I felt… I didn't mean to… please forgive me."

Trying her best to force the memory from her mind, Elinore continued to explain, "The note is from Rose, the necromancer. I received it just before your sister arrived back at the castle. I was sent here to help find out what the king plans to do in the southern parts of the kingdom. Most of the rebel attacks aren't actually *rebel* attacks at all. They are attacks carried out by men and women from the isle to the east that were hired by your father. We think he is trying to eliminate any powerful magic wielders in Viridia that he cannot control. I'm here to find out where he is going to strike next in order to warn the people of this kingdom."

"You're a rebel?" Andrew said, confused

"Yes, but we aren't the villains the king paints us to be. We want the same things I believe you and the princess want," Elinore admitted.

"And what is that?" Andrew asked.

"A unified people that are safe in their homes despite what power they possess or what value the king believes them to have," Elinore's voice rose slightly.

Andrew held up the note once more, "And what weapon is Rose referring to here? She wrote *'They have received their weapons. I hope they reach Addie soon'*"

"Rose commissioned my father to forge two swords and an ax from enchanted steel for her daughter, William Banks, and Grant Anderson. Her daughter, Cora, had a premonition that they would find Addie and Rose wanted to ensure they had the best chance possible of saving her," Elinore concluded.

"Why didn't you tell me sooner?" Andrew asked, sounding almost hurt.

Elinore shrugged and shook her head, "I needed to make sure you were someone I could trust and I wouldn't be at the end of a rope or sword if I told you."

"And you trust me,"the prince stated as a fact.

"Yes. More than I trust most actually," the last several words came out in a mumble.

"I'm sorry I invaded your privacy and caused that memory," Andrew placed a hand on Elinore's shoulder, "My gift only allows me to see a person's current thought through their eyes. I had no intention of forcing you to see what you saw."

"I believe you. It's happened a few times these past few days and I have no idea what to do about it. I never know what is going to trigger it either. Yesterday, one of the guards dropped a stack of parchment on a desk in the map room. It sounded like a snap and all I could see or hear was that fucking whip," tears fell slowly down Elinore's face.

"The fucker *whipped* you?!" Elinore could hear Andrew's jaw clench, "I'm going to kill him."

"I'll race you to it," Elinore let out a humorless laugh.

"If that is what you need, my lady, I will gladly give you my sword to do it," Andrew bowed.

"Thank you for not judging me," Elinore's voice was soft again.

"Judge you for what? Nothing that happened was your fault. If anyone other than that monster is to blame it would be me. I antagonized him and gave him you as a target. And for that I am truly sorry. I will never forgive myself for that," Andrew admitted.

"But why me? I don't understand. I am insignificant and of no importance to you or this kingdom, as far as he knows. Why would Vern care about me?" Elinore rambled.

"Because I did. Because I do. I find you stunning and intriguing. He knew hurting you would hurt me," Andrew's brows pulled together forming two perfectly parallel lines between them. "I will not let that happen ever again. I promise you, Elinore."

The sincerity in Andrew's words warmed Elinore to her

core. Apart from her own father, no other living person in this world had cared whether she lived or died. The prince's words felt like a confession from the depths of his soul, spoken directly to hers.

A soft smile spread across her face, "Thank you, Andrew. And just so you know, I do not hold anything that happened to me against you."

Gently, Andrew collected Elinore's hand into his own and placed a small kiss atop her knuckles. Together they rose to their feet and Andrew tentatively pulled her in for a hug.

"Um, Andrew," Elinore whispered into his ear.

"Yes, my lady," Andrew breathed deep into Elinore's hair.

"You are still mostly nude and Addie is standing in the doorway," Elinore replied sheepishly.

"Do you not knock either, Addie," the prince chided playfully before turning to his sister.

"If you two are finished here, can you get dressed so we can get to Grant?" Addie lifted a knowing brow at her brother.

Quickly, Andrew grabbed a white tunic from the back of a chair near the window and pulled it over his head, followed by dark blue linen pants from the floor. Addie stepped to his side and kicked over one of his boots from beneath the chaise.

As he slipped into his boots, all traces of lightheartedness faded, "How is mother?"

"She's alright for now but she is dying. I can't heal her," Addie admitted.

"How did we not know?" Andrew asked himself.

Elinore shook her head thinking aloud, "If the king has been dosing her for as long as you think, there is no way you would have. Her symptoms probably started to appear the same way any illness would, with fatigue and shortness of breath. I think the king intended to kill all of you tonight. That's why the castle is empty; no one would accidentally find you and save you."

"We need to get to Grant as soon as we can and let them know everything. Are you ready?" Addie turned to her brother.

"Let's go," Andrew stood, sword in hand, and opened his patio doors into the gardens beyond.

Chapter 30

Grant

Grant tucked himself into the shadows beneath the old willow with Will and Cora and waited for the sound of Addie's approach. She should have been to the meeting point nearly an hour ago and everyone's nerves were high. The echo of hurried feet crept through the swaying branches. Cora and Will moved out from behind the tree's large, twisted trunk, weapons drawn.

"That's more than one set of boots," Cora whispered and stepped between Will and Grant.

"Do you think it could be Elinore *and* Addie?" Will asked skeptically.

"I hope so," Cora replied, "We are in serious trouble if it's castle guards."

The thick curtain of foliage opened slowly before Addie stepped into the wide open canopy. The small lantern in her hand cast flickering light across Grant's scowling face. The sight of her friends prepared to attack stopped her short.

"It's alright. It's me. Elinore and my brother are right behind me," Addie said, raising her hands high.

"Thank the gods," Grant exhaled, face softening. Relief flooded his heart and he dropped his sword to the ground before racing to Addie's side.

"Sorry we're later than expected," Andrew's voice was deep and still slightly raspy.

"What happened?" Grant asked, pulling Addie into his arms.

Elinore breathed out a hard breath, "Someone tried to assassinate Andrew, Addie, and the queen tonight. We believe the king poisoned them all at dinner."

Fury burned in Grant's eyes as he pushed Addie's shoulders out far enough for him to get a better view of the length of her body. His eyes made frenzied paths up and down her frame before resting on her face. With both hands, Grant cupped Addie's cheeks and pulled her face toward his own and searched for any sign of trauma.

"I'm going to kill him," Grant's voice was thick with the wrath that brewed in his chest.

"That would be unwise. We are fine— for now; although our mother is much worse off. We think our father has been poisoning her for some time and she is not truly sick from some *incurable* illness," a single tear ran down Addie's cheek as she spoke.

"What do we do about it?" Will asked hopefully.

Andrew shook his head, "We don't know if the damage that has been done can be undone. Perhaps with time, she may recover if we can stop the king's further doses. As for the king, we need to find a way to remove him from his seat on the throne without an uproar and without innocent people dying."

"What do you suggest we do, brother? We can't kill him," Addie stated, shaken.

Cora cleared her throat before she spoke, "Actually, I think we probably could. I mean, if he has been poisoning the queen, why can't we get a powerful sedative into one of his drinks and take him out the same way?"

Elinore shrugged, "I could get close enough to him to do it as his healer. If anyone thinks there has been foul play I can tell them he has been struggling with the same illness as the queen but is too proud to show weakness."

"That could work but you would need to do it over a prolonged period of time so people see him getting progressively worse before the final, you know, *gluk*," Will said, running his index finger across his throat, gesturing to the king's impending demise.

Andrew frowned, "Elinore, would you be okay with doing that? You would be putting yourself into even greater danger. You already risk too much."

"Holy shit, I do know you," Cora snapped her fingers in Elinore's direction. "You're Talos's daughter."

Grant and Will both turned to face Cora and spoke simultaneously, "Who is Talos?"

"Henry Talos. He is the smith that forged your swords and my ax. I've met you once before, when we were younger," Cora again turned and spoke to Elinore. "Why do you serve the king?"

"I am here to keep *our* people and your mother informed of the king's plans. I moved into the castle almost two years ago but had to wait until now to become the king's personal healer," Elinore explained.

Silence descended over the group. The weight of every recent spoken truth hung heavy in the air. Grant held Addie's hand in his own and relished in her closeness. Had he known how close he was to losing her tonight, after just finding her again, Grant felt he would have done anything to get to her, no matter how reckless.

"We need to be kept informed on everything that is happening in the castle," Grant stated, facing Addie, "Could you meet us here in the evenings after dark?"

"That isn't going to be a wise idea," the prince spoke.

"Unfortunately, my brother is right. Once a week might be our safest option," Addie reluctantly agreed.

Grant knew his request was selfish but wasn't sure being separated from Addie for long stretches of time wasn't going to drive him insane with the constant fear that something horrible could happen. "I would be more comfortable knowing you are all safe. Is there no way we would be able to meet more frequently?"

Elinore smiled and shrugged, "I am of no real importance to the guards and many of the servants here harvest from the forest's edge every few days. I could meet at the cabin a few times throughout the week to ease your mind, my lord."

A near inaudible groan of frustration escaped the prince's mouth before his words fell from his lips, "Elinore, you need to stop with the self degradation, please. You are not unimportant or insignificant."

"What I mean is, I will not be watched to the extent you and Addie are," Elinore clarified. "If either of you were to wander through the wood's, you would be followed. I, on the other hand, will not be."

"She's right, Andrew," Addie placed a gentle hand on her

brother's shoulder. "No matter how much I would rather meet more often myself, it is far too risky."

"Fine, " Andrew agreed finally, "but you are going to be armed at all times."

With a small, broken smile, Elinore reached into the hidden pocket of her skirts and unsheathed the dagger that had been strapped to her thigh, "I always am as of late, your highness."

The prince knit his brows together and sighed, "As you should be."

"Then it's settled," Cora exhaled, "We will meet here once a week starting this night. Elinore will frequent our cabin as often as safety allows."

In a nod of agreement from everyone, Andrew and Elinore stepped out into the night followed by Cora and Will, leaving Grant and Addie alone. Despite the years spent apart, the flutter in Grant's chest he remembered as a young man had bloomed to life once again over the past several days. The look in Addie's eyes told him she too felt the same.

"I don't like not knowing whether or not you are safe in that place," Grant admitted.

"Nor do I with you out here,"Addie rested her head on Grant's chest. "I need to know you're safe but risking being followed into the woods every night isn't a chance I can take."

"I know, princess. I will promise to stay out of trouble if you do," Grant rested his chin on the top of Addie's head.

"I will do my best," Addie smiled.

"That doesn't give me much reassurance," Grant jokes lightly. "Just be safe and look after the queen until we can make a move."

"I will. I think if Elinore and I work together we may be able to speed up some of her healing," Addie stated hopefully.

"Then I will see you in a week, your highness," before Addie could reply Grant grabbed her chin between his thumb and index finger, pulling her lips to his. Grant's heart thrummed so loudly in his chest he was sure the rest of their companions outside of the confines of the willow's weeping branches could hear. With one final embrace, Addie and Grant separated and stepped out into the darkness blanketing the forest beyond.

Chapter 31

Elinore

The week following Addie's return to the castle filled the halls with a nervous energy Elinore couldn't seem to escape. King Colvin had become exceedingly paranoid following his toast to his children and had demanded Elinore examine him daily for any sign of illness. He had attempted to frame his sudden fear for his health around his wife's declining condition but Elinore knew better. His actions were truly in fear of retaliation from his children. The fact that he hadn't discovered her involvement and the true roll she played made her almost joyous.

Each morning, Elinore provided her 'healing aid' and issued a clear bill of health despite the death she could feel slowly encroaching upon him. Every time her glowing golden hands rested on his skin, she could feel the growing poison in his system from the night cap he poured himself each evening. With a pleased smile, she found any small scrape or bruise on the surface of his skin to heal in order to maintain the illusion that she was keeping him safe.

It had been almost two weeks of secret meetings and Elinore had still not heard any notable news to pass along to Grant and the other's regarding Lord Anderson. The sun had already made its descent beyond the horizon and the dark sky overhead seemed to house an unending storm. Having concluded her daily tasks, Elinore made her way back through the servant hall that ran along the length of the king's personal quarters. The whisper of an unfamiliar male voice drew her attention.

"Your Majesty, are you alone?"

Elinore instantly stopped and pressed her ear to the wall separating the two chambers.

"*Not here,*" King Colvin's voice was filled with disgust. "This way."

The sound of hurried feet shuffled past Elinore's vantage and moved deeper into the king's study. Quickly, Elinore moved down the main servant's hall on silent feet and tucked herself into the impossibly tight crawl space between the far wall of King Colvin's study and his adjoining bedchamber. Pressing her ear to the cold stone, Elinore listened with bated breath.

"Have you lost your fucking mind completely?! I thought I made myself very clear. Our correspondence must never happen here. You cannot be seen." King Colvin hissed. "What do you need so desperately that you would come here? If you are seen, I will have no choice but to execute you. My people cannot know."

The stranger's voice was filled with what sounded like terror, "There has been movement in the forest."

Several seconds passed in tense silence before King Colvin

responded, "Is it him?"

"My men only saw the creatures, your Majesty. But, we believe they are the beasts Lord Anderson created. They were moving south toward our encampment near Onyx Hollow," the man's voice was shaky.

"How many are there?"

"I do not know. At least three hundred from what we have gathered, possibly more in hiding. We cannot continue with our agreement. My people are not equipped to fight the dead."

A loud crash reverberated through the wall, startling Elinore back and sending flecks of broken stone and dust through the air around her in the confined space. The king's voice was much closer now as she pressed in again.

Just on the other side of the wall he spoke with malice coating his every word, "Listen to me. I own you. Your king has given you and *your* people to me and you will do as *I* command. If your usefulness has come to an end, I will have every one of you dismembered slowly and leave you to the beasts of the forest."

A chill ran down Elinore's spine and she swore she could hear the stranger's skull grinding against stone.

When he finally spoke his words were gargled by what Elinore could only assumed was a mouth filled with blood, "My apologies, your Majesty."

A soft thud on the ground at her feet let Elinore know King Colvin had let the man fall to the floor. "To my displeasure, I still need you," the king spoke through clenched teeth, "My family has spent centuries reclaiming this kingdom from the retched unworthy. I will not let everything fall apart now, not after what has been done. History will be written in

259

my favor and my family's legacy will not be tarnished. Even the genocides of our past will be seen in glory once I have succeeded in ridding the kingdom of those unworthy to wield power."

"Then we shall move on Shepherd's Glen and Onyx Hollow in the coming weeks as planned then?" the man sounded defeated as he pulled his body from the floor.

A pained gasp left Elinore's lungs. She threw her hand over her mouth to silence her outburst too late. The king's study fell silent just before King Colvin's calamitous steps rushed through the room, headed for the entrance to the servant's hall in his bedchamber. In an instant, Elinore squeezed back into the main servant's corridor and sprinted towards the passage that would lead her past the kitchens to her hopeful escape. She was nearly certain King Colvin's size would hinder his ability to move swiftly through the tightly constructed maze of servant passages throughout the castle but she refused to slow her pace until she was no longer in his path.

As she reached her next turn, King Colvin's voice boomed and echoed off the wall's, "I know you're in here, little rat!"

Elinore's lungs burned but she forced herself on, down the passage and around several more turns until the flickering light of her safe haven shown below a narrow wooden door. She ran full force through the door and landed with a clatter on the floor of a large sitting room. At the opposite end of the room, Prince Andrew leapt to his feet in shock, knocking the book he had been reading to the ground as he drew a throwing knife from his vest.

"Help me," Elinore pleaded breathlessly. "Your father is in the passageway. He's coming."

Instantly, Andrew was at her side pulling her to her feet. With one arm, he swept Elinore from the ground and moved to collect the lamp he had been reading by, from the table. In several long strides, they reached his bedroom. Quickly, he shut the door and gently placed Elinore on the large bed at the center of the room.

"Take off your shoes and gown and get under the blankets," Andrew directed as he pulled his shirt and vest off.

"What?" Elinore balked.

"If he is coming this way, I need him to think whoever is here with me is... *occupied*," Andrew lifted a brow and proceeded to remove his pants. "Do you trust me?"

With a subtle nod, Elinore proceeded to follow the prince's instructions and tuck herself under the thick blankets out of sight in only her thin linen shift. Her bare feet showing below the bedding. The room went dark as Andrew blew out the lamp and his warm hands found her beneath the sheets.

In a gentle whisper, the prince spoke into her ear at her side as he climbed into the bed with her, "I promise you I am not naked. I still have on my braies. I don't want to scare you in any way, but I am going to need to prop my body over yours. Is that alright?"

Elinore inhaled deeply and nodded into the dark before realizing the prince was most likely unable to see her response.

"Alright," her voice sounded more breathless than she had expected.

Slowly, Andrew settled his left knee at her side and pulled his body over hers. Heat radiated from his chest just inches from her own. She knew if she breathed in too deeply her bust would most likely graze his. She had expected to feel fear but instead her heart began to race for another reason.

Above her, Andrew's breathing grew heavy and she could hear his heart racing as well.

"Elinore," his voice was ragged and filled with what she thought sounded like longing.

Before he could continue, the door to his bedchamber flew open, smashing into the wall with a bang. King Colvin crashed into the room, sword in hand. A terrified shriek escaped from Elinore as Andrew whirled on his father. Keeping her blocked from sight, Andrew covered his lower half from view as he got to his feet.

"Father! What are you doing?! Get out!" Andrew barked. "I'm in the middle of something, if you couldn't tell."

King Colvin diverted his gaze back toward the two guards now standing in Andrew's main sitting room and let out an angered groan. "They must have gone through the kitchen!"

"What are you talking about?!" the prince continued to protest, throwing his free hand into the air.

"Never mind. Finish with your *whore*," the king grunted as he walked back through the prince's door. "But know this, son, I will not tolerate illegitimate heirs."

The door slammed shut behind King Colvin and silence settled over the room. Flickers of moonlight broke through the dark clouds overhead, casting shadows through the window. Elinore slowly stood from the bed and stepped to Andrew's side.

"Thank you," her voice was a whisper.

"I told you before, Elinore. I am *always* here for you. Any time, day or night," Andrew replied. "I do, however, need to know what just happened though. Are you alright?"

Elinore quickly told Andrew everything she had heard as they both dressed and collected themselves.

"We're meant to meet at the willow tomorrow. I can tell the others everything then but I need to get back to my room and get word to Rose and my father tonight if I can," Elinore concluded.

"My father was supposed to be meeting with Gavin just south of the northern front tomorrow. If he chooses to stay after everything tonight, Addie and I will need to stay behind," Andrew thought aloud, "Can you get to their cabin in the morning if he does not leave?"

"Yes, I believe so," Elinore nodded.

"Good. Find out what Cora can see but please, be safe. Tonight was too close," pain stained Andrew's confession. "Had he found you... He would have done far worse than kill you, Elinore."

Chapter 32

Cora

"My mother will be the easiest for me to see. As for Onyx Hollow, I may be able to see your father but I'm not sure how helpful either vision will be," Cora shrugged sympathetically, her mouth twisting to the side.

Will, Grant, and Cora sat around the small table in the kitchen of General Banks's hunting cabin while Elinore paced the length of the room.The sun had just crested the tree tops, the sky above was still darkened by thick storm clouds.

Roughly ten minutes ago, Cora and her companions woke to the sound of Elinore signaling with a hurried dove call from the tree line. To their surprise, she quickly explained what had transpired the night before in the confines of the servant's passageway. Shortly after waking this morning, Elinore heard word of King Colvin's decision to remain at the castle from one of the other women in the kitchens. Grant's obvious disappointment at Addie's absence was overshadowed buy his desire to know any information Cora could add about his father's possible location.

"I have already received word from your mother. She intends to leave for Shepherd's Glen as soon as she is able," Elinore pulled a small, rolled scrap of paper from her pocket and passed it to Cora. "My father hasn't responded to my raven and I fear the worst."

Slowly, Cora read over the small slip of paper before handing it back to Elinore, who proceeded to toss the scrap into the small fire burning in the hearth. Grant shifted impatiently in his seat. Responsibility weighted heavy on Cora's shoulders. Subconsciously, she gnawed on her bottom lip.

"Anything you are able to see will be helpful, Cora," Will wrapped his arm around Cora's shoulders.

"This is the first possible news we have heard about my father since the cave. We need to know where he is going and what we face," Grant squeezed his eyes shut and pinched the bridge of his nose.

"It's not that simple," Cora exhaled. "There are so many factors that can impact what I see. Plus, visions that find me, like the one you saw in my nightmare, are far more reliable than the ones I search for. But I will try. You know I need to know as much as possible just as badly as you do, Grant."

Elinore finally halted her pacing entirely and leaned against the basin sink at Cora's right. "What do you need from me in order to see my father?"

"Just your hand," Cora held out her arm towards Elinore with her palm facing the ceiling.

Elinore's smaller hand fell into Cora's and slowly Cora closed her eye's in concentration. When her eyes opened again, clouded white replaced the beautiful green of her irises.

265

She spoke in an eerily calm tone, "The smith stands with his people. Onyx Hollow readies to move north as one."

"Are they going to make it here before the king's rebels strike?" Elinore squeezed Cora's hand tightly, discoloring the tips of her fingers a deep red.

"Danger looms at their back. The smith will protect his people and lead those he can north," Cora blinked hard and shook her head clearing here eyes to their natural emerald green.

Elinore quivered at her side, slow tears rolling down her cheeks, "So they are going to make it out?"

"Everything was so unstable. I think they are preparing to leave together but I don't know when. My vision was distorted and jumped from image to image. It looked like Onyx Hollow is loading all of the children to leave but its going to be close."

"Was there any sign of my father or the death wraiths?" Grant pressed.

"Not that I could see in Onyx Hollow. If the man Elinore heard was correct though, Shepherd's Glen is the only other township that far south," Cora furrowed her brows. She rolled her shoulders before laying both of her hands flat against the table in front of her and again closed here eyes.

"The necromancer meets weary travelers on the road. The dead move south. The lord waits in sorrow."

Again Cora's eye's cleared. She blinked hard and pushed herself from the table, "I can't see clearly. Lord Anderson looks to return to his home. That much I can see. I don't know what he intends or when he will reach Shepherd's Glen."

"What do we do now?" Will asked skeptically.

"We can send a raven to Ren but if my mother meets

266

them on the road they may already be preparing to move. Unfortunately, I can't tell what the timeline is for anything," Cora groaned in frustration.

"Then we send ravens. My father wouldn't hurt innocent people."

"The man he *was* and the one he has *become* are not the same," Cora refuted.

"I know," Grant admitted, "I think all we can do at the moment is try to keep everyone informed and vigilant."

Chapter 33

Addie

Time passed in a blurred facade of normalcy. Addie returned to her expected role as princess, being seen but rarely heard. Andrew once again stepped into his place as heir and sat at his father's side for every council and war meeting; all the while Elinore secretly monitored the toxin the king consumed in his poison laced nightcap after dinner each night. Despite their need for discretion, Andrew struggled to keep quiet as reports flooded the king's desk daily of attacks in the southern most parts of the kingdom. Small towns and villages called repeatedly for aid but their cries continued to fall on the king's deaf ears.

Two days after Elinore's encounter with the king in the servant's passage, Addie and her brother sat atop the dais beside their father and listened as two young men gave first-hand accounts of the tragedies their homes were experiencing but the king only offered his condolences for the gruesome attacks the poor families endured.

"I do understand. But I cannot, at this time, send aid with you. We are at risk of losing the northern border to the kingdom of Alizari if we separate our forces," King Calvin's voice was empty.

"Father!" Andrew interjected, unwilling to hold his tongue any longer, "We are losing *our* people in the south. We can't continue to stand by and do nothing. They aren't asking for an army of troops. They are asking for resources necessary for their families to survive the winter after being robbed of everything they have worked for this past year," Andrew argued.

"Enough," King Calvin's voice was level and stern.

"You mean to continue to ostracize your own people for what?! A war with Alizari that you instigate?! How many more of your citizens have to die before you correct the mistakes *you* are making?!" Frustration laced every one of the prince's words.

Cold, calculated rage filled the king's eyes, "You sound like a sympathizer."

"Then my point is being made as intended," Andrew spoke through clenched teeth.

"Andrew is right, father. Your people are dying and we are sitting on our hands here," Addie added.

"Neither of you know the struggles of ruling this kingdom! It would be wise for you *both* to follow my direction," the king rose from his seat dismissing the two men seeking his counsel, fatigue evident in his steps down the dais.

"But your direction is killing innocent citizens that are begging for your help," Andrew followed behind his father through the great hall.

"That is enough, Andrew! I will not entertain your ramblings anymore. Tomorrow I am sending you to the front with Gavin so you too can see where the true danger resides," the king bellowed.

"No! Father, please," Addie hurried to his side.

"I would have sent you north too, long ago, if I thought you could be of use. You are unhelpful in war and I'm afraid you must remain here for me to *deal* with," the king spat the words out like venom.

"So instead you aim to send both of your male heirs into the one place you have deemed so dangerous you can't spare any resources to aid in the south? You are either a foolish king or a mad one," Addie shouted.

King Colvin's rage erupted. Turning swiftly, the back of his hand collided hard with Addie's face, throwing her to the floor, blood splattering from her mouth across the tile. The symphony of shocked inhales from the men standing guard throughout the hall was cut short as the king stood taller and cleared his throat.

"Ahm. You are right, child," her father spoke, smoothing out his robes, "Sending your brother north tomorrow *is* foolish." Turning toward the guard closest to the door, her father gestured with a single hand. "Send word to Prince Gavin. Tell him his brother will be arriving by morning."

"What?!" Andrew shook his head in disbelief. "You cannot seriously believe this to be a wise choice."

"This is my only choice, *boy*. Unless you would rather I got Vern and the healer involved?"

Addie looked at her brother wide eyed. She had known Andrew had been forced to endure Vern's punishments again but the dread that flashed across Andrew's face made her realize something had changed. Addie knew what horrors her father's interrogation inflicted, having suffered through them herself more than once when she was younger, but something told her it wasn't just his own well being her brother feared for.

"Fine," Andrew conceded, "I'll leave as soon as I get my things packed."

"You will leave now. We will have your things sent after you," the king corrected.

"You can't do this," Addie snapped as she pulled herself to her feet.

"It is done," her father said sharply, exiting the great hall.

"Addie, you need to make sure Elinore is kept far from Vern while I'm gone. I'll get back as soon as I can. I would have loved a game in the gardens tonight but it looks like you are on your own for a while. Be safe, please," Andrew spoke low.

Quickly, two younger guards step to Andrew's side. Their own distaste for the king's decision and outburst evident on their faces.

"Your highness, let's get on the road as soon as we can," the younger looking guard said; his bronze skin glistening with sweat as he leaned closer for only Addie and Andrew to hear, "For what it's worth, many of the guards feel as you both do."

Addie and Andrew gave a subtle nod of thanks before Andrew was whisked into the hall, leaving Addie to walk back to her rooms alone. Once inside her bathing chamber, Addie washed the remaining blood from her face, having healed her busted lip immediately after her father struck her to the ground.

Less than an hour later, Elinore burst through the double doors to Addie's room, "Andrew is gone! I was just outside the stables when he and two guards rode away. What is happening?"

"The king has decided he is of better use to him in the north, defending Viridia from the Alizarin people, for now," Addie grit her teeth at the words, "He will try to get back as soon as he is able."

"But why?" Elinore shook her head.

"My father was tired of Andrew speaking for the people. When Andrew protested, he threatened to involve you and Vern," Addie answered and her eyes softened.

Pure terror was written all over Elinore as she spoke, her words shaken, "Did Andrew tell you then?"

"He hasn't told me anything but I think that was the most fear I have ever seen in my brother's eyes in my entire life," Addie admitted.

"Vern... Vern attacked me in his chambers after beating your brother a month ago," Elinore spoke with conviction. "Andrew thinks it was because he defended me and Vern wanted to prove a point."

"Elinore, I'm so sorry," Addie took her friend's hand, "Is there anything I can do? I'd be more than happy to dismember Vern if you'd like."

Elinore gave a weak smile, "Although I appreciate your offer, I am working through it all. I will keep you in mind though if I need anything. But back to your brother, what are we going to do to get him out?"

"I don't know. Do you think Rose's ravens could keep us in contact?" Addie asked.

"Of course. I can get a message to Rose tonight about what has happened and I'm sure she will be happy to lend us a hand," Elinore said calmly, "We need to let the others know tonight."

"I know. I don't think I can stay in the castle any longer without Andrew here," Addie rubbed her face, "I think the king is planning something. How have his drinks been going?"

Elinore smiled wickedly, "I've just upped the dose. If we keep this pace, we can eliminate him completely in the next few weeks without anyone being too suspicious, I think."

"Good. Hopefully Andrew is able to return before then," Addie stated, "Tonight we need to be more cautious than normal just in case the king has anyone watching me more closely. Grant isn't expecting us this evening. We are going to need to get to the cabin unseen."

Elinore nodded her agreement before striding back toward the door, "We can leave through the service tunnel near the kitchen so we are closer to the tree line. I'll make sure I'm the last to leave the kitchens after everything is cleaned and tomorrow's breakfast has been prepped."

"Just be careful and stay out of my father's sight if you can help it," Addie advised before Elinore returned to her daily duties.

With dinner service only a couple hours away, Addie walked the hallway of the floor below her rooms and made sure every window was left open and the discreet service door to the kitchen tunnels would open silently. At dinner, Addie sat with her head down and ate quickly before excusing herself early. She hoped her father would see her behavior as nothing more than a spoiled princess pouting over her discomfort with her brother's unexpected departure.

In the confines of her rooms again, Addie waited for the rustling in the castle to settle and for the residents within to drift into oblivion so she might make her escape. As she climbed through the window and down to the floor below, Addie knew this may be her last chance to leave the castle unseen. In the leather pack strapped to her back was a collection of the few things she would need to make an escape she may not be returning from any time soon.

The small window on the landing below Addie's room did not budge as she tried to push it open. A slight panic raced through her chest. She was sure she had double checked every window on this floor. Tentatively, she moved along the stone ledge to check the next window. Again the window did not give. Window after window stayed tightly shut. If Addie could get to the other end of the wall, the hillside sloped upward along the side of the stone building, she was certain she would be able to get into the castle once again through Andrew's chambers on the ground level on the opposite side of her home.

A light rain began to fall making the stone beneath Addie's feet slick. She wasn't sure how much farther she had to go before a fall was no longer dangerous. Slowly, she stepped around a larger protrusion from the wall but as her left foot lifted from its perch, her right slipped free sending the princess falling to the ground below. A scream caught in her throat as the too short drop knocked the air from her lungs. Standing once again, Addie couldn't help but chuckle to herself as she ran her hand over the waist high ledge she had been standing on only moments ago.

Quickly, she ran up the steep embankment and rounded the corner to the large glass doors to her brother's room. Addie gently turned the gold filigree handle and pulled the door open with a sigh of relief. The eerie darkness of her brother's room sent a chill down her spine. Addie quietly made her way through the sitting room and laid her ear to the door. Total silence greeted her. Opening the door, Addie slipped into the hall and made the short walk to the kitchens.

"Holy shit, Addie! You scared me! What happened?" Elinore whisper-shouted as she jumped at the sight of the princess walking into the kitchen from the main doors.

"All of the windows were locked. I had to come in through Andrew's room. Lets go," Addie whispered back.

Elinore looked Addie over, "You don't intend to return, do you?"

"I hope not to. You shouldn't either," Addie replied.

Elinore shook her head, "No, I need to be here. No one knows my involvement with you but if I leave now everything I have done will be lost. I need to stay."

Addie's shoulders rose, "What about Vern? Will you be alright here with Andrew and I both gone?"

"I'll be fine. If I feel like I'm in danger, I will leave. I promise," Elinore smiled unconvincingly, "Now we need to hurry before the next guard rotation."

Elinore moved to push the large door to the gardens open. The cold wet air assaulted their faces instantly. The tree line lay just beyond the garden's edge. Both young women dipped into darkness on silent feet and were quickly swallowed by the canopy of trees, unseen. The hike from the castle gardens to the cottage took just under an hour. A dim light flickered on the pale curtained window.

Elinore grabbed Addie's hand and pulled her to a stop, "They don't know we're coming. We need to signal them first to let them know it's us and not to cut our heads off the second we walk through the door."

Elinore brought her cupped hands to her mouth and blew

between her thumbs creating the rhythmic coo of a morning dove. After several seconds of silence, the sound echoed back from the cottage. Quickly, Addie and Elinore swept to the open door before it was closed tightly behind them.

"What the fuck happened? Why are you both here?" Cora snapped.

Grant rushed through the door from the bedroom. "Is everyone alright?"

Addie shook her head, "The king sent Andrew north this afternoon and I don't think the castle is safe for me anymore."

"You can both stay here. We can figure out how to get Andrew home as soon as possible," Grant pulled Addie in close.

"I need to go back," Elinore shrugged. "We need someone inside to know what is going on and the king doesn't know I'm working against him. Plus I need to keep the doses up or his strength will recover."

Cora stepped close to Elinore's side, "Give me your hand."

"What?" Elinore looked around skeptically.

"Let me see your future so we all can have a little peace of mind knowing you are going to be alright," Cora answered and gently took Elinore's hand. Her eyes glazed and her breathing slowed.

"This part is always fascinating," Will's voice came from the doorway to the bedroom, "I mean as long as she doesn't say a bunch of ominous shit anyway. Ha, who am I kidding? That's pretty cool too."

Several deep breaths later, Cora's eyes returned to their natural green, "From what I can see, you should be safe in the castle for now but things get a little hazy in about a week. If you're alright with it, I can look again in a couple days and see if I can figure out why that is."

Elinore exhaled, relieved, "That would be much appreciated. For now, I need to get back so I can get another message to Rose about Addie and Andrew leaving the castle."

Addie moved in and wrapped her arms around Elinore, "Please be careful and do not hesitate to come here if you are in trouble, alright?"

"Of course. I will see you all in a few days under the willow," Elinore squeezed Addie tightly one last time before stepping back into the rain.

Chapter 34

Grant

In the days following the stranger's sighting of the death wraiths, Lord Anderson's movements seemed to stall entirely, as if he and his creatures had vanished while traveling south through the kingdom. Grant lived in an ever present state of anxiety. Cora's premonition for Will lingered in his mind like a dark cloud. Addie had taken residency with the three companions in the cabin nearly a week ago and Elinore continued to report limited movements from the king. Shortly after she divulged who she truly was, Grant asked Elinore to send word to Ren and Maggie to let them know he was safe. After their initial response of relief, Grant had not received any other communications back. Tomorrow was set to be another meeting and Grant hoped to hear reassuring news from anyone.

The sun sank low behind heavy, dark clouds that would most likely bring with it dangerous winds and possibly rain and snow in the coming days. A foreboding sense settled over the forest as darkness descended.

Stepping into the cabin with a load of wood, Grant cleared his throat, "I have a terrible feeling something bad is going to happen soon."

"Well that's one way to enter a room," Will joked while stoking the fire he had just sparked to life.

Cora set the knife in her hand down on the cutting board next to the vegetables Elinore had snuck out of the gardens for them. "I think he's right, Will. I have had this sinking feeling I misjudged how much time we have before Lord Anderson reached the castle with his army. I need to sit with you tonight for a while Grant and see if I can find him more clearly; I can't see him on my own but perhaps with you I can see what his plan is."

"Is now a good time or is there anything you need first?" Grant stacked the pile in his arms near Will.

"I think I will need something in my stomach. This will most likely require quite a bit of energy and none of us have eaten well in a few days," Cora replied.

Addie stepped through the cabin door, hands tucked behind her back and a large, satisfied grin spread across her face. Guilt struck Grant hard as he watched Addie's expression shift at the tension in the room.

"Is everything alright? Has something happened?" Addie looked from Grant to Cora and back again.

Will answered light heartedly before Grant or Cora could, "Well, Mr. Doom and Mrs. Gloom over here, seem to think the world might end soon but nothing new really."

Addie gave a small snort at Will's comment before resting the large rabbit she held behind her back inside the sink basin, "Well hopefully this might brighten their moods then."

A resounding clamor of excitement echoed through the cabin. "Was that in one of the traps?" Grant asked, picking up the soft furry creature by its hind legs.

Addie nodded, "It was in the one closest to the creek. I haven't ever skinned anything so I just brought it back here so one of you could show me how."

"I can show you," Cora picked up the knife she had used for the vegetables, "We will need to head back to the creek though, so we can keep predators away from the cabin."

Both women, bundled in their minimal winter clothing, departed for the creek quickly, leaving Will and Grant in the small cabin's living space.

"Do you really think your father is going to attack the castle soon?" Will asked Grant hesitantly.

"The man I knew wouldn't hurt anyone intentionally, unless it was absolutely necessary. The man we found in that cave was not my father," Grant sighed. "After my mother's death he changed so much but I would have never expected any of this."

"I don't think I ever knew their gifts," Will stated to himself.

"My mother was very good at growing things. She could get even the most delicate flowers to bloom through the coldest snow if she wanted. As for my father, he could wield water. I think they paired really well together. My mother grew her gardens and my father kept the soil moist."

A look of realization lit Will's expression, "Could he impact the weather?" a lace of panic in his tone.

"I don't know. Why?" Grant looked at his friend confused.

"Cora said her premonition showed heavy snow like it was winter, correct?" Will prompted.

"Yeah, she said we would probably have close to two, maybe

three months," Grant answered.

"If your father can manipulate water, maybe after everything that happened in the caves he tapped into some sort of power to control the rain as well. If that's true, he could attack the castle at any point and we won't be ready," Will explained.

Grant's heart sank, "I think you may be right. We need to find out as much as we can when Cora and Addie get back."

As if summoned, Cora stepped through the door with Addie close behind. The princess walked over to the cutting board and continued to process the rabbit into a pot along with the vegetables for a stew.

"Did we interrupt something?" Cora asked, looking into Will's stunned expression.

"We think Grant's father might be able to control the weather…" Will sighed uncomfortably.

Cora pinched the bridge of her nose between her brow with her thumb and index finger, "That would mean my timeline was incorrect and we have no idea how soon we could face what I've seen"

"We know," Grant took a deep breath, "Is there any dried meat left so we can try to see what my father's future might be?"

Will shook his head slowly, "No we finished that yesterday along with the cheese."

"I can have this stew ready in about an hour," Addie placed the large pot over the fire.

"Then we will wait," Grant ran his hand through his hair, leaving the longer than normal strands disheveled.

Just under an hour later, Addie pulled the boiling pot from the fire and dished the steaming stew into several small wooden bowls. Quickly, all four companions took various seats throughout the small space to eat and each one nearly inhaled their meals in silence.

"I'm ready when you are, Grant," Cora stood and placed her dish in the sink.

"I'm as ready as I can be," Grant's hands shook slightly as he took a seat nearest Cora at the small dining table.

Cora placed both hands palms up and closed her eyes. With a slow exhale, Grant rested his own hands in hers. The moment Grant's skin touched hers, Cora's eyes flew open. They all sat in complete silence for a short time before Cora furrowed her brows and a tear ran down her cheek.

"There is nothing left. The old maple blazes crimson.. The buildings are overrun. Shepherds Glen has been reduced to ash and smoke but he is not alone. Another has betrayed this kingdom. Lord Anderson knows when to strike. We are out of time," Cora's words were filled with terror as tears flowed freely down to her chin and splashed on the rough table top. The green of her eyes returned and she pulled her hands out from beneath Grant's.

"Can we save Shepherd's Glen?" Grant asked, voice full of heartbreak. "I can ride south now and—"

Cora shook her head subtly and wiped the tears from her face despite the fact that she continued to weep, "The damage to Shepherd's Glen is done. Many were able to flee but not all. My vision from before... It was incomplete. They are fleeing to seek refuge here."

Will stood at the head of the table and placed a hand on Cora and Grant's shoulder's, "Who was with Lord Anderson?"

"It was hard to see his face but I think it was Lord Stevens. He was marking locations on a map," Cora's tears slowed,

"They are coming. We don't have months, I fear we have days."

Heavy silence thickened the air. Addie was the first to speak after what felt like an eternity, "I will go to the castle armory tomorrow after nightfall and we can leave for the survivors. If my father won't listen and defend his people, we must rally anyone fit to wield a sword."

"Then we should all get as much rest as we can. Tomorrow we build our forces, however small they may be and we prepare for war," Grant held his shoulders firm as he stood from the table and made his way out of the main living space, Addie close behind.

Gently, the princess closed the door behind them and placed her hand on the center of Grant's back, "How are you feeling?"

"Like all of this is my fault. Like more innocent people have died because of me. I never wanted any of this," Grant sat down on the edge of the cot against the wall opposite the door and buried his face in his hands.

"You aren't responsible for any of what Cora saw and you aren't responsible for what your father has done," Addie dropped to her knees in front of Grant's bowed head and placed a hand on both of his thighs.

"We may all meet our end soon and there is little I can do to stop it," Grant spoke into his hands.

"You aren't doing any of this alone, Grant. But if we do face our end, let's not waste what time we do have," Addie ran her hand up Grant's leg.

Dropping his hands, Grant looked down at the princess on her knees before him, "What are you doing, Addie?"

"Reminding us both that despite the darkness we face, there

283

can still be moments of light and life," Addie's tone was rich.

Grant grabbed Addie's wrists, stopping her slow progression up his leg. Eyes filled with longing, Grand's voice was low and sultry, "Not like this, Princess. You. Deserve. Worship." Each word enunciated by a kiss starting at Addie's palm up to her collar bone

Standing quickly, Grant pulled Addie to her feet with him and spun them both until she stood where he had just been. Stepping closer until the back of her knees hit the frame, Grant settled Addie onto the cot slowly and leaned in to press his lips to hers. His heart began to thrum in his chest like a war drum.

Their kiss deepened and Grant explored Addie's mouth wildly. Each stroke of his tongue filled with the words he was afraid to admit aloud. If this was all the time they had left, he wasn't going to let his self-depreciation interrupt them. His hands traced the curve of her breasts before coming to rest at the top of her thighs.

"Are you sure this is what you want?" Grant pulled away slightly. The warmth of her skin on his made it nearly impossible for him to separate himself from her any further.

Addie ran her hands up Grant's chest and cupped his face in her palms. "More than anything," she whispered against his mouth.

Without further hesitation, Grant made quick work of the laces at the top of her pants and lifted her lower half from the cot, tossing her clothes to the ground. Dropping to his knees, Grant reached up and gently guided Addie until she was propped on her elbows and her bare half sat perched at the edge of the cot's cushion.

"Spread your legs, Highness, so I might show you how

pleasant these types of relations can be," Grant purred.

Obediently, Addie spread her knees to either side of Grant's shoulders, bearing herself to him. Slowly, he laid a path of kisses and gently nipped up past her knees until he reached the apex of her thighs and devoured her completely. Grant licked the length of her center before stopping to indulge in the taste of her on his tongue. Addie arched her body into his movements. Quiet moans slipped from her lips. Grant traced his right hand up her leg to her core.

Groaning with pleasure, Addie begged for more and moved fervently against his hand. Gently, Grant repeatedly stroked the inside of her body. Both breathing heavy, Addie tried to keep her pleasure contained until she couldn't any longer. Lacing her fingers through Grant's hair, Addie ground her body against his mouth, pressure building low in her belly. Grant curled his fingers slowly until every muscle in her body began squeezing tight before finally releasing in a shutter.

"Oh gods! Fuck!" Addie swore as she shattered to pieces below his touch.

Grant pulled back and stood again to unbuckle his belt and pants, dropping them in a heap on the floor next to Addie's. He quickly threw his shirt off over his head exposing every inch of his warm tan skin and collected the bottom hem of Addie's tunic, tugging it off as well.

"I'm not done with you, your Highness," Grant hummed, pulling Addie to her feet, "Lean forward and put your hands on the wall."

Grant grabbed her hip with one hand and used the other to run his tip through her wet core. Stopping at her entrance, Grant slowly pushed into her inch by inch until he was fully sheathed. A small high pitched squeak sounded from Addie.

"Gods you're beautiful," Grant leaned into Addie's hair and whispered in her ear. Slowly he began pulling out before easing back in over and over. Holding tight to her hips Grant thrust into her carefully several times before withdrawing completely and spinning her to face him. Lifting her against the wall, he sank into her hard. Addie rested her legs in the crooks of Grant's arms as their bodies collided again and again. Her body shuddered as she tumbled over the edge once more into an all consuming bliss.

Gently Grant lowered Addie to her feet. "Now on your knees so you can see how good you taste on me."

Without hesitation, Addie dropped to the floor and wrapped her lips around Grant's considerable length.

"Gods Addie," Grant groaned as she pulled all of him into her, hitting the back of her throat. "You look so good on your knees." Grant's body twitched and pulsed in Addie's mouth as she repeatedly worked her way up and down his shaft until he was spent.

Grabbing his shirt from the floor, Grant held it out to her, "If you'd like to, you can use this; it needs to be washed anyway."

Confused, Addie stood and wiped her mouth with the pad of her thumb, "Why would I need to do that?"

"Never mind," Grant smiled a coy smile and chuckled sweetly, "You're certain you've never done that, Princess?"

Addie's cheeks flushed a beautiful pink, "Did I do something wrong? I've never done that before. I mean some of it I have but not the mouth part. Did I make a mistake?," Addie began rambling.

Taking her hand, Grant eased her racing mind, "You didn't do anything wrong, Addie. Although, I don't much like the thought of you and anyone else doing any of that," he admitted.

Addie smiled softly before stooping to collect her clothes from the floor. "How are we going to clean ourselves a bit without Will or Cora knowing?"

Cora's voice sounded from the living space beyond the door, "There's no need for discretion. These walls are thin. There is some warm water and a clean towel by the door."

Addie froze instantly with embarrassment, "They heard everything."

"Not everything," Will laughed,"just the last couple minutes. We were getting cold outside waiting for you two to finish and Cora figured you'd want warm water to wash up with."

"I'm absolutely mortified. I'm so sorry," Addie replied.

Grand stepped to the door and opened it enough to peak out and collect the supplies. "Thank you, Cora." Grant said with a playful wink.

Chuckling, Grant placed the water at Addie's feet and offered her the towel.

"How are you not embarrassed!?" Addie asked as she dipped the towel into the bowl.

Grant smirked and shrugged nonchalantly before Will once again answered, "Probably because, from what we heard, you both were *thoroughly* sated."

"Will!" Cora barked, holding back a laugh followed by the sound of her hand smacking his arm.

Addie quickly cleaned herself and passed the rag to Grant while she dressed. In a few short minutes, both stepped out into the main sitting room where Will and Cora rested in front of the fire.

"We filled your water skins as well. They're on the table,"

Cora nodded to her left, "And, if you'd like, you both can share the larger pallet Addie and I have been using.".

"Thank you, Cora. I would very much appreciate that," Grant ran a gentle hand down Addie's spine as they both stepped over to the table for their drinks.

"Well, I'm ready to turn in. I'm sure you both are too," Will teased before standing and making his way into the adjacent room. Close behind him, Cora rose to her feet and followed him through the open door.

Together, Grant and Addie returned to the bedroom before settling into their cot and bundling up for the night. With a soft breath, Cora blew out the lantern on the table by the door.

"Sleep well everyone," Grant wrapped Addie against his chest and stated into the dark. "Tomorrow is going to be a challenge for us all."

Chapter 35

Cora

Cora had been pacing the length of the small kitchen since just before sunrise. Despite her best efforts, her dreams were again plagued by her vision of Will's death. Each time the premonition replayed in her mind, her heart broke a little more. In the past month, only one aspect of her vision seemed to change. In some versions she watched from her knees as Will fell in his human form, while in others, he was brought down as the large dragon she had seen in the forest. Cora couldn't keep the knowledge of Will's future a secret from him any longer. She had been trying to work out the best way to have such a difficult conversation with him this morning but continued to fall short.

Will groggily stepped through the wooden door separating the two small rooms. "Good morning, beautiful," he said with a yawn and rubbed his hands over his eyes. "Those two are probably going to be asleep a little longer. Did you want me to find something for us to eat? There's still stew in here." Will stirred the wooden spoon in the cast iron pot still hanging over the coals in the fire place.

Cora shook her head and took a deep breath before blurting, "I need to talk to you about something important and I need you to really listen, alright?"

All traces of drowsiness disappeared from Will's eyes as he took a seat and patted the chair to his left for Cora. "I'm listening," his tone was sincere, "but if you have been pacing here for over an hour because you are worried about telling me that we are mates, you can relax a little, Cora. I already know."

Shock exploded through Cora's chest, "What? How? Did Grant tell you?"

Will shrugged, "No, not exactly but he helped me get to that conclusion. And before you go murdering him, I knew there had to be something between us. The day I first saw you in your garden ... It's hard to explain but something in my soul told me I was meant to see you there."

"I'm not going to kill him and I know what you mean," Cora took a deep breath, "That wasn't the first time *I* saw *you* though. Did you know that?"

Will shook his head before Cora continued, "The day you and Grant fell from the tower, I slowed your fall. I was at the castle with my mother and something in me shouted that I was needed out there. It woke me from sleep, actually. When I stepped outside, I watched you slip and I instinctively reached for you. That was the first time I slowed time for anyone other than myself. My mother told me what it all meant once we left the castle. I hated how much it felt like I was losing control."

"I'm sorry, Cora," Will's voice was soft.

"Why are you sorry? You had no clue you were even gifted. How could you have possibly known anything?" she asked, puzzled.

"Because you deserve better than me, Cora. I have no money. No home. I am nobody. You deserve someone far greater than I will ever be," Will admitted.

A frustrated tear rolled down Cora's cheek, "You are truly a fool, William Banks, if that is what you believe! You are the bravest person I have ever met and it is my honor to have you as my partner, if you'll have me. I'm the one who is unworthy of *you*. I have been lying to you for so long."

"It's alright, love," Will placed his hand on hers, "I'm not upset at all that you were worried about telling me. I get it; it's a big deal to be nervous about."

"That's not the only secret I've kept from you," Cora inhaled a deep breath, "Do you remember the night we were attacked at the edge of the woods?"

"Of course I do. That was a pretty significant night for me, if you remember," Will said with a cocky grin.

Cora gave Will a proud half smile before her grin faded, "What Grant and I saw wasn't just a premonition about the battle we are going into. It was a vision of you."

Silence lingered for several seconds, "And?" Will asked, prodding her to continue.

"I watched you die, Will. For weeks now, I have watched you die in my sleep every night. You die while trying to get to me," several more tears escaped down Cora's face.

Will's chin jerked back slightly and surprise splashed across his face before it was replaced by a warm smile, "Cora, I couldn't possibly imagine a greater death than one earned saving someone I love."

The final shred of Cora's control on the floodgates of her emotions snapped, sending a cascade of mixed feelings through her. Pain and pride were coated in love and anger. Someone she had known for such a short time loved her beyond what she could ever have thought possible.

"I won't let it happen, Will. I wont lose you for real," Cora said, determined.

"We can cross that bridge when we get there. Until then, I need you to know that I truly do care for you and nothing will change that," Will wrapped his arms around her in a tight embrace.

Cora nestled her head into the warmth of Will's body and reveled in the security she found there. In each other's arms, she felt like she was strong enough for anything. For the first time in her life, Cora let her emotions take the reins and lead her to where she longed to be.

Her serenity was short-lived as the front door to the cabin swung open without warning. Instantly, Will was on his feet pulling Cora behind him and picking up the closest item within reach to defend them both against the unexpected intruder. Standing in the door frame, drenched from the pouring rain, stood a terrified Elinore.

"Fuck, Elinore! I could have killed you," Will snapped.

"With a wooden spoon?" Cora joked playfully before getting a solid look at the fear etched into Elinore's expression.

A groggy Grant and Addie shoved through the door beside Cora, blades in hand.

"What's happening?" Grant bellowed.

Elinore's words came out in a rush, "They're going to kill Andrew. I, I overheard several of the guards just now say the king sent Vern north to 'handle a problem for the king.' He's going to kill the prince!"

"We have to stop him!" panic filled Addie's voice.

"None of you can be seen in town," Elinore panted hard like she had run the entire distance to the cabin, "But I can. I just need a horse fast enough to catch up to them. I don't know how long ago they left. I need to get to Andrew first."

"Take Shea," Cora offered without hesitation, "She's fast and knows how to handle tough situations."

Pushing past Elinore into the rain, Cora brought her fingers to her lips and whistled loudly. From just inside the densest tree coverage near the stream, Shea stepped forward and approached Cora's waiting hand.

"I need you to help a friend of mine, Shea," Cora gestured for Elinore to come closer, "This is Elinore and she needs you to get her to Prince Andrew in the northern camps as quickly as you can. He's in danger." Shea dropped her soft, white muzzle into Elinore's hand before bowing her head lower. "Her saddle and gear are in the wood shed. They may be a bit wet but they will do just fine."

Addie stepped next to Elinore, "In my chamber's there are some spare clothes you can change into. They will most likely be a bit large for you but I think you'll need to wear something less cumbersome than your skirts."

"I do hope you don't mind, but I've already taken the liberty of borrowing a few things," Elinore pulled the small pack from her back and opened the top, revealing a pair of folded black pants and a dark green tunic. Lifting her skirts, Elinore wore an old pair of Addie's boots.

"I do not mind a bit, my friend. Be safe and save my brother," Addie's voice was stern.

In a matter of minutes, Elinore was changed and mounted

Shea. "If you two get separated for any reason, whistle as loudly as you can and she will find you," Cora said to Elinore. "Good luck." Cora and Will stood beside Grant and Addie in the wood shed as they watched Elinore disappear into the rain.

"Do we continue with the plan for tonight?" Will asked tentatively.

"I think it's more important now than ever, that we do," Addie replied. "If she fails to reach him in time, the people of Shepherd's Glen will need to find refuge in hiding until the king is dealt with. I don't think he will welcome them with open arms but will greet them instead with swords"

Chapter 36

Andrew

Andrew spent nearly a week in the gods forsaken valley just south of the Alizarin border and had only spoken to Gavin twice. The morning following his arrival, the eldest prince met with his younger brother to discuss the challenges they would be facing from the north before he was sent to guard the border. The information he was given had been cursory at best and did not seem to provide any real detail about the supposed enemy their kingdom was at war with. Their second conversation had been brief regarding troop rotations at the front. Andrew hoped to meet with his brother in private tonight about their father. He had assumed Gavin had been sent here for the same reason he had. The king had ultimately sent Andrew north with the hope that he would not have to entertain his son's demands to send aid south as well as give him a first hand look at the 'true danger' the soldiers in the north faced.

Although they were said to be under constant threat,

Andrew had yet to see any aggression from the Alizarin people that was not provoked by Viridian attack. He could not fathom why the king refused to spare men to protect the people that truly needed aid. After a daunting day, Andrew left the mess tent and headed in search of his brother. As he crossed the camp, he couldn't help but notice the vacant looks and sense of restlessness that lingered on the faces of the soldiers that had been stationed here.

The dark flaps of Gavin's tent shifted slightly as a frigid gust of wind blew through the camp. Two shadows danced across the rugs strewn across the floor of the tent from the flickering light inside. Stopping just outside the entrance, Andrew waited for his brother's company to depart so he might have a private audience. Gavin's voice carried through the canvas, catching Andrew's attention.

"I understand your concerns, but we cannot act until my father gives the word," Gavin's voice was full of authority.

An unfamiliar male voice spoke, "But sire, your brother is a liability and he has become far too suspicious of our movements here. The men…"

Gavin's voice rose loudly, cutting the unknown man off, "You know as well as I do that I want him eliminated but he still serves a purpose. When he is no longer of use we will remove him and make him the martyr he was sent here to be."

Andrew's heart sank as the truth of his and his brother's rolls became clear. Gavin was not the ally he thought he would be but instead his intended executioner. Quickly, he turned and headed back to his quarters hoping to collect his belongings and get back to Addie and his friends near the castle unnoticed until after dawn.

He was stunned in place the moment he passed through his tent opening. Perched atop his cot sat a raven as dark as a moonless sky. Attached to its leg was a rolled parchment. Tentatively, Andrew knelt down and removed the paper with deft fingers. The moment the twine fell free the dark plumed bird took flight through the billowing tent flaps causing Andrew to jump in surprise.

Slowly the prince unrolled the note. Rose had written in hurried scribe:

The king's rebels aim for Onyx Hollow. Few will survive.
Make haste for the castle, prince.
Addie is in danger.
-R

Dread pooled in the pit of Andrew's stomach. Addie was in trouble and Elinore's home was under attack. Throwing on his vest, Andrew strapped several throwing knives to his person before tossing his sheathed sword over his shoulder. If he hurried, he might be able to reach the castle before midnight and perhaps get help to Onyx Hollow before catastrophe struck the small village.

The tents outside had begun to quiet for the evening. Several soldiers sat around the fire roughly ten yards away. Sticking to the shadows, Andrew made his way around the men to the corral at the outer edge of the camp. A spotted mare stood quietly, still saddled and tied to the post outside the enclosure. Looking around quickly, Andrew untied the horse and led her into the darkness before mounting.

In fear of discovery, Andrew pushed his stolen mare hard through the freezing rain. Small shards of ice pelted his skin.

He knew the moment his brother realized he was gone, word would be sent to the king. The sparse light from the sun faded beyond the horizon and the already treacherous ride became impossible at his current speed. After nearly an hour at a hasty trot, Andrew slowed his horse and tried to focus on his surroundings. Through the onslaught of wind and icy rain, murmured voices seemed to sound from every direction.

The whistle of an arrow snapped his attention to his right, narrowly avoiding a lethal impact. Battle cries sounded as several armed assailants bounded into sight. All four masked men quickly surrounded the prince, weapons drawn. Among them stood a behemoth of a man. Andrew realized at that moment this was more than a chance encounter but instead an assassination attempt.

"This is the end of the line, Prince," a familiar foreboding voice left the large man's covered mouth.

"If you expect me to lay down my arms and die quietly, you are gravely mistaken," Andrew pulled free his long sword.

"Good. I do enjoy this part," the man replied and charged forward.

Pulling tight on the reins, Andrew's horse reared back and brought its powerful legs down on the large man, throwing the attacker to the ground. The prince swung his sword through the air deflecting the first blow from another to his left. Spinning his mount, he attempted to keep the men surrounding him at bay long enough to find an exit that didn't involve either himself or the mare being seriously wounded.

Below the horse's feet, the large man pulled his injured body to the roadside. "Kill the damn horse and bring him down, you useless swine."

In a barrage of blades, Andrew was unable to defend both

himself and the horse he sat upon. With a swift swipe of their sword, one of the attackers ran his blade across the horse's chest, causing her to throw Andrew to the ground, before sprinting into the torrential downpour. Pulling himself from the mud, Andrew lifted his blade and deflected several blows. Kicking his foot out, the prince threw one of his attackers to the ground and ran his sword through his heart. Spinning on his toes, he brought down two more men with the throwing knives he pulled from the harness in his vest.

The monstrous man finally pulled his massive frame to his feet, "I've wanted to do this for a long time, *Prince*," he spat the final word like an insult.

"Are you here on my father's behest or have you already become my brother's tool as well?" The prince taunted.

Angrily, the large man ripped the black fabric from his face. In a voice full of hatred, Vern laughed humorlessly, "This *tool* is going to enjoy tearing you to pieces and leaving your entrails for the birds."

Vern, blinded by rage, rushed forward and swung his sword hard through the air, shattering the prince's weapon into smaller razor sharp shrapnel. With nothing but the jagged remnants of his blade, Andrew blocked Vern's next strike and slid across the muddy ground on his knees before burying the broken shard of his sword deep into Vern's calf. Andrew quickly pulled one of his throwing knives from the body beside him.

Throwing hard, Andrew's blade flew wide of its mark striking Vern in his shoulder. An animalistic bellow erupted from him as he dropped his sword and threw himself wholly onto the now unarmed prince.

"I've always hated you," Vern held tight to the prince's throat and repeatedly slammed his head into the ground below. Mud and gore splashing over their faces.

Andrew's vision began to blur with each impact. In a final effort to save himself, Andrew managed to free one arm and reached for Vern's face. Vern refused to relinquish his hold on the prince's neck even after Andrew dug his thumb deep into the man's eye socket, completely destroying his eye.

As Andrew began to feel his imminent death creep in, his only thoughts were of Elinore and the unexplored feelings he wished he would have been able to pursue with her and the kingdom they could have built together. With what he assumed would be his final breaths the prince let her name escape his lips.

Suddenly, the pressure on him shifted. The colossal man perched on his chest instantly became heavier for several moments before his entire body went limp and fell to the ground. Breathing in a distressed breath, Andrew rolled to his side and out from under Vern's legs.

The prince heaved haggard inhales on his hands and knees. Lifting his head, he couldn't comprehend what he was seeing. A small form sat perched atop Vern's lifeless body. It took Andrew several moments to register what had happened. Someone had saved him. Clumsily, the small form dismounted and hurried to the prince's side with glowing palms. Elinore's beautiful golden hair parted the rain and her hazel eyes stared down at him.

"Elinore," her name was just a rasp as he sat in the rain.

Was this death? Had he been granted peace or was this some illusion before him? The searing pain in his body and the terror in Elinore's eyes told him this was not death.

"Don't talk yet," her voice was kind, "let me try to fix your throat first."

The instant Elinore's hand rested on the prince's face his labored breath began to subside.

"How are you here?" Andrew managed.

"When I heard one of the guards say Vern was sent north, I knew he would be coming for you. Cora offered me her horse and I came as quickly as I could," Elinore brought her hands to the several gashes on his chest and abdomen he had not noticed.

Every moment since they were separated this past week tugged at his emotions.

"May I kiss you?" The words left his mouth before he could think wiser. Despite the rain and lack of light, Andrew watched Elinore's face brighten.

"I think I would like that very much, your highness," she replied nearly inaudibly.

Gently, Andrew cupped the back of her head and pulled her into him. Their kiss started tentatively then evolved into one full of passion and longing; as though both of their very souls collided. With heavy breath, they broke apart and Elinore rested her forehead against Andrew's.

"I hate to ruin this dream worthy moment but we need to get moving. I need to get to the castle and warn everyone. I think my father aims to take out Onyx Hollow and Addie is in danger," the prince's words cut through the moment like a blade

"What's happened to Addie? We heard word that Onyx Hollow was in danger and we've already sent a raven to warn my father. The village is preparing to leave as we speak," Elinore explained.

"Rose sent a raven. Her message wasn't clear but I know it

was urgent. Where is your horse?" Andrew turned his head and peered into the dark.

Elinore rose to her feet and brought her index fingers into her mouth and whistled loudly. From the south, a whinny echoed through the trees just before Shea ran into sight.

"That's handy," Andrew raised a brow and helped Elinore mount before settling down behind her.

"Are you healed enough to ride?" Elinore asked.

"Thanks to you, I am," Andrew landed a soft kiss on the crown of her head.

As they stepped over the bodies around them, Andrew watched Elinore's unease intensify. "No matter what anyone says, taking a life is never easy, even if the person was a monster."

"I couldn't let him kill you. I never imagined I would be capable of cutting a person's throat but I had to stop him," Elinore's voice was filled with tears.

"I'm sorry that you had to do that but I am eternally grateful that you were here for me when I needed you," Andrew collected the reins around her side and quickly nudged Shea south.

Chapter 37

Addie

Addie waited until the sun had begun to set before she made her way onto the castle grounds. As a child, she learned every entry point into and out of the massive stone structure and could hopefully get inside without being seen. The guards had always followed the same rotations and paths throughout the halls and if she timed everything correctly she could get what she needed and back to the cabin completely unseen in just a few hours.

An icy rain had been falling for hours and the sound of her booted feet crunching against the paved stone walk near the northern entrance slowed her approach. Near the great hall there was a small service entrance that would allow her to use the paths throughout the castle meant for staff.

Getting into the armory through the service door would not be an issue. Once she collected the weapons she needed and the items from her room, she would have to find a way back through the castle without notice. If she left too soon, the rotating guards near the great hall would see her return. If she was delayed more than five minutes, she risked her father's personal guards seeing her make her way through the gardens toward the forest.

As always, the doors to the great hall service entrance were unguarded and unlocked. Addie slipped inside easily and walked in total darkness through the small tunnel. She counted each turn until she made her final right and ran her hand along the wall, feeling for the wooden door that opened closest to the armory. Her hand slipped over smooth stone for several feet before the uneven grain of wood grazed her finger tips. With a gentle push the door slid open silently. The hall outside the armory was dimly lit by a small sconce at the far end of the carpeted corridor. The large ornately decorated double doors to the armory were kept locked but unguarded. Luckily, Addie had become quite skilled at picking open most locks throughout her home.

Dropping to her knees, she pulled several pins from her cloak pocket and got to work releasing each bolt from within. The subtle click of the final mechanism signaled that she had been successful. Addie pushed the door open just enough to sneak inside and closed the door softly behind herself. She made quick work of lighting one of the lanterns near the door with one of Cora's matches before she tossed her large canvas duffel bag onto the floor in the center of the room and began to collect several weapons from the walls around her. In less than three minutes, Addie had stashed several daggers, a crossbow and arrow along with over a dozen throwing knives into her sack and slung the strap over her shoulder.

She moved like a shadow through the room and back into the service hall. The staircase leading to her room was to

304

her left several yards down from where she had just entered the dark tunnels. With her looted goods in tow, she pushed herself up the steep stairs and stopped short at the door leading to the hall connected to her rooms. The dim glow of candlelight passed slowly under the door in front of her exit. Addie finally released the breath she had not realized she held the moment the light slipped from view.

After several minutes in silence, Addie braced her body against the heavy door and pushed out into the hall. In three short strides, she stood in front of her unguarded bedroom doors. Placing an ear against the wood she listened for any sound from within but heard nothing. From down the hall murmured voices sounded, sending her already racing heart into a frenzy.

Quickly, she swung the doors to her rooms open and silently closed them. Frozen in place, she rested her head against the door and prayed to the gods that she had not been seen. Heavy rain and ice pelted the large window on the far wall of her sitting room. She let the heavy bag slide from her shoulder and rest on the floor with a gentle thud. It took several seconds for Addie's heart to steady slightly and for her to notice the snap of the fire blazing in her hearth. Spinning on her heels, she realized she was not alone. King Colvin stood with his back to his daughter facing the roaring flames, hands locked behind his back.

"I knew you would make your way here at some point before you left," the king's voice sounded mournful.

"How did you know I was in the castle," Addie took several tentative steps around her father.

"I know everything that happens here, child. My guards see everything. Your mother would have been ashamed of what you have reduced yourself to," the king turned to look his daughter in the eyes.

Addie clung to her father's words, "What do you mean 'would have been'? What have you done?"

King Colvin shrugged nonchalantly, "I have done what is necessary for the safety of my bloodline; for any royal with a gift. Do you know what your mother's gift was?"

Angry tears began to pool in Addie's eyes, "She is a telepath."

"Oh, Addie, your mother was far more than a telepath. Had I known what her true gift was before we were wed, I would have killed her the day I met her. You see, your mother had a very rare, very potent, gift for mind manipulation. She could make anyone do anything she wanted and they would think *they* wanted to do it. When I first discovered what she could do, she was already with child and I had hoped she would be my greatest tool in creating a unified kingdom. Then I realized her vision for our people and my own were at odds with each other. I couldn't allow her to ruin what I was building. I started dosing her with a small amount of poison made from hemlock pollen."

Addie wailed, "She is your wife! How could you!?"

"Were you not listening at all, child? Let me be clear, for nearly the past three decades I have kept Viridia safe by limiting your mother's abilities to corrupt my work. Do you understand?" the king's voice rose slightly as he stepped closer to his daughter.

"You are killing her," the words were a broken sob in Addie's throat.

King Colvin's brows knit together before he spoke like he tried to restrain the emotions that raged behind his eyes, "Wrong, Addie. She lays in her bed as we speak, breathing her last breaths, if she has not done so already."

Addie lunged for the door but was quickly stopped short by her father's large frame. "Let me help her please!" she begged between sobs.

"I'm afraid I can't let you leave this room. My secrets will die with you three tonight, I am afraid," the king's tone once again filled with sorrow. "I had hoped my eldest would have seen the vision I saw for him. But, Gavin will have to suffice and uphold my line, I suppose."

"You can't do this!" Addie yelled and slammed her fists hard into her father's chest.

"I am the *king*, Addie. I can and will do what I deem necessary," her father said, shoving her to the floor.

Addie hastily shuffled herself back toward the large window and pushed herself to her feet. "You are a monster! What other atrocities have you justified? For years, I believed you to be this kingdom's salvation. Now I know what you truly are. You are our damnation."

"I am keeping our kind alive and thriving in positions of power. You could not see past your silly bleeding heart to realize that burning down towns like Onyx Hollow are a necessary evil to protect *you*!" Addie's father stalked across the room.

"Is Onyx Hollow truly lost?" Addie said, stunned.

"I received word this evening that it has indeed fallen. Rebel forces throughout Viridia will take the fall once again for my soldier's work and the fall of another city filled with magic wielding *peasants*. The people in Onyx Hollow were a necessity to lose," King Colvin said forebodingly.

Addie felt like her heart was shattering, "They were innocent people; women, and children and you've killed them all!

307

You are responsible for so many unnecessary deaths! Lady Anderson, all of Shepherd's Glen, it's falling apart because of you."

"They were traders and a danger to my kingdom!" Her father snapped back at her bitterly. "I am not responsible for Lady Anderson's death. Your dearest Grant was my target, not that woman. She simply tried to protect a stupid boy with far too much power. I knew he was hiding something the day he and his stupid friend fell from that tower. In the eyes of our kingdom, my hands are clean. Records will show that her death and the attack on Onyx Hollow tonight were the work of rebels."

"But your hands are *not* clean. Their blood coats them, as would mine, if Grant and Will and Cora, people you deemed *unworthy* of existence, had not come to find me. Does my life not mean enough to you for you to put your own fears aside?" Addie's voice shook with rage.

King Colvin droned, "I would have mourned you but it would have been a casualty of war and it would have rid my conscience of what I must now do myself. You were lucky your friends came for you, but they too are a danger to our kingdom."

"They are not a danger to our kingdom, they *are our kingdom*. They are our *people*! And you have chosen to turn on them, to abandon them. Lord Anderson has committed atrocities, yes, but they were done out of love and loss and grief. You commit atrocities because of fear and your own selfishness. I fear I may have let rose colored glasses impede my vision for far too long with you, father." Addie replied.

"I knew you were going to be a problem the moment you destroyed that stupid fucking teacher of yours. I should have ended you then," the king's voice was low as though he spoke to himself.

"Then why didn't you?! If you could have killed me, why let me be a risk to your insane ideas?" Realization shown on Addie's face. "You've tried ... haven't you? A few weeks after the accident with my magic my carriage was attacked on its way back from town. That was you... And when my lady's maid was poisoned last year that was meant for me also, wasn't it? When I returned, you poisoned me again; I knew it was always you but somewhere, in my heart, I had hoped I was wrong. You've tried and failed!"

"I should have done it with my own hands!" her father bellowed.

"You are afraid of me, aren't you?! You didn't do it yourself because you *fear* me," Addie scoffed in disbelief.

Rage boiled in her father's eyes before he lunged. Large hands wrapped tightly around her throat and began to squeeze and shake with her father's fury.

Struggling for breath, Addie reached her hands up and grasped at her father's knuckles. His flesh under her hands began to darken and rot away but his grip only tightened. The veins in the king's head pulsed along his temple. Panic began to sink deeper into Addie's gut. She knew it would be her life or his. Lifting her hands higher, she reached for her father's face and focused on the darkness in her soul and the grief she was drowning in. The feeling of death and decay filled her senses. She finally let her true power go. For the first time she completely freed the darkness she had suppressed.

The king's eyes widened, "Addie. Stop," he croaked out just before his grip loosened on her throat.

"You should have listened to your fears," Addie's voice was

detached as she let her rot sink its talons into her father's brain and take everything from him. "You should have killed me before I learned what I'm truly capable of."

The king's wide eyes blinked rapidly before putrid yellow bile spilled from his mouth and blood poured from his eyes, nose, and ears. Bright green, glowing light filled the room. Moments later, King Colvin's body hit the floor of Addie's room with a reverberating thud. A part of her soul splintered into shards like a fine porcelain at the impact.

The door to Addie's room swung open and slammed against the wall, the ornate brass handle crashing into the stone sending a web of cracks through the marble. Andrew stood breathless, sword in hand, Elinore at his side in the doorway. Addie's stunned gaze met her brother's. Sheathing his sword, Andrew stepped into the room.

"Addie, are you alright?" Her brother spun quickly closing the door behind Elinore before facing his sister. He was at her side in several long strides and gently collected her face into his hands.

"We need to get to mother," Addie's monotone voice matched her blank expression.

"What?" Andrew looked over his sister, confused.

"I think father killed her but we need to get to her if we can," Silent tears poured from her eyes.

Quickly, Andrew grabbed Addie's hand and followed Elinore out the double doors and down the hall to their parents' rooms. One of the large carved doors sat ajar slightly, casting a strip of flickering light across the narrow carpet in the hall. Elinore gently pushed the door open and followed the prince and princess into the sitting room and the bedchambers beyond. Addie's heart sank deeper in her chest

310

at the sight of her mother's still body atop her bed. Andrew exhaled a deep, grief riddled breath before dropping to his knees at the queen's bedside.

"She didn't deserve this," Addie wept as she lay next to her mother's cold body. Several minutes passed, Addie and Andrew's mourning the only sound echoing through the silence.

Clearing his throat, Andrew drew himself to his feet, "We need to deal with the king's body. It has to look like he died without foul play."

"Why?" Elinore ran a gentle hand down the prince's spine.

"I will not be allowed back into this castle if it is believe that the king was executed the night I fled the camps in the north," Andrew clarified. "It will look like a regicide and the throne will pass to Gavin."

"I didn't mean to kill him like that but I don't regret it. I hope he felt everything," Addie sat up and wiped the tears from her face.

"What do we do now?" Elinore exhaled.

"We need to clear Addie's chamber and move his body into his room. We must make it seem as though he passed in his sleep," Andrew replied. "Then I will need to send word to Gavin and let him know I was summoned back to the castle by the king because he felt ill. Elinore, do you think Rose's raven could leave a forged summons from the king in my tent?"

"Timing might be tight but if you get me the letter in the next hour I can get it to Rose and into your tent before dawn. What about Onyx Hollow?" Elinore replied.

Addie shook her head, tears once again rolling down her face, "The king received word before I arrived that Onyx

Hollow is gone. I don't know if there were survivors."

Elinore swallowed hard and held back her shattered heart, "Then I will go in search of survivors at first light."

"We had planned on leaving for Shepherd's Glen once I return tonight," Addie breathed, "Come with us and we will help you find your people."

"I'm coming with you," Andrew wrapped his arm over Elinore's shoulder.

"How will that work with father's death?" Addie asked skeptically.

Andrew shook his head and looked down at Elinore, "I don't know but I am not going to let you face Onyx Hollow without me."

"In your father's summons, write that he needs you to defend Onyx Hollow. And say he can't go himself because he is feeling ill and he doesn't trust anyone else to go. His armory is filled with my father's work and it would make sense for him to want to protect his assets, right?" Elinore offered.

"I think that may work, Andrew," Addie nodded.

"Then we need to move the king and get going," Andrew made for the door.

"Grant, Will, and Cora are waiting at the tree line. I can inform them of our plan and we can all meet under the willow in an hour," Addie followed Andrew back down the hall.

"Perfect, I can signal for Rose's raven from my room and get the forged letter off as soon as we are able," Elinore agreed, sending all three companions off into the night.

Chapter 38

Elinore

Standing under the willow, ice coated Elinore's hair and coat. The shifting wind blew the leaves on the branches surrounding her together creating a symphony of sound that, under any other circumstance, would have been beautiful. Addie joined Elinore and Andrew in the confines of the tree shortly after they arrived and let them know the other's would be along shortly.

Will and Cora had devised a plan to sneak several horses out of the stables while Grant stood guard at the tree line. If something were to go wrong, Grant's nightmares would be able to stop anyone before an alarm was raised. Most of castle staff had been ordered to the great haul this morning after the discovery of the king's body just before dawn.

From beyond their safe haven within the willow, the sound of hooves steadily approached. Slowly, Grant's voice slipped through the hanging ice crystals coating the leaves, "All clear. Let's go."

Elinore moved first and stepped into the frigid wind. The pail light from the rising sun peaked through the dark clouds overhead, casting ominous shadows across the forest floor. Next to Grant, Will and Cora stood holding the reins of two horses.

Will shrugged, "We were hoping to snag another mare but there were several guards patrolling the grounds. These two will have to do."

Andrew stepped beside one of the horses, "This is more than we could have asked for."

Cora cleared her throat, "Here's the plan then — Elinore, you and Prince Andrew will take the red stallion. If you're alright with that?"

"Perfectly," Andrew responded quickly.

"Good," Cora nodded, "Addie, you and Grant will ride the darker mare and Will and I can ride Shea."

"If that doesn't work for anyone, I can shift and carry a single rider," Will offered and scanned over the faces of his companions.

Grant shook his head in protest, "We don't know what we are going to find. You shouldn't waste your energy."

"Grant's right. I can't see much beyond glimpses of injured people on the main road, and I think my mother may be with them soon but we don't know if they are being followed," Cora added.

"Then let's hurry," Will said, throwing a pack Addie brought from the castle over his shoulder.

Snow flurries swirled around the group as they mounted and set out into the woods surrounding the castle. If they cut through forest as they moved south, they would reach the main road leading back to Shepherd's Glen in a matter of hours. Apart from being discovered by guards, Elinore feared encountering any of the dangerous creatures she knew prowled the deeper parts of the woods.

The group traveled in silence for nearly the entire journey through the forest before Cora spoke. "The snow is sticking," her voice was a whisper that cut through the air like a blade.

Will pulled her body closer to his, "It's going to be alright, Cora. We still have time."

From ahead, Grant cleared his throat, "We should be at the main road soon. Once the sun is high enough, I hope we will have a little better visibility, but I don't have much hope for that."

Large clumps of snow began to stick to Elinore's lashes, sending a shiver down her spine. Andrew's arms held her firmly against his chest. The press of his body against her own quickened her heart.

The prince's lip grazed her ear, "Would you like my cloak?"

"Thank you, but I'll be alright. If you lend me your cloak you will freeze," Elinore tucked her arms in at her sides.

Andrew shifted behind her to pull the dark heavy fabric from his shoulders anyway and draped it around her. Without another word, he collected the reins again and continued forward. Elinore breathed in his soft floral scent.

"Lavender?" Elinore wondered aloud.

A warm burst of air rose the hairs all over her body. Andrew's chest vibrated subtly as he laughed low, "It's my favorite. Most of my soaps and oils at the castle are either lavender or citrus."

"Lavender's were always my mother's favorite too," Elinore admitted. Since her mother passed when she was a child, Elinore rarely spoke about her in fear it would hurt too much for her father.

"She was a woman of good taste then. With a daughter like you, I'm sure she was a kind woman as well," Andrew spoke graciously.

Elinore smiled to herself at her mother's memory, "She was the kindest person I've ever known. It's been just my father and I for a long time but sometimes when my father says some of the things she used to say I can almost hear her voice." Several tears froze on Elinore's cheek.

"We will find him, Elinore. I promise," Andrew spoke with determination.

"That isn't something you can promise," her voice cracked, "Once we find the refugees from Shepherd's Glen, I need to continue on to Onyx Hollow and find him; even if it is just to give him the burial he deserves beside my mother."

"Addie will be able to get those we find to a safe place. I'll be right beside you the entire way," Andrew pressed a kiss to the top of her head.

Through the canopy above, faint light from the rising sun pierced the dense foliage and thick clouds overhead. Larger clumps of snow began to fall more steadily. Grant pulled him and Addie to a stop and lifted his right hand to silence their group's movements.

Will cocked his head slightly, two pointed bat-like ears forming on either side. His normal rosy skin blended to a near translucent, fleshy gray. Small wiry tufts of black hair sprouted from the finely pointed tips. His voice was just above a whisper, "The road is just ahead and it sounds like there's a lot of feet." Will shook his head, shifting his ears back to his own.

The party slowly dismounted and stalked to the tree line

316

several yards away. Elinore squatted next to Andrew and Addie and peered down the road. A strange flickering glow emanated from over the hill.

"Is that them?" Elinore whispered.

"There's only one way to know for sure," Will said, pulling off his clothes.

"What the hell are you doing man?" Andrew blocked Elinore's view.

"I don't want to ruin my clothes," Will responded, handing his folded shirt and pants to a red faced Cora before he shifted into a raven in a burst of warm air.

"Holy shit," Elinore peeked out from behind Andrew's arm.

"That was crazy!" Andrew blinked in shock.

Will took flight and quickly shot down the snow coated path; his black wings a stark contrast to the untouched snow. In a few short moments, Will's raven form landed at Cora's feet squawking profusely.

Again, Will shifted and turned to face them all with Cora at his side desperately trying to cover his nude body. "It's them," Will said breathlessly, "There are more than a hundred people and many of them need aid."

Jumping to her feet, Elinore moved quickly into the road, stopping abruptly the moment Andrew gently grabbed her wrist.

"We need to help them and I need to know if anyone from Onyx Hollow is with them," Elinore's voice was pained.

Andrew frowned slightly, "I know Elinore, but we need to approach with caution. Addie, can you help those at the front so Elinore and I can work our way to the back? We can see if we can find anyone from Onyx Hollow as we move through the crowd and help who we can from there."

"Grant and I can see who is in charge and get everyone taken care of," Addie nodded in agreement.

Cora stepped forward, "Will and I need to look for my mother."

Andrew stood next to Elinore, "Direct everyone to the castle and let them know the kingdom offers them any aid they require. We are most likely not going to be well received by most, Addie. Please, watch your back."

"No one is going to hurt her," Grant vowed.

With a bow, Andrew turned to Elinore and gestured her forward. Instantly she raced over the pristine snow leaving hurried steps in her wake. Stumbling over the hill, Elinore skidded to a stop before diving head first into the procession of carts and bodies droning forward. Everywhere she looked, fatigued and sorrow soaked each soul to the bone. Not a single individual in the throng of people around them was clean. Every face and body was marred by an ambush none of them were prepared for. Nearly every person she passed was in need of a healer's aid, making her feel like she would suffocate. Heavy snow continued to fall as she searched each face for a single familiar one. With each step forward, her despair only grew. At the edge of the crowd, Rose knelt next to a small child covered in dried blood and dirt. Shuffling around folks absolutely dead on their feet, Elinore made her way to Cora's mother.

"Is he here? Did he survive?" Elinore nearly shouted, Prince Andrew approached close behind.

Both Rose and the child at her side looked to Elinore. The moment Elinore saw the small child's face a spark of relief coated in pain struck her. The small child grinned widely before leaping into Elinore's arms.

"Eli! You're here! Your daddy is helping my sister in the wagon," the child beamed as Elinore held him tight, letting her healing magic course through him and repairing every scrape and bruise.

"I'm so happy to see you, Max. I'm going to see my father then come back to find you, I promise. Can you stay here with Ms. Rose?" Elinore held her tears at bay.

Max squeezed Elinore one last time before releasing her and stepping back into Rose's waiting arms.

Elinore offered a gentle nod to Rose before she and Andrew sprinted for the wagon at the end of the procession. The rear door to the rundown cart was missing, giving them a look inside as they rounded the back corner. Elinore's father, Henry, knelt low, one elbow propped on his knee as he rang blood from the cloth in his hands into a small basin at his side.

"Father," Elinore's voice shook as she stepped onto the small platform on the slow moving structure. "Are you alright? What can I do to help?"

Henry's head spun at the sound of his daughter's voice. He jutted to his feet, rocking the trailer. Lamp light flickered across Elinore's face.

"My sweet girl," tears cut clean lines through the filth and blood coating his cheeks, "Just a few bumps and bruises. I'm so glad you came. We need as much help as you can offer."

"How many from Onyx Hollow are here?" Elinore looked to the several other people crammed in the small space and recognized only her father and the small girl he had been tending to, her eyes closed and skin a sickly pale.

Henry shook his head, "Max and Gwen were the only ones I could reach before the entire village was overrun. I feared

319

we would lose Gwen before you arrived."

Tears silently streamed down Elinore's face and neck. Dropping to her knees at the small child's side, Elinore's hands began to glow, brightening the cramped space. The moment her hands rested on Gwen's arm and face the girl's color started to return. The large gash up her leg slowly knitting closed.

"She will be unconscious for a while still, and may walk with a limp for the rest of her life, but she will live," Elinore declared after several tense minutes, "Are these the people with the worst injuries? I can heal most of them to a stable point but it was a long ride to get to you. I will do everything I can though. Princess Addie is at the front mending those she can."

"There are several men and women that should be here as well. They gave their seat for Gwen when the folks from Shepherd's Glen found us on the road. They are in the cart just ahead of us," her father spoke as she made her way to each of the five other men and women among them.

The light emanating from Elinore's hands flickered and dimmed with each wound she healed. Clumsily, she stood and braced her hand on the wall to steady herself.

"Rest for a moment Elinore, please. This was far too much for me to ask of you," her father stepped forward, worry coating his every word.

"Your father's right, Elinore. You need to slow down," Andrew's voice sounded from just outside the door. Walking behind the wagon, the prince's long strides made it easy for him to keep pace with their movement.

"I need to help them," Elinore protested and stepped onto the platform outside the covered wagon's door. As she dismounted, Elinore's knees buckled beneath her, pitching her forward into Andrew's waiting arms.

Stunned silent, Elinore stumbled over her words, "You're, ah, I'm... thank you," she managed as Andrew settled her feet to the ground.

"As long as I breathe, I will not let you fall," Andrew looked deep into Elinore's tear soaked, bloodshot eyes. Her heart skipped at the promise behind his words as she stared back into his deep blue eyes, the brilliant flecks of gold more prominent than she had noticed before.

"People still need help, you highness," Elinore finally found her voice.

"That is true. But not from you, my lady. Now you can either walk with me back to our horses or I will pick you up and carry you. It's your choice but I will not let you drain yourself into unconsciousness. You have done enough," Andrew crossed his arms over his chest authoritatively.

Elinore looked to her father several yards ahead for support but received none.

"Rest, Eli. You must do as he says. He is *your* prince after all," her father said dramatically over enunciating her possession of the man at her side.

Elinore turned back to Andrew and rolled her eyes, "Fine but only for a short time so I can catch my breath and eat something. Then I am going to continue," Elinore amended.

"Fair enough, *Eli*," Andrew grinned. "You are incredible, you know?"

Elinore turned and walked back into the crowd, Andrew just a step behind. "What are you talking about?" She snipped, her exhaustion making her more irritable.

"Your commitment to helping other people even at your

own detriment is honorable. That eye roll was pretty cute too," Andrew admitted.

Elinore scowled at the prince over her shoulder.

"That's a cute look as well, my lady. I must admit you look quite stunning no matter your mood," Andrew gave her a playful bump with his shoulder, his words sending a flurry of butterflies through her stomach and staining her cheeks a soft pink. "I will say this is my favorite though," Andrew leaned in and whispered in her ear, darkening her flush from pink to a deep crimson.

Elinore took several silent steps through the crowd before the rest of their group came into sight. Rose and Cora held each other tightly as they approached. Elinore inspected Addie's posture and expression of exhaustion as she rested her head against Grant's chest. She was sure, she too, looked as drained as the princess but did her best to hide how close she stood to collapsing into the snow below their feet.

"What is it with healers?" Andrew's voice startled her, "Addie, you look like you are about to faint too."

Lifting her arm slowly Addie raised her middle finger and settled further into Grant's hold. "At least some of us are useful here," she chided playfully.

"You've got me there. We need to get these people out of the cold," Andrew turned to Will and Cora.

Will nodded in agreement, "If you are sure we won't be executed the moment we enter the castle, you and I can ride ahead and enlist more aid so we can get everyone back more quickly. Some of these carts aren't going to make it if the snow continues to pile. People are going to freeze to death."

"Excellent, but we must act surprised about my father's death when we arrive. If we are convincing enough, I can round up men and women that can help to get everyone to the castle," Andrew stated with a small shrug.

Andrew turned to Elinore and pulled her hand to his lips placing a soft kiss on her skin, "Be safe and rest, *please*. I will be back in a few hours."

"I can get us there and back quicker if I fly," Will interjected, "but I will need to shift back before we get too close to the castle. I don't want to get blown out of the sky."

"What could you possibly shift into that could carry me with you?" Andrew asked in disbelief.

Will grinned wide and began to take off his clothing once again before Rose stopped him, "Whoa there young man! What are you doing?"

"I don't want to ruin my clothes again," Will shrugged.

Cora's mother shook her head slowly, "First, don't shift here in the nude; there are children present. Second, when we get a minute I need to get a few of your measurements. I think I can enchant something for you and possibly have Elinore's father, Henry, forge something semi-decent for you so you aren't running around in the buff."

Will's cheeks blushed before he leaned in and whispered something in Cora's ear that caused Cora's cheeks to flush. Andrew kissed the crown of Elinore's head before he and Will departed on foot over the hill and out of sight. Moments later several shouts drew everyone's attention to the sky. A large black dragon soared into the clouds, Prince Andrew perched atop its shoulders between two of the large spikes protruding along the creature's spine.

Rose spun to face the crowd, "Please do not panic, friends. They are going to get us help." A resounding echo of relief flowed through the people.

"While Addie aided the injured, I was unable to find Maggie or Ren," Grant spoke to Rose, her back still to him.

"I am sorry, Grant. They are not here. From what I have heard, Ren held off the dead so the folks that are here could escape," Rose's tone was sorrowful.

Elinore watched as Grant's face hardened with grief. Addie turned to him fully and wrapped her arms around his neck. Several silent tears fell as he bent and buried his face in the crook of Addie's neck.

"Thank you, Rose," Grant's voice was muffled.

"What do we do now?" Cora asked her mother.

Looking around, Rose sighed, "They need to keep moving but they have nothing left in them. Our best option is to move forward as quickly as we can until the prince returns. At our current pace, we won't reach the castle until nightfall."

"Then we power through as best we can and help those who begin to fall behind," Elinore pulled her shoulders high. "I am happy to offer my horse."

As quickly as they could in the thickening snow, Cora, Addie, Grant, and Elinore helped several people mount their horses and continued on. In just under an hour, a dark shadow eclipsed the sun through the dark gray clouds for several seconds before descending and disappearing on the main road farther north.

The sound of large, heavy feet in the snow approached before a massive dragon's head crested around the corner up ahead, the prince at its side. As her bone deep exhaustion settled over her, Elinore nearly wept in relief at the crowned prince's return.

Chapter 39

Andrew

Andrew and Will faced minimal scrutiny from castle guards when they arrived in search of help. Several dozen men and women hastily departed toward the coast after realizing Gavin would not be taking his father's seat atop the throne. Now that the too few survivors of Onyx Hollow and Shepherd's Glen were fed and settled in the castle, Andrew stood in his rooms alone, ready for a moment to catch his breath for the first time in what felt like forever. A loud knock pulled him away from his reprieve.

"Your Majesty," a young guard's voice sounded from behind his door; the new title throwing him off balance.

"Come in," Andrew replied.

The guard that had delivered him to the northern war camps entered the room, "An older gentleman and woman just arrived. They're demanding to speak with the king. What would you like us to do?"

Andrew inhaled a deep breath to steady himself. "I'll see

them in the great hall. What are their names?" He exhaled as he pulled his vest back over his shoulders and followed the young man back toward the door.

"I believe his name was Ren, sire. I apologize, I'm not sure of the woman's name. They say they are from the Anderson estate," he said, bowing his head.

Andrew spun abruptly to face the guard, "Ren? Where is Grant?"

"Lord Anderson is looking for research in the library with the princess, your Majesty," Andrew's second guard replied from his position just outside the threshold to his rooms.

Andrew stepped into the hall and faced the second guard, "Could you have him join me in the great hall, please. I believe he will want to be there." Once again he turned to look at the younger man on his right, "What is your name?" he asked as the other guard departed in search of Grant.

He bowed low, "David Ettor, sire."

"How long have you been a member of the king's guard?" Andrew gestured for him to rise.

"Less than a year, your Majesty," David responded nervously.

"I need someone I can trust at my side, not someone my father had in his pocket. Can I trust you, David?" Andrew asked with the authority of a king. His gift peered into the young guard's mind. Surprise washed over David's nervous expression, his copper skin paling lightly.

"I do hope so. I only want what is best for this kingdom. I believe you do also."

"That, I do," Andrew reached forward and shook David's hand firmly before continuing toward the great hall.

It took Andrew and his new companion nearly ten minutes

to make their way from his rooms to the other side of the castle. As the prince approached, the guards on either side of the grand entryway pulled the large double doors to the hall open and announced Andrew's arrival before the prince stepped into the large space. Two individuals stood to their feet and offered a deep bow despite their fatigue and visible wounds that adorned their faces and hands.

Before addressing either newcomer, Andrew turned to David, "Please fetch medical aid and ask the kitchen to bring up food and water for our guests." Andrew returned his attention to his guests and gestured for everyone to be seated, "Ren, I presume?"

Bowing his head, Ren nodded, "Yes, your highness. We were hoping to speak to the king. We have difficult news from Lord Anderson."

"King Colvin is dead. You may speak with me," Andrew replied dryly.

Ren jerked back slightly in shock, "I, I'm sorry for your loss, your *Majesty*."

"Thank you," Andrew showed no emotion.

"How is the queen holding up with her husband's passing?" the woman at Ren's side asked.

"My mother is no longer with us either. I'm afraid," Andrew swallowed hard and did his best to keep his grief from his face but failed. "Her death is a great loss to us all."

"Prince Andrew, I am so sorry," the older woman reached across the table and rested her hand atop his.

Before Andrew could continue, the doors to the great hall opened abruptly, Grant and Addie just beyond. Grant's pace quickened the moment his eye's met Ren's.

"Ren! Maggie!" Grant wrapped his arms around them both,

"Why weren't you with the rest of the people from Shepherd's Glen? We thought you were dead."

"That is why we are here," Ren faced Prince Andrew. "Lord Anderson has done something terrible."

Andrew's brows pulled tightly together, "We are aware of what he has done. We're currently trying to find a way to undo what has happened. Do you know where he is now?"

Ren shook his head, "He and his creations took Shepherd's Glen. We were captured while defending the town center. He gave us a message for the king. That is now you, your Majesty. He is coming in three days if the crown is not handed over to him and his wraiths."

"I refuse to willingly relinquish the crown to whatever he has become," Andrew's voice was deep. "His grief does not give him the right to take this kingdom."

"Then we fight," Grant startled them all. "The man that was my father is gone. Addie and I believe we may be the only ones that can stop him."

"How?" Andrew asked, surprised.

"Rose believes together we will be able to destroy whatever has consumed his soul," Grant's words were vague.

"How are we meant to fight those creatures? They do not fall," Maggie spoke, voice haunted by the horrors of Shepherd's Glen.

Elinore's voice rang out from the service entrance, "My father can begin work on inspecting weapons in the armory. We will need weapons if we hope to keep them subdued long enough for Grant and Addie to stop Lord Anderson for good."

"Elinore, you should be resting," Andrew's voice was far gentler than just a moment ago.

"David said you needed food and medical aid. So, here I

am," Elinore approached Ren and Maggie and set bowls of stew before them both.

"Are either of you injured?" Addie said confused.

"No, we are alright, Princess. Thank you. Nothing a little rest and some food can't help," Maggie smiled kindly.

"I called for medical aid as a precaution but I do not want you *or* Elinore healing anyone else until you have both *slept*," Andrew stood next to Elinore. "You've done enough in the past forty-eight hours. You've earned your rest."

"We are both fine, miss," Ren reassured, spooning a healthy ladle of stew into his mouth with a groan.

"Fine, but as for weapons, what do we need and how many," Elinore stood tall.

"Unless they are completely dismembered, the wraiths just keep getting up. Even that might not be a permanent end for them," Ren shook his head discouraged.

"Then we need to create a barricade and try to keep them at bay from a distance," Andrew surmised.

"My father can forge supplies for crossbows and catapults if Cora and Rose can collect supplies for explosives," Elinore pulled a slip of paper from her pocket and began to write a list.

"At first light we will prepare for war then," Andrew exhaled, "Get your rest everyone. Elinore, would you walk with me alone for a moment, please?"

Elinore followed Andrew into the hall, "There were others David could have gone to," Andrew spoke skeptically. "Why did he seek you out?"

"David is from Onyx Hollow," Elinore explained, "He's a good friend. He's lost everything."

A small pang of jealousy rose in Andrew's chest, "I'm sorry.

Is he a sympathizer too then?"

"He is. There are more of us here than you would believe," Elinore shrugged, "David and I grew up together. I trust him."

"Then I will too," Andrew nodded before turning past the kitchen toward his rooms. "If you are alright with it, I would like you to stay closer to my quarters"

"Why?" Elinore said lifting a brow in surprise.

"It would give me peace of mind knowing you are sleeping safely just beyond the walls of my room, not in the staff quarters. In fact, I don't want anyone in those conditions. There will be major renovations to the castle once this is all over," Andrew mumbled the last confession.

"I didn't realize there were other rooms near yours," Elinore wondered aloud curiously.

"Technically speaking… there aren't. You would sleep in my room and I would set up a place for myself in my study in the adjoining room," Andrew clarified. "That is, if you are alright with that. If not, I can have you move next to my sister on the other side of the castle."

"I don't want to force you out of your own bed, Andrew," Elinore stopped just in front of the prince's chamber, "But, I would also feel more at ease closer to you. I'm happy to take a cot in your study if that's acceptable?"

"First, Elinore, I am offering, you are not taking anything from me. Second, you deserve so much more than a cot in an old study," Andrew kissed the top of her hand.

Scarlet stained her cheeks as Andrew pushed the door to his suite open. Elinore stepped into the large space and Andrew softly closed the door behind himself. The door to his bedroom was wide open. Atop the plush cream colored bedding sat a neatly folded stack of satin sleepwear.

"You sleep in satin?" Elinore stepped closer to the bed and ran her finger tips over the delicate fabric.

"No, my lady. Those are for you, no matter where you choose to sleep," Andrew smiled wide, showing off a small dimple in his left cheek.

Tears welled in her eyes, "I don't think I've ever owned anything so fine. Thank you, Andrew. Is there already a place for you to sleep in your study tonight?"

"Yes," the prince lied. Every spare bed in the castle was currently being occupied by refugees. Andrew refused to take a bed from any one of them. "I have sleeping arrangements for myself prepared if you choose to stay."

Raising a brow, Elinore cocked her head to the side, "Why do I have the feeling you aren't being truthful, your Majesty?" Andrew shrugged slightly before she continued, "Show me."

"What?" Andrew nearly choked.

"Show me where you will be sleeping and I will happily take your bed for the night," Elinore demanded sweetly.

Andrew fidgeted with the bottom of his vest, "Ah, alright then." Stepping past Elinore back into the main room, Andrew walked several paces and pushed open the large wooden door to his study before pointing to the small leather couch near a large bookcase. "I will sleep there tonight and have a more permanent bed brought in tomorrow."

"No," Elinore pulled the door shut. "If I'm not being too forward, I would rather you slept next to me in your own bed so I do not feel like I'm putting you out in any way."

Elinore's words caught Andrew by surprise. Without filtering his thoughts, the prince blurted the first thing that came to mind, "But I sleep in the nude."

"Hm," a small embarrassed giggle escaped from Elinore's

331

lips.

"I mean, normally I do but I have sleep clothes that are, *in fact*, satin," Andrew watched as Elinore's cheeks flushed a beautiful shade of pink as he fumbled with his words. "I can wear clothes if you'd like."

Standing on the tips of her toes, Elinore gently kissed his cheek, "That will be preferred… for now, your Majesty."

Chapter 40

Will

Will scoured the halls of the castle for Cora's mother. He wasn't sure how much Rose knew about Cora's vision of his future but he was certain she would know if there was anything he could do to ease her daughter's troubled heart. As he entered the great hall, Will caught sight of Rose at the end of the long table.

"Ms. Rose, could we speak in private for a moment?" Will asked low.

Cora's mother looked up into Will's hopeful expression, "Of course, William. And please, it is just Rose."

Stepping back into the commotion in the hall, Will struggled to find where he should begin. "I'm not sure if you and Cora have had a chance to discuss her premonition regarding my fate but I would like to know if there is a way to change the future she has seen or, at the very least, help her accept the reality we may soon face?"

Rose nodded her head in acknowledgment as they continued down a quieter corridor. With a deep breath, she smiled kindly, "Magic is a fickle thing, William. There is always going to be influence from the user. You, for instance, are a shifter that has spent the majority of your life wielding your gift blindly and adopting other's features and traits. I believe this is because you fear rejection. Cora, on the other hand, fears her loss of control. That fear is probably my doing, I am ashamed to admit. But, for Cora, you *are* that loss of control."

"What do you mean?" Will's brows knit together.

"When she is around you, she cannot control her emotions or their impact on her gift. As a result, when she looks into the future, all she sees is you. She cannot see any other possible outcome." Rose explained.

Will stopped mid stride, "Can the future she saw change?"

"Nothing is ever written in stone. Things change all the time. Cora's visions just provide the most *probable* future we face," Rose smiled weakly. "Your death may not be the only possibility. It is just the most probable future she can see."

The small spark of hope Will had been stoking dimmed slightly in his heart. He wasn't ready to leave Cora, but if he had to choose his life or hers, he would always choose her.

Rose slowly began to walk again and motioned for Will to follow. Clearing her throat she asked, "Do you know where magic comes from? Most in Viridia do not."

"No, I can't say I do," Will matched her pace as they both passed through the doors leading to the glass walls of the sun room.

"Alderbrooke Forest is the home of a well of magic. The water and soil itself is rich with it. At its core, our world is filled with power. Places like the caves in Alderbrooke exist on many continents," Rose began, "Centuries ago the castle was built atop a sacred spring just like the one that runs through the cave where you found Lord Anderson and the princess. The spring that once flowed below our feet was one of the last few in the northern kingdom that had not run dry. The water at many of the springs once nourished the land and the creatures in it. Long ago, an ancient king discovered that consuming the water or vegetation and animals that drank from the wells could give them great strength and even give their children greater gifts. Our borders were once open to all surrounding kingdoms for trade. That same ancient king's youngest daughter was gifted and was drawn to a visiting farmer's son who too possessed a gift from the land. He had the power to wield fire. The magic in our world is like a living thing that wants to grow and spread. Many of those gifted are fated to find another with gifts of their own so the magic can grow stronger with each generation."

"So, Cora and I are connected so the magic can continue?" Will wondered aloud.

"Yes, at its core. When the old king became greedy, he closed the borders. He feared his daughter's love for a commoner and acted on that fear. Soon, trade stopped, those with magic vanished, and the fire wielder was lost. The ancient princess was devastated. Her father did not understand why magic had chosen someone for his child that was not noble by blood. The magic could sense the king's darkness and fear. He attempted to tailor power for his own benefit. The few wells that had remained, sank deep into the soil. Creatures began to appear in the forest to guard the land and its riches. Darkness spread like rot through Viridia.

Over the past several decades, those in the southern parts of the kingdom started to show greater strength in their abilities, like they once had. I believe it was to prepare for what we are about to face once again because of a king's greed. I do not think King Colvin found the wealth of power in and near towns like Shepherd's Glen and Onyx Hollow very settling. He feared he would lose the control he had on his kingdom if those in the south were allowed to prosper from the forest's gifts. That is why there was never any aid sent south. That is why the *'king's rebels'* have infiltrated the forest. If others did his dirty work, VIridia's *'devoted king'* could still parade the kingdom as a good honest, man while he committed genocide behind closed doors."

"What does that have to do with Cora and I though?" Will asked calmly.

"When gifted folks find their other half they are far more powerful together. You and Cora are both children of the southern region of this kingdom and were given great gifts that may be vital in the coming battle, as will Grant's and Addie's. The magic of this world needs to balance out the pain King Colvin has caused," Rose paused and exhaled a heavy breath.

"Could you look and see what *you* can predict?" Will asked.

Rose sat down on an iron chair before a small table. "I would be happy to. Please, take a seat. I wasn't *born* with Cora's magic and using blood magic is far less clear but still useful when used appropriately."

Will took a seat and offered his hand to Cora's mother, "Whatever you can tell me would be appreciated."

Drawing a small dagger, Rose sliced the blade over Will's palm and brought his hand to her lips. Instantly, Rose's eyes went a pale white and her hold of his hand stiffened.

336

Dragon fire clears the way for our salvation but there is a cost
Someone dear will pay with their life but who that is, is lost
The end approaches but for whom I cannot see
For in the coming days all goes dark for thee

"What does that mean?" Will whispered low.

Releasing his hand, a troubled look grew in Rose's eyes, "I, I do not know... In all the years I have been alive, I have never seen so much uncertainty. I know one thing for certain however, William. Cora's vision is *not* a guarantee, but death will claim many in the coming days."

"Thank you, Rose," Will stood slowly.

"Make the most of your time, William. Let my Cora know you love her just in case *we* do not get another day," Rose's eyes began to water. "Before you go, I need to get some measurements. I might be able to enchant clothing you can shift with and Henry may be able to forge enchanted armor for you as well if there is time."

"Of course," Will nodded his head. "What do you need me to do?"

Tapping her index finger against her chin for a moment Rose thought aloud, "I will need your standard measurements of course, as well as your alternate form."

"I can shift into many creatures... I shifted into a gnat in Alderbrooke Forest and at my largest, thus far, I have been able to become a dragon. We may need to step into the garden for that," Will gave a sheepish smile.

"That is *quite* the range, young man," Rose stated, stunned. "Most shifters had but one alternate. A dragon I can work with but a gnat... that may be too difficult for even myself to manage. Would a creature the size of a small raven be

337

satisfactory for you?"

Bowing his head low, Will smiled graciously, "Any aid would be greatly appreciated, Rose."

"Then let us begin outside quickly so we might get things moving along," Rose stood and made her way to the large glass doors.

In less than ten minutes, Rose collected the number's she needed and Will bowed at the waist before quickly making his way through the castle toward his and Cora's rooms. The door to Cora's room was closed as Will searched for the courage he needed to speak to her about what he had learned from her mother.

"Will, if that's you out there please stop pacing and come in here. You're making me nervous," Cora spoke through the door.

Seated at the small table and mirror near the large bed in her dressing robes, Cora ran a comb through her wet hair. Will took a seat on the bed next to her and ran his finger over the small cut on his palm.

"I just spoke with your mother," he began. Cora spun to face him and waited for him to elaborate. After several long moments Will cleared his throat and continued, "She believes your visions are biased because you love me."

"That's ridiculous, Will," Cora rolled her eyes.

Will's voice rose in frustration, "Which part, Cora? That you could be *wrong* or that you *love* me? Because you said it yourself, I will be your undoing."

"I *pray* I am wrong. Gods, do I hope that I am. But, I'm afraid that I am not! I'm more afraid now than I have ever been! I'm afraid I have lost control and I'm afraid it is because of you!" Cora shouted. "Is that what you want me to say?"

338

"I want you to tell me how you feel, Cora. Because I love you. I knew I loved you the moment I saw you. I will be damned if I die knowing you never heard those words from me," Will admitted, his passion lacing every syllable.

Will watched Cora struggle to hold back tears. "Will— I love you more than I ever thought I could and I don't know what to do about it. I feel like it's eating me alive knowing your death will be because I love you and you love me."

Springing forward, Will grabbed Cora's face, his lips colliding with hers and they kissed without abandonment. Will's hands slid over her shoulders and down her back as she wrapped her arms around his neck. Each frenzied movement was filled with their desires no longer restrained. Pulling her to her feet Will lifted Cora by the back of her thighs and wrapped her legs around his waist. Gently, he spun and laid her down atop the soft mattress adorned with more pillows than any one person could need.

"I love you, Cora," Will whispered into her ear as he placed a trail of kisses down her neck and collar bone and untied her robe.

With skilled hands, he slid the thin strap of her night gown from her arm and pulled the thin cotton dress over her head. Cora less delicately ripped the buttons free of Will's tunic, sending them scattering across the floor.

"That was my last shirt," Will joked, bending in to kiss her peaked nipple.

Cora quickly unlaced his pants, chuckling to herself. "Take these off, please," her voice came out husky and breathless.

"Hand me that pillow," Will's voice was low as he obliged her request, letting himself free of his dark leather pants.

Taking the pillow from Cora's hands, Will lifted her body

and settled her down gently, hips propped up slightly. Her eyes widened longingly as she took in his entire body more fully than she had allowed herself to do before.

"Is this alright?" Will asked, as he perched himself on his knees between her legs.

"Gods, yes, please," Cora groaned.

Will lifted one of her knees with one hand as he guided himself closer with the other. Slowly, he thrust into Cora's body causing her to arch off the mattress and fist the sheets at her sides.

"Would you like me to be gentle, my love?" Will's voice was a caress in her ear as he drove into her again. "Or would you like me to make you *scream* my name?"

A soft moan slipped free from Cora's lips as she grabbed Will's hips and pulled him against her hard. Will pulled his bottom lip between his teeth, a low growl rumbling in his chest, and he began to thrust into her at a rhythmic pace. Licking his thumb, Will reached between their bodies and stroked the sensitive bud at the apex of her thighs before pulling out completely and flipped her over onto her stomach. Propped up on her knees, Cora pushed back against him. Tucking his arm under her hips, Will ran his fingers over Cora's skin before once again stimulating the most sensitive part of her with small circular motions, matching the cadence of his body against hers.

"Oh. Gods. Will." Cora pleaded, "I need more, please."

Pulling her back against his chest, Will laced one arm through hers behind her back and gently wrapped his other hand around her throat.

"Look how good you take me," Will nipped her ear lightly, "Such a good girl." At his praise, Cora unraveled completely, body shaking in ecstasy. "That's my girl," he whispered before laying them both down on the bed; his body spooning hers.

Breathlessly, Cora rested her head on Will's arm, "Give me a minute."

"You can rest, my love," Will kissed Cora's bare shoulder.

"Oh no, I'm not done with you yet, William Banks," Cora's tone was filled with desire as she leaned forward and blew out the candle by the bed, "A little bondage doesn't frighten you does it, *love*?"

"Anything you wish," Will's heart was full as he smiled wickedly into the dark.

Chapter 41

Addie

The sun had just begun to rise behind the dark clouds above the castle. Addie stood and admired the grandeur of the map table before her in what was once her father's council room. So often growing up, she had dreamed of being worthy of standing next to the king in this spot. She knew now she had deserved a place here far more than her father ever had, even if he had not believed that to be true. The mountains jutted from the table to scale and Addie couldn't help but notice her home seemed to sit higher on the map than any town in the southern parts of the kingdom. She wondered to herself if that was a true representation of the topography or was her father so contemptuous that he had his castle depicted higher than those around him.

Andrew cleared his throat from the head of the table, drawing the attention of everyone in the room. A chosen few stood in a circle around the table. Grant stood to Addie's right followed by Will, Cora, Rose, General Banks, her brother's guard David, Henry, and finally Elinore to Andrew's left.

"According to word from our friends from Shepherd's Glen, the army of death wraiths will be here in less than two days. I will not let this kingdom fall because of my father's greed and misplaced sense of self importance. We need to prepare ourselves as best we can." Sliding a small fence over the table, Andrew drew a line across the map between the edge of Alderbrooke Forest and the western sea at the edge of the castle grounds.

"We need to keep them out of the city long enough for Lord Anderson to be stopped for good," the prince looked to Rose, "Do you truly believe my sister and Grant can put an end to all of this?"

"They are the only ones that I believe can," Rose nodded.

"I don't understand? We can't just kill him?" Elinore asked, confused.

"No," Rose breathed. "The moment he offered himself to the curse that resurrected his army, he became like them. He is not entirely living, nor is he dead. His soul needs to be freed from the hold his anger and grief has become consumed by before he and his beasts will fall."

"How many do we think we face?" Henry asked. "I can work quickly but the time we have is not enough for much more than sharpening blades and possibly building a handful of crossbows if I have the right materials."

Andrew shook his head, "We don't know. From the accounts we have heard from survivors, the number varies drastically. It could be as few as a couple hundred or as many as several thousand death wraiths."

"My mother and I can collect supplies for healing drafts and explosives today in the forest. It will be tight on time for

343

a few elements," Cora admitted.

"I have some of the components in my belongings that will keep us from the deepest parts of the forest," Rose addressed her daughter.

General Banks cleared his throat, "When I received word of King Colvin's death, my men and I came straight here. Prince Gavin has abandoned his post in the north with a handful of *his* men and is fleeing to the coast. He aims to cross the sea, your Majesty."

Will faced his uncle, "How many have you brought with you?"

"Less than a thousand, I'm afraid," General Banks faced Will directly. A look of relief filled his gaze before he continued with a discontented shrug. "We may have more soldiers coming from other camps throughout the north but the previous king spread us far and wide to keep us occupied."

"That is far better than we had yesterday," Andrew bowed his head in gratitude.

"We can begin preparations immediately," Rose bowed at the waist.

"If that is all, we will reconvene here after sunset to discuss where we stand," Andrew said, dismissing his companions from council.

Addie watched as the room cleared, leaving her alone with her eldest brother, "What are we going to do about Gavin?"

"I don't know?" Andrew ran his hands through his hair. "You should have heard him in the war camp, Addie. He sounded so much like our father."

"If it came to it, could you kill him?" Addie asked tentatively.

"I don't know if I would have a choice. I would hope he would be willing to listen to reason but I don't know how much of a hold father had over him," her brother admitted.

"I know, whatever happens, you will do what is best for this kingdom but I pray he does not have to die by your hand," Addie sighed.

Stepping to the door, Addie turned to her brother before she left, "I think mother would have been proud of how you have handled all of this so far."

"Thank you, Addie," Andrew nodded before returning his attention to the map table.

Addie made her way to the library in search of Grant. The weight of what they both must do felt nearly insurmountable. Pushing the glass door to the library open, she watched Grant from a distance for several minutes before she approached. Every muscle in his body seemed to be coiled just as tightly as her own.

"How are we meant to prepare for what we are expected to do, Grant?" Addie asked as she made her way to his side.

Grant shook his head, "I have no idea. I've read through dozens of tomes looking for anything about either of our gifts but I can't find anything useful."

"My father had a collection of ancient relics from some of the first kings. We can see if they say anything of note," Addie realized.

"Where are they kept?" Grant paused his pacing.

"They should be in his personal study in his and my mother's rooms," Addie's heart splintered at the memory of the last time she had been in her mother's chamber.

"I can get them, Addie. If you aren't ready to go back in there, no one would judge you," Grant's voice was kind as he squeezed her hand tightly in his own.

"No, I need to do this," Addie insisted.

With tentative steps, Addie and Grant made their way through the castle. She attempted to reassure herself with each step that she could handle walking back into one of the darkest moments of her life.

"Let's just collect the books. We can sit *anywhere* else to read through them," her voice was unsteady.

Grant rubbed comforting circles over her back as they pushed open the doors to the king and queen's chambers. To the right, sat the king's private rooms and Addie's mother's to the left. The air inside was far too cold. No fire burned in the hearth. No lamps had been lit since the queen's death.

Quickly, Addie made her way to her father's study and pulled the door open letting herself and Grant enter before slamming the door shut, panting slightly.

"You can do this, princess," Grant commended.

Taking in a deep breath, Addie pointed to the large bookcase near the window, "The books on the second shelf are the ones we will probably want, and the maroon colored stack on the shelf below that as well."

Tucked in the corner of the room, sat a gold bar cart the king once used for displaying his most refined liquor.

"I'm sure no one will mind if we clear this," Grant said, moving the cart toward the bookshelf and relocating the beautiful glass decanters and glasses to the desk at his side.

Picking up two bottles from the cart, Grant lifted a brow, "Are these the bottles Elinore laced?"

"That would be them. We should probably dump those before anyone decides they want to drink them?" Addie confessed.

"We can dump them when we leave," Grant placed the bottles back on the lower shelf of the cart and began loading the books.

Several minutes later, Grant pushed the heavy cart into the main sitting room of the royal suite.

"Let's dump the bottles here so no one sees us leave with them," Addie picked up the bottles and stepped into her mother's bathing chamber.

Several of the queen's personal belongings still littered the room. The scent of her perfume filled the air with a warm sweet smell that broke Addie's heart. Swallowing hard, she stepped to the small window ledge and pushed the stained glass open and dumped the liquid out onto the ground below. The thick white snow below the window turned a dark amber as the final drop of liqueur fell.

"We need to hurry," Addie said and stepped back to Grant's side, wiping away an errant tear.

The next several hours seemed to slip by quickly. Book after book Grant and Addie came up short until an excerpt from a small leather bound book that resembled Rose's manuscript drew Addie's attention.

"Grant, read this," Addie passed the small book to Grant on the other side of the table in the library.

"What is it?" Grant picked up the yellowing pages and began to read the handwritten scrawl aloud.

> *A healer's hand has its pros*
> *But don't discount its twin*
> *Rot can be a greater gift*
> *If one just lets it in*
>
> *A Soul Tender can repair*
> *But Reaping is a prize*

Though darker than its counterpart.
Combined their power lies.

"We knew this already though," Grant shrugged.
   "Read the next lines," Addie pointed to the next page.

When focused on the brightest light
A soul can be saved
But if that soul is too far lost
The hosts must decay.

"What is this book?" Grant turned the leather cover over in his hands.

Written in gold lettering up the spine was a single word: *'Prophecy'*

"I think we need to take that to Rose and see if she knows anything," Addie stood from her chair, "they should be headed to the council room soon."

Chapter 42

Cora

The ride into Alderbrooke Forest was quiet as though even the trees had stilled. Cora sat atop Shea, Rose riding at her side. After nearly a quarter of a mile into the thick brush, Cora's mother broke the silence.

"I spoke with William yesterday. He is a good man," her tone was soft.

Cora looked to her mother, "I know, probably better than all of us."

"Loving him doesn't make you weak, you know?"

"It makes me foolish and blind," Cora bit out, "I do love him and it frightens me how much it makes me fear what we face. I've never feared death. Not until now. Death is meant to bring a soul peace. His will only bring mine anguish."

Rose tisked, "This battle may not play out as you expect, my child. You are right that your love for the shifter has blinded you but you cannot let your fear of losing him force your vision to come to fruition. Knowing he would gladly sacrifice his life for you should bring you immense pride."

"It does. But it also devastates me," Cora admitted.

"Embrace how you feel for him. Do not run from it," Rose advised.

Once again mother and daughter fell silent as they rode deeper into the forest. The mid-morning sun hung tucked behind heavy, dark clouds casting the world around them in an ominous gray. To their right several branches snapped, halting their progression.

Cora leaned in toward her mother and whispered breathlessly, "Do you hear that? Something is coming."

Through the thick foliage, several large pale pinkish-gray bodies moved through the brush like phantoms. Cora's heart nearly stopped as she watched a hoard of skin-walkers pass as a collective. Not a single one made any attempt to attack. Every hair on Cora's body stood on end. In her entire life she had never witnessed anything like what she now watched cut through the forest with an unnatural, predatory determination. The final creature paused for a moment as it crossed their path and looked over both women. Rose rested her hand on the hilt of the curved blade at her side. With what could have been a bow of respect, the creature snarled low and continued.

"What the *fuck* was that?" Cora let out a breath.

"I think the forest is preparing for war," Rose said in awe. "Let us make haste. I do not wish to linger here."

Cora and her mother quickly reached a small brook and dismounted to collect their supplies. In a matter of hours, both women began their ride back to the castle, goods in tow.

"We need to let the others know about the skin-walkers," Cora told her mother.

"Yes, so our own forces do not inadvertently start a war with this place as well," Rose gestured to the world around them.

"When we meet the others tonight, we can let them know we may not be alone in this fight. But first we must prepare what we have gathered," a chill ran down Cora's spine at the memory of her last encounter with creating acid bombs.

"We can show others how to build our arsenal while we work, that way we can stock as much as our cash of supplies will allow," Rose amended.

The remainder of their ride fell silent as Cora mulled over her mother's wisdom regarding Will as well as the challenges they would face once they began manufacturing the acid bombs. She attempted to focus her thoughts on other possible outcomes for tomorrow but continued to see only Will's impending demise.

Shortly after reaching the castle, Cora and Rose rounded up nearly a dozen men and women from Shepherd's Glen that were eager to help in any way they could. Within an hour, Rose had built a well oiled assembly line on the far edge of the royal gardens. With only a few minor injuries, every drop of acid sap and pollen was loaded and stored. While Rose oversaw their team's work, Cora built a fire and began to brew a massive batch of healing draft with what little skin-walker venom Rose brought to the castle. The sun began to sink as Cora finished capping the final bottle of elixir.

"The others will be waiting," Rose exhaled and stood to Cora's left.

Both women walked through the accumulating snow into the castle halls and beyond into the map room where Grant and Addie stood alone. The moment Rose entered the room,

Grant approached and held forward a small leather bound journal.

"What is this?" Cora took the book from Grant's out-stretched hands.

"We believe it is a personal ledger or manuscript of some sort from someone like you, Rose," Addie stated hopefully.

"We weren't able to find much on how we are meant to stop my father but there is a page marked in there we believe may be a push in the right direction, even if we don't really know what it means," Grant pointed to the tabbed pages.

A thin line appeared between Rose's brows as she looked over the pages before her, "Where did you say you found this?"

"It was in King Colvin's personal study," Grant stated, "Why? Do you know it?"

"No, but I know who wrote it. This was written with my mother's hand," Rose explained, "but I do not know how it came to be in the king's possession."

"Do you know what she meant here," Addie pointed to the prophetic scripture. "I can't decay a *soul*, only flesh and bone."

Rose silently read over the passage several times before she spoke, "I believe my mother may have meant that *together* you can do just that. Grant, I believe you are going to have to find a way to hold yourself in both Addie and your father's minds long enough for the princess to use her gifts to eliminate the darkness that has plagued your father's soul from within."

"What if you are wrong? What if I can't do that?" Addie's words were filled with dread.

"Then I fear we may all be doomed to whatever fate Lord Anderson sees fit," Rose contended.

Behind Cora, the door swung open softly. Andrew and

352

David entered together followed by Elinore and her father and Will with his uncle.

"Please, everyone, have a seat so we can discuss where we stand and hopefully get some sleep tonight if we are able," Andrew made his way around to the large chair at the head of the map table.

Rose was the first to speak, "We were able to collect and assemble one hundred and fifty seven acid bombs and brewed enough healing elixir to aid several hundred minor to moderate injuries. We did encounter something quite unusual while we were in the forest, however."

Andrew cocked his head to the side, "Unusual as in dangerous or simply bazaar?"

Will quickly shifted in his seat and searched over Cora's body from head to toe. "Are you both alright? What happened?"

A small smile of appreciation at Will's concern spread across Cora's face, "We are fine but we encountered several dozen skin-walkers headed west toward the edge of the forest."

"They were not interested in us but that is not the most peculiar part. At most I have seen perhaps two or three beasts roam together. Never have I seen them move in this magnitude," Rose admitted, perplexed.

"What does that mean?" Elinore asked, concerned.

"My hope is that the magic that gives life to the forest and the land is preparing for the battle we will face," Rose replied hopefully.

"Let us hope you are correct, Ms. Rose, and we are not about to face an army of unbelievable strength from the forest as well," General Banks remarked. "As for my men, Will and I have barricades in place from the sea to the forest's edge and have built camps just inside the castle grounds for weapon staging as well as in-field triage if needed."

"We have also set up as many cots as possible in the great hall for more serious injuries," Elinore continued. "My father and several members of the guard were able to build two catapults, as well as nearly a dozen crossbows."

"Most of the weapons in the armory are my own work and have been well maintained," Henry assured the prince, "It appears we have far more weapons, at this point, than we have men and women able to wield them."

"We will have to make due with the manpower we have," Andrew held his head high and rolled his shoulders back. "We have far more at stake to lose if we should fail. Fighting for those we love is a far greater motivator than grief and anger could ever be, no matter the unnatural odds we face tomorrow."

Henry stood and stepped to the large case he had carried in with him, "I do have one last thing I was by some miracle able to complete." Dropping to a knee at the prince's side, Henry unlatched the brass clasp on the box and lifted the lid revealing a beautifully crafted long sword. "Elinore informed me that your sword was destroyed. I forged you a new one. It is simple but sturdy. I hope it serves you well."

"This is a stunning blade, Henry. Thank you," Andrew wrapped both hands around the fine leather grip and hoisted the sword from the case.

"It is not my most beautiful work but I do believe it is some of my best and most balanced," Henry admitted.

"Thank you again, my friend," Andrew said graciously and slid the sword into its scabbard.

354

Rose turned to face Will before reaching into the satchel at her side. "I was able to create this for you to wear tomorrow," she said, resting a leather vest and trousers into Will's hands. "Armor was not something we could manage in such a short time, I am afraid. However, *dragon scale* is some of the most powerful armor in nature."

"Thank you, Rose," Will said, accepting the gift.

Andrew spoke then to the group, "If there is no other news to discuss, I advise we all find whatever rest possible tonight, for tomorrow war will be upon us."

Chapter 43

Addie

Icy wind whipped Addie's braid over her shoulder, several loose strands grazing her cheeks. Grant stood at her side, head held high as they both looked to the hillside and main road beyond from the balcony in Addie's room. After a fitful sleep, plagued by worry and fear for what they all must face in the coming hours, Addie did her best to remain optimistic. In the early hours of the morning, just before sunrise, the storm outside seemed to intensify nearly tenfold, blanketing the world in a thick layer of snow and frost several feet deep. Now the sky paused its assault as though it held its breath for the true storm that approached from the south. A knock at the door pulled both Grant and Addie back into her suite.

"Your highness, Prince Andrew has requested that everyone meet near the main doors," Addie could hear the fear that laced the young guard's voice as he spoke. "He asks that you ready yourself quickly. There's movement south of the castle gates."

"Are you ready, Grant?" Addie squeezed his hand gently.

"I don't know if I will ever be ready but we are out of time and my father is already lost to me," Grant sighed.

Together, they walked through the castle halls and out into the snow. The frigid air cut deep beneath Addie's skin. Will and Cora moved at Rose's side and strapped the last of their weapons to their bodies as they walked.

Cora gave a weak smile to the prince as he approached, "Soldiers near the barricade have been armed with as many bombs as possible, your Majesty."

"Thank you, Cora," Andrew gave a subtle nod. "How much time do we have, General?"

General Banks dismounted his horse quickly, "It looks like we have less than an hour before they reach us. We have sent several ravens in an attempt to end all of this before any bloodshed as you requested, your Majesty. The couriers have not returned."

From Grant's left, Ren approached leading two beautiful horses. "When Maggie and I were on the road back to the castle we found a couple of old friends," Ren spoke to Will and Grant as he placed both Whiskey and Brandy's lead ropes into Grant's hand.

A small smile graced Grant's previously stoic expression, "I fully expected to never see either of you again."

Will let out a low laugh, "As did I but I believe Brandy may serve you better than she will me today, Addie."

"That is much appreciated, Will. Thank you," Addie ran her hand down Brandy's forehead to the soft fuzz of her muzzle.

Silently, Andrew mounted his horse beside David and General Banks, "Let's move into position and pray we all meet again once this is over, my friends. No matter what happens today, I am honored to fight alongside all of you."

Pulling herself into her seat atop Brandy, Addie looked over the grim faces of her friends and family as they rode to their possible demise. No one spoke for the journey to the front. As they reached the soldiers stationed near their hurried barricade, men and women bowed low to show their respect for her brother leading them all forward into battle. A loud high pitched bellow sounded in the near distance, halting everyone's movements moments before the headless bodies of all three ravens crashed to the earth at Andrew's horse's feet.

Andrew drew the long sword from his side, "Arm yourselves everyone and show no fear. If we die today, we die for those we love and for a kingdom we hope to rebuild."

"Archers to the ready," General Banks's baritone voice carried over the crowd. The sound of bow strings being pulled tight echoed down the line of soldiers on either side of Grant and Addie.

Just beyond the treeline, hundreds of grotesque monsters crawled forward on all fours. Eerie groans and shrieks emanated from their snarling faces. No trace of humanity remained in any of the beasts.

"There he is," Addie could hear Grant's heart break as she scanned the hoard for his father.

Nearly dead center, standing next to Lord Stevens, Lord Anderson stood tall. From this distance, it would have been nearly impossible to distinguish him from the monsters at his sides if it had not been for his posture. His skin had paled beyond any natural shade for the living and his face was gaunt beyond any real recognition. The once graceful man now towered over his army of death wraiths with an unnaturally thin build, arms and legs stretching far longer than they should. With a guttural wail, Lord Anderson and his army swarmed toward the makeshift wall separating them from Addie and her loved ones.

Overhead, a large shadow swept over the soldiers as Will soared into the air and laid down a wall of indigo dragon fire, slowing the legion of beast's. Arrows cut through the air moments before a cacophony of screams echoed from beyond the flames as many arrows hit their mark. Drawing their swords, Addie and Grant raced forward atop their horses, David and her brother on either side.

Grant's voice cut through the ringing in Addie's ears, "I love you, Addie."

"Tell me again after this ends," Addie shouted back.

Several of the wraiths pulled their blistered bodies over the barricade and stormed toward the prince. David and Andrew held the creatures at bay while Addie and Grant attempted to reach Grant's father.

Moving slowly, another creature approached Addie and Grant, its body still burning along its arms and spine. Grant swung his blade through the air, separating one of the once human creature's arms from its torso. Addie spun Brandy to defend Grant's unguarded side and stopped abruptly the moment Lord Stevens blocked their path. An ugly rage stained the lord's scared face.

"Do you really think you can stop Lord Anderson with your pitiful party trick," Lord Steven hissed.

"I don't know if I will be strong enough to stop him, but I assure you, *you* will not be the one to keep me from him," Addie spoke through clenched teeth.

"You are no one, Addie," Lord Stevens provoked, "I will not allow you any further. I will be your reckoning."

Addie scoffed loudly, eliciting an outraged grunt from the man before her, "Stevens, moments from now you will be nothing more than a stain on this kingdom's history not even the *gods* would care to remember."

Unable to restrain his rage, Lord Stevens lunged for her swiftly, forcing Brandy to rear back and knock Addie to the ground. Swinging again, the tip of Lord Stevens's blade grazed Addie's shoulder as she rolled from his attack. Pulling herself to her feet again, she blocked his next strike before lifting her booted foot forward. Kicking his abdomen with full force, she drove Lord Stevens to double over long enough for her to bring her elbow down on the base of his neck. He hit the ground on his hands and knees as Addie brought the toe of her boot to his face. Blood from his nose and mouth splattered across the fresh white snow at her feet.

"It seems I will be *your* reckoning, *my lord*," Addie mocked a bow before collecting the pitiful excuse for a man's face in her hands. "I do hope you feel *every* moment of this."

The normal golden hue from Addie's gift shifted to a putrid green as several dark veins of her magic crawled across Lord Stevens's skin. For several moments, his mouth opened and closed in silent screams of agony. The whites of his eyes slowly shifted to a soft pink before they were bloodshot completely and a thin trail of yellow-green pus oozed from each corner down his face. Letting him fall to the snow, he began to shake uncontrollably before he vomited a foul black substance down the front of his body and stilled.

"Holy fuck, is that Lord Stevens?" Grant stepped to Addie's side breathless and coated in blood from the dismembered creature left in the snow behind them. She looked over his shoulder and watched as Whiskey and Brandy sprinted back toward the castle.

"It's not anything anymore," she remarked and wiped her hands on her pants. "Let's keep moving."

Will, once again, circled overhead and expelled a ring of fire at the edge of the wall ahead of Grant and Addie before screeching loudly to them both. Swooping low enough for his wings to lessen the flames still burning along the barricade, Addie got a glimpse of Lord Anderson and nearly a dozen wraiths at his side. Reaching low, Will's massive taloned claws ripped several of the beasts from the ground while his barbed tail threw the remainder into the ring of fire and beyond.

"Will has found him," Grant stepped to the edge of the wall of flames and quickly jumped blindly to the other side.

Addie followed him closely and found the large, nearly empty space, completely corralled in an unending blue glowing heat. The snow that had been piled within the makeshift arena had all but melted away to nothing more than a few small puddles and steam. Sweat immediately began to bead across Grant and Addie's foreheads.

A voice full of vitriol spilled from the man that had once been Grant's father, "I seem to have missed something very crucial in my planning. Had I known you had a dragon, I would have just killed the two messengers from Shepherds Glen and brought you all to your knees in the dark."

"Those two *messengers* were once your closest friends," Grant interjected.

"It makes no difference to me who they were or that I must now deal with the beast in the sky as well. It all only delays the inevitable," Anderson's voice was cold.

"And what do you think that is?" Addie stood with two smaller daggers in hand.

Anderson shrugged his shoulders nonchalantly, "Your demise, Princess Addie, yours and, unfortunately, Grant's."

"I may not leave this battlefield today," Grant began, "but neither will you or the monstrosities you have created."

Addie held one of her blades by its tip and sent it soaring through the distance between them. With preternatural speed, Lord Anderson deflected the projectile with his sword, sending it crashing to the ground before rushing toward Addie. His blade swung erratically through the air. Addie dodged several lethal blows then dropped to the ground to avoid the lord's frantic motions. Grant grabbed Addie's ankle and pulled her across the dirt on her back, narrowly missing his father's sword smashing to the ground just above her head.

On her feet once again, Addie spoke low to Grant, "Get him between us. I have an idea."

Grant dipped his chin in agreement and the two separated the moment Lord Anderson lunged for Addie. Now several feet apart, the princess dropped her dagger and wrapped both hands around the length of the lord's blade and held tight, the edge biting into her skin. In just a matter of seconds, Addie pulled the sword closer to her body, burying the end deep in her thigh. Grant's screams behind his father were muffled in her ears by the loud thrumming in her chest. Releasing the blade, sickly green light refracted off Addie's face from her palms as she grabbed Lord Anderson by his throat and began to rot away flesh.

Grant's dark wisps of nightmare caressed Addie's subconscious and instantly his father dropped to his knees and the three froze in place.

* * *

Addie could feel Grant in her head but it was not like it had been in the cave. Like a constricting serpent, tendrils of the nightmare they were currently entangled in wound themselves around her soul for what felt like an eternity. A sharp pull yanked her painfully into the darkest pool of despair she could imagine. Every fiber of her being felt as though it was being shredded apart.

"Addie!" Grant's voice was far away, "Addie hold on to my voice! Come find me, Addie!"

Just before she was lost to the all consuming darkness around her, a warm, bright light wrapped itself around her and pulled her soul from the frigid sinking abyss. Grant's form radiated a brilliant white against the void surrounding them in her mind.

"I don't know how long I can keep him restrained, Princess. I need you to rot us *both* away," sorrow filled Grant's words.

"What?! No," Addie protested.

"I don't know how to get you to him here. But if you are able to rot my soul away while I hold onto his, I think I may be able to bring him down with me," Grant explained with agony in his voice.

"I can't do that, Grant! Please don't ask me to do that," Addie's soul wept.

"I'm sorry I won't be able to tell you I love you after everything is over. This is the only way I can see anyone walking away. It's the only way *you* walk away," Grant's resolve hardened. "I love you, Addie. I wish you did not have to be the one to do this."

"Please, Grant. I love you too," Addie begged.

"*Now*, Addie, or it will be too late!" Grant ordered, restraining the sob Addie could feel in every word he spoke.

Screaming into the emptiness, Addie pushed her gift forward into Grant. The light in her soul shattered as Grant too roared in pain. Unlike every other time Addie had used her darkest gift, no blisters formed and no grotesque lesions ruptured. She just held tightly and pushed every ounce of power she had in her soul through the man she loved and watched him dissolve into darkness like smoke and ash in the wind.

* * *

Blinking hard and struggling for breath, Addie tried to take in the world around her. Blood dripped from her nose and ears as well as her leg and the cuts that mangled her palms. Laying before her was the motionless, decaying body of Lord Anderson. She spun to her left only to find Grant face down at her side, arms outstretched toward her.

"Grant!" She screamed, dragging herself toward his body. Lord Anderson's sword protruded from her leg.

His chest did not rise or fall as she rolled him over and pulled his head into her lap, her own blood staining his midnight hair. Tears streamed down her face. Pressing her glowing hands to his body, Addie searched for any injury she could heal to bring him back to her but found nothing. Grant's beautiful face was calm, eyes forever closed.

"Please, Grant. Don't leave me. I'm not ready for you to

leave me again," Addie pressed her forehead to his, tears rolling down her cheeks. Footsteps sounded from somewhere behind her but she made no move to defend herself from whatever approached. In her heart, she readily awaited the death she hoped would claim her too.

"Addie, I need you to get up. Let me take you into the castle. You aren't safe here," Andrew's voice was gentle but firm as he knelt by her side. "He's gone, Addie"

"I know," Addie's heart splintered into a million pieces as she wept over Grant's motionless body and pulled his face into her chest. Her tears dripped from her chin before splashing against his cheek.

"You do not need to die here too," Andrew carefully tucked his arm under his sister's legs and lifted her from the ground. Grant's head silently slipped back to rest against the blood stained soil. "I will send David to bring his body back once you are inside."

Chapter 44

Will

Will soared above the chaos exploding on the ground. Shortly after clearing a path for Grant and Addie and separating Lord Anderson from his creatures, he went in search of Cora. Below, soldiers stood side by side and worked to keep death from reaching the kingdom's citizens sheltered beyond the castle. Waves of gray, mangled flesh crashed against the wall of flames. Trees swayed and rustled near the edge of the forest just before dozens of skin-walkers in their natural form sprinted out from the brush and leapt from the canopy, tearing through the horde of the undead. Like a thick black mist, blood from the creature's Lord Anderson had created filled the air.

Sweeping low, Will caught sight of several large explosions. At the center of the havoc, Rose stood, sword drawn but Cora was nowhere in sight. Will landed with a ground rattling crash next to Rose as panic raced in his heart. Ducking his body low, he spun his colossal tail behind himself and cleared a large space for Cora's mother. A blood curdling scream cut through the animalistic shrieks from the wraiths around them.

"Cora needs you!" Rose shouted and pointed to Will's right.

Over the snarling faces of the monsters around them, Will watched Cora's body tumble through the air and collide hard with the ground. A guttural roar bellowed from deep within Will's chest. His massive claws tore through creatures as he leapt and glided his way over the crowd to stand at Cora's side.

"You shouldn't be here, Will!" Cora screamed, "You have to leave this place."

Hot air from Will's nostrils blew back Cora's hair as she stood to her feet and cut down another wraith. Will watched as its body hit the ground and stilled. With his nose, he pushed the lifeless corpse, eyes widening with the realization that the creature did not reanimate or show any sign that it would rise again. Will let out a steamy chuff of air and once again pushed the creature toward Cora.

"Holy shit. They did it," Cora's voice was stunned. "It's truly dead."

In their distraction, a large swarm of wraiths pushed through the flames surrounding them. Nearly a dozen blistered and burning beasts mobbed Will, shredding everything they touched. Will pulled his wings in tightly and slammed his body into the ground in an attempt to dislodge the piling creatures but failed. More wraiths seemed to manifest from thin air. Sharp teeth tore into the soft flesh of his membranous wings and clawed hands ripped through the scales along his back.

Dread pooled in his belly the instant he caught sight of Cora.

Completely outnumbered, she threw her last acid bomb and held firm to her ax. The look in her eyes broke Will's heart as he realized this was the future she had seen in her vision. If he could just get to her side, he could clear a path for her to escape and get to Rose. If he could just push a little longer, he could save her, even if it was the last choice he ever made in this life.

Breathing hard, Will attempted to drag his tattered body toward the woman he loved. Pain radiated through every cell. Digging his talons into the blood stained snow, Will pulled his belly across the ground. Cora spun to face him now only a matter of yards away, sorrow filling her expression.

"Run!" Cora pleaded before turning and swinging her ax hard to meet the beasts now nearly on top of her.

Will shook his massive head slightly in protest and wished he could tell her one last time how much he loved her. He needed her to know she was his reason for existing and was honored to die at her side. He knew the longing in his eyes wouldn't be enough and he hated knowing his end was near.

The death wraith that had reached Cora swung its massive hand and blocked one of Cora's assaults, sending her ax flying from her hand before it skidded to a stop far outside of her reach. Faster than she could recover from the blow, the creature slammed its razor sharp nails down, slicing through skin, muscle and bone. All the air in Will's lungs left his chest the instant the lower half of Cora's left leg separated from her body and she tumbled to the ground, blood pouring over the snow. With every ounce of strength he had, Will spewed dark, black flames from his lungs, turning the monster standing over Cora into nothing more than ash in an instant. Then, Will was overtaken completely.

Chapter 45

Cora

Cora watched on in horror. Wordless screams shattering the world around her as her greatest fear materialized before her eyes. No matter how much she had wished these past weeks something would change to prevent this future, Will still stood at the precipice between life and death. The distance between them never felt more colossal as she again attempted to pull her broken body from the ground. There could be no life for her in a world that Will didn't still draw breath. If he was determined to die protecting this kingdom and the people he loved then she would be damned to let him die alone.

On a single leg, Cora rose to her full height and focused on Will just yards away and began to slow time as much as she could. The swarm of creatures covering Will's shredded wings slowed to a crawl and his dark scaled head snapped in her direction. Every trace of fear she had seen a moment ago in Will's expression shifted as he realized what was happening. There would be no way to escape the fate they both now faced but with the time Cora could give them, Will would have the window he needed to take down the largest hoard of wraiths left standing.

Spinning free of the creatures' hold, Will slunk through the beasts surrounding him with clumsy movements. One by one, he tore heads from bodies and limb from limb, blood and rotted gray flesh falling from his maw, until Cora's strength failed her.

Falling to her hands and knees, Cora felt the cascade of moisture pouring from her face and wasn't sure if it was tears or blood that ran from her eyes and nose down her chin. Time returned for all those around Will that he had not been unable to bring down. In an instant, he was once again facing a half dozen unnatural foes. Cora swore a look of gratitude crossed Will's expression just before he turned away to charge head first into death's waiting claws.

From somewhere behind Cora, a high pitched whistle cut through the chaos around her. As swift as a crashing wave, Shea sprinted past Cora into the fray. Seated atop Cora's trusted companion, rode Cora's mother, sword sheathed at her side and armed from head to toe with every known weapon Cora could imagine. Swiftly, Rose threw her final two acid bombs past Will's massive form, casting two of the wraiths in flames.

Like a weapon honed for war, she threw herself from Shea directly onto one of the beasts closest to Cora. A battle cry echoed through the air the moment her body left Shea's saddle. Immense pride filled Cora's heart as she watched her mate and her mother fight side by side. Will tore through a creature's deformed leg before throwing it to the ground and setting the remainder of the monster ablaze. Cracking

370

his tail hard behind him, he smashed in the chest of another wraith, splattering its viscous blood across the already stained snow.

Movement from Cora's left drew her attention in time to see the final death wraith lunge for her mother still perched atop the creature she tackled to the ground. The curved blade in Rose's hand cut deep into the monster's chest below her, stopping its frantic movements just before the second monster blocked her mother from Cora's view. Leaning forward, Cora pulled the dagger from the boot still on her severed foot on the ground before her and sent the blade spiraling through the air. An animalistic wail exploded from the beast as Cora's aim rang true. Blood pouring from its grotesquely broken jaw, the creature turned to face Cora fully. Rage and despair filled Cora's heart at the sight of her mother's body in the snow coated in blood.

The final wraith didn't make it more than two feet in Cora's direction before Will's massive dark scaled body collided with the monstrosity and tore the creature to ribbons. The world around her tunneled as she drug herself to her mother's side, leaving a path of her own blood behind her in freshly falling snow.

"Mother," Cora wept, grabbing Rose's limp hand. "I'm so sorry. Please. You'll be alright."

Rose's voice was broken as she spoke, "Oh, my sweet girl. This was always meant to be my fate. I will always be with you."

Cora leaned forward and placed her forehead against the fatal gash through her mother's bleeding chest, "I can't do this alone."

"You never will be," Cora's mother choked. "Take care of

her, young man."

The heat from Will shifting at Cora's back enveloped them both in a warm embrace. He slowly leaned in close over Cora's shaking body and placed Rose's and her daughter's hands in his own, "It will be my honor, Rose."

With a final shaking breath, Rose's body stilled under Cora's hands.

"No, no, no! Please," Cora begged.

After several moments, Will gently pulled Cora from her mother's still form and tucked her head into his body, the heat from his chest a stark contrast to the frigid world around them.

"We need to get to a healer or her death will be in vain, my love," Will spoke softly as he pulled Cora into his arms as he stood. Her tear filled breaths began to slow and she struggled to remain conscious. Gently, Will hoisted himself and Cora atop Shea and turned for the castle gates.

Closing her eyes, Cora felt as though only a few seconds had passed. When she opened her eyes once more, she found herself in the buzz of the great hall, tucked beneath a clean white sheet with Will nowhere in sight.

Panic surged through her. Shooting up into a seated position, Cora's head began to spin.

"Oh, dear!" A young voice spoke, "Can I get some help here!?"

Soft hands firmly took hold of Cora's shoulders from behind. "Miss Cora, dear, we need you to lay back down. You've lost a lot of blood, sweetheart," an older woman added.

"Where is Will!?" Cora demanded, struggling to free herself from the hands that held her still.

"He is alright, Miss Cora. He is being tended to now and

will be by your side shortly. I promise. That boy has always been a handful. It's no surprise that his *mate* would be too," the older woman said sweetly.

Relaxing slightly, Cora turned to face the older woman directly.

"My name is Maggie and it is a pleasure to finally meet you," a warm smile spread across the plump woman's face. "Amy, could you go see how much longer for Mr. Will? And let him know Cora here is awake, would you?"

"You're Maggie…" Cora held back a flood of tears. After Will's mother had died, Will had told Cora about how much Maggie had cared for him and seeing her here, now, seemed to break loose something inside Cora's heart.

"I am," Maggie gave a small bow of her head.

"Is Ren here too?" Cora asked, looking around, recalling Will's description of the two being together in all of his memories.

Maggie's eyes glassed over as she shook her head, "He hasn't made it back to me yet. But he will. I'm certain."

"I do hope he does," Cora held tightly to Maggie's hand.

With a loud slam, the two large doors to the great hall flew open and crashed into the stone walls on either side. Will, shirtless and still covered in gore, sprinted through the hall toward Cora and Maggie, followed by an angry looking woman shouting in protest for him to stop.

"Cora!" Will exhaled, dropping to his knees at her bedside and cupping either side of her face. Frantically, he pulled her lips to his, "I have never been more afraid of anything than I was of losing you today."

Tears fell from Cora's eyes, "I thought I lost you too!"

"I'm so sorry, love— for everything," Will wiped tears from

her face as he spoke.

"I'll let you two be. If you need anything, I'll be around," Maggie said standing to leave.

"Thank you, Maggie, for looking after her while I was gone," Will stood and pulled Maggie into a tight embrace. "I think you should head to your rooms. I just sent Ren that way."

Soul deep joy and relief radiated from the smile that spread across Maggie's face. Without another word, the older woman lifted her skirts into her hands and ran from the hall.

Kneeling, Will faced Cora once again. "How are you feeling, love?"

"I don't know? What's happening out there? Is it over?" Cora asked.

"It's over. You've been unconscious for about four hours. I expected you to be out a lot longer, actually. Elinore is making sure Addie is being taken care of. From what the Prince has divulged, Lord Anderson is dead and the wraiths did not rise again after he fell. They are burning their bodies now."

"And my mother?" Cora asked quietly.

Will help Cora's hand gently, "She was brought into the keep and her body is awaiting your instructions."

Cora shook her head in disbelief, "I don't know. I will need to bring her home to be buried with the rest of my family but I don't know how…"

"I will be here with you and will help in any way I can," Will promised.

Will gently rubbed up and down the length of Cora's spine. The echo of the injured around them filled the silence for several moments.

"You didn't mention Grant—" Cora realized aloud.

Sorrow filled Will's eyes, "No, I did not."

"What happened to Grant, Will? Where is he?" Cora wiped a tear from her face.

"He, ah" Will swallowed hard and took a deep breath, "he is with Rose."

Cora wrapped her arms tightly around Will's neck and refused to let him go, "I am so sorry, Will."

After a long moment, Will spoke through his tears and redirected their conversation back to her, "Cora, I need to know how you're feeling physically. I'm not sure what you've been told or how much you've seen."

Cora took a deep breath before she spoke, "I uhm, I haven't seen my leg yet but I," Cora closed her eyes tightly, "I know it's gone and I'm scared."

"We can look when you're ready. The medics did a really good job saving what they could," Will ran a comforting hand down Cora's arm.

"I'm not ready yet," Cora breathed.

Will nodded slowly, "That's alright. You have time."

"How are *you* feeling?" Cora furrowed her brow.

"Physically, I'll be alright. I'm missing a kidney and my breathing will be shit until my lungs recover. Elinore said I probably shouldn't shift into anything for a while. I'm worried that I may never fly as a dragon again. But, that's a future problem," Will attempted to appear indifferent but Cora knew how much he had loved soaring through the clouds and could see the heartbreak in his eyes.

"You know dragons aren't the only beasts that can fly right? Do you know what a wyvern is?" Cora smiled.

"No?" Will's brows raised in confusion and a spark lit in

his somber expression.

Cora leaned in and placed her head against his chest, "Think slightly smaller dragon with two legs instead of four. I can show you some in my books when we get home."

Will's heart sputtered in Cora's ear, *"Home?"*

"Yes, *home*, you fool. I'm not about to try to climb stairs at the cottage without you," Cora joked with a broken smile. "I need you."

"Anything you wish," Will inhaled, placing a gentle kiss atop her head.

Epilogue

Grant

For a moment, Grant stood completely petrified as he watched his father's blade slice through the soft skin of Addie's palms and sink deep into her thigh. Her hands were instantly wrapped around his father's throat, dark lines of rot trailed up toward his face and her blood dripped from her hands down below the collar of his tunic. With a deep breath Grant pushed his gift out completely shrouding his father and Addie in shadow.

* * *

Deep in the darkness of what was once his father's soul, Grant searched for the single shining light he had seen in the cave in the Alderbrooke Forest. Far in the distance, a faint glow flickered weakly. The weight of all of his father's pain and despair crashed against Grant's own anguish and agony like a tidal wave reaching to pull him under.

Grant used every ounce of strength he could muster to keep moving through the thickening sludge of corruption that surrounded him. Inch by inch, he made his way to the dying spark of hope and joy that struggled to survive.

His father's warm voice was weak as it cut through the roaring in Grant's thoughts, "You have to end this, son. I'm sorry for all of the pain and havoc my grief and selfishness have caused."

"I don't know how to end any of it. How am I meant to bring Addie to this place in your mind? This world only exists in my dreams and my nightmares," Grant pleaded with his father.

"If you are linked to me, I think you know what you must do," sorrow filled his father's voice.

"I don't want to leave her yet," Grant admitted as he acknowledged his grim fate. "If I am destroyed here with you, I can bring your soul with me but I'm afraid. I didn't have a chance to truly love her."

"Hold on to your love and find her in the next life," Lord Anderson sighed.

Grant's gift wrapped his father's spirit close and pulled him along into the sanctum of his own mind. The memories that flooded Grant the instant he opened himself up were bright and vivid and vibrant. Moments shared between him and Addie from throughout their adolescence flashed before his eyes. Her radiant smile engraved itself onto his soul.

"Now, son!" Lord Anderson's voice filled with panic as tendrils of corruption leaked from their shared connection, as though the darkest parts of him were reaching out with clawed hands to stop Grant.

Grant dove head first into Addie's mind and was instantly plunged into darkness. Murky, dark water pulled him under for a moment before he was able to compose himself.

"Addie!" his voice echoed into the emptiness, "Addie, hold on to my voice! Come find me, Addie!"

Reaching deep into the water, Grant pulled Addie's soul to the surface. Warm light illuminated her beautiful face. "I don't know how long I can keep him restrained, Princess. I need you to rot us *both* away," sorrow filled his words.

"What?! No," Addie cried, shock coating her voice

"I don't know how to get you to him here. But if you are able to rot my soul away while I hold onto his, I think I may be able to bring him down with me," Grant restrained the tears he could feel building behind his eyes.

He could feel the agony that filled Addie's soul, "I can't do that, Grant! Please don't ask me to do that."

"I'm sorry I won't be able to tell you I love you after everything is over. This is the only way I can see anyone walking away. It's the only way *you* walk away," Grant forced more courage into his voice than he truly felt. "I love you, Addie. I wish you did not have to be the one to do this."

"Please, Grant. I love you too," Addie's voice shook.

"*Now*, Addie, or it will be too late!" Grant pleaded through his pain.

He could feel Addie's gift flow into his soul. A pain he had never known tore through him as her darkness cut deep. His hold on his father's soul began to pull taught as rot began to fester in his mind and tear Lord Anderson apart. Like smoke in the wind, Grant's father's soul dissolved into nothing more than a memory lost to time. His hold on Addie weakened as his heart slowed and the light from his soul drifted into the darkness.

* * *

He wasn't sure how much time had passed or where his soul lingered before a tug pulled him through the fog that concealed him. Filled with warmth and joy from Addie's memories, Grant's soul stirred in the shadows of a cold dark room. Blinking open his eyes, Grant stood, stunned in the doorway as he took in the scene before him. Laid out on a large wood table was his own body covered by a beautiful emerald quilt, Addie snuggled in close to his motionless form. Her head rested over his chest as golden light radiated from every inch of her skin.

"You can't be gone," her voice was rough with tears, "Please, Grant."

With a shaky breath, Grant stepped closer to her, "Addie, can you hear me?" Instantly, Addie snapped her head in his direction, eyes wide and red as she took in Grant's nearly translucent form only feet away.